Sultana

By Lisa J. Yarde

Cover Artwork
A Jewish Girl of Tangiers, Charles Landelle, undated
File source: Creative Commons, Attribution License
http://commons.wikimedia.org/wiki/File:Landelle.jpg

Innenhof der Alhambra, Adolf Seel, 1892
File source: Creative Commons, Attribution License
http://commons.wikimedia.org/wiki/File:Adolf_Seel_Inne
nhof_der_Alhambra.jpg

Cover design and Alhambra Press logo by Lance Ganey
www.freelanceganey.com

Also by Lisa J. Yarde

Dedication & Acknowledgments

To Anita K. Davison and Mirella Sichirollo Patzer, dear friends who have always believed in this story

This book has been a labor of love and commitment. The members of my critique groups were invaluable sources of help, especially Anita Davison, Jen Black, Philip Essely, Jennifer Haymore, Laura Hogg, Sheila Lamb, Mirella Patzer, Rosemary Rach, Ginger Simpson, Steve Vissel, and Anne Whitfield.

To the readers of the final manuscript, Judith Arnopp, Victoria Dixon, Kristina Emmons, Mirella Sichirollo Patzer and Tricia Robinson, you have my enduring thanks. Lastly, I appreciate the skill and patience of Cindy Vallar, who worked on this book in the early stages.

As always, to my loving family, my work would not be possible without you.

Foreword

Dear Reader,

The events in this book take place during a turbulent period for thirteenth-century Moorish Spain, in the kingdom of Granada. Historians have referred to the rulers of Granada as princes or kings. I refer to them as Sultans. While the first four Sultans of Granada are members of the Banu'l-Ahmar family, and other clans were the Banu Ashqilula and Banu Marin, I have chosen the more commonly accepted names, such as the Nasrids for the Banu'l-Ahmar, then the Ashqilula, and the Marinids. Many of the male characters bear the name Muhammad. I have distinguished between them by using titles where possible. I have used Arabic words for Moorish cities, regions and certain terms. The chronology of events differs in a variety of sources, but I have kept the narrative close to the best-documented dates in the Moorish period.

I am indebted to invaluable research materials for an understanding of thirteenth-century Spain and its inhabitants, including Simon R. Doubleday's *The Lara Family: Crown and Nobility in Medieval Spain,* Shirley Guthrie's *Arab Women in the Middle Ages,* and L.P. Harvey's *Islamic Spain 1250 to 1500.* Other vital sources of information on the detailed history of the Alhambra and Moorish architectural achievements came from Antonio Fernandez Puertas' masterwork, *The Alhambra: Volume 1 from the Ninth Century to Yusuf I,* and Michael Jacobs' *Alhambra.*

Months of the Hijri Calendar

Dates approximate the equivalent periods of the Hijri and Gregorian calendars. The sighting of the crescent moon determines dates in the Hijri calendar. The term AH refers to events occurring in numbered periods after the year of the Hijra or the emigration of the Prophet Muhammad from Mecca to Medina in September AD 622.

Months
Muharram: the first Islamic month
Safar: the second Islamic month
Rabi al-Awwal: the third Islamic month
Rabi al-Thani: the fourth Islamic month
Jumada al-Ula: the fifth Islamic month
Jumada al-Thani: the sixth Islamic month
Rajab: the seventh Islamic month
Sha`ban: the eighth Islamic month
Ramadan: the ninth Islamic month, a venerated period of abstinence and fasting from sunrise to sunset
Shawwal: the tenth Islamic month
Dhu al-Qa`da: the eleventh Islamic month
Dhu al-Hijja: the twelfth Islamic month, a period of pilgrimage to Saudi Arabia

Characters

The Nasrids

Fatima bint Muhammad, daughter of Abu Abdallah Muhammad II of Gharnatah

Muhammad I ibn al-Ahmar of Gharnatah, the first Sultan of Gharnatah (r. 632-671 AH), Fatima's grandfather

Abu Abdallah Muhammad II of Gharnatah, the second Sultan of Gharnatah (r. 671-702 AH), Fatima's father

Muhammad ibn Muhammad, Fatima's elder brother
Muna bint Muhammad, Fatima's first sister
Alimah bint Muhammad, Fatima's second sister
Azahra bint Muhammad, Fatima's third sister
Tarub bint Muhammad, Fatima's fourth sister
Nadira bint Muhammad, Fatima's fifth sister

Abu Said Faraj ibn Ismail, nephew of Muhammad I ibn al-Ahmar of Gharnatah and Fatima's husband
Muhammad ibn Ismail, nephew of Muhammad I ibn al-Ahmar of Gharnatah and Faraj's brother

Faridah, sister of Muhammad I ibn al-Ahmar of Gharnatah, mother of Abu Muhammad

Maryam, daughter of Muhammad I ibn al-Ahmar of Gharnatah

Hamda, the second wife of Muhammad I ibn al-Ahmar of Gharnatah

Qamar, the third wife of Muhammad I ibn al-Ahmar of Gharnatah

Lateefah, the favorite of Muhammad I ibn al-Ahmar of Gharnatah

The Ashqilula

Abu Ishaq Ibrahim, a chieftain of the Ashqilula, former son-in-law of Muhammad I ibn al-Ahmar of Gharnatah, Raïs of Qumarich

Abu Muhammad, a chieftain of the Ashqilula, maternal nephew of Muhammad I ibn al-Ahmar of Gharnatah, Raïs of Malaka

Aisha bint Ibrahim, Fatima's mother, first wife of Abu Abdallah Muhammad II of Gharnatah
Abdallah ibn Ibrahim, Fatima's maternal uncle, Raïs of Naricha
Saliha bint Muhammad, Fatima's maternal grandmother

The Marinids

Abu Yusuf Ya'qub al-Marini, the Sultan of the Marinids (r. 656-685 AH)
Abu Zayyan ibn Abu Yusuf Ya'qub, son of Abu Yusuf Ya'qub al-Marini
Shams ed-Duna bint Abu Yusuf Ya'qub, daughter of Abu Yusuf Ya'qub al-Marini, second wife of Abu Abdallah Muhammad II of Gharnatah

Ibn Yala, chief minister to Abu Yusuf Ya'qub al-Marini

Umar of Mahalli, the *Shaykh al-Ghuzat*, commander of Marinid forces in al-Andalus

The Royal Court of Castilla-León

Alfonso X, the Wise, the king of Castilla-León (r. AD 1221 – 1284)
Violante de Aragón, wife of King Alfonso X, the Wise

Doñ Nuño Gonzalez de Lara, the chief advisor of King Alfonso X, the Wise

Retainers, Slaves and Others

Ibn Ali, chief minister to Abu Abdallah Muhammad II of Gharnatah, former royal tutor, head of the Sultan's chancery

Abu Omar, minister to Abu Abdallah Muhammad II of Gharnatah

Nur al-Sabah, Galician favorite of Abu Abdallah Muhammad II of Gharnatah

Hasan, chief eunuch of Abu Abdallah Muhammad II of Gharnatah

Halah, governess of Abu Abdallah Muhammad II of Gharnatah's children
Ulayyah, a maidservant of the Ashqilula, Halah's sister

Niranjan al-Kadim, Fatima's eunuch-guard
Leeta, Fatima's maidservant, Niranjan's first sister
Amoda, Fatima's maidservant, Niranjan's second sister and twin of Leeta

Marzuq, Faraj's chief steward

Baraka, Faraj's Genoese concubine
Hayfa, Faraj's Nubian concubine
Samara, Faraj's Provençal concubine

Ayesha, a Sicilian slave girl

Abu Umar of al-Hakam, a pirate chieftain

Sitt al-Tujjar, a Jewish merchant

Chapter 1

Pawns in the Game

Princess Fatima

Gharnatah, al-Andalus: Muharram 664 AH (Granada, Andalusia: October AD 1265)

A hot, dry hand covered Fatima's mouth, smothering the scream in her throat. She awoke to a nightmare unfolding in the darkness of the bedchamber she shared with her siblings.

A lone figure in a black hood and cloak hovered in silence next to her on her pallet. An unwelcome weight and warmth from a burly hand held her pressed against the pillow beneath her head. The odor of saffron and rosewater filled her nostrils. In the fading glow of a dying iron sconce on the wall, she could hardly tell where the folds of the cloak began or ended. She guessed the rough touch and strength of the hand on her mouth, as well as the husky shape in the darkness, meant her captor was a man. Raspy breaths escaped the stranger's throat, as if he had been running and fought for each breath now.

Though her heart pounded steadily, she forced herself to remain calm. She did not know what this stranger intended or what he might do to her. As her eyes grew accustomed to the dimness of the shadowy chamber, she made out the images of three others, cloaked and hooded like the one who held her captive. Two of the intruders stood on either side of the olive wood door, occasionally peeking through the slats of the entryway. Another who stood taller than the other two walked toward the window

1

and closed the lattice, shutting out the sounds of crickets chirping and owls hooting at night, before the figure crossed the room and lingered beside the boy who slept closest to the door. The intruder bent and moved closer to Muhammad ibn Muhammad, peering into his smooth, olive-skinned face.

Fatima froze, paralyzed in horror. Her brother Muhammad, only a year older than her, slept peacefully on a pallet below the wall sconce. The ebbing light revealed the disheveled mass of his dark hair on the silken pillow. Thin and lean like her, he stretched out on his back and snored lightly. He must have kicked off his woolen blanket during the night. One arm dangled off the pallet and touched the floor immediately below, while he had thrown the other back behind the pillow. In a deep slumber, he did not know the danger they faced.

One thought filled Fatima's mind, mirroring her whimpering plea behind her captor's hand. "No! Don't hurt my brother!"

Muhammad was only nine years old, the eldest child of her parents and her father's heir. She could never let anyone harm him.

She clawed wildly at the hand pressed against her mouth, but her little fingers could not fight off the heavy hold. Then her captor pinched her nostrils closed with his other hand. A choking wave of terror swelled in her throat and squeezed her chest. Tears trickled beneath the lashes, blinding her.

On a low table at her side, the sparrow in its gilded cage whistled cries of alarm and battered its wings against the metal bars.

The person beside her brother stood and approached her pallet, bypassing the white marble alcoves where her younger sisters Muna, Alimah, Azahra, and Tarub also slept. Only the baby Nadira, born two months before, was absent. Fatima prayed Nadira's wet-nurse would keep her safe and out of danger.

Each noiseless footfall brought the intruder closer to Fatima. Her fingers still scratched at the hands that cut off her breathing. The tightening sensation grew inside her throat. Her body went limp and her limbs slackened.

The silent figure knelt beside the cage and withdrew a square of black cloth. Fatima panicked, fearing for her pet as much as she worried for her family. The cloth went over the cage and covered it. The sparrow quieted except for a few clicks and chirps.

Then thin, almost womanly, fingers rested on her captor's shoulder. At this silent command, the one holding her nostrils released the brutal grasp, though the other hand remained on her mouth. Wonder at whether this was the leader of the intruders died, as the first blessed lungful of air burned at the back of her throat. Despite the burning, she sucked in the next breath with a heavy wheeze, before she stared at the trespassers. Tears spilled from her eyes, but she immediately swiped at them. She was not going to let them see her cry or show them that she was afraid.

She could not make out their features in the darkness, except that both had heavy lidded eyes lined with kohl, gazes that returned her watery stare. The one standing by her side had a smaller frame than his companion did, but beyond the differences in their shapes and the size of their hands, she could not discern anything else. Who were these people? She felt sure they hid their characters further by not speaking. She would have known any of the eunuchs or retainers in her father's palace by the sound of their voices alone. Had their servants risen against her father and betrayed the family?

Fists tightening at her side, she trembled with fear and a growing rage. If they had hurt her father or kept him captive like her, not knowing of the danger to his children, she would.... She sagged against the pallet. What could she do, a girl who might now not live to see her ninth birthday?

She glared defiantly at the cloaked intruders. If they had harmed her father, she prayed Allah would give her some means to avenge him.

The tall man bent toward her. His eyes were large and luminous in the dark. Soft fingertips glided across her wet cheek, startling her. She jerked her head away, pulling back from the unfamiliar touch.

"Take her."

His nasalized voice barely rose above a whisper. The hand over her mouth withdrew for the course of one breath. In the next, a cloth, thick with the smell of horse manure and camphor, covered her lips and nose.

***

Fatima awoke to the glare of lamplight. She blinked against the golden glow cast by iron brackets hanging from a wall. She rested on a pallet in one corner of an otherwise empty room. At its center, the lamplight shimmered and reflected in the depths of a pool lined with marble. Fatima trembled anew at the unfamiliar surroundings. She could not be at home in her father's palace.

As she sat up and tucked her legs into the folds of a silken coverlet, a brisk wind raced inward and rippled through her curly hair. A shudder ran through her, as the chill penetrated the thin, calf-length tunic she wore. She looked around her, wondering where the breeze had come from. There were no windows in the room. She pushed aside strands of ink-black hair from her face.

A water channel connected to the pool, carrying the liquid around a corner. From that direction, a feminine voice echoed.

"... She wanted to see her, Abdallah. How could I have refused her request?"

A man answered, "You risk too much. You should not have brought the girl here, all for the whims of an old woman."

"A dying woman, Abdallah. My mother."

"Still, it is a heavy burden you bear. Now, to involve the child and expect her to...."

"I ask nothing more from her than her grandfather has already demanded. He knew the risks when he married her off. If you had seen her earlier today at the wedding.... She is barely eight years old and already a bride. She cannot begin to understand the consequences of this union, what it may mean for her and for us all. This husband of hers," the woman's voice rose a pitch. "Prince Faraj has his father's selfishness. He shall ensure his own protection, not Fatima's. The Sultan and his son are responsible for her final fate. She is a mere child, not a pawn in this game of her father and grandfather."

Fatima frowned at the woman's words. How could a person be a pawn? Pawns belonged on the chessboard with which she and her father played in the evenings. She did not recognize the voices, though each person knew of her. Had they brought her to this unknown place? Even more, she hated the way the two talked about her, her grandfather and father. Who were these people?

The man continued, "It is finished now. The girl has done her duty."

"Duty! She had no choice. Just like me. My husband thinks I am a fool, who knows nothing of the Sultan's plans. He thinks to keep me an unwitting fool, a prisoner caged within the walls of his palace. I have been nothing more than his broodmare, forced to endure birthing after birthing. I can hardly bear the sight of the children, knowing they are his."

"They shall not understand your actions."

"By the blessings of Allah, the Compassionate, the Merciful, they are too young to know why I must leave this place, except perhaps for the boy. His eyes have seen things... he is always watching, like his grandfather. When the children are older, their father's lies shall comfort them."

"We must leave the city at first light when the gates are opened. My coming to Gharnatah cannot remain a secret for long. Are you certain of this course? Your husband shall believe the worst of you, that you have betrayed him. He shall hate you."

"No more than I have hated him."

Fatima pushed off the cover on her legs and crept across the marble floor. She winced at the coldness of the tiles and peeked around the corner into an antechamber.

A copper brazier pierced at the sides cast a shadow against the wall. The smell of ambergris and musk wrinkled her nostrils. Opposite the brazier, a rectangular channel at the base of the floor held copper bowls, each connected at the top by a thin, metal shaft. A bronze water clock dripped fluid from a tiny hole at its base, which collected in the bowls below. Three of the vessels already overflowed with water. The last of these dribbled its runoff into a fourth bowl.

The man and woman had settled before a lattice-covered window, where the pool's water channel disappeared under the wall. Behind them, yellow damask curtains edged with gold filigree flapped in the breeze. The man knelt beside his companion while she sat on a low, wood carved stool. Deep pockmarks pinpricked his cheeks. She wore silver silk robes and a black *hijab* covered her hair. The opaque veil trailed to the floor. The man placed his large, olive-brown hands over her smaller, slender ones. Her sun-browned skin glistened with health and vigor, and her cheeks tinged pink. She inclined her head toward him, dark brows flaring beneath the fold of the *hijab*.

"There is hope for Fatima. You have given it to me, Abdallah, the means to save her from the schemes of her father and grandfather."

"Neither of them can trouble you here. Still, I regret my part in this. You risked too much in coming. I should never have asked it. I have placed you in grave danger, Aisha, you and your daughter."

Fatima drew back and pressed a hand to her chest. A sudden tremor pounded in her heart. She recognized the woman. She had seen her only briefly in the past. She could never forget the familiar face, yet the woman was like a stranger to her.

The woman withdrew one hand from her companion's grasp and smoothed a lock of his thick, brown hair away from his forehead, where deep lines burrowed. "I have known danger most of my life, Abdallah, ever since I married the crown prince of Gharnatah. Why should tonight be any different?"

He brought her hand to his lips and kissed the fingertips. Fatima smothered a cry behind her hands, but not quietly enough. The pair jerked toward her.

The woman's wide, green eyes, lined with kohl and painted with malachite, sparkled like emeralds. At first, Fatima imagined those eyes filled with tears, but that could not be true.

A sharp pain dug into Fatima's brow. Her hands fell at her side, shaking. "How could you do this to my father? Steal me from my home? Be here with another man? Why are you letting him," she stabbed her finger at the stranger, "touch you?"

The woman rose and approached, her bejeweled fingers clasped together. A lock of her hair slipped from beneath the folds of the *hijab,* in a thick coil of burnished copper. The warming pink flush of her face faded to a muted, cream-colored sheen. She seemed like a stone carving in the garden – beautiful, but cold and hard.

The pockmarked man behind her stood. He towered taller than any other person Fatima had ever seen. "Ignorant child, you know nothing of what you are speaking. You are being disrespectful to your mother."

The woman hushed him. "Do not chide her, brother. If Fatima is ignorant or willful, it is because her father and grandfather have allowed her to be so." She paused and held out her hand. "Come, daughter, it is time you learned the truth."

Fatima drew back. "Don't touch me! You're not my mother, you never were."

***

Prince Faraj

Brass lanterns sputtered in an orange haze of fading light. Evening shadows lengthened as defeat cast its grim pall over Faraj. He faced his opponent on a familiar battlefield. Muhammad ibn al-Ahmar, the Sultan of Gharnatah leaned toward him and smiled a predatory grin, before he delivered the deathblow. "Do you yield, nephew?"

Faraj stared at his adversary. The Sultan's piercing hazel eyes looked at him from a careworn, olive-skinned face, with laugh lines around the mouth. Faraj shared similar features with the old man, family traits like the heavy brows and the hawk-like nose. The Sultan covered his thinning hair with a *shashiya*. He rarely wore any head covering except the brown skullcap.

Faraj returned his attention to an ebony wood chessboard, inlaid with mother-of-pearl, his father's last gift to the Sultan. Despite the passing of several years, Faraj still admired this elegant piece of handiwork. A wall of his white pawns now lined the other side of the board. He shook his head in dismay, recognizing how the earlier, reckless positioning of his cavalier had heralded his downfall. He rubbed at the corners of his burning eyes and wracked his mind for a counter-move. Yet, he could not deny the truth. As in all other things, his uncle held the advantage.

He barely recalled the time when he had not lived by the Sultan's whim and desire. After his arrival in Gharnatah nine years ago, a wearied and bloodied boy, the old man raised him alongside his own royal sons. At nearly seventy-four, the Sultan's mind remained formidable. Despite his advanced years, he appeared rested and focused, but then, he probably slept well most nights.

For his part, Faraj could not remember the peace that sleep had once brought. The memory evaded him, just as easily as contented slumber had for nearly ten years.

"Do not succumb to idle thoughts, nephew. You have already lost pawns, as a result."

"I do not have my father's skill. How was it that he was able to best you every time?"

The Sultan exposed a gap-toothed smile. "Is that what he told you? Your father's gift for exaggeration was always incomparable, but perhaps in this, he did not lie. You may not have his talent, but each day you grow more in his image. If he had lived, my brother would be very proud of you. My only regret is that he was unable to witness your union with my granddaughter today."

Faraj kept his stare fixed on the board. He dared not raise his gaze for his uncle's eager scrutiny. Otherwise, the hawk-eyed glint in the Sultan's expression would pierce the heart of him and reveal the turmoil brewing inside.

Throughout the day, unrelenting fear had roiled in his guts, warning him against the path he now trod. As before, the same concerns that had plagued him earlier returned now. He pushed them aside, but swallowed audibly before daring an answer. He prayed his voice would not betray him.

Jaw clenched tightly, he muttered, "I share the same regret, my Sultan."

His uncle leaned forward in his cedar chair, as though he had not clearly heard Faraj. "Your father would say to both of us that regrets are best left in the past. In that, as in other matters, he would be right. Still, I believe he would have been proud that you have attained your manhood and taken a royal bride."

Faraj nodded, though he believed his father would have viewed the marriage with the same circumspect opinion he once held of his own wedding: a means to an end. As with his father, Faraj had not chosen his own wife. At least his father had made a better bargain, with an alliance that benefitted their family. Faraj was not certain how his own marriage gave him any advantage. Likely, it would result in his quick death.

The Sultan showed no awareness of his companion's discomfort. "Your union with Fatima surely surprised many people. I suspect it has angered others, particularly the Ashqilula family, but they shall accept it."

"And if the Ashqilula do not accept this marriage?" Faraj gasped at his own carelessness and gripped the edge of the chessboard until the nail bed of his thumb whitened. He chided himself. Only a fool revealed his fears so easily, especially before another who would play upon them.

As he anticipated, the Sultan paused and cocked his head. Faraj perceived the change in him instantly, like a hawk sighting prey. He knew their game of chess was at an end. He released the side of the gaming board and steeled himself, feigning courage he did not feel.

"Do your ties to the Ashqilula family still burden you, nephew?"

The attack came sharp and swift, tearing to the core of him. The roughened nails of his hands cut into the palms, unseen by the Sultan's persistent gaze. How dare the old man even ask about burdens? Faraj cursed him inwardly, for having burdened his family generation after generation. Likely, the Sultan's machinations had brought them to the brink of ruin.

Still, Faraj waved a trembling hand over his chest, as though flicking away dinner crumbs from his black tunic. He controlled the fluttering at his breast with even breaths, before he glanced at the Sultan. He hated and loved this old man, who always pierced to the heart of a matter. Faraj could almost admire the skill, if the Sultan had not turned it against him.

"Why should old ties impede me?" He despised the unsteady warbling in his voice, but the unbreakable cord still encumbered him – blood ties to the Ashqilula family.

Their blood coursed in his veins by virtue of his mother, an Ashqilula chieftain's daughter, who had wed the Sultan's brother and loved him until her death. Faraj shuddered at his last memory of her, bloodied and ruined, and drew a deep breath before continuing.

He forced the words from a dry throat. "I couldn't care less about my ties to them. The Ashqilula mean nothing to me."

The lie hung heavy in the room. Faraj gritted his teeth as the weight of it bore down upon him. A burdensome encumbrance, but one he undertook for his own sake. The Sultan expected it. He would never accept anything but unwavering loyalty from his family.

"What are your thoughts on my granddaughter, then?"

Faraj swallowed at the sudden change of topic and pronounced a swift reply. "I hardly know her. We had never met before I married her today."

"That is common enough. Yet, surely, you must feel something about this union. You have barely spoken of it since the oaths made during the ceremony. When my heir congratulated you before all our guests, you did not acknowledge his acclaim beyond a mere polite nod."

Faraj cursed the old man again. Why did he keep pretending that this wedding was anything other than a declaration of war against his enemies? Why did he appear so unconcerned that those enemies would now retaliate against him and embroil Faraj in their feud?

Still, he steeled himself against showing any further weakness. He began, "My Sultan, I perceive the great honor you have bestowed upon me with this union betwixt myself and the daughter of the crown prince."

"Bah! Do not dissemble. You do not have your father's skill for it. Not yet. Tell me, truthfully, what did you think of my granddaughter as you beheld her for the first today?"

Through the haze of his bewilderment, Faraj recalled the image of the pale, stick-thin girl whom everyone expected he would acknowledge as his wife. She had worn

gaudy jewelry, garish cosmetics, and rich robes -
extravagant wastes for such a scrawny, waif-like child, in
his opinion. The weight of her finery overwhelmed her, as
she had sat apart from everyone on a red damask cushion
trimmed with gold filigree. Her features were markedly
angular and gaunt, similar to her father's in appearance,
though not as sallow. If the sight of her had not stirred
Faraj's revulsion for the prospect of marrying a child, he
might have pitied her. Except in one instance.

When the evening breeze had filtered in from the open-
air courtyard, torchlight flared and cast its glow upon her
dark hair in an eerie halo. At that moment, her sharp chin
rose and her stark gaze met his, unflinching. Brilliant
flecks like the embers of a fire glittered in her brown eyes.
The sight took him aback for a moment. Then she looked
away. Even now, his lips curled at the memory of how she
had turned and ignored him, with the neglect reserved for
menials.

He tamped down the abhorrence souring in his belly.
"Forgive me, but she is merely a child of eight years. What
can I, a man ten years her senior, be expected to feel
regarding her?"

After a moment, the Sultan shrugged and nodded, as
Faraj had hoped. "I suppose you have years, Faraj, in
which you may come to know my granddaughter better.
For now, she shall remain in her father's house until she
can bear your children. I rely on her father to protect her."

"Your plans shall tear the Sultanate apart."

"Your union with Fatima shall heal the rift. Can I rely
upon you?"

Though Faraj doubted how a union with a child might
preserve the land, he kept those thoughts to himself.

"You may." He held the Sultan's gaze without wavering.
Not for the first time, he thought the old man burdened
him unduly with inopportune vows.

Raised voices echoed beyond the closed doors of the
chamber. Both the Sultan and Faraj turned toward the
sound. Two sentries stationed beside the door opened it at

a curt nod from their master. Faraj stood as torchlight revealed the sallow face of Fatima's father, the crown prince of Gharnatah, Abu Abdallah Muhammad.

The crown prince stood tall and sneered at the guardsmen outside the chamber before he approached. He sagged on one knee before the Sultan, his dark leonine head bowed. When his father touched his shoulder, he stood unsteadily. Faraj scratched his thin beard and eyed the men intently.

A frown marred the crown prince's brow, aging him beyond his thirty-one years. His deep-set eyes, another family trait, were red-rimmed and his mouth, bounded by a dark beard and moustache, was a grim, fixed line. He spoke in low tones with his father. When he finished, the Sultan grasped his arms, as though propping his son up.

"Are you truly surprised by this betrayal? It is only your wounded pride that cannot accept it."

"She belongs to me! I shall never give her up."

The Sultan sighed. "You insist upon this obsession."

"I love her!"

"Yes, despite her feelings. If you must have her back, we shall find her. There are few places within *al-Qal'at al-Hamra* where she can hide."

"She has escaped the palace!"

The Sultan cocked his head and chuckled. "She possesses a quick wit, far greater than you anticipated. Of greater concern to me is that she also has allies to aid her cause. We must eliminate all those who remain loyal to the Ashqilula."

"They have too many spies here!"

"It is a concern that we shall deal with in time. We have our own spies within their walls, too."

"My chief eunuch is questioning Aisha's servants now, in the presence of the executioner. How could she do this to me? I have given her my heart."

"Women weaken the heart. Do not trouble yourself, my son, we shall find her before she leaves Gharnatah."

"When I have her in my arms again, she shall regret this night." Thinly veiled rage seethed from the crown prince's embittered lips.

Faraj wondered who could have made him so angry. From the import of their conversation, it was likely some favorite. He sneered and shook his head. The Sultan was right. Women weakened the heart and any man who allowed a woman such power over his emotions was a fool. How disappointing that the crown prince possessed poor control of his passions and his household.

The Sultan strolled toward Faraj. Looking down at him, he gestured at the chessboard. "The pieces are set. The game can begin."

The last embers within the brass lanterns crackled and died, as Faraj pondered the meaning behind that enigmatic statement. His mind swirled with myriad thoughts. Foremost, he must ensure his uncle's plans would not threaten his own survival or interests. He was not about to become anyone's pawn again, not even that of the Sultan.

Chapter 2

The Ways of Men

Princess Fatima

Gharnatah, al-Andalus: Muharram 664 AH (Granada, Andalusia: October AD 1265)

Fatima trembled, a sharp breath paining her side. Princess Aisha's lips were pressed tightly together, nearly bloodless. Something in her eyes seemed sad, before she waved off the man at her arm.

He touched her shoulder, his hand almost like a caress, leaving Fatima uneasy and repulsed. She shuddered at the sight of the deep scars from the pox that marred his otherwise handsome features. His hair was darker than Aisha's locks, but otherwise he possessed the same olive skin she did, with her dark brows and lashes, aquiline nose and small mouth. Although Aisha had called him her brother, his boldness was unexpected, especially when Fatima had never heard of or seen him before.

He said, "Do not be too harsh with her, sister. She doesn't know what she is saying."

Aisha shook her head. "My daughter is the image of her father in many things. Like him, she has learned how to wound with words."

Fatima swallowed loudly and looked away, the nervousness bubbling inside her stomach. When the man glanced at her and shook his head, her chin jutted forward.

"I shall go to her now, Aisha. Summon me if you need me."

She waved him out again. Fatima's stare followed him from the room.

Aisha smoothed her thin hands across the skirt of the silken robe. She gestured toward the wooden stool at the window. "Please sit."

Fatima shuffled on the tiles, the white marble like a gleaming sheen of ice beneath her feet. Still, she stuck out her chin further and remained rooted to the spot. "I want my father."

Aisha turned to the sole window. "I am unused to your disobedience, but stand if you prefer."

Fatima glanced at the stool before she noticed Aisha eyeing her over her shoulder.

"Where is my father?"

A strong gust of wind whipped through the lattice, carrying aloft Aisha's sigh. She pushed aside the damask curtain. Her fingers traced circles on the plasterwork wall, her eyes fixed on some point in the darkness. When a dog howled, she trembled and rubbed her arms.

"Do you know why your grandfather married you off to your cousin, Prince Faraj?"

"Father told me to marry him."

"You are so obedient that you do anything your father tells you?"

"Father says children must listen to their parents."

Aisha turned to her. "Would you do so now? I shall tell you the truth your grandfather and father have concealed, about why they made you marry Prince Faraj."

Fatima avoided the plea shining in Aisha's dark eyes. She wanted something from her, though Fatima did not know what it could be. Whatever it was, she swore she would not submit easily.

"Father says you are a great liar. He said I must never believe anything you say."

A soft gasp escaped Aisha, who suddenly faced the window again, with her head bowed. Her shoulders shook and she did not speak.

Fatima swallowed past the heavy lump wedged in her throat. Something about what she had said had disturbed her mother... no, she must not think of her in that way.

From her earliest memories, the palace servants had told her never to call Aisha 'Ummi' or speak with her unless the princess spoke first. Fatima had never forgotten the warning. Still, her words had clearly upset Aisha and that bothered her. Was Aisha right? Had Fatima told the truth because she knew it would hurt? Was it possible to harm a woman who never showed her feelings? Did she even have any feelings?

Fatima hugged her arms as a sudden breeze tore through the folds of her silk tunic. Despite the brazier and Aisha's presence at the window, she felt cold and alone. Were other women as unkind and uncaring to the children they bore? Did they ever hug their daughters or wish them sweet dreams at night? Did they love their children? Did those children know it?

"By tradition, your grandfather has always sealed the alliance with the Ashqilula through marriage."

Aisha's low, bitter tone broke the silence. Fatima jerked back to awareness.

"It has been so, child, since my aunts Leila and Fatima married the Sultan's brothers. Even the Sultan took an Ashqilula wife, your grandmother the Sultana Muna. He gave his sister Faridah in marriage to my uncle. The Sultan's daughter Mu'mina wed my cousin, the chieftain Ibrahim. Then your father demanded me for a bride. Now, everything is different, but the blood ties remain."

She paused and glanced over her shoulder. "Do you understand the significance of the blood, Fatima? It has bound the Nasrids and the Ashqilula for two generations."

Fatima crossed her arms over her chest. "I know my family's history."

Aisha faced her, lips thinned, shoulders back. She showed no hint of her earlier unease.

"Yet, your young mind cannot fathom the damage that has been done, now that you have married at the whim of your grandfather. He has placed you in grave danger."

"My father can protect me."

Aisha shook her head. "You're so young, too young to understand how much your future has changed because of this marriage. Your father cannot protect you forever, Fatima."

"Because you took me from him! Why have you stolen me away?"

"You may not believe me, but I did it for your protection, to keep you safe. I won't let your father and grandfather use you to start a war with my clan."

"Father and Grandfather would never do anything to hurt me. They love me!"

"Fatima...."

"No! What do you know of love? You don't even look at us, your own children. When my sister Muna has bad dreams and cries at night, you're never there to hold her and rock her to sleep again. Only our governess is. You don't know how to show love."

Aisha drew back and pressed against the wall. Her eyes glittered for a moment, before she looked away.

"Your father must have told you that. How strange it is to hear his accusations from another's lips. If my words cannot convince you otherwise, then my actions must. I know all too well the dangers you face. I want you to know that I... sympathize with you. I know what it is to be subject to the will of a powerful man. Such is the fate of those who suffer under the dominion of your grandfather and father."

Fatima's eyes watered, even though she willed the tears away. Any show of weakness before this woman would not help her get home. "Why do you hate Father so much?"

She sniffled and wiped her nose with the back of her hand. "He gave you a home and children. Don't you care about any of it?"

"It is because I care for you that we must leave this place." Aisha's voice barely rose above a whisper. "You cannot stay here. The danger is too great. If I must take you away from everyone and everything you have ever known for your own safety, then so be it."

She edged closer and Fatima pressed against the wall behind her, burying her face in her hands. Bitter cold pierced her back, but the pain tearing her heart felt worse. "I want my sisters and Muhammad! I don't want to leave them."

She could not go and never see her family again. Aisha asked for too much.

"Daughter...."

Aisha's words trailed off and Fatima's sobs filled the silence that followed.

"Fatima, your love for your family is great, one of many among your qualities that I admire. One day, when this is over, I promise you shall see your brother and sisters again. I know you do not want to leave them, but you must for now. I know your grandfather's wishes for you, but you cannot rely on Prince Faraj, either. He is ten years older than you are. He is a man already. He shall look to his own interests first."

Fatima peeked between her fingers. "How do you know?"

"People marry for alliances, land, and treaties. Some women grow to love their husbands dearly, if they are lucky. This marriage has robbed you of that chance, for how can you love a man who shows no concern for you? Your grandfather wed you to your cousin, instead of one among my clan, to break his alliance with the Ashqilula. Your father bears the blood of an Ashqilula woman, as do you. Your descendants shall not. Your grandfather shall never allow anyone in his line to marry among the

19

Ashqilula again. The men of my clan shall go to war with the Sultan. Your youth cannot protect you."

Fatima sobbed harder. "Father could!"

"He cannot. Please trust and obey me in this. You are the dutiful child of your father. Yet, you are as much my child, as his. He may think he can protect you from any harm, but I cannot trust in his power, when danger surrounds you. No mother could allow her child to face this peril alone."

When Fatima lifted her head, Aisha knelt before her and took her face between her bejeweled hands.

She smiled, though the corners of her eyes did not crinkle like those of Fatima's father. "Look at the mess they made of your hair." She smoothed the dark tresses. "My servants must have frightened you. I am sorry for that. Do I ask too much, daughter... I want to brush your hair, if you would allow it."

Fatima stared without blinking. She did not know what to say.

Aisha crossed the room and reached into a satchel at the base of the wall below the window. She pulled out a brush. When she gestured for her, Fatima joined her on trembling legs and sank on the low stool.

Aisha ran the bristles through the length of her hair. For a while, only the slow scrape of the brush disturbed the tranquility.

Fatima drew her knees toward her chest and rested her chin in the valley between them. Her heart filled with new, unspoken feelings. Did she dare speak them?

Then the motion of the brush stilled. Aisha rounded the stool and knelt at her feet. She cupped Fatima's cheek. "You have the beauty of women in your father's family, but remember this: all beauty fades with time. What shall never fade is the power of your mind. It is your greatest strength, especially in your relations with powerful men, like your grandfather and father. Perhaps, even your husband."

She set the brush on the low windowsill. Fatima followed the gesture and then their gazes held. "Why are you telling me this?"

Aisha smiled again, but it seemed sad. "Hush now, child, listen well. Understanding shall come. Even when you must do what others command, never forget the power of your own reasoning. One day, your husband may rule your body, he may even come to rule your heart, but your mind is and always must be your own, where none but you may rule. Promise me that you shall never forget these words."

Fatima swayed slightly. Her throat hurt, but she whispered, "I promise."

She returned Aisha's intent stare, for the first time, unafraid. Aisha's eyes glistened like gems in the lamplight.

"This is the only measure of advice I can give you, Fatima. You must learn the ways of men, as I have. Do not trust in men alone. Love, be dutiful and respectful, but trust yourself and your instincts first. They shall always guide you rightly."

Fatima looked away, her throat tightening. She fought against it, but a tear fell, followed by another, each smoothed away with a gentle touch. She turned to Aisha again. Tears welled in her beautiful eyes, too.

"I would see you safe, but also happy in life, daughter."

With a shudder, Fatima clasped the hand against her cheek in her smaller one. Aisha sighed and her smile widened, despite her tears.

She started when the man returned, his face downcast. "It is time, sister." He looked past her at Fatima.

When Aisha rose, her hand slipped from Fatima's grip. Fatima balled her fingers into a fist, stifling the urge to reach for her again.

Aisha said, "Come, child. Someone here can help us. Perhaps if you listen to her, you may believe in me."

***

Prince Faraj

Faraj accompanied the Sultan and his son through the doors of the Sultan's bedchamber. Torches glistened among the shadows outside. Mute guards lined the walls like stone sentinels. A garden of oleander thrived in the courtyard.

The Sultan said, "We must move quickly against the Ashqilula now."

The crown prince halted beside him. "What of the delegation to the Marinid Sultan in al-Maghrib el-Aska?"

The Sultan paused and smiled at Faraj, who stared back at him, wondering what lay behind that gesture. "They shall leave soon, but other matters concern us."

"Father, if the Marinids intervene, our family shall have a strong ally."

The Sultan raised his hand and stilled further argument from his son. "There is the danger of interference from Castilla-León and Aragón. Our last treaty with King Alfonso of Castilla-León has ended. We cannot allow our old enemies to ally with the new ones."

Faraj frowned at this. "Then, why talk of the Marinids at all? The allies you seek are across the sea and over the mountains. Can they aid us against the Christians who are at our borders?"

The Sultan smiled. "You're quick to give your opinion, for one who shows no obvious interest in daily court life. I had thought you weren't paying attention at all."

Faraj ducked his head. "My father taught me foremost to observe."

His uncle nodded. "He was right. Consider what we know of the Christians and their ambitions. Gharnatah weakened by a civil war is an easy target for them. The Ashqilula family shall become even more dangerous with Christian help."

The crown prince sighed. "You know what you must do?"

The Sultan patted his shoulder. "They are only words, my son."

Faraj wondered when empty promises and broken vows had become acceptable. Surrounded by such people, was there anyone he could trust?

The crown prince continued, "You risk a great deal for your throne, Father."

"Is it not worth it? The Ashqilula would undo everything I have done. We shall strike on both frontiers. First, we shall make an attractive proposition to the Marinids that includes two strategic ports and the offer of your newly widowed sister, the Sultana Maryam."

"She shall rebel against being bartered away so soon, Father. She loved her Ashqilula chieftain."

The Sultan rolled his eyes heavenward. "Still your favorite sister, humph? How pleased she shall be to have your support. If only you might undertake her financial burdens, as well. She should be grateful for this union. She is not in the flower of her youth, but like her mother, Maryam's beauty is timeless. As with his ancestors, the Marinid Sultan would love nothing more than to meddle in the politics of al-Andalus. I know the danger of foreign warriors with a foothold on my land, but the Ashqilula pose too great a threat."

"Wisdom suggests Ibrahim shall move swiftly once he learns of your overtures to the Marinids."

The Sultan chuckled, a hollow sound. "Wisdom has no influence here. Had I been wiser, I might have never allied with Ibrahim's father. Another, rather than Ibrahim's aunt, might have been my first wife. My brothers and my own beloved firstborn daughter would have wed others. You would not be enduring a sham marriage...."

When the crown prince ground his teeth together and cast a dark look at his father, the Sultan paused. "Well, that is best left unsaid. I have sacrificed my family's futures in favor of the Ashqilula's ambitions, but no longer."

Faraj shook his head. "No man can know the future, not even the Sultan."

The Sultan suddenly rounded on him. "Only a fool perceives a trap and walks blindly into it!"

Faraj bristled, for he had often wondered whether he was a fool for perceiving the danger posed by this union with the Sultan's granddaughter. Yet his ambition had overpowered all reasoning.

The Sultan muttered, "I did not care for the future. I wanted power and secured it with the support of the Ashqilula. I bound my blood to theirs. Now civil war shall ensue, but we cannot avoid it. My first wife's greedy nature signifies all I find intolerable about her clan. Now they plot against me, secure in the power bases I have given them. They would steal my throne."

He stabbed a finger at Faraj. "Your marriage shall check the ambitions of our enemies. Fatima has a special significance to our foes. A union between her and the Ashqilula would have continued our alliance. Now, there can be no more marriages between my heirs and the Ashqilula. Your union with my granddaughter has secured my legacy."

Faraj said nothing, though he deeply resented the responsibility. His uncle played them all like pieces on a gaming board.

The Sultan studied him. "I have spoken with the royal tutor about you."

When he paused, Faraj hung his head a little.

With a sigh, the Sultan continued, "I would think your entire education a waste, but for your aptitude with languages, in particular Latin and the Castillan tongue. Ibn Ali praised your skill."

Faraj raised his eyebrows at this. "The royal tutor was too kind."

"I would hope not. I am dependent on your skill."

When the crown prince gasped, both men turned. Identical twin girls holding hands ambled past the oleander hedges, both rubbing their eyes. The crown prince knelt before the children. "Alimah, Muna. Why aren't you asleep, my darlings?"

"Father, where's Fatima?" one child asked.

"What do you mean? Isn't she abed?"

"I thought she went to use the chamber pot, but she hasn't come back."

The crown prince stood and looked at the Sultan, his eyes bulging. The Sultan rushed toward his granddaughters. "Return to bed, I'm sure Fatima shall join you soon. Go now."

The pair bowed stiffly before leaving the courtyard. The Sultan turned from all of them, his hands shaking at his sides.

"Father...."

"No! She made her objections clear to you, but I never imagined she would dare take that child from here!"

Faraj looked to each man's face with a frown. "What has happened? Who has taken Fatima?"

The crown prince said, "My wife, Aisha of Ashqilula."

Faraj drew back. "Your wife? What sort of woman steals her own child?"

Equally troubling, what sort of man must the crown prince be if his wife had willingly abandoned him and taken their daughter?

The crown prince glared at him. "Do not dare speak ill of her! You have no right." He turned to his father. "I shall go to Aisha's servants. They shall tell me the truth."

He hurried from the courtyard, but paused for a moment, glaring at Faraj over his shoulder. "Do not speak to anyone about this night."

The Sultan said, "I do not doubt my nephew's ability to keep secrets."

When Faraj tried to speak, the Sultan waved him away and withdrew inside his chamber, muttering, "Bitch! More trouble than she is worth, just like the rest of her family."

Faraj shook his head. What had he gotten himself into with this marriage? Emotions warred inside him; confusion and worry coupled with an inescapable sense of relief. He tamped down that latter feeling almost immediately as it sprang. He could not allow anyone to know his real thoughts on the union. His uncle and his cousin, who was also now his father in-law, must perceive that he shared their concerns for Fatima's well-being and safe return. With a frown directed toward the Sultan's doors, he escaped to his own residence.

After his parents had died, he arrived in the capital with his half-brother and three sisters, and received his own household upon reaching thirteen years of age. He enjoyed every privilege, for the Sultan had admired and loved his father. The royal tutor had educated him, but the man wasted his efforts. Faraj had no interest in intellectual knowledge. Only power, wealth, and mastery of his destiny offered security.

When he entered his house, the warmth of the first chamber enveloped him. The source of heat was a metal brazier, emitting the fragrant scent of sandalwood. Green and white cushions lined the base of pale yellow, stucco walls. A low table stood in the center of the room and underneath it, a plush, multicolored carpet covered the floor. Brass lanterns glowed hot, illuminating the windowless room. An arch to the left led to the courtyard from which his steward, Marzuq, approached.

Marzuq bowed, thick blond curls falling over his youthful face. His sky blue eyes glowed with pleasure and admiration. "Congratulations on your marriage. We didn't expect you so early, master."

Faraj grimaced. "Tell my women I'm waiting."

He bypassed the servant and headed for his apartment in the harem. Soon his concubines, the *jawari*, appeared outside the door. They were three of the most beautiful women in his estimation. Rarely did a night pass where at least one of them did not tempt him to call her to bed. They were each around his age, but their differences were stark. Baraka was Genoese with dark brown hair, skin like alabaster and a petulant nature. Hayfa was a beautiful Nubian, tall and lithe with a sweet disposition. Samara was a Provençal with white skin and black hair.

While she behaved like a mouse, she was a lioness in his bed.

Frowns and downcast eyes greeted him, instead of welcoming smiles and limbs.

"Why do you look so forlorn?" He forced a measure of concern into his voice.

"How can you wonder? You're married now." Baraka's pink lips pouted.

"Why should my marriage displease you? You have always had my affections. This won't change."

"But your wife may not like us, master." Hayfa whimpered.

"What if she tries to sell us?" Samara added, her words ending on a sob.

He groaned aloud. "You are mine. My wife would never dare sell any of you."

Baraka said, "Bad enough we must share you with each other, but now you are married. Is she more beautiful than me, your princess?"

Exasperated, he rolled his eyes. "Princess Fatima is a child, with several more years to pass before she reaches womanhood. Then she'll be my true wife, subject to my will and whims. She'll accept your presence because she has no other choice."

Baraka said, "Still, master, you do not answer me. You do not tell us if she's beautiful."

Her impudence made her the most disagreeable of his *jawari*, but she excited him beyond measure. For the entertainment she provided, both in and out of his bed, he forgave her much.

"You're all slaves. I don't have to submit to your questioning. I do so simply because I don't wish to hurt you. Lest you forget yourselves, remember I am your master and you have no right to question me. Each of you would do well to keep that in mind, lest you find yourselves at auction soon."

As he expected, Samara and Hayfa burst into tears, while Baraka's pout grew defiant. He dismissed the others and tugged Baraka to the bed. He banished her displeasure with kisses along her throat and shoulders until she surrendered.

Later, he rolled on his stomach, replete in the enjoyment of the concubine's charms. Baraka traced a nail across his shoulder. "I can stay if you like, master."

"You'll leave now. You know the custom."

He waited for her sigh before she stood and wrapped her alabaster body in silk. When none of this happened, he dragged the coverlet from her. "Go, Baraka."

Her arm snaked around his shoulder, fingers at the nape. "Why do you send me away? I only want to comfort you, master."

"And you have. Now you may go."

She brushed a pert nipple against him and kissed his ear, nibbling on the lobe. Her other hand threaded wispy curls of hair on his belly and drifted downward. "Your body cannot say no to Baraka."

He pushed her back among the pillows. Her throaty laughter, her scent, and her desire enthralled him. She wound her limbs around him and tugged his face to hers. She proved more intoxicating than her perfumes.

Much later, he collapsed on her body, but her legs tightened around his waist. Loosening her possessive hold, he rolled on his side. "Leave off, Baraka."

She stroked a curved nail across his back. "Rest, master, for you have pleasured me well. You need to regain your strength. I shall stay with you until you do."

She was impudent, but he was too tired to chastise her. Eyelids heavy, his head sank on the pillow. Before sleep claimed him, he managed a weak protest. "I don't want you here."

"Yes, master, you'll always want Baraka."

He closed his eyes, as the powerful lure of sleep claimed him.

The dreams came unbidden, as they always did. Violent, vivid images ripped from the depths of his buried past, a child's worst nightmare.

His father slumped over the low dining table. Viscous blood pooled under his face, stained the golden silk tablecloth, and ran red trails to the cedar floor. Mother cradled the body in her arms. His father's head lolled against her shoulder and fell backwards. The gaping gash at his neck seeped blood from a red, jagged line torn ear to ear.

Mother closed his sightless, gray eyes and kissed the dark brown hair, matted against his skull. Then she removed his bloodless *khanjar*, the jeweled hilt of the dagger gleaming in the torchlight. She plunged the weapon into her chest. Only a brief spasm betrayed her pain. She never screamed, no – his cries were the ones to fill the room, as they did now.

Shuddering, bathed in perspiration, Faraj opened his eyes. Despite his fears about Baraka or anyone else seeing him in such a vulnerable state, the *jarya* snored beside him. Pale moonlight filtered through the lattice windows. It traipsed across the thick woven rugs covering the olive wood floor. The light illuminated the recesses of a carved niche where a fountain and basin held water for morning ablutions.

Cloying, fragrant, jasmine permeated the thick, curled locks of the woman who lay beside him. Her pale arm encircled his chest. Even now, with her rounded, full breast pressed against him, her leg draped possessively over his, her allurements and charms were a temptation. He wanted to wake her and take his pleasure upon her willing body. As if in doing so, he might chase the nightmares away forever.

Disgusted, he shrugged off her arm before extracting himself from her embrace. Naked, he stood at the window and peered through the lattice to the south, in the direction of the place he had once called home. His head bowed, he whispered into the darkness, "Father, protect me. Mother, forgive me."

Chapter 3

The Prophecy

Princess Fatima

Gharnatah, al-Andalus: Muharram 664 AH (Granada, Andalusia: October AD 1265)

In silence, Fatima followed Aisha. They crossed a darkened hallway with shuttered windows near the ceiling. Fatima glanced at the man who fell into step beside her.

He said, "Princess, I am your uncle Abdallah, brother of Aisha."

She eyed him, from the collar of his *jubba*, a wave of azure silk, to its hem skirting the floor. She was no longer leery of the scars on his cheeks. "Why haven't I seen you in Gharnatah before?"

He halted and showed even, white teeth in a smile. "Your mother was just as direct in our childhood."

She waited for an answer.

He replied, "I visited several years ago, in the days after your birth. I held you and proclaimed you were a child of my sister's spirit. You remind me of her."

"I look like my father."

"You resemble him, but you have your mother's dignity and strength." At her puzzled frown, he continued. "When you are older, you shall understand my meaning."

When he walked on, she followed him. "You never came back to Gharnatah after that visit?"

He stopped again and rubbed the back of his neck, looking away from her steady gaze. "It was... difficult, at times, to see you and Aisha. I had given up all hope, until today."

The hesitation in his voice told her that he hated the long absence from his sister, but she did not know who or what could have kept him away. A doubt nagged at her. Had her father done it? Had he kept Aisha locked away from her family, like a prisoner?

She shook her head and asked, "Is this your house?"

"The only one I own in the foothills of Gharnatah." He looked around as though seeing something in the shadows along the alabaster corridor. "I shall miss it."

She sensed some hidden meaning behind his answer, but she struggled with the understanding of so much already. Besides, the palace servants had always taught her that children never asked adults to explain themselves. Children had a duty to follow orders.

Up ahead, a dark-skinned servant approached Aisha, bending at the waist. A rounded belly jutted under her tunic. When she straightened, her veil slipped back, revealing dark hair cropped close to her skull. Fatima stared, recognizing something familiar in her rounded features. The servant spoke in whispers with Aisha, who turned back to Fatima and Abdallah.

"She wishes to see us alone, brother, before speaking with Fatima. Please arrange for my daughter to have something to eat. We don't have much time."

Abdallah waved the servant forward. "Ulayyah, have the cook prepare the morning meal for the child."

Aisha approached. "Fatima, return to the room."

"But I don't want to be there alone."

Aisha patted her head. "Nothing and no one can harm you here. I promise."

"How long must I wait?"

"For as long as it takes. Now please, do as I say."

Fatima spun away in a huff and dragged her feet across the marble, looking over her shoulder at almost every step.

31

Abdallah followed and closed the door on her last glimpse of her mother in the hallway. She sat down on the stool, her chin in her hand and waited.

***

The scent of freshly baked bread alerted her even before the door latch clicked. The same dark-skinned slave entered and padded across the floor, her bare feet hardly making a sound. She sank to her knees and lay flat on the ground, her forehead touching the marble.

"My princess, I am the slave Ulayyah. I serve the Ashqilula." Her voice quivered.

Fatima frowned at her. Only the Sultan deserved such a respectful bow. She did not expect it from a servant among the Ashqilula.

As the slave moved to a sitting position, her legs bent beneath her, two other women entered carrying a platter of flatbread, boiled eggs, cheese, olives, grapes and pomegranates, with a pitcher of water. They set the food and drink on the windowsill and left.

"May I serve you, princess?" Ulayyah asked, though she did not wait for an answer. She reached for the platter.

"I cannot eat all of that!" Fatima exclaimed. "Just the eggs and flatbread, please."

Ulayyah held the platter while Fatima chose the food she wanted. The flatbread was warm and thin, but not dry like the cooks in her father's kitchen made it. After eating it and the eggs, she plucked a few grapes from the stem.

She said, "You look like my old governess Halah."

The slave replied, "I am her younger sister, my princess."

Fatima remembered her governess had spoken of a sister who served the Ashqilula, one who had left Gharnatah years ago.

"Princess Fatima, I was the servant of the Sultan's daughter, the Sultana Mu'mina, until her death. Then I was sold to the lady Saliha."

"Who is that?"

"My lord Abdallah's mother."

"Then, she must be my grandmother." Fatima wondered why Aisha had brought her to meet her grandmother now. She had never thought of whether Aisha had any family. In truth, she had never wondered anything about Aisha's life before her marriage to Fatima's father.

Her hand fell from the platter and she twisted away from the slave, peering out through the lattice.

Despite the gloom of nighttime, she made out swaying tree branches lining both sides of an empty courtyard. The city was silent, except for the occasional hooting from an owl in the trees. The smell of dew-soaked grass and a flower garden, perhaps below the window, reached her nostrils. She inhaled with a sigh and leaned forward, her forehead pressed against the wooden screen. She could not tell where the heavens touched the earth on a night as black as kohl, except for when glimmering beams of light beckoned from a distance.

"Ulayyah, where are we?"

"In the foothills of Gharnatah, my princess."

"Am I close to the Sultan's palace? How far is it from here?"

"I'm not supposed to tell you that."

She jerked back toward the slave. "Who said so?"

Ulayyah's shoulders sagged and she hung her head. "My lord Abdallah. Forgive me, princess. I know you have been brought here against your will."

Fatima's jaw clenched. She swung toward the window and stared out into the darkness again, focused on the flickering lights.

"Would you like some more of the fruit, princess? You have eaten so little. It would displease the lady Aisha if she knew."

Fatima ignored the slave at her feet. Angry tears welled in her eyes, but she swiped them away impatiently. Would she ever see her father, brother, or sisters again? If Aisha had her way, it might be a long time before that happened, or perhaps never. Aisha had not explained where she intended to go after leaving Gharnatah. Was she truly doing this for her daughter's protection? Could Fatima's father have been right in warning her never to believe the princess? Her gaze clouded with more unshed tears. Whom should she trust – the father who had always adored and sheltered her, or the mother whose love she had long desired?

Just the evening before, everything had been different, as the household slaves prepared her for the wedding. Fatima's governess had brought her to the *hammam* where four female attendants awaited them. They undressed Fatima, while she studied a frieze of glazed tiles, in hues of yellow, blue, red, green, and black.

She had bathed and relaxed in the water. The attendants scraped her hands and feet with pumice stones. They toweled her dry and massaged her skin with rose oil and myrrh. They dried her hair with silk cloths perfumed with ambergris. Her governess dressed her in a *qamis*, a thin cotton shirt. Even now, she shivered in the cool room at the memory of the nearly transparent material against her bare skin.

She looked down at her hands, still painted with henna. Like all Andalusi brides, she had undergone the rituals of *al-laylat al-henna*. She remembered the heady fragrance of aloe wood, as her governess led her from the *hammam* to the garden where the women of the Sultan's household had gathered. Only Aisha remained absent, but then, Fatima had not expected her to be there. One of her grandfather's favorite concubines, his *kadin* Lateefah had painted her fingers and palms, even the soles of her feet.

Fatima traced the fine lines and swirls, with which the tip of the thin brush had colored her skin. When the henna application had dried, Lateefah bound her hands in white cotton. Fatima's governess returned her to her chamber, but she hardly slept that night. A woman's voice rose above the rhythmic sounds of *zaggats*, clanking finger cymbals made of brass and bowl-shaped, wooden *kāsatān*. The noise of the festivities drifted through the lattice windows of the harem until the coming of the first prayer hour, *Salat al-Fajr*.

The governess had returned in the morning with the slaves who brought her wedding garments, a palette of white, silver, and lavender colors. Over another white cotton undershirt and ankle-length trousers, the slaves dressed Fatima in her lavender silk *jubba*, over which they drew another robe of white, brocaded cloth, the *khil'a*. Ermine trimmed the neckline of the garment. The slaves had sewn embroidered *tiraz* bands in silver silk around the sleeves.

The jewels were even more beautiful than the clothes. Heavy silver anklets, rings inlaid with pearls, and multiple strands of amethyst bracelets had weighed down her limbs. Of all those ornaments, she kept only the *khamsa*, a charm in the shape of an upturned palm, known also as the Hand of Fatima.

Now, she reached beneath her tunic and fingered the silver necklace looped through the charm. Married women wore the *khamsa* for blessings of patience, wealth, and faithfulness from their husbands. She gripped the *khamsa*, struggling against a desperate need to return to her family and let them know she was safe. She needed no charm for good fortune, only a way to escape. Then, her hold on the charm loosened and faltered. If she returned to her father's palace, she would be choosing everyone over Aisha, who promised protection and, more importantly, the mother's love she had never felt.

"My princess, I beg your favor, please. Does my sister still live? Please tell me. I have not seen her for over twenty years."

Fatima's gaze returned to the slave. She had almost forgotten Ulayyah remained at her side.

"Halah takes care of us, my brother and sisters and me. If she knew where I was, she would want you to help me go back to my father."

Ulayyah set the platter on her lap, with her head and shoulders bowed. Her lower lip trembled. "I cannot do it, princess. Please do not ask me."

"Then, if you can't help me, leave me alone!" Fatima hid her sobs behind her hands.

***

Soon, Abdallah returned and led Fatima from the room to another part of the house. Servants stood on either side of a shuttered olive wood door. It opened onto a dimly lit room with windows covered in lattice and torches in iron sconces flickering near the low ceiling. Rugs covered the floor and colored silken cushions lined the base of the walls.

At the heart of the chamber, a woman reclined on a black pallet, her head lolling on red and silver striped pillows. Aisha knelt beside her, hands clasped. The woman on the pallet waved her off and crooked a finger toward Fatima, who shuffled across the floor.

For the first time, she gazed upon the face of her maternal grandmother. Dark brown hair curled about the woman's timeworn countenance. Her eyes, like a cat's own, resembled Fatima's, though there were crinkles in the leathery flesh surrounding them. She was small and slim. Her red and black robe, bracelets and rings shimmered with gemstones.

"Your bloodlines bear out too much, child, for me to call you kin. You belong to the Nasrids, much to my regret. I would speak with you alone, princess of Gharnatah."

Fatima glanced at Aisha, who nodded toward her before retreating to the doorway. Soon, Fatima stood alone with her grandmother.

At a gesture from her, Fatima sat and handed her a water pipe on a silver gilt tray.

The woman inhaled and set it aside. "I am Saliha bint Abu Abdallah Muhammad ibn Yusuf, the last rightful Hud lord of Ishbiliya."

Fatima frowned. "I never knew the Hud family married among the Ashqilula clan."

The Hud tribe had been her grandfather's enemies until he helped the Christian kings destroy them. Yet, he had chosen Aisha as a bride for his eldest son. Fatima drew back, realizing that she bore the blood of her family's enemies through her mother.

"I never said I married by choice, girl. Your grandfather raided Ishbiliya and forced me to marry an Ashqilula chieftain against my will. Such blood ties would not have existed in the days of my father. Your grandfather murdered my father at the gates of al-Mariyah."

Fatima snapped, "It's not true. That's not what my father told me!"

"Then, he is a liar who shall burn in hell-fire, just like his accursed father."

"Don't say that. You don't know anything. Father said my grandfather rose against the Hud clan because they were cruel masters of al-Andalus. That is why Grandfather helped the Christians conquer Ishbiliya."

The woman closed her eyes. "One day, you shall have to learn about your family. Your grandfather is not the benevolent savior of al-Andalus. Your innocence and youth blind you to the truth about him now, but one day, you shall be a woman and the truth shall become clearer in your mind. Your grandfather has betrayed his brothers of the Faith, because he is greedy and corrupt."

Fatima stared at her in silence, although her heart pitched violently inside. How could this woman say such things about her family? It could not be true. At night, her father often lulled her brother and sisters to sleep with stories of his father's raids along the Christian frontier and tales of how he protected the people of Gharnatah from Christian and Muslim enemies. Her father would never lie to her, it was impossible.

Fatima muttered, "I don't believe you."

The woman opened her eyes and returned her intent stare. "Believe what you must, child. It shall not comfort you. I have wept for my Ishbiliya, a once great and cultured city. Now, the faithful live in squalor in the Christian Sevilla. Allah, the Compassionate, the Merciful, calls to me, but even death cannot grant me comfort. Thoughts of how much my family has lost because of yours plague me. I would fight on and live, if only to see your family's end."

"Are you dying?"

"There is a canker growing in my breast. My useless physicians can do nothing. Each day the pain grows and I swallow more opium."

Fatima looked at her feet, unsure of what to say.

"Are you concerned for me, child?"

"I don't feel happy when anyone dies. I've never met you before, but I'm not happy to see you suffer."

"Then you have more kindness in you than any member of your clan. The treachery of your family defeated my father. My one satisfaction comes in seeing you at last, for in you, I have beheld the ruin of the Nasrids."

Fatima frowned. "I don't understand."

"Your children shall destroy your grandfather's line of Sultans. Neither the Ashqilula, nor the Christians kings shall claim the victory over your family. No, that line shall end with the tyranny of the children you bear, and their sons, and the sons of their sons. My father always said, the blood shall bear out in the end and what is rotten at its core cannot yield better." She moaned then sagged against the pillows in shudders that visibly wracked her body.

Though puzzled, Fatima could hardly bear the sight of her pain. "Can I help you? Do you want me to call your son?"

"Abdallah cannot help me."

Fatima waited for a moment before asking, "What did you mean when you said my children would destroy the line of Sultans?"

Her grandmother made no reply. After a long silence, Fatima thought she was dead. Leaning closer, she listened for labored, shallow breathing.

The woman's birdlike hand caught her wrist, nails digging into the skin. "You shall see the end of your family name. You cannot prevent it. You shall remember my words and know the truth of them."

Her grip relaxed, arm falling at her side. Her chest still rose and fell, though slower than before. She did not speak again. Fatima fled and found Aisha and Abdallah waiting in the darkened corridor.

"My mother lives?" he asked. At her nod, he said, "I do not think she shall return with me to Naricha."

Aisha asked Fatima what her mother had said.

"She told me that she was born into the Hud family. Did my father know that when he married you?"

"He did. His desire for me outweighed any thought of my blood ties. What else did Saliha say to you?"

"She said my children would destroy the Sultan's family. I don't know what she meant."

With a faraway look, Aisha whispered, "My mother has always had an understanding of things, beyond the comprehension of others. When I was a child, she always knew with certainty of events occurring miles away. When tragedy struck, she never seemed surprised. She has the gift of prophecy and she is never wrong."

Abdallah pressed his fists to his temples. "I shouldn't have done this. I shouldn't have told you to bring the girl here."

"I am pleased that you did, kinsman, even if your secrecy is an affront to me. How else might have I have seen the bride I shall claim for my own?"

They turned at an unexpected voice coming from the shadowy hall. Abdallah drew back, his hand going to an empty sheath belted at his side. When he seemingly realized the weapon was not there, his whole body sagged.

Aisha drew Fatima into her arms and pressed her close, enveloping her in silken skirts. Fatima shuddered despite her fervent hold and stared into the darkness.

Heavy footfalls heralded the emergence of two bloodstained strangers. The taller, thinner man hefted a crimson-stained blade. As he approached, tiny droplets dotted the marble floor. Deep lines crisscrossed his leathery complexion, where coarse, dark facial hair did not cover him. His bold gaze pinned them in the corner.

"What other secrets have you been keeping from me, Abdallah? You have brought your aged mother all the way from Naricha. What could have been so important for you to drag a dying woman to Gharnatah? Only this reunion with your sister and her daughter?"

The man behind him stepped closer. Aisha's gasp echoed along the length of the corridor. "Abu Muhammad! What are you doing here?"

His likeness reminded Fatima of the Sultan and her father. He even had the same hazel eyes, hooded under heavy brows like the Sultan's own and the hawk-like nose.

He looked down the length of it at her mother, then at her before spitting on the floor near Abdallah's shoe.

When the first intruder cackled and brandished his sword, Fatima's skin crawled. Flecks of blood from his weapon spattered the walls.

"I promise, Aisha, this shall not be a sweet reunion between you and Abu Muhammad. You should have married him when you had the chance. Now, you are tainted, cousin, with the blood of those who have turned against us. Abu Muhammad has accepted the truth about you."

Aisha trembled so violently that Fatima clutched her tighter. She realized these men must be the Ashqilula chieftains, Abu Ishaq Ibrahim of Qumarich and Abu Muhammad of Malaka. If so, what cause did her mother have to fear these two men so much? They were kin, after all.

Her mind grasped that Ibrahim was a cousin to Aisha, but the news that Abu Muhammad had wanted to marry her startled Fatima. She truly did not know the woman who had given birth to her.

Abdallah stepped between them and the men. "Please, my lords Ibrahim, Abu Muhammad, my kinsmen. Let us speak in private. My lord Ibrahim, your bloodied sword frightens the princesses."

"Did you know they were coming to Gharnatah, too, Abdallah?" Aisha's voice was shrill. When Fatima looked up at her, her bosom rose and fell rapidly and her olive skin paled.

"Go back to the room across the hall, sister. Take Fatima with you." He spoke without looking at either of them.

Aisha rounded him, still clutching Fatima against her. "Did you know, brother?"

"Go, damn you, before you make things worse. I should not have asked you to come. Go, Aisha!"

She dragged Fatima with her and Abdallah followed. When he slammed the door shut in their wake, Aisha turned and rattled the handle. The door would not budge. She collapsed on the floor, cradling her head in her hands. Her scream pierced the silence of night, carried on the breeze that stirred the damask curtains.

Chapter 4

Blood Ties

Princess Fatima

Gharnatah, al-Andalus: Muharram 664 AH (Granada, Andalusia: October AD 1265)

Fatima crouched beside Aisha on the marble floor. Her hand rose in mid-air and fell. She did not know if she should comfort her mother, as her governess often did when her sister Muna had nightmares. Would it be better if she left her crying alone? Lost in uncertainty, she lapsed into cold silence.

Aisha rose and clasped her hands together. "I shouldn't have brought you here. I should never have trusted...."

She hesitated at the first step, but after regaining her footing, she walked to the window. She sat on the sill and gestured for Fatima, who joined her on the stool. She peered through the lattice and Fatima followed her gaze, seeing little in the shadows of night. Even the flickering lights were gone.

"Forgive me, child. I thought I could have saved you, but it seems it is your destiny to remain at Gharnatah."

"What are we going to do?"

"You shall return to *al-Qal'at al-Hamra.*"

"What about you? You mean, we shall return to *al-Qal'at al-Hamra*, right?"

When Aisha looked at Fatima, her sad smile returned. "Dawn is almost upon us. We don't have much time. Abdallah told me he had hired the help of a Jewess, the

Sitt al-Tujjar. She is a widowed merchant's wife, who sells silk and other goods in her husband's stead. She travels throughout al-Andalus, even to *al-Qal'at al-Hamra*, where your grandfather's wives and other courtiers rely on her trade and her gossip. I could persuade her to help. She would do it, for the right fee."

"But we're locked inside the room. How can you talk to her?"

"Have you eaten?"

"Yes, but...."

"Do not be fearful, my child. Allah, the Compassionate, the Merciful shall watch over you, all of your days."

Aisha opened her arms and beckoned her close. She hesitated just before flinging herself into that embrace, finding the comfort she had never known.

**

Fatima stirred groggily. Opening her eyes, she realized her head rested on the leather satchel from which Aisha had retrieved the brush. The pallet cushioned her again, though someone had moved it next to the brazier. With a quick glance at the water clock, she realized the fifth copper bowl was nearly full.

The slave Ulayyah stood with a platter of uneaten food before Aisha at the window, their heads bent together. Fatima closed her eyes and listened to their conversation.

"... Life is forfeit, but you can help me save my daughter. Go to the Inn of the Merchants in the heart of the marketplace. The Sitt al-Tujjar arrived there two days ago. Give her my message."

"Mistress, my lord Ibrahim shall surely know that I am missing."

"Why should he care?"

"Because, my lord Abdallah sent me to him after they met. He always sends me to him, to be his... companion."

Silence followed. Fatima kept herself very still on the pallet, though she did not think either of the women were paying attention to her.

"Ulayyah, is Ibrahim the father of the child you carry?"

"Yes and of the son I have already borne, though he would never acknowledge him." The slave's voice was low and bitter. "I have every reason to hate him."

"Then, do this to thwart his intentions. He shall take Fatima to Qumarich. His fortress is impregnable, on a rock promontory with sheer sides except for one that is gated and heavily guarded. If he steals her away, her family shall never see her again. I cannot bear to think of my child in his clutches. It would truly be a worse fate than even her grandfather would have in mind for her."

A little squeak escaped Fatima's throat. Surely, her grandfather could never be as cruel as Ibrahim.

Aisha continued. "If you want me to believe Abdallah's vow that he did not betray me, save my daughter."

Then silk swished across the floor.

"She's awake. She's listening to us," Aisha said. Silk rustled again before long fingers cupped Fatima's chin. "Open your eyes, my girl."

When Fatima did so, Aisha hovered at her side, with a watchful Ulayyah behind her.

"Mistress, I must go," she said, glancing over her shoulder at the door.

"Leave the food, Ulayyah, or they shall become suspicious. Go to the Sitt al-Tujjar. If Abdallah would prove himself to me, he should give you the payment for the Jewess."

"I understand, Mistress." Ulayyah glanced at Fatima before she left the room.

When they were alone again, Aisha sat down on the pallet. She tore the flatbread and broke a piece of cheese. She gave the rest of the meal to Fatima. "Eat. You shall need strength at dawn."

Fatima chewed the hard cheese, nearly choking on it. "What's happening? What are you doing?"

"I intend to save your life and get you far from this place. Eat and stop asking questions I cannot answer."

Just then, the door latch clicked.

44

Fatima stopped chewing. Her breath escaped in a short gasp as the Ashqilula chieftains entered.

Ibrahim said, "There. You both look much better now that you are eating."

Abu Muhammad crossed the distance between them and stopped at Fatima's feet. Although she trembled, she stared up at him in silence and would not retreat or move closer to Aisha.

"This one has strength, but it is clear she is the crown prince's whelp."

Ibrahim bent and reached for her, fingers tangling in her curls. His dark eyes gleamed. He jerked her forward. Wisps of hair tore from the roots. Pain seared her scalp, but she pressed her lips together and smothered her cry.

Aisha dropped the flatbread. "Don't dare touch my daughter."

Ibrahim swung his hand wide. The blow connected with Aisha's cheek. She crashed with a sickening thud against the alabaster wall behind her. Fatima reached for her, but Ibrahim's cruel grip tightened. Aisha clutched the side of her head and righted herself. Blood smeared the wall.

"Soon enough, she shall be the least of your concerns, woman."

Ibrahim leaned closer to Fatima and smiled. His breath smelled of cinnamon, his teeth white and even. "Yes, this one shall breed strong sons and beautiful daughters for the Ashqilula. Not like her aunt Mu'mina, who managed to bear me only one weak-willed son."

When he released her, she jerked away and hugged Aisha. "Are you hurt?"

Aisha groaned. "Do not worry for me."

Fatima glared at the chieftains. "My father shall kill you for hurting her and me."

"No, little Fatima, your father shall never see either of you again."

He stood and wiped the hand that had slapped Aisha on the side of his trousers. "The preparations for our wedding feast are at hand."

Still clutching her head, Aisha whispered. "She is already married, you must know that."

Ibrahim laughed at her. "Ismail's boy? He is of no consequence, just like his dead father. Besides, I know the marriage remains unconsummated. It seems Faraj has qualms about bedding his child bride."

His gaze fell on Fatima again. "I have no such reservations. Her blood shall stain my bed soon enough."

She huddled against Aisha, who clutched her tightly.

Ibrahim knelt before Fatima once more. He framed her face in his large hands and forced her to look at him.

"I shall sire beautiful daughters on you, ones with eyes of fire like yours, but you shall first give me sons, strong sons to claim the throne of Gharnatah. What do you say, my princess?"

She clamped her mouth shut again. His grip on her flesh tightened. She sucked in all the spittle she could and spat. A white blob landed on his face. He grabbed her hand, crushing her tiny wrist. He used the back of her hand and wiped the spittle from his cheek. Then he shoved her back against the wall.

At his side, Abu Muhammad said, "Do not taint her too much, cousin."

Ibrahim stood "No bruises shall ever mar her face, but when she is disobedient, she shall learn never to test my patience. When I have her in my bed as my lawful wife and my child is in her belly, her grandfather the old fool shall know I have defeated his plans. Now, what shall we do about her traitorous mother? Honor demands a decision."

Aisha's trembling coursed through her body and Fatima felt her shaking, before Aisha stood and stared at both men.

"Do what you must with me, but I pray, do not let my daughter see it."

Fatima clutched at the folds of her *jubba*. "No, stay with me! We have to stay together."

Ibrahim chuckled. "Foolish girl." He turned to his companion. "Take her for a while, if you still want her. Do not deny yourself a little pleasure, before the end."

Although his gaze was hard and his mouth a thin, firm line, Abu Muhammad shook his head. "I am sorry, Aisha, but it truly would have been better if you had died years ago. Instead your father broke our betrothal and wed you to the Sultan's son." He glanced at Ibrahim. "I want no part in her fate. I am returning to Qumarich in advance of your wedding feast."

Ibrahim replied, "Coward. Take that wretch, Abdallah, with you. I don't trust him."

Abu Muhammad bowed and turned. Halfway to the door, he spun on his heels.

"And, what if he should ask after his sister's welfare?"

Ibrahim laughed, throwing back his head covered in a black turban. "I do not doubt your ability to tell lies, cousin."

When Abu Muhammad left, Ibrahim eyed Aisha. Then he drew his long sword from its sheath. Traces of dried blood coated the metal. "Kneel, woman."

Fatima's heart lurched inside her. She covered her mouth with her trembling hand. "No, my lord! Please, you can't."

Aisha hushed her. Fatima grabbed at the hem of her mother's robe again, her cries buried in the silk. "Please don't leave me, *Ummi*. Don't...."

Aisha crouched beside her and held her shaking hands. "How sweet you are. At the end, I finally hear you call me 'Mother' as you should have always done. Forgive me for never letting you say it before now. It is the most beautiful word I have ever heard.

"Have courage, this shall soon be over. Never show your fear before the enemy. He shall only use it to defeat you. Keep your wits and survive another day and the next. Be happy in your marriage to Faraj, unlike mine. Above all else, love your children. Show them your devotion every day of their lives. Tell them how precious they are to you, always. Never leave them in doubt of your love. Never doubt my love for you again. It is unending, not even death can stop it. And, remember your promises to me."

She backed away even as Fatima reached for her desperately. "Now, close your eyes, child. This horrid night has been naught more than a bad dream and soon you shall awaken, in your father's palace."

"No! I won't pretend."

"You must heed me in this, the last request I shall ever make of you."

"No, *Ummi*! I cannot."

Ibrahim growled low in his throat and hauled Aisha against him by the collar of her robe, before he shoved her to the ground. On her hands and knees, she bowed her head, leaving her neck exposed. "Avenge me, daughter."

Despite the tears blurring her vision, Fatima stared straight ahead. When she blinked, the terrible whoosh of Ibrahim's sword came down in a terrifying arc. His eyes glittered like black opals, lips pulled back over his teeth in a savage growl. Warm blood sprayed her face. Aisha's body sagged and sprawled forward. A viscous blotch spilled and drained from the still form. It trickled between the tiles and into the water channel. Fatima drew her knees up, rested her chin on them, and covered her face with her arms.

Chapter 5

Vows

Princess Fatima

Gharnatah, al-Andalus: Muharram 664 AH (Granada, Andalusia: October AD 1265)

Heavy footfalls on the marble barely warned Fatima. As Ibrahim roughly seized her and threw her over his shoulder, her limbs flailed. Her tiny fists battered his back, as he stepped over the headless body and headed for the door.

Fatima's screams pierced the rafters, as she stretched out her hands toward the murdered figure. "No, *Ummi*, *Ummi!*"

Although she struggled and twisted, Ibrahim's firm grip encased her. "She can't help you now."

He took her down the darkened hallway and turned to the right, just before reaching the room where she had seen her grandmother. Did the lady Saliha remain alive? If she had the gift of prophecy, had she already guessed her daughter was dead?

Ibrahim brought her down two flights of stairs. They entered a narrow corridor lit with a few torches. There were no windows, only satchels made of hemp stacked up along the wall.

He hefted her into his arms. She dug her teeth into the only exposed area, his bare neck. He screamed and released his hold.

The base of her skull exploded in splinters of shuddering pain. Orbs of light danced before her eyelids. She went limp. He raised a heavy boot and ground it into her hand, flattening it against the cold floor. When she cried out, he pressed harder. "I'll break every bone, if you don't stop screaming."

He bent and grabbed her by the neck, hauling her up. She clawed at his hand with her tiny fingers, her legs thrashing through the air.

"Open the storeroom."

Someone unseen behind her jangled keys and turned a lock. The room brimmed to the ceiling with wooden crates and more hemp sacks. Ibrahim dropped her inside the doorway. Her elbow jammed against the hard tiles. Rough hemp pressed against her back through her silken tunic. A painful wheeze tightened her chest and she coughed, gasping for air.

Outside the room, Ibrahim jabbed a finger at the person whom she still could not see. "Give me all of the keys. No one enters. She does not leave until I come for her. If she escapes, I shall kill you and every last slave in Abdallah's service."

"Yes, master."

A lean, bronze-skinned man stepped into view. As he bowed and handed the keys to Ibrahim, his dark eyes met Fatima's own. Then he turned away and walked the length of the hall.

Ibrahim wiped a smear of blood from his neck and looked at his stained fingers with widening, dark eyes. They narrowed as he turned his gaze on her. "You shall regret that. Your father has obviously spoiled you. When we are married, you shall learn the ways of a proper wife."

"I hate you! You killed my mother!"

He pulled the door shut with a heavy thud and left her in darkness.

She reared up, her chest and throat burning each time she inhaled. Something small and furry squeaked and rummaged between her toes. She drew her knees up.

Although it was safe to cry, when no one else could see her, she swiped at each tear before it could fall.

Crying would not help her. She had to escape, return to her father, and let him know her mother had died. The horror of all she had seen did not frighten or make her sad. Something had awoken inside her that she did not understand. It exploded when she had bitten into Ibrahim's throat. The power of it left her shaking, but also aware that she had to live, if only to destroy Ibrahim by whatever means she could manage.

Raised voices came to her from beyond the door. "I don't care what he's asking for, Abu Muhammad! I'll kill him if he becomes too suspicious."

"Enough blood has stained our hands today, Ibrahim. We have to find another way out of the city. The guards have not opened the southern gates."

"But it's nearly dawn. We can't leave with the trade caravan, unless they open those gates!"

"I know. There can be only one reason they haven't done it. The Sultan knows the child and mother are missing. He thinks if he keeps the gates closed, Aisha cannot escape."

"There's no escape for her or for her daughter."

Keys jangled in the lock. Fatima pitched forward, ready for Ibrahim's return. If her grandfather knew she was gone, there was still hope. She had to try.

The door did not open. She frowned into the darkness.

"Leave her here, cousin."

"What?" Ibrahim's fury set Fatima shaking, although she was outside his reach. "Are you mad? She's the reason I snuck into this city."

"Would you risk our lives for her? I won't!"

"You'll do what I tell you, Abu Muhammad. You may be the *Raïs* of Malaka, but never forget, I made it possible for you to attain that honor."

"The debt has been paid, several times over."

"You need a reminder of it. Without me, the Sultan's brother would still be alive, or Prince Faraj might hold the governorship in his stead. Now see to Abdallah and his mother. Ease his fears and tell him to make her stop blubbering."

"He's tried. She keeps beating her breasts and muttering Aisha's name."

Fatima slumped against a sack. A wedge formed in her throat, but she swallowed hard against it.

"Hide the truth, until it is no longer possible. I am not ready to kill him, yet. He still has his uses. Many of our warriors remain loyal to his father's memory."

"You should have thought of that before you murdered his sister, Ibrahim!"

"I told you before, honor demanded it. Should I have released her, let her escape back to her husband? You harbor some feeling for the woman, I think."

"I do not. I am reconciled to Aisha's fate. I am going to Abdallah. What are you going to do?"

The keys jangled and heavy footfalls sounded, moving away from the door. Fatima strained to hear Ibrahim's answer, but silence had fallen.

She sat in the shadows for an uninterrupted time, with the mice her constant companions. She jerked and squealed each time one of the rodents brushed too near.

Then, there was a faint scratching at the base of the door. "Princess?"

She covered her mouth with a hand, too frightened to answer the raspy voice beyond the walls.

"Princess Fatima? I've returned."

She sobbed at the sound of Ulayyah's voice. Her throat ached, but she forced the words out. "I'm here! Help me."

Ulayyah whispered, "Niranjan, hurry. If he knew there was another set of keys, he would kill me."

Keys jangled before the door creaked on its hinges. A shaft of light pierced the darkness. A large, black rat bolted into the hall, darting between the feet of the man and woman who filled the doorway.

Fatima launched herself at Ulayyah. "He killed her."

The slave held her close for a moment and whispered against her hair. "Hush, child. He can't hurt her anymore."

She drew back and wiped Fatima's face with the trailing edge of her veil.

"I grieve with you, princess, but I must fulfill my vow to your mother. You must go."

"I can't leave her here!"

Ulayyah set her down, jarring her. When her hands enveloped Fatima's smaller ones, Fatima whimpered.

"If you don't want your mother's death to be meaningless, then go now, with Niranjan al-Kadim. You can do nothing more. Abu Muhammad sent his men to clean up the blood and hide the body from my lord Abdallah."

"You must tell him what happened to my mother."

"It would destroy him! He would rise against Ibrahim and it would mean his death. One day, he shall see the truth about his family for himself. He can never know how Princess Aisha died."

"No, *Ummi* said...."

"Hush now. Your mother would want you to trust in me and Niranjan, as she once did."

The bronze-skinned youth stepped into view again from behind Ulayyah. Fatima frowned at him. He wore the iron collar of a slave, the same as all the slaves of her father's palace wore.

She asked, "What can he do? He's just a slave."

Ulayyah shook her head. "He can sneak you in a hemp sack up to the courtyard. I heard Ibrahim and Abu Muhammad whispering in the hall above. Abu Muhammad has bribed guards to open the northern gate of the city. He shall go first with my lord Abdallah. If he makes it out, Ibrahim shall follow. He shall tell my lord Abdallah that Princess Aisha delayed them and the Sultan's guards captured her."

"No! He cannot hide what he has done."

53

Ulayyah patted her hands. "You are the only witness to your mother's sacrifice. Do not let it be in vain. Go with Niranjan now. No one shall notice him in the courtyard. Abu Muhammad and my master prepare to leave with many pack animals."

Niranjan entered the room and grabbed one of the burlap snacks, surprising another rat that scrambled between the crates. Niranjan emptied a cascade of grain on to the floor and motioned for Fatima. She stepped into the hemp sack and he pulled it up to her shoulders.

Ulayyah knelt and pressed her forehead against the ground for a moment. "Know that I am loyal. I hate Ibrahim and if it is ever within my power to help you destroy him, I shall do it. Now go, princess, go! Go with God."

When Niranjan tried to close the sack, Fatima grabbed Ulayyah's hand. "What about you? Ibrahim said he would kill the slaves if I escaped."

"When my master Abdallah leaves, I shall be with him and his guards. I shall warn him to prepare for any treachery. Do not worry for me."

"But...."

"I must return to Naricha. I have a child there. My son Faisal is very sickly. I cannot be without him and I am heavy with another babe. Promise me only this – live and reach your father's house. Let your father know of your mother's sacrifice and tell my sister that I am still alive."

"I shall never forget you!"

Ulayyah lifted her fingers and kissed them, before she turned to Niranjan. "Close the sack. I go ahead of you to ensure the way is clear. Once you reach the courtyard, do not stop. Put the sack over the donkey's back and leave at the end of the caravan with the others. Lag behind them. My master's steward is old and his eyesight and strength are failing him. He shall not notice if you are careful.

"The caravan travels unguarded. My master does not have enough warriors to spare a portion for the safety of his goods, but he and Abu Muhammad shall catch up to the caravan. You must break away from it the moment you can. When you see the orchards in the hills above, you must turn south to the marketplace."

She poured a fistful of jangling coins from a small, red pouch into her hand, murmuring under her breath before she put them back inside. She pressed the pouch into his hand. "For the Sitt al-Tujjar. I shall ensure Ibrahim does not see you leave."

"How?" Niranjan raised his eyebrows in a questioning slant. Fatima glanced at him, recognizing something familiar about his nasal tone. They had never met before this but she was certain she had heard his voice before.

"I'll go to him. If I am with him, he won't be thinking of what is happening elsewhere."

Niranjan tied the hemp sack. Enveloped on all sides of its stifling warmth, Fatima fought for calm, even breaths. When Niranjan hefted her over his shoulder, a shrill wheeze escaped her.

He murmured, "Not so loudly, princess."

"Don't tell me how to breathe!"

He chuckled. "You sound just like your mother."

"What?"

"Niranjan, don't provoke her. This night has been very difficult." Ulayyah's voice came from up ahead.

Fatima groaned when Niranjan maneuvered her at an odd angle. She realized they must have started up the stairs. She could not see anything from within the dense, fibrous hemp.

"The courtyard is clear. Go with God."

Ulayyah's whisper preceded her hasty footsteps before they faded. A little light penetrated the strips of fiber. The air thickened with the scent of juniper and rosemary. Voices bellowed instructions, but above the cacophony came the sound of water murmuring in unseen channels.

Such a peaceful sound, so unlike anything Fatima had experienced in the last hours. She closed her eyes, but still, tears squeezed out beneath her lashes.

Deep inside, she silently vowed, 'I'll never forget, *Ummi*, never.'

She stifled a grunt when Niranjan set her across the back of a swaying animal. When thick rope secured her at the waist, it was nearly impossible to breathe.

"Open the gate! Get those sacks out of here and onward to Naricha."

Fatima recognized the voice of her mother's brother. He would never know the truth of what had happened to Aisha.

***

When Fatima finally stood and the sack opened, she wobbled slightly. Niranjan and two identical young women wearing slave collars bowed before her. She looked around, realizing she was in a sparsely furnished tent, with only a chair and table. Outside, the people talked and argued and coins jangled.

She asked, "Are we in the market?"

"Yes, my princess." Niranjan gestured to the chair. "Please await the Sitt al-Tujjar here."

"I want to go home."

"You shall." He grabbed the chair and set it in front of her. "Sit."

"Don't tell me what to do! You're not my father. You're just a slave."

He grinned, showing yellowed teeth with a few gaps in his mouth. "You remind me so of her. When I see you, I imagine what she was like as a child."

"Who?"

"Princess Aisha."

"Don't talk about my mother! You didn't know her."

"I did. I have served her since I was a child, long before she married the crown prince of Gharnatah."

Fatima sank into the chair and folded her arms across her chest. She did not want to hear from anyone who knew her mother, who might have known her better than she did.

56

Niranjan pushed the two women forward. Their coloring was the same as Niranjan, except they were thin and looked as though they had not eaten in a week with bellies caved in and ribs peeking through the flesh. Their narrow features were stark, bulging dark eyes, high, hollow cheekbones and buckteeth jutting forward between their thin lips.

"These are my sisters, Amoda," Niranjan patted the arm of the one who wore her braid on the left shoulder, "and Leeta." He gestured to the other girl, her dark hair falling over her right shoulder. "If you're hungry, they can bring you food."

"I don't want anything from you! When can I see my father again?"

Niranjan shook his head.

A morning breeze whistled through the tent, just before a woman in a blue cloak entered. She swept back her hood with a fat, bejeweled hand, revealing a white cloth with two blue stripes that covered her hair. A small ring-shaped patch of yellow cloth decorated the shoulder of her cloak. She bobbed her head.

Niranjan bowed to her, before turning to Fatima. "The Sitt al-Tujjar."

Fatima scowled and leaned forward on the chair. "Why is your name the 'mistress of the merchants'?"

"It is best for my business that no one knows my real name, princess. I am a widow who manages her late husband's trade. I am free to travel throughout the Muslim and Christian lands. People pay for my silk and wares. They pay me even more to keep their secrets."

She held out her hand. Niranjan pressed the red pouch into it. She cupped the weight and nodded. "We leave for *al-Qal'at al-Hamra*. Once there, I shall send word to Prince Faraj's steward that we have very special merchandise, for his master's eyes only."

Fatima jerked from the seat. "What? Why aren't you taking me to my father?"

The Sitt al-Tujjar tucked the bag of coins into the unseen folds of her garment. "I receive large sums of money because I am careful and can follow precise instructions. Your mother commanded me to deliver you only to your husband, Prince Faraj. She said he would understand the need for discretion, rather than arousing the curiosity of others by your sudden appearance outside your father's harem."

Fatima shook her head. "My mother trusted Prince Faraj? She didn't even like him."

The Sitt al-Tujjar shrugged.

***

Once again bound and stifled in the hemp sack, Fatima could hardly breathe. The bounce and sway of the camel caravan stole each breath, as rope held her securely on its back again. She rode up a sharp hill. When the camel finally sank to the ground, she waited for the opening of the sack.

"Send word to Prince Faraj's steward of my arrival."

She stayed quiet listening to the Sitt al-Tujjar giving other instructions. Soon, the camel swayed again and she gripped its sides tightly, fighting against the urge to vomit.

"Sitt al-Tujjar! Welcome."

A deep voice boomed in greeting before the beast sank to the ground again.

"Marzuq, I greet you in peace," the Sitt al-Tujjar said. "Your master collects rare and beautiful treasures. I bring him riches beyond measure."

"My master's moods are fickle, of late, but I shall summon him. You honor his house by granting us first choice and I recognize the value of that esteem."

Fatima bit her lip as she was lifted and lowered in the sack. Cold marble seeped through the hemp fibers.

"Marzuq, what is this?"

When the sack opened, Fatima gasped the first lungful of fresh air.

Faraj stood beside the fountain in his inner courtyard. The first rays of sunlight twinkled off the burnished copper roof and cast a halo around his dark, straight hair, which curled slightly at the nape. In the sunlight, his dark olive skin glowed like bronze. His jaw dropped and showed even, white teeth behind his thin lips.

"By the Prophet's beard... Fatima."

She stumbled slightly and Niranjan righted her. Shrugging off his hold, she swayed on her feet. She glared at Niranjan as he hovered beside her, his hands at the ready.

She asked, "Where is my father?"

Faraj gestured to the yellow-haired man beside him. "Marzuq."

"At once, my prince." The steward rushed from the house.

The Sitt al-Tujjar bowed before Faraj. "My task is completed. God be with your house."

She withdrew without looking at Fatima, who still staggered, as shards of pain knifed her legs.

Niranjan's fingers closed on her wrist. "Give yourself a little time. The ordeal has weakened you."

She snapped. "I'm not weak!"

Tiredness weighed down her limbs. It seemed like forever that she had feared she might never see her father or family again. The hated tears welled up and spilled.

Niranjan's gentle touch glided across her wet cheek. She pulled away and whispered. "It was you."

He raised his brows.

She continued. "In my room that night, it was you. She sent you to take me away. You said 'take her' to the other man who tried to keep me from warning my brother and sisters. I remember your voice."

"Princess, I was your mother's guard, the only one she relied upon. I have never left her side, until now."

"I have heard your voice before. I didn't remember where until you touched my cheek. Now I know you."

"I once served your mother in the palace. I do not doubt you may have heard my voice there."

"You're lying, I know you're lying." She licked away the salty years, as Faraj approached, eyeing both of them.

He asked, "What happened to you, Fatima?"

Before she could think of an answer, her name floated on the wind. Her father dashed from the entryway and across the cobblestone square. He lifted her from the ground and held her as if he would never let go.

"Oh, my dearest one, how I feared I would never see you again."

She hid her tears in his shoulder. In his embrace, she threaded her fingers in his dark reddish-brown hair and inhaled the familiar scent of him.

***

Later, she returned to the harem with her father, via an underground passageway from the citadel. She had never seen it before, but her father assured her, it was necessary to keep her absence and return a secret from everyone outside the family. She looked over her shoulder, wondering why he had allowed Prince Faraj to join them.

She waited with Niranjan and his sisters in the harem's garden courtyard. Overhead, the sun rose on another Gharnati day. Birds chirped in the trees and scented flowers filled the space. Water bubbled from the pomegranate-shaped fountain and surged along the channels that lined the walls. Everything looked the same. Yet, it would never be the same for her again.

Her brother appeared first, rubbing his eyes. He seemed indifferent to her presence, yawning loudly. While her sisters were also bleary-eyed, they were happy to see her.

Muna hugged her. "We didn't know where you were. Why are you so dirty? Your throat is all red."

Fatima swallowed past the lump in her throat, stomach roiling. Her brother and sisters stared. She reached blindly and Niranjan caught her hand. Burying her wet face in his tunic, she gave in to his gentle soothing.

He said, "I have ever served your mother. Now, I shall serve you. I shall protect you until the end of my days."

Behind her, Alimah asked, "Fatima, what's wrong?"

Their father cleared his throat. Fatima looked up just as the Sultan arrived. The princes and princesses fell to their knees.

"Fatima, come to me." When the Sultan held out his hand, she withdrew from Niranjan's hold and knelt, kissing the hem of her grandfather's robe. The Sultan raised her up and cupped her face, looking down at her in a steady hazel gaze.

"Rest, bathe and eat, for now. Afterward, I want to know everything."

***

After the slaves Leeta and Amoda had bathed her and her governess wrapped her in clean garments, Fatima went to her father's apartments in the harem. Niranjan trailed her silently.

"Go back!" she whispered over her shoulder. "I am only going to my father. I don't need a guard for that."

His stubborn footfalls echoed hers. She scowled over her shoulder at him. She bypassed a garden ringed with myrtle trees. At the center, multicolored fish swam in a marble pool. When she reached the entrance of her father's residence, she turned to Niranjan. He bowed and stood next to a column, hands clasped behind him.

From within, the sound of her father's weeping echoed. She had not told him of her mother's death, but he seemed to know it.

When she entered, he sat hunched over his writing desk, while the Sultan and Faraj stood on either side of him. The Sultan lifted his hand before letting it fall limp at his hip.

He asked, "Where were you kept, Fatima?"

She answered, "In the house of Abdallah, Princess Aisha's brother, my Sultan."

"Who else was there, other than the princess and her brother?"

"The Ashqilula chieftains, Ibrahim and Abu Muhammad followed Abdallah to Gharnatah."

61

Her father lifted his head. His eyes were wet and puffy. "Did Abu Muhammad hurt Aisha?"

"No."

The Sultan approached. "Did Ibrahim do it?"

When she nodded, her father jerked to his feet, knocking the chair over. "I'll kill him myself."

The Sultan patted his shoulder. "In time, my son, all in good time."

Chapter 6
The Bond

Prince Faraj

Gharnatah, al-Andalus: Muharram 664 AH (Granada, Andalusia: October AD 1265)

Faraj turned toward the window, as Fatima and her father embraced. He considered the consequences of the previous night. The child kidnapped. Her mother murdered. If her captors had no qualms about killing a woman, their own kin, what might they do to him, now that he was Fatima's husband? The death of the crown prince's wife was the first hint of the threat the Ashqilula posed.

"I have dispatched guards to the foothills, to search for the body. When they return, I want the rest of your children brought here, my son. They must know the truth."

When the Sultan spoke, Faraj turned toward him with a frown. What could his master be suggesting?

The crown prince pulled back slightly from his daughter, though his arms still encircled her. She kept her face buried in his shoulder.

He said, "I intend to tell them, Father."

"That is not enough. Let them come and see the body."

The crown prince stood, his reddened eyes widening. Still, he hugged Fatima close to him. Faraj felt a tiny pang of jealousy stirring his memories. No one had remained to comfort him when his mother had died.

63

Sultana

"Father, you cannot mean it."

"Don't I? Let them see what comes of treachery and disloyalty to this family."

"I won't do it. You cannot be so merciless, not even to your own grandchildren. I shall not burden them with such a sight! It would destroy them. Would you have Fatima endure it again? Hasn't she suffered enough in this ordeal?"

"I was there." Fatima murmured against the folds of her father's robe. "I was there, when Ibrahim killed her."

Faraj drew closer, his heart pounding. When the crown prince knelt before her again, she rushed on, "He took out his sword. She told me to look away, but I wouldn't do it. Then, he cut off her head."

Faraj staggered slightly, drawing the sudden interest of both the Sultan, who studied him and his son, who sneered. Her matter-of-fact description pierced his very soul.

He had informed the Sultan of the deaths of his parents in much the same way, over ten years ago. He gripped the bottom of the crown prince's writing desk, where the men could not see his shaking hand. At length, both of them looked away. He sagged slightly, but kept a steady hold on the furniture.

The crown prince hugged his daughter again, as she renewed her sobs. Over Fatima's head, he murmured, "I hope you're pleased with yourself, Father. Look at what has happened to Fatima, what she has endured. Would you ask her to do it again?"

The Sultan waved a dismissive hand. "I predicted your union would only bring discord and it has done just that. Your lust led you to want a woman who belonged to another. I indulged your desire, like a fool. You shall soon find another woman to comfort you."

"How dare you!" The crown prince glared at his father. "Aisha was my wife, Father, and regardless of our relations, I loved her. Do you understand anything of what

64

it is to truly love a woman, or do you only recognize her value in wealth or alliances?"

Although he addressed the Sultan, Faraj felt a small spark of concern at his earlier thoughts. He did not love Fatima – indeed, how any man could love a child bride confounded him – but he recognized that for him, her only value existed in her relationship to the Sultan. Was it right to use this marriage only to further his own interests? What about Fatima?

He pushed aside worry for her, as the crown prince continued, "My wife's blood is on your hands, Father. She died because of this feud between you and Ibrahim."

"My son, be reasonable. The Ashqilula did what anyone should have expected. If we held the kin of one of them in our clutches, we would have done the same. They killed her as one of the enemy."

"Yes, all because you made my daughter marry that boy!"

When the crown prince turned his glower on Faraj, he shrank back under the scrutiny.

The Sultan muttered, "Don't blame Faraj for your failures. You should have controlled your wife and kept her locked up."

"She was never my prisoner, Father!"

"If she stood here, she would say different." The Sultan sighed. "Grief and sentiment clouds your judgment. This night, while tragic, is also advantageous to our cause."

"That my children should be motherless is advantageous?"

"You've oft said she never showed them a mother's love. She is no great loss and if you put your feelings aside, in time, you shall see that. Her death aids our cause. It shall sway other families still loyal to the Ashqilula. If they learn our enemies have killed one of their own, a woman whose only fault was to marry you, they shall rally against them! I shall be the victor, in the end."

"Then, have your hollow victory, at the expense of my pain and tragedy. What of my children? How am I to raise them, motherless? You have all the answers, Father, but none for that."

***

Later, the rest of the crown prince's children assembled before their father. The Sultan's guards had found the mangled body of his son's wife and returned with it. Faraj still barely believed that the Sultan would have countenanced his grandchildren witnessing such a grisly sight, but mercifully, he had rescinded the command.

He remained in the room with the Sultan, both of them at the window. The crown prince sat at his writing desk with the children gathered at his feet. A little baby snuggled in his arms. The children's governess, a tall Nubian, hovered behind them. There was elegance in her appearance that he had never seen in a slave. He suspected she might have been very beautiful in her youth, with wiry, graying hair cropped close to her skull, large eyes and smooth lips. Her nut-brown complexion glowed with vitality and reflected a good diet. Her slim fingers cradled the youngest child against her. She quieted the fussy child as the crown prince began speaking.

"Children, Allah, the Compassionate, the Merciful in His infinite wisdom protects us, but He has taken one from among us. The enemies of your grandfather have stolen away your mother, the Princess Aisha. She has died, gone to Paradise."

Stunned silence followed their father's announcement. Their governess hugged the smaller children, while the twin girls he had seen earlier, Fatima's younger sisters, hugged each other. Fatima stood apart from all of them at the side of her brother, Muhammad ibn Muhammad. After a moment, he turned and faced the wall.

When Fatima wrapped her arms about his waist and laid her head against his shoulder, Faraj edged closer. He had never seen such intimacy between siblings and it fascinated him. The children appeared close in age, each perhaps no more than a year older than a younger sibling. They each had dark brown or even dark red hair and their

66

father's brown eyes or the Sultan's hazel ones. Except for the boy Muhammad, each had inherited their father's sallow-skinned complexion. They looked thin and lean, as if none of them ate enough, but surely, the Sultan's grandchildren were not starving. Only Fatima had black hair. No other feature distinguished her from her brother or sisters.

As Faraj neared her and her brother, Muhammad said, "She left us."

"The Ashqilula took her away from us, brother," Fatima murmured against his tunic.

Muhammad pulled away. "She never wanted us. Now she's finally rid of us forever."

Faraj frowned at their exchange. Why was this little boy so angry? He looked around and realized that despite the news only Fatima showed any sadness. Her sisters appeared confused and surprised more than anything else. The death had brought strong, but opposing emotions to the surface in the two eldest children. Perhaps the others were too young to understand the impact of their loss.

Fatima shook her head. "You don't know what you're saying. The Ashqilula killed her."

"Good. I hope she suffered, I hope it hurt."

Her face reddened with blotches and she curled her tiny hands into fists. It seemed as if Faraj could see into her heart, the turmoil building inside her. He had never felt such a strong awareness of the feelings of another in his life.

"Don't say that, Muhammad. She was our own mother."

"Not mine. I never had a mother! She never cared for us. Never a kind word! She hated us and I hated her. I'm glad she's dead."

She pushed Muhammad with such force, that he sprawled on the marble. Faraj's heart thudded when. She threw herself upon her brother, tiny fists raining down blows.

Faraj scrambled across the room, without thinking and pulled her off. She fought against him now, her legs flailing. She kicked Muhammad's nose and blood spurted. Faraj held her close, despite her squirming struggles.

"Hush, hush now! It's over, you're safe, Fatima, safe with your family again."

"No! No! No!"

He twisted her in his arms and lifted her off the ground. Her eyes were wild and bloodshot. His heart cleaved in two, for he recognized the hurt inside her. He had once felt the same way.

"Unhand her, give her to me."

When the crown prince reached for her, he hesitated to relinquish his hold. The man's icy glare pinned him in place. Fatima's screams gave way to sobs and she buried her face in his neck. Her hot tears soaked the collar of his tunic.

He said, "Forgive me, but I understand better than any of you what she must be feeling."

The crown prince sneered. "Truly?"

"Yes. I saw my father killed and my mother dying when I was but a year older than she is now. Only one who has witnessed such things could understand what it does to a person. Please, let me comfort her."

The Sultan eyed him and then nodded to his son. "He has the right."

"I am still her father! Are you saying I can't be a comfort to my own child?"

"I am saying Faraj shares the same, terrible bond of grief with your daughter, at the violent loss of a parent. He has seen the things she has seen. Let him console her. Instead, help your son up."

Until now, it seemed everyone had forgotten about Muhammad. He shrugged off his father's hold and smeared the blood on his nose with the back of his hand. With a silent glare at Fatima, he left the chamber.

"I'll talk to him later," the crown prince said. He glanced at Faraj. "For now, take Fatima to her room. I shall lead you."

Holding her against him, Faraj followed the crown prince out, past the myrtles and slender, carved columns of the buildings. He looked over his shoulder when the bronze-skinned slave, who had delivered Fatima to his house earlier, fell into step behind him.

At an archway, turquoise-colored damask curtains embroidered at the hems with gold lace fluttered along the walls. The silky cloth billowed with each gust of the morning breeze. They crossed the threshold into a long corridor, with eight niches. Within each, a eunuch-guard stood with a spear in hand and a short dagger in its sheath. Each man inclined his head as they walked.

They entered a room with four alcoves. The crown prince gestured to a pallet in the far left corner. "Put her there. She needs to sleep."

"It may be difficult for her to sleep. Sleep brings dreams, the terrible things she has seen, to life again. If you would permit it, I shall remain with her until she calms and closes her eyes."

Faraj stared straight ahead and avoided the crown prince's darkening expression.

"Now, you believe you can judge her needs better than I can? Do you think because you claim her as a wife that you know her? I am her father!"

"I have not forgotten. I only want to help her."

"Then help her!" The edge of impatience that had crept into the crown prince's voice rippled through the air.

He raked his hands through his hair. When he sighed and nodded, Faraj carried Fatima to her pallet.

"I shall do what I can."

Her cries had subsided to tremors. When he bent toward the pallet and relinquished his hold, she whimpered and gripped the folds of his garment with a claw-like hand. He silently understood and scooped her up. He lowered himself to the ground next to the pallet.

Her grip slackened, her body went limp, and she resumed weeping on his shoulder.

The slave who had followed them now stood at the end of the pallet. He bowed before the crown prince, who shook his head and left them.

Faraj sighed wearily and briefly shifted his hold on Fatima. Her hand swept up and tightened around his neck. He murmured against her hair. "Hush, you are safe. I am here with you."

She trembled against him. Unthinking, he nuzzled her hair and cradled her closer. He leaned back and looked up at the ceiling. Seven knots of lapis-lazuli and gold filigree encircled the domed heights of the room. Fatima lived amid such beauty, but now she had witnessed the ugliness of life also, a sight he knew she would never forget. The Sultan was right – a terrible bond connected them.

"*Ummi.*"

He raised his head at the sound of her plaintive whimper. His hand slid from her shaking shoulder down her back. Her tears pooled at the nape of his neck. His stomach knotted and contracted into a tight ball. He curled and uncurled his fingers at her back.

Each sob tore at him, tearing open deep wounds buried within his soul. Memories cluttered his mind and clouded his voices, violent images from a past he could never forget.

"You, come here," he said to the youth who hovered at the foot of the pallet. "Take her from me."

The slave's eyes narrowed with suspicion and he hesitated.

"Damn you, I said take her." Faraj struggled against the quaver in his voice.

The slave recoiled, his expression pinched. Despite the wrinkles furrowing his brow, he approached and scooped up Fatima in his lanky arms. "I thought you said you wanted to help her. Was that a lie?"

"I won't tolerate questions from a slave."

"I may be a slave, but I have more strength than one too cowardly to bear this child's pain."

Faraj lurched to his feet, his hand upraised.

"Would you do it, strike me down knowing I hold the crown prince's beloved daughter in my arms?" The slave swung Fatima away from him. "What is she to you? A mere child, the granddaughter of our noble master, beyond your caring or concern? Why did you marry her, if you think it too much to be there for her when she needs you most? Is that not the duty of a husband, to comfort his bride in times of sorrow? You cannot imagine the horror she must have seen, or how bravely she has borne this pain."

When Faraj laughed, the sound seemed hollow and pathetic to his ears. "You couldn't be more wrong. It's a pain I understand all too well."

"Then help her, as you promised her noble father that you would. She needs you, as much as she needs him and the rest of her family."

Faraj's heart palpitated wildly, as his vision swam. "Don't you understand? I can't! Not anymore."

He waved the slave away and left them.

"Then you're a coward, my lord." The slave's echoing condemnation chased him from the room. "Forgive me for saying it. May God help my mistress bear the burden of being wed to a weakling like you. You do not deserve her. She may be a child, but she is stronger than you...."

Faraj blinked harshly as he emerged in the full glare of the sun. Shielding his eyes behind his hands, he noticed the Sultan and his son in conversation beside a column.

The Sultan looked at him. "Is Fatima asleep already?"

He shook his head and stumbled before he backed off.

The crown prince glared at him. "What have you done with my daughter? You left her alone. I thought you wanted to stay with her."

"I cannot...." His voice was a low moan, brimming with all the pain and confusion churning inside him.

71

He turned on his heel and escaped the demands of the crown prince. He broke into a run, fleeing the demons of his own violent past. He could not aid Fatima against the nightmares that would soon assail her. It was useless to try, when he did not know how to help himself.

Chapter 7

Kings and Counselors

Prince Faraj

Gharnatah, al-Andalus: Ramadan 664 AH (Granada, Andalusia: June AD 1266)

Ten days into the holy month of fasting, Faraj stood on the battlements of the citadel. The midday sun beat down on his head without mercy. He could not escape the heat, anymore than he could escape this meeting between his master and the Marinids.

A detachment of Marinid warriors streamed through the western gate, under the watchful gaze of the Sultan and the crown prince. Their commander, Umar of the family Mahalli, rode at the forefront. The Sultan of al-Maghrib el-Aska had promised Umar was the fiercest defender of the Faith in all the Islamic lands. Faraj understood this to mean the Marinid warrior was a religious fanatic, but he wondered whether the commander was the right sort of fanatic for what the Sultan of Gharnatah had in mind.

Nine months on, the conflict with the Ashqilula had escalated. According to the Sultan's spies, they now offered their allegiance to King Alfonso of Castilla-León, who supplied them with a thousand Castillan knights for their protection. Provocation indeed – but the Sultan hoped the arrival of the Marinids, the new allies he sought, would prove the downfall of his enemies.

The last of the retinue entered the precincts of *al-Qal'at al-Hamra*. Faraj followed the Sultan and crown prince, descending stairs winding from the citadel to an underground passage, flanked by bodyguards. The passageway led under the citadel to an exit in the courtyard. From there, stairs offered an approach to the recesses of the throne room.

When the Sultan and his entourage mounted the stairs, guards patrolling the area bowed in reverent silence. One soldier opened the door and everyone, except the Sultan, hung back. The women of his household gazed at them in surprise, with cries of alarm.

The ladies sat concealed from view behind their *purdah*, a latticed screen. The Sultan's two remaining wives, the Sultanas Hamda and Qamar, and his *kadin* Lateefah greeted him first.

Faraj relied on the Sultan's previous descriptions to identify each woman now. Sultana Hamda smoothed her dark blue, brocaded robes and smeared a thick berry stain on her thin lips, before she acknowledged her husband. Faraj did not doubt she was as vain as the Sultan had once remarked. Then she reached for a water pipe filled with opium. She drew deeply upon the pipe, inhaling the sickly sweet scent of the poppy. Faraj sneered and thought it a disgusting habit.

Hamda's counterpart Sultana Qamar sat with her thin hands in her lap, delicate golden brows flaring over her doe-like, brown eyes. She offered her husband a shy glance, which made Faraj wonder how she could be so reticent before a man whom she had been married to for more than twenty years. Her fair skin glowed and a faint scent of lemon drifted from the folds of her *jubba*.

The *kadin* Lateefah sat beside Sultana Qamar. Although no longer in the first blush of youth, she remained the favorite, the most honored of the Sultan's concubines. She offered him a coquettish smile. It seemed foolish from a woman who was perhaps only a few years older than the crown prince was. Her heart-shaped face, full, stained lips and honey-brown complexion held the Sultan enthralled before he moved on. His daughter, Maryam the widow, also offered him a winsome smile before she lined her gray eyes with kohl. Faraj suspected the Sultan returned her welcoming gesture with feigned pleasure. Only this morning, he had complained to anyone who would listen about her excessive spending on silks and damasks at the market. However, if his plans succeeded, his spendthrift daughter would soon be gone from Gharnatah.

With the Sultan's permission, his retinue passed beyond the *purdah*, eyes averted from the women. Sycophants comprised of Gharnatah's wealthy elite filled the rest of the room, whispering their latest intrigues in hushed tones. When the Sultan appeared without warning at the forefront of the throne room, the din of murmurs died.

To the left stood his counselors, who advised him upon all political and religious matters. Most of them were sons of non-nobility who had earned the right to become permanent fixtures of the court by their intellectual prowess. The crown prince preceded Faraj into the room, while the Sultan's bodyguards fanned out along the walls.

The Marinid delegation stood just outside the open brass and oak doors, waiting while the aged court herald shuffled forward. "In the name of Allah, the Compassionate, the Merciful, bear witness and render homage to the presence of the Appointed of Allah. He, who is like the mighty and invincible lion in times of war and like the generous water giving life to the dry earth in times of peace. His great deeds shine brilliantly for all to see. The happiness of men and the jubilation of women precede his coming. He is *al-Ghalib bi-llah*, the Sultan Muhammad ibn al-Ahmar ibn Yusuf ibn Nasr. Give praise to Allah for his justice. Give praise to Allah for his peace. By the blessings of Allah, know there is none but Allah and the Prophet, may peace be upon him, is His messenger. *Amin.*"

Suppressing a yawn, the Sultan sank into the chair behind him. Faraj stifled a laugh, but the crown prince glared at him.

Umar approached, leading his Marinid delegation. He was a broad-chested man of Nubian stock, heavily built with bowed legs. His moon-shaped face with its heavy jowls reflected a rich diet. His eyes were small dots. It seemed as though he might be squinting. "Peace be with you, the appointed of God, exalted Sultan of Gharnatah. I greet you in the name of my noble master, Sultan Abu Yusuf Ya'qub al-Marini, the Commander of the Believers and the Anointed of God. My master sends greetings and well wishes for your continued prosperity, and gifts to honor your household."

Faraj smiled. This military man had the smooth tongue of a diplomat, too. Umar beckoned slaves, who presented tokens of leather, precious metals, spices, and silks. The Sultan showed the appropriate interest and appreciation, but Faraj guessed he did not care.

Umar stated, "There is one more gift, but it is a delight meant only for the Sultan."

The Sultan tugged hair on his gray beard, while Faraj leaned toward the crown prince. "It must be a woman. At seventy-five years old, our master needs a pleasure slave like he needs another wife to annoy and harass him."

Though he chuckled, the crown prince stared at him without saying a word. Then Faraj remembered - his uncle never complained about any of his wives, except for the crown prince's late mother, Muna. Embarrassed, Faraj cleared his throat and looked ahead.

The Sultan stood, his legs shaking a little with the effort. His son took a step forward, earning him a disapproving glare. Then the Sultan said, "The court shall withdraw. Only my guard, the Marinid commander, my heir and Prince Faraj may remain."

Chattering, the courtiers retreated. The royal wives peeked from behind the *purdah*, but the Sultan waved them off. The doors to the throne room slammed in a resounding thud.

"With your permission, may I show you the gift?" Umar gestured to the antechamber just off the throne room. The Sultan walked with him, while Faraj followed beside the crown prince.

A delicate girl knelt in the center of the marble floor. She appeared to be no more than twelve years old, swathed in gold cloth and strings of pearls. Her face was heart-shaped and lily white and her ice-blue eyes at first seemed almost sparkling. Then, she swayed slightly. Pale golden curls tumbled free from the confines of her veils. Faraj realized her captors had drugged her. He snorted with disgust. She was nothing but a child bought for an old man's pleasure.

The Sultan and the crown prince glared at him. He averted his eyes from her.

Umar said, "She is from Galicia, captured earlier this year. She has been well-trained and is very skilled, I'm told."

The crown prince drew a step closer to the girl. "A blonde. Such rare magnificence." He cleared his throat. "What is her name?"

Umar answered, "We have called her Nur al-Sabah, noble prince."

The Sultan said, "How fitting, for she's the embodiment of 'the light of morning' with her golden hair. Tell your master I accept his gift with pleasure, Umar. My son, summon the chief eunuch of my harem to see to this girl."

The crown prince asked, "You... intend to keep her, Father?"

"I shall keep her. I may be an old man, but I suspect she could make me forget my age if she is indeed skilled. Would you suggest I do otherwise, son?"

The Sultan watched his heir like a hunting hawk studies its prey, looking for weaknesses. The crown prince stared at the girl, with something akin to reverence. She lifted her chin a little, her gaze straight ahead, trained in the crown prince's direction. A sigh escaped him, whispering of some inner turmoil and burgeoning desire. He looked to his father then, with a pitiful expression of appeal, almost despairing. His lips trembled.

Faraj shook his head, wondering whether the crown prince dared ask for the girl. Lust could easily rule a man. He vowed no woman would ever hold sway over his heart. Burdened with a bride who could not be a true wife to him, he saw no reason to fear.

The Sultan smiled and diffused the tension. "Commander, my household has prepared a reception for you and your highest-ranking officers this evening. Shall we adjourn until then?"

When Umar assented, he nodded toward the crown prince. "Do as I have asked, son. Come, nephew."

When they left the room, Faraj trailed behind the Sultan. Before they reached the entrance, he looked over his shoulder. The crown prince still stared, fascinated with the girl. Oddly enough, despite her torpor, she seemed focused on him, too.

***

After sunset and the observance of the fourth daily prayer, *Salat al-Maghrib*, Faraj accompanied the Sultan. They led the Marinid delegation to the gardens north of the palace. There, a feast awaited them, inasmuch to entertain their guests as to break the day's fasting.

A festive atmosphere already pervaded. Musicians played in a secluded corner. The crown prince arrived last, with his three younger brothers. Faraj wondered at his delay, but could not allow himself further speculation, as the Sultan motioned for the meal to begin.

The royal family sat on the left and to the right Umar joined five of the Marinid officers, including his younger, sinewy brother, Talha. Slaves placed dishes of lukewarm rosewater and a towel at each table setting. After everyone washed their hands and toweled them dry, the Sultan blessed the meal. The waiting slaves revealed the contents of great gold and silver platters inlaid at the edges with mother of pearl.

Faraj ate with gusto, enjoying one of his favorite dishes, roasted lamb, and rice stir-fried together with onion, lemon, and carrot. There was flatbread and an eggplant dip, which the lemon juice made too bitter, in his opinion. Lentil soup and a salad of mint and parsley accompanied the main meal.

Umar praised the Sultan on the taste of each dessert that followed, eating date balls and pastries with almonds, sugar and rosewater, or others with a mixture of sweet white cheese, nuts and syrup.

While slaves removed the remnants of the meal, everyone dipped their fingers in the water bowls and dried them.

The Sultan addressed his guests. "In honor of your arrival, I've chosen six of my most beautiful slaves, all virgin maidens whose perfection I've only seen, but never touched. Each of you shall take a slave for your pleasure. These women are my gifts to you."

The men murmured their appreciation and approval. Then the Sultan turned to Umar. "Join me on a tour of these magnificent gardens. Your men may remain and enjoy the hospitality of my household. My heir shall ensure they lack for nothing."

He and Umar left the others, followed at a discreet distance by his bodyguards. Faraj chewed at his lower lip and stared long after they disappeared behind a row of juniper trees.

***

When they returned to the banquet area, Faraj and the others stood to greet the Sultan and his guest. The Sultan remained cordial with Umar. But during the ritual of the water pipe which followed, Faraj noted whenever his uncle eyed Umar, the commander appeared flustered. He even dropped the pipe twice.

The yawning Marinid officers prompted the Sultan to dismiss them. Slaves escorted them to their quarters and the waiting slave girls.

The crown prince leaned toward his father. "What did Umar say, honored father? Will his master aid us against the Ashqilula?"

The Sultan took the water pipe and inhaled deeply. "Umar told me that his master honors me as a brother of the Faith. However, he cannot pledge an alliance with me."

Sighs of dismay issued from everyone. The crown prince asked, "Did you appeal to his heritage? Our intelligence confirmed his mother was Andalusi, from near our home in Aryuna."

The Sultan drew on the pipe again. "I mentioned it."

"And he responded in what manner?"

"His mother left al-Andalus as a girl and could not recall her birthplace with any clear memory or affinity."

"Did you tell him how his master would do well to support us? In thirty-five years of your reign, you've made Gharnatah a haven for those who live under Islamic rule. Did you explain how civil war would destroy his mother's birthplace?"

"He knows this, too."

"Did you speak of the Castillans? Did you say that if Gharnatah should ever fall to the Castillans, nothing shall stop them from conquering other Moorish lands? Gharnatah alone stands between Castillan ambitions and the subjugation of Islam. Did you say none of this?"

The Sultan set down the water pipe and glared at his son. "Would you like to try with him? You might have better luck."

The crown prince stammered. "I could never match your skill in diplomacy. You're my teacher, Father."

Despite his son's contrition, the Sultan continued to frown. Then the heir mumbled, "At least my sister Maryam won't be bartered away."

"Then perhaps you should take her into your harem and let her drain your treasury, like she's done with mine."

"We have gambled and lost," the Sultan's third son, Prince Nasr, interjected. "If the Marinids cannot help us neutralize our enemies, what can you do, noble father?"

The Sultan smiled. "Now, we deal with the Castillans."

Expressions of confusion and concern greeted him. As usual, the crown prince voiced his opinion first. "But, the Castillans are allied with the Ashqilula."

"For now, it would seem to be the way of things." His father stroked his hennaed beard.

"I don't understand. Were your reports wrong?"

The Sultan gestured to Faraj. "Perhaps my nephew can explain."

Expectant eyes turned to him. Faraj said, "The Marinids would have been powerful allies and could have helped us end the Ashqilula revolt. But they're across the sea, while Castilla-León is at our back. We can't afford for the Castillans to aid the Ashqilula in a civil war."

The Sultan added, "After the wedding, when I discussed Faraj's marriage to my granddaughter with him, he reminded me of the Castillan threat. They concerned me, too. At my behest, Faraj wrote to the Castillan king. I have promised to renew the tribute paid under the old Castillan king's regime. The new one is greedy like his father. He'll take the money, but I'll hold him to renouncing the alliance with the Ashqilula. One way, by fair means or foul, I shall be rid of them. Now, we journey to Castilla-León."

***

Al-Qal'at ibn Zaide, al-Andalus: Ramadan 664 AH (Alcala la Real, Kingdom of Castilla-León: June AD 1266)

One week later, the Sultan's entourage, including Faraj, journeyed to the Castillan city of Alcala la Real, where the Sultan would meet with King Alfonso the Wise.

The rugged terrain offered opportunities for bandits. The men traveled under a heavy retinue of guards. They neared the city once known as al-Qal'at ibn Zaide, famous for its healing mineral springs. Then a dust cloud billowed on the horizon. Heavy hooves pounded the earth.

The Sultan ordered the halt. Faraj shielded his eyes with his hands.

"A portion of royal guard, my Sultan, with your messenger and his horse in their midst."

The Sultan nodded. "Is our messenger still alive atop his horse?"

Faraj squinted. "He appears unharmed."

The Sultan rubbed his hands together. "This bodes well for our meeting."

One man led the Castillan riders. Without a proper greeting, he addressed the Sultan in coarse Latin. The Sultan smiled, but the crown prince's hand went to the short dagger at his side.

"Noble father, this son of a dog must not be allowed to speak to you in this manner!"

The Sultan shrugged. "What would you have me do? This isn't the Sultanate. I can't just cut his head off."

He gestured to Faraj. "Address this Castillan dog and remind him that we are here at the invitation of his master Alfonso. My Latin is as fine as yours, but I'd never demean myself by answering this oaf."

After Faraj spoke with the guard, the man wheeled his horse about and the Sultan and retinue followed, flanked closely by the king's guard.

When they entered the gates, the townspeople appraised them under hooded eyes. Fair women made the sign of the Cross while children hid their ruddy, dirty faces in their mothers' skirts. The Sultan chuckled at this ridiculous behavior, as the riders from Gharnatah trotted in rows of three over cobblestone streets paved by their Moorish ancestors.

They entered the fortress and dismounted in the outer courtyard. A waiting page led them into a great hall where the king, his nobles and the Castillan parliament, the Cortes awaited them.

The Sultan and the Castillan king had met many years before during the siege at Ishbiliya. Gharnatah's existence then had been precarious. Even with the Ashqilula alliance, the Sultan had not achieved a substantial victory over his then foes, the Hud family. In an agreement with the Castillan king, the Sultan had offered to recognize him as an overlord and pay him an annual tribute of gold coins, if King Fernando destroyed the enemy at the Hud base in Ishbiliya.

Yet when King Fernando took Ishbiliya, he had held it for Castilla-León. To the Sultan's undying shame, he had lost the greatest of Muslim cities. When he returned to Gharnatah, he refused the acclaim his people offered, saying, 'There is no Conqueror but God.' From then, those words had become the motto of the Nasrids.

Now, Fernando's son, Alfonso the Wise sat with several courtiers who flanked either side of his gilded chair. King Alfonso had brown hair that curled at the nape of his neck. He wore his crown on a pale, smooth brow. His features were stark and plain, like those of an un-bearded youth, although he had to be at least forty years old. His rich robes, red mantle trimmed with gold tassels and gleaming crown distinguished him from his rich noble. The Sultan and his entourage bowed before him, but remained standing. There was the expected grumbling among the nobility.

An iron-muscled, fair-haired man, also without any facial hair, who stood closest to the king bent and whispered in the monarch's ear. Alfonso waved him forward.

The courtier bowed before the Sultan. "I am Doñ Nuño Gonzalez de Lara. I greet you in the name of my honorable master, King Alfonso of Castilla-León, son of the great King Fernando of Castilla-León. My master welcomes you to his court. I shall serve as his interpreter and you may speak with me as you would him."

The Sultan's face became etched in stone. His displeasure at the sight of this man was extreme. Before Faraj might wonder at his reaction, he gave him a curt nod and Faraj stepped forward.

"I am Prince Faraj, nephew of the Sultan. I greet you in the name of my humble master. I shall serve as his interpreter and I pray you would speak with me as you would with him."

Through his interpreter, King Alfonso said, "We pray you and yours have come in peace to Alcala la Real, Sultan. Granada exists only as a vassal of Castilla-León. Our nobles do not like how you and your companions remain standing before the royal presence."

Through Faraj, the Sultan replied, "I assure your nobles, we meant no such disrespect. Indeed, my retinue and I have brought gifts to show how much we honor you."

At his behest, Faraj presented his gifts of precious gems, leather, silks, and brocade to the Castillan king. After a lengthy examination, Alfonso seemed mollified and ordered their removal.

Faraj's negotiation with the Castillans lasted long into the evening, during which their hosts never offered refreshment. Not that he would have accepted anything lest they sought to poison him. Hours later, the two sovereigns signed a new treaty before the Sultan and his retinue withdrew.

***

While Faraj adjusted the bridle on his horse, the crown prince argued with his father. "For two hundred and fifty thousand Castillan gold pieces, you have submitted to these dogs again."

The Sultan grinned. "I have bought peace for my people and ensured fair dealings between the Ashqilula and me."

"But Alfonso's forced you to put off hostilities with the Ashqilula for a year...."

"... And thereby spared my people the devastating consequences of a civil war, while giving me time to persuade the Marinids. Umar may have disappointed me, but the Ashqilula shall not. They shall continue their crusade against me. I must be vigilant if I am to defeat them."

"Father, when the king doesn't withdraw his support of the Ashqilula, what recourse remains?"

"If the Castillans actually keep their word, my enemies shall not have the powerful backing of the Christians. If the Castillans have lied...."

The crown prince stared at him expectantly, but the Sultan chuckled. "Such concerns are the Sultan's own. You are not Sultan yet, my son."

The crown prince growled low in his throat and mounted his horse, as the Sultan did the same.

He maneuvered his bay stallion next to Faraj's horse. "You did well. I have further use for you."

He led the way home, while Faraj pondered the meaning of that inscrutable statement.

Chapter 8
The Walls of Malaka

Prince Faraj

Malaka, al-Andalus: Dhu al-Hijja 665 AH - Muharram 666
AH (Malaga, Andalusia: September - October AD 1267)

Faraj shielded his eyes with a hand, as the Sultan ordered
the advance slowed on the outskirts of Malaka. Olive
groves stretched toward the walls of the city. Faraj inhaled
the long-remembered scent from his childhood.

He gritted his teeth as a memory of the chieftain Abu
Muhammad blazed in his mind. He had first seen him at
Gharnatah upon his arrival as a bloodied and frightened
boy, one of five refugees escaping the carnage at Malaka.
Abu Muhammad, only son of the Sultan's sister, Princess
Faridah, strongly resembled his maternal uncle. The
hawkish nose and brown-gray eyes were the same. The
Ashqilula chieftain had also come to Gharnatah with
many supporters and received the honor of Malaka. He
had taken Faraj's birthright.

Faraj had never returned home since that terrible
night. Yet, Malaka remained as unchanged as in his
thoughts. The craggy landscape rose and fell in a series of
undulating brown hills. Under the sapphire skies in his
memories, the sandstone walls of the castle and the
citadel of *al-Jabal Faro* glowed atop two promontories.
Golden beaches fanned out from the base of the slope and
greeted the azure-colored waters of the sea. All of it
belonged to the Ashqilula now.

A mild wind from the sea and rough chainmail chaffed his skin where his tunic did not cover flesh. Despite the sudden chill, perspiration trickled under his helmet and stung his eyes. A cotton tunic clung to his back under the leather coat and chainmail.

No activity occurred at the city walls. The same flat, red-roofed houses as he remembered rose on steep slopes behind the bastions. To the south, the land, thick with more olive groves and almond trees stretched toward the sea. On the highest promontory jutting from the city center, its eastern hillock supported *al-Jabal Faro*, still towering under the heavens. He had played at the base of its inner walls as a child, darting between pine and eucalyptus trees from the servants who scrambled to catch him. More than ten years had passed since he stood in this place. Now, he had returned with his uncle's army to destroy it.

When the crown prince glanced at him, he ducked his gaze. He could not afford for anyone to guess at the conflict brewing inside of him. In his heart, this was his city. It would always remain so, even if his father's murderers had tainted memories of it.

The Sultan had come to wrest it from Ashqilula control, after learning that they had sought separate promises of Castillan and Marinid aid. He intended to eliminate them before any help materialized.

It was a dangerous gambit. Faraj's father Ismail had strengthened the ramparts of his city before he died. Surely, the Ashqilula had improved upon those foundations in the months since the civil war started.

The crown prince snarled at him. "Well, what more can you tell us of this city?"

Faraj returned his intent gaze. "I have told you everything I knew of its defenses from when I was a child. Surely, you don't believe the Ashqilula are unprepared for this assault."

His gaze swept over the Sultan's army at their backs, nearly seven thousand strong. "They won't give up the city so easily."

The crown prince grinned and drew his scimitar, raising it above his head. Sunlight gleamed off the edge of the blade. "I hope not. I owe Abu Muhammad for the death of my wife. A cut for a cut."

His slashing weapon whistled through the air. The detachment of warriors under his command clanked their swords against rounded shields. Their rousing cry spread across the plain.

Inside the city, a mirroring cry echoed, but not the sounds of jubilation. Screams of panic vied with the din of the Sultan's army. Faraj could only imagine how his father's people had reacted to the appearance of thousands of Nasrid warriors.

Then the commanders of Gharnatah's army shouted, "The gates! Look to the gates!"

Faraj could not see what brought shouts of triumph to the various ranks. The glare of the sun, the noonday haze, and sweat almost blinded him. He pushed back his mailed hood roughly and wiped his face.

The flag bearing the colors of the Ashqilula lowered from sight. Soon the Nasrid flag unfurled on the battlements, proclaiming the surrender of the city. Faraj could hardly believe his eyes. He reeled in the saddle and the horse shied under his sudden movement. He glanced in the direction of the Sultan, mired in the midst of his commanders. It seemed that without a ram brought to bear against a gate or even one shot of an arrow, he had already won the contest. Without caution, the Sultan urged his horse toward the gates in a circle of his commanders.

As he and the crown prince approached to within a short distance from the ramparts, a volley of flaming arrows shot over the walls of Malaka, barely missing his position. His stallion snorted and panicked.

Faraj spurred his horse. He bored through the ranks of mounted men and reached the Sultan's side. The Sultan cursed wildly. In his euphoria, he had removed his mail mittens and helmet. Now, he struggled with them. Faraj shook his head at such carelessness and drew his sword. His shield locked tightly with those of his companions. The commanders protected their furious leader. Three bodies catapulted over the wall, bouncing and crashing to the earth below. One figure stirred and tried to stand, but arrows sliced through the air and pinned the body to the ground, never to rise again. Whoever might have betrayed the Ashqilula and helped the Nasrids was now dead.

The defenders and besiegers of Malaka traded volleys. Soon, siege weapons battered the stout masonry. The commanders ordered towers braced against the walls. Infantrymen tried to scale the heights, with the defenders raining arrows down upon them. A tower caught ablaze. Its screaming occupants tumbled to the ground. The Sultan emerged from his protective cocoon and urged his army onward. He ordered the battering ram brought up against the northernmost gate.

From the west, dust clouds rose in the distance. Faraj turned in the saddle. His jaw dropped and he jerked the reins of his mount. A black swarm of riders on light mounts rumbled across the plain. He gaped in stunned silence as they closed the distance, pressing the Nasrids between them and the walls of Malaka. The land trembled under pounding hooves.

Archers on the walls fired down on the heads of the Nasrid soldiers. Volley after volley flew from Malaka's ramparts, piercing armor and flesh, man and beast. Gharnati crossbowmen had weapons within range and answered the Ashqilula volleys. Deadlier than an arrow, the bolts from Moorish crossbows also had a longer scope. The defenders vaulted over the walls in their death throes, but more in the front ranks of the Sultan's army fell.

The riders bearing down on them unleashed arrows and crashed into the warriors at the vanguard. The

Sultan's commanders berated their men, cursing and driving them into formation.

Having weakened their attackers at the forefront, forces inside Malaka sallied forth from the city gates. Hemmed in on both sides, the Nasrid crossbowmen fired wildly, bringing down horses and riders, but also many among their company. Battle drums vied with the screams of dying men and horses, as metal and flesh came together.

Faraj faced the warriors who rode out. His mind raced with lessons. Memory told him that a sharp stab to a horse's chest or neck would bring the animal and its rider to the ground. He threw his javelin and embedded it in a horse's belly, then drew his scimitar, slashing at the rider who had fallen, but scrambled to his feet. Faraj stabbed him through the heart, twisted the blade, and yanked it free. An almost primeval scream echoed from the man's throat before he reeled back from the fatal blow. Faraj leaned forward and thrust his feet into the stirrups, retrieving his javelin. All around him, the metallic smell of blood permeated the thick air. The men of the Sultan's army fought desperately for their lives. He had lost sight of the Sultan in the swirling ranks.

A horn blared through Nasrids ranks. Across the plains, the crown prince shouted until he sounded hoarse. "Retreat! Retreat! Flee for your lives."

Drummers rallied the Gharnati forces. Faraj's heart sank, but he rushed headlong with the charge back to Gharnatah.

***

In the first week of a new Muslim year, Faraj sat brooding on the steps of the southern terrace at his house. He had not spoken to anyone in the aftermath of the failure at Malaka, especially the Sultan, whose hatred for the Ashqilula knew no bounds. Faraj had even more reason to regret the ill-starred venture than his master did. He deserved Malaka. Yet, he had not helped defeat those who held it. The knowledge of his failure and a continuing lack of action gnawed at him.

Slaves interrupted the haze of his reverie, clanging ceramics on the low table beside him. When he snapped at them, they scurried like frightened rats. An idle hour later, flies buzzed noisily over a platter of cold, uneaten flatbread and boiled eggs.

Marzuq approached with a rolled parchment. "The Sultan summons you."

Faraj growled at his steward, "What does he want? I'm not in the mood!"

Marzuq bowed low. "You cannot refuse, master."

Faraj waved his steward away, knowing the man was right. When he was alone again, he muttered a curse under his breath and left the house. His half-brother Muhammad ibn Ismail awaited him at the gate. Though they resembled each other and their father, Faraj thought there was no one else in the world who was more different from him, than his brother.

Both had lost their mothers on the same night, except the mercenaries had taken Muhammad's mother with them. Muhammad could hope she was still alive while Faraj relived the final fate of his mother every night.

"What are you doing here, Muhammad?"

His half-brother looked at him with eyes that mirrored their father's own. Everything about him reminded Faraj of their father, but he could never forget that Muhammad's mother has been his mother's rival.

"I heard what happened, Faraj. The entire court knows. I wished to see how you fared."

Faraj chuckled and shoved past him. "I think it is too late for brotherly concern."

Muhammad grabbed his arm. "How can you quarrel with me eternally over an issue not of my making? It is not my fault our father loved my mother and yours equally."

Faraj shrugged off his hand. "You shall never mention my mother again! Don't speak of her in the same breath as your mother. You're the son of a slave. I'm the heir."

"So you keep reminding me. Do you think I've forgotten? And where is your inheritance, brother? Have

91

you regained your birthright? Or is it still in the hands of Abu Muhammad of Malaka?" He shook his head, dark waves of hair cascading over his eyes. "One day, this rivalry between us must end, but I see it shall not be today. I should have known better than to think you would welcome my comfort. I shall never understand what our uncle was thinking when he wed you with his granddaughter."

"You don't have to understand it, only accept it."

Chapter 9

The Bargain

Prince Faraj

Gharnatah, al-Andalus: Sha'ban 665 AH (Granada, Andalusia: May AD 1268)

One week before Faraj's nineteenth birthday, he joined the royal hunt at the height of spring. The Sultan's sons and their families gathered within the southern precinct of the royal *madina*. Slaves accompanied the hunters, prized hawks and peregrines held tightly with jesses. Fatima stood at her father's side, while he bent on one knee and embraced the girls surrounding him.

Stiff-backed, Faraj bowed before the royal heir and his family. Fatima glanced at him, her gaze expectant. He mumbled a greeting for her. A spark of anger lit in the girl's gaze. One of her sisters whispered something in her ear. She offered him a curt nod.

His lips pressed tightly together, he leapt on his horse and stared straight ahead. She turned away and spoke with her sisters. More than a year after their marriage, he and his child bride shared no affinity for each other. Try as he might, he could not put aside his reticence. Each time he looked at her, he remembered the child whimpering in his arms, crying out for her murdered mother. He shied away from his own painful memories evoked by her suffering.

His uncle bore the blame for all their misery. The Sultan had forced his hand, bound him in this dangerous union, which threatened his fortunes and safety. It was an enticing trap, baited with the promise of royal favor and riches beyond expectation, but it had already claimed the life of Fatima's mother. He would not become the next victim.

He returned his attention to the crown prince, who admonished his children. "Be mindful of your governess."

Fatima replied. "Father, come home to us soon."

Faraj sneered at her blind, childish devotion. How could she love a man who had inspired such hatred in his own wife that she had betrayed him? Fatima's youthfulness prevented her from comprehending the magnitude of her grandfather's schemes, but Faraj did not enjoy such merciful bliss. His bride remained an innocent, ignorant child. He welcomed, yet dreaded the day her father or grandfather's actions shattered her illusions. He had suffered cruelly from life's harsh lessons and in truth, he did not wish that kind of pain upon anyone, not even the little girl his uncle had forced on him.

The Sultan mounted his horse and waved a salute for three women in white garments, his wives, and *kadin.* Then he ordered the departure of the hunting party.

They exited the southwestern gate, their mounts ambling along the cobblestones. The crown prince and his younger brothers followed their father. Against his choice, Faraj rode beside his half-brother. He pointedly ignored Muhammad.

The searing mid-morning sun tracked their progress down the slopes of the Sabika hill. They entered the precincts of the *madina*, bustling with activity. The royal guards cleared the route, while slaves brought up the rear with hunting birds and provisions. The denizens of Gharnatah waved and bowed. The Sultan accepted their acclaim with brisk nods.

The riders turned south where they anticipated good hunting. They camped near the river Xenil, a suitable site for its fresh water supply. Luck eluded Faraj on the first day. His peregrine snared only a meager grouse. Later, he listened with silent envy as his half-brother recounted how his hawk had brought down four fowl. By evening, the men feasted on roasted and stewed game, with flatbread, cheese, and fruits from their provisions.

The next morning, Faraj left the encampment and relieved himself, before performing the prayer ablutions. When he returned, the Sultan and his heir sat on the ground outside the Sultan's tent, speaking with a messenger.

Faraj joined his half-brother beside the fire. "What has happened?"

Muhammad looked up, dark, wavy hair like their father's own falling over his eyes. "A rider came in but a moment ago. We must wait."

Across the camp, the crown prince flailed his hands, his face a dark mask of fury. The Sultan demanded silence before addressing the messenger again.

Muhammad chuckled low and scratched his scraggly beard. "Look at you, so intent on their schemes. Life at court suits you. You vie for the Sultan's favor with the best of them."

"Is it envy I see in your eyes? Are you jealous of what I have?"

"You see pity. I could never be jealous of you. I do not share your ambitions. My pity is not for you, but for your wife. She cannot know the sort of man our uncle has united her with and I pray you never disappoint her."

"My future is not your concern. Think of your own."

When he stood, Muhammad grasped his arm. "You shall never have Malaka. It is lost to us forever. The Ashqilula have it and they shall never give it up."

"We'll see." Faraj shrugged off his grip.

When the messenger left, the Sultan beckoned all his relations, who joined him around the campfire.

He said, "We have had strange tidings this morning. Doñ Nuño Gonzalez de Lara has arrived at the frontier. He is one of King Alfonso's most trusted Castillan commanders and advisors. He seeks to parlay with me. He shall join us here. After prayer and the morning meal, I require the presence of my heir and Prince Faraj, who can translate. The rest of you may go."

The royal princes and Faraj's half-brother scowled in his direction, but he shrugged. Why should they be angry with him, when his uncle could do whatever he wanted, including commanding their stay or departure?

The Sultan's third son, Prince Nasr asked, "Honorable father, who is this Castillan who thinks himself worthy of meeting with you?"

His father stared into the fire. When he spoke, it seemed he imagined another time and place. "You should remember him from our negotiations with the Castillans at al-Qal'at ibn Zaide two years ago. I first met him in battle during the siege at Ishbiliya. He is the master of Istija now, which the Castillans call Ecija. I have fought against him, too. He conquered my ancestral home at Aryuna."

"For this and more, he should die!" The crown prince drew his *khanjar* and angrily drove the dagger into the ground.

Murmurs of assent followed from his brothers.

The Sultan called for silence. He stared hard across the fire at his heir. "In life, I've borne many troublesome burdens. A Sultan must think of his people first, before his own desires. Although my hatred of the Castillans and Doñ Nuño Gonzalez has great cause, I shall bargain with him, if only to know whether his words may benefit me. Now, I demand an oath from each of you. Swear by the blessed name of the Prophet, may peace be upon him, no one shall harm the Castillan commander."

He stared at each man sternly. Prince Nasr first swore the oath, albeit grudgingly. Faraj followed, as did others, last among them the crown prince. Afterward, when he met his father's eyes, something interminable passed between them. Faraj wondered at the new machinations each might be plotting. Both had proven they could be cunning and unpredictable, even dangerous.

***

The Castillan commander and his company arrived at the encampment the next morning. The Sultan's bodyguards remained, joined by a detachment of forty soldiers from the fortress of *al-Quasaba*. The Sultan and crown prince waited inside the tent, while Faraj greeted the arrivals.

Doñ Nuño Gonzalez de Lara rode into the camp at the head of his men. He dismounted, as did the three others who directly followed him. Faraj approached and bowed, introducing himself and greeting them in the name of his master in Castillan. The inflections of the Castillan language and the rapidity of their exchange required dogged concentration.

"Where is your king?" Doñ Nuño asked impatiently.

"My master awaits you in his tent. Please follow me."

He led the men into the shelter of dried animal skins dyed green and black. The Sultan and his son sat in the recesses, while the royal guard lined the walls. After the men exchanged greetings, Faraj continued his role as interpreter.

The Sultan leaned forward. "You have brought many men to Gharnatah, Doñ Nuño Gonzalez, yet you claim you wish to speak in peace. Why should I hear what you have to say?" He gestured for Faraj to translate.

"I would answer, but I request we speak directly," Doñ Nuño replied in Arabic. "We do not need an interpreter. My news is important, I assure you."

"Such remains to be seen."

"I would not have made the journey otherwise. I have always known you to be a man of excellent reasoning, great Sultan. I pray you shall permit me to speak to you with complete candor and privacy."

"While I might agree to speak with you, I can never agree to dismiss my guards." The Sultan chewed a handful of dates from the low table beside him. Pointedly, he offered no hospitality to the commander.

Doñ Nuño Gonzalez frowned. "Your Sultanate is the only power in the peninsula that can withstand Castilla-

León. There are others who would join me in rebellion against the Crown."

The Sultan asked, "To what end?"

"The king had denied me several profitable estates, which I wish restored to my family and if you would aid us...."

"Ah, so it is coin you're after. How can I be sure this meeting is not an elaborate ruse to entrap me? You must know I have concluded another treaty with your king only a year ago."

"Great Sultan, let me prove my worth. I know the exact number of forces under the command of your enemies. I can give you information your spies would never have, such as the Ashqilula's ability to withstand siege, where their vulnerabilities lie and the number of Christian knights in their retinues."

"Indeed, you could tell me all about the knights, for you led them. Are you not the commander of the Christian knights who've reinforced the Ashqilula territories?"

"I have their loyalty. If I command it, no Castillan warrior shall remain in the influence of your enemies."

The Sultan did not reply. He slowly twirled wisps of hair in his beard.

Then Doñ Nuño added, "If you agreed to my request, I would offer you these same men to rid yourself of the Ashqilula."

The crown prince frowned, his dark eyebrows knitted together. The Sultan threw back his head and laughed, his voice filling the tent with a rich tone. Doñ Nuño smiled and chuckled. Faraj shook his head, unable to believe the audacity of Doñ Nuño. He doubted the Sultan and his guest were laughing for the same reason.

His uncle said, "You would offer me the very same Castillan knights to thwart the Ashqilula as your king offered to the Ashqilula to undermine me?"

"I assure you, the king's present behavior has forced me to this course."

Faraj's heart thrummed inside his chest. His uncle's capricious nature warned of danger. Would the Sultan slaughter the Castillans now for their daring?

Instead, the Sultan said, "I shall consider it. You and your company may remain at our campsite until I have made my decision."

Faraj heaved a sigh. Who could understand the myriad ways in which his uncle's mind worked? It was useless to speculate.

Doñ Nuño continued, "We await your command."

When he exited the tent, the Sultan turned to Faraj. "What's your opinion of him?"

"He is... complicated, as was his tale," he cautiously replied.

The crown prince added. "He is a greedy, disloyal man. Alfonso is welcome to him."

His father nodded. "I agree."

The crown prince grinned, his smile admiring. "If you don't trust him, then surely you've decided not to aid him? Let me kill him, Father. My blade would pierce the dog's heart and send him to the Christian hell where he belongs."

The Sultan said, "Your *khanjar* shall remain sheathed. I shall aid him, for my own interests. Doñ Nuño is one of the best military strategists in Castilla-León. As he uses me to pester Alfonso, so I shall use Doñ Nuño against the Ashqilula and the Castillans. Before I give him one gold *dinar*, he shall give me all the logistical and tactical information I need to defeat my enemies on both fronts."

The crown prince's expression lapsed into a troubled scowl. Faraj kept his silence, though he feared these intrigues were becoming too dangerous.

He withdrew to his cool tent in the lingering heat of evening. At the entrance, a slave with a glistening, baldpate offered him a rolled parchment.

"Forgive me for disturbing you. I have a message for your eyes alone."

Faraj looked over his shoulder toward the Sultan's tent. Satisfied no one watched him, he broke the hardened, red wax seal on the scroll. He committed the Castillan words to memory and then tossed the parchment into the small fire at the center of the encampment. Flames devoured it entirely.

He returned to the slave. "Does the Sultan know I have received a missive?"

"No, my prince, I was told to bring the message in secret."

Faraj tapped the hilt of his dagger with a thumb. "Who approached you with it?"

The slave swallowed. "One of the Christians gave it to me. My prince, I'm a loyal servant of Gharnatah, please don't harm me."

Faraj ducked inside the tent, grasped his satchel, and withdrew a small pouch of *dirhams*. He returned outside. The silver coins jangled as he pressed them into the slave's hand. "See that you forget about the message."

Following the instructions of the missive, he left the encampment. A circuitous route took him to a clearing at the base of the Sabika hill. Juniper trees shadowed him. From behind a copse, Doñ Nuño Gonzalez de Lara stepped out, alone.

"I thank you for coming, worthy prince. It's an honor to speak with you."

Faraj rolled his eyes at the attempt at pleasantries and switched to the Castilian language. He despaired of listening to Doñ Nuño speak Arabic, as though he was Moorish. He could not be more different.

"My lord de Lara, my master does not know I'm here, but if we tarry for long, I shall be missed."

"Then, I shall keep you no longer than necessary. I am aware of your blood ties to the king of Granada, how he raised you from boyhood. He has been like a father to you. I would have you ease the... ill feelings between your uncle and me. As you may know, we fought each other many years ago at Arjona. The Sultan doesn't trust me."

"He has his reasons."

"You have great influence with your uncle, perhaps enough to make him see beyond those reasons."

"You want him to war with you against Castilla-León. Why should he risk it?"

"Sway your uncle's decision in my favor. Allow me to influence the opinions you offer your master, and I would reward you well."

"Any boon you might give is still no guarantee my uncle shall listen to me."

"Surely, you underestimate your skills and my resources. Name anything you want. You can have it, if you would look favorably on my claim."

"You can't give me what I want. You waste your time and mine. I bid you both good-day and the peace of God be with you."

As he turned to go, Doñ Nuño called out, "If you were able to influence your master, the Escayola might release their hold on your ancestral home at Malaga."

When Faraj continued undeterred, the Castillan added, "Your father built a mighty fortress, which the Escayola have improved upon. With my help, perhaps your uncle could retake the city. Indeed, the Escayola would never have held it in the first place, except by their treachery."

Faraj halted. "What do you mean 'treachery'?"

Doñ Nuño closed the distance between them. "Do you want to know the truth about your father's murder?"

"I know it. I was there! Marauders attacked our home. They sliced open my father's throat and raped my mother. She killed herself rather than live with the shame."

"Do you know who commanded those men in their attack?"

"The Sultan told me his old enemies, the Hud family, did it. He had driven them from power in Sevilla. They avenged the loss by killing my father, the governor of Malaga."

Doñ Nuño shook his head. "The Hud family is partly responsible, but they had help. Have you never wondered why the citadel guards didn't raise the alarm?"

"The Hud warriors attacked too swiftly from the sea. Malaga is protected on all sides, except the south facing the deep water."

"The marauders came looking for you in the nursery. How did men in the employ of the Hud clan, your uncle's avowed enemies, know the layout of the complex and its weakest points of entry?"

"I was a child, I didn't think of those things. I only thought of survival."

"You are a man now and deserve the truth. The Escayola conspired with the Hud marauders to take Malaga."

Faraj backed away and nearly stumbled on a stone. "The Escayola were loyal, until two years ago. The Sultan made them rich. They gave their oaths in turn."

"Yet, your uncle withheld the prize of Malaga, the city with the richest trade, the greatest tax wealth, rivaled only by Granada herself. Imagine the anger among the Escayola, when your grandfather drove the Hud family from Andalusia with their help and then gave the pearl of his kingdom to his favored brother, your father, Ismail. A man who contributed no money or men to the campaign."

"My mother was an Escayola princess. Why would they have killed her?"

"She wed your father for love. From that day onward, she was no longer part of the Escayola clan. They ordered everyone killed, including her, your father, your brother and sisters, and you."

Faraj swayed on his feet. His mother had died by the command of her own family for loving his father. Through her, he bore the blood of the Ashqilula clan.

"How do you know this, Doñ Nuño?"

"My father brokered the meeting between the Hud and the Escayola. You have more reason to hate the Escayola than anyone does. You have the right of vengeance against the current governor of Malaga."

"Why would I want revenge against Abu Muhammad? Did he order the murders?"

"No, Ibrahim of Comares did, but Abu Muhammad bargained with the Hud and planned the killing of your father, so he could claim your inheritance."

"I need more than your word."

"What further proof could convince you other than the reality of your circumstances? Your parents murdered. You and your siblings orphaned. Abu Muhammad in control of Malaga. The price was the death and destruction of your family. Abu Muhammad got what he wanted in the end, didn't he?"

Chapter 10
Secrets in Silk

Princess Fatima

Gharnatah, al-Andalus: Ramadan - Dhu al-Hijja 666 AH
(Granada, Andalusia: June - September AD 1268)

While Fatima sat on a low stool in her room with Leeta brushing her hair, Niranjan entered, a long garment draped over his arm. Purple silk glittered with *tiraz* bands sewn in silver thread. Amethyst and mother of pearl trimmed the hems.

"A present had arrived for you, my princess, a beautiful ceremonial robe."

"Another present for my tenth birthday?" She fingered the fine silk. "Who brought this for me? Is it from Father?"

He replied, "The Sitt al-Tujjar brought it, all the way from Naricha."

She shook her head. Why would the Sitt al-Tujjar send her anything?

When she glanced at Niranjan again, he held her gaze and nodded.

Then she remembered who lived in Naricha, her mother's brother and the slave Ulayyah.

Niranjan set the cloth on her bed, bowed and went away. Leeta finished and Fatima dismissed her.

Alone, she dashed to the bed and grabbed the robe. She studied the cloth. The silk had come from Ulayyah, her governess' sister, who served Grandfather's enemies, the Ashqilula. Why did the slave send her a present?

104

Then, she noticed an overlay of lavender silk sewn with rough stitches that seemed to serve no purpose in the garment. Trying not to ruin it, she picked at the threads until they loosened. A thin, folded sheet of parchment fell. She opened it, her heart racing with each word.

'Greetings in the name of God, may peace be upon you. I write to one whom I have never forgotten. Those who are disloyal to Gharnatah are plotting the end of the Sultanate. There was a meeting between the Sultan's enemies at al-Hisn Qumarich on the second day of Ramadan. My lord Abdallah does not know I listened at the door to the raised voices. There were four men inside my lord's chamber, three whom I recognized: my master Abdallah with the chieftain Ibrahim and the governor of Malaka, Abu Muhammad. The fourth man, they called Doñ Nuño Gonzalez de Lara.'

The last name held no significance for her, but her jaw tightened at the mention of Ibrahim and Abu Muhammad. Ibrahim might have killed her mother, but Abu Muhammad was just as responsible for her death. She realized Abdallah still did not know the truth of Aisha's death. Shaking her head, she continued reading.

'I had never seen this Doñ Nuño before. My master and his kin wanted assurances they could trust him. The governor of Malaka asked this Doñ Nuño if he was there to seal the new alliance between the Ashqilula and the Castillan king. Doñ Nuño said it was his purpose in coming. I do not pretend to understand all they spoke of, but I know the Ashqilula seek powerful allies against the Sultan. They must pay for their treachery. Tell the Sultan. He shall know what to do. With respect, a loyal servant of Gharnatah.'

Fatima's head pounded with the knowledge Ulayyah had shared. She called for Leeta. "Please, fetch my father at once."

Clutching the precious letter, Fatima waited for him.

Quick strides brought him to her room. "Daughter? Your servant said you needed me. Are you unwell?"

"I am well, Father, but please sit."

She gave him the letter. He read it once, his eyes widening. He glanced at her and then read it a second time. "What's this about, Fatima?"

"Father, it's from my governess' sister, the slave Ulayyah. She serves my mother's brother Abdallah at Naricha."

She reminded him of the story of Ulayyah's kindness to her.

He replied, "Despite all you have said, I fail to understand why this slave would take such a risk? She owes no loyalty to our family and truly, there is no proof, just her words. Did you consider she might be a spy put forth by our enemies to provide false information?"

"Father, you don't know her as I do. She helped me. You must believe her!"

He shook his head, but she knelt at his feet and grasped his hand. "She gave her loyalty to me and my family, also."

"What of her master? Doesn't he also deserve her loyalty? Yet she betrays him."

"Ulayyah serves her lord Abdallah but she also said Ibrahim of Ashqilula was cruel to her."

"Reason enough for her to be bitter and write this letter, Fatima. It is not enough." He scratched his beard. "It's not for me to decide. I shall speak with the Sultan in an hour, after public audience has ended." He paused and his hand within hers shook. "What if the Ashqilula find out what she's done? I don't know why this woman contacted you, but you must have no more dealings with her. If she sends you another letter, promise me you'll destroy it."

He kissed her brow and left. He did not wait for her to make the promise.

An hour passed on the water clock. Fatima went into the bedroom, asking Leeta for her black hooded cloak. She left the harem with Niranjan.

Secreting themselves behind a high row of hedges, the pair did not have to wait long.

Soon her grandfather, her father, and the Sultan's counselors marched past where they sat hidden. The Sultan ordered the throne room's doors closed behind them.

Niranjan and Fatima left the garden and went down the stairs at the edge of the garden. The door to the tower creaked slightly. Down a long, dark passageway, which ended with a door, they then made their way up one level and hid again, behind the *purdah* where the women of the Sultan's household usually sat during public audience. The meeting inside the throne room had already started.

"... Can we believe the words of a disgruntled slave? She has suffered at the hands of the Ashqilula and clearly bears them no loyalty."

That was her father's voice. Words of agreement followed, all soon hushed by the Sultan. "Yet, you brought this slave's story to me, son. We must weigh the consequences of any action. I cannot risk the Sultanate on the basis of rumors, but neither shall I allow the Ashqilula or Castillans to make a fool of me in my own land."

The Sultan fell silent as the tower doors opened. His other sons and Prince Faraj entered. Fatima shrank back next to Niranjan, who placed a comforting arm over her shaking shoulders. She listened to the ensuing argument.

In the months after her mother's death, she had reasoned that Aisha was right. Her union with Faraj had been a part of the Sultan's plans. Gharnatah's future would determine her fate. She could not remain ignorant of events in the Sultanate, or her father and grandfather's actions.

The Sultan said, "Even if we did not have the claims of this slave, I have enough reason to convince my allies the Ashqilula should be destroyed. Doñ Nuño Gonzalez de Lara came to me in peace months ago. I gave him coin to aid his rebellion. Nothing has resulted. My coin, my trust bartered for so little. I shall not lose in this affair. We must be cautious."

After the men finished and departed the throne room, quiet descended on the tower again. Niranjan and Fatima crept from their hidden location. When they exited in the garden, a sudden downpour surprised them. Niranjan led her across the darkened paths.

When he stumbled and cried out, she peeked around him.

Faraj eyed them. "What are you and your little mistress doing here, slave?"

She stepped out from behind Niranjan. "The Sultan has never forbidden his grandchildren in any part of his palaces. I go where I please."

"With a shadow in tow, I see. Your father said he left you in your room, Fatima."

"We are going there now."

Niranjan bowed and she followed him.

At her back, Faraj said, "Tread carefully, Fatima."

She called over her shoulder. "I have nothing to fear in my grandfather's *madina*."

***

A second letter from Ulayyah arrived within a few weeks. Torn silk in hand, Fatima stood in her father's garden at sunset with Niranjan beside her. When he finished reading the letter, she asked, "When does the Sitt al-Tujjar return to Qumarich?"

"Soon. I'm sure she'd be pleased to undertake any request you may have."

"Good. I want to thank Ulayyah for her gift."

"It shall be done, my princess."

She dismissed Niranjan. He ripped the parchment into fine pieces, and feed them to the fire at the edge of the garden.

Fatima folded her arms across her waist, and hugged her body against a cooling breeze. She could not turn back from this course, despite her father's admonitions. She suspected Ibrahim kept spies in their household. Now she would have a spy in his.

Chapter 11
A Small Measure of Peace

Prince Faraj

Gharnatah, al-Andalus: Ramadan 670 AH (Granada, Andalusia: April AD 1272)

Showers burst from the morning clouds, catching Faraj on a morning ride in the hills above Gharnatah. The sudden rain turned his mood sour. He nudged his horse back down the sloping hills and entered the courtyard of the citadel.

Thunder rolled as a steady rain soaked him to the bone. With a shudder, he dismounted and found shelter under the redbrick Gate of the Merchants, where he four other people stood, including Fatima.

The stick-thin, sylphlike girl had changed in the six years since they had wed. She stood just shy of his shoulder now. An opaque blue-black veil hid her dark hair. Tiny *dirhams* with holes drilled at the center of each silver coin decorated the fringe of the veil.

"It's a terrible time to be riding your horse, my prince. The poor animal is soaked." She rolled her eyes at him and pulled her multicolored linen wrap tighter about her shoulders.

He groaned, in no mood for her droll observations. "I'm pleased you care so much for the beast's welfare, even if you think so little of mine. Besides, it was not raining when I left home. Why are you outdoors?" He paused and glanced at the slaves sheltering behind her. "And why has your escort not gone ahead to arrange for your safe conduct?"

The eunuch edged closer and cast a baleful stare full of insolence at him, before he bent and whispered to Fatima. She hushed the slave, her fingers alighting on his forearm. "Remain at my side, Niranjan. There is no need for you to be drenched on my behalf."

The eunuch dared glance at Faraj, who tightened his fingers into a fist, stifling a fervent urge against striking the impertinent wretch. Had Fatima stimulated such a violent reaction in him instead?

"I had hoped to reach home sooner than this, my prince." She waved a slim, bejeweled hand at the gathering puddles at their feet. "My lesson in *al-Quran* was not finished until late."

"Humph. Aren't you past the age where princesses are tutored?"

She shook her head, mumbling something under her breath. Then she said, "Memorizing *al-Quran* is a duty. I may be fourteen, but Father has given permission for the continuation of my lessons."

He sneered, eyeing her steadily. "How generous the crown prince is. Do you enjoy your studies?"

"Just because you didn't like the princes' school doesn't mean I can't appreciate Ibn Ali's teachings."

"How did you know I didn't like my lessons with Ibn Ali?"

"I asked him about you. He said you were the worst student he has ever had."

"You questioned the royal tutor about me?"

"You're my husband. Isn't it right that I should want to know about you?"

He clenched his fists. "If you want to know anything, I'd prefer if you asked me. I'd never hide anything from you."

"Humph. I don't believe you."

"Are you calling your husband a liar?"

She glanced at him briefly. "You keep secrets. Always, your eyes are watching and observing what others do, yet you remain silent. Something lies hidden in you. You do not speak of it, but sadness and pain haunts your gaze. What secrets are you hiding, Prince Faraj?"

"If I had any secrets, why should they concern you?"

"As I have said, you are my husband. Everything about you is a matter of interest for me."

He crossed his arms over his chest. "I wonder, what provokes this wifely concern? You've never shown it before."

"When have I ever had the chance to do so? As I have said, you keep secrets."

She turned her gaze to the sky. An arc of lightening illuminated the darkening clouds, highlighting the curve of her cheek. As he continued staring, a deepening blush suffused her skin. Suddenly, he wondered at how the softness and texture of her flesh might feel against his.

She asked, "Why did you refuse Grandfather's invitation to dine this evening?"

Startled at the impulsive thought of touching her, he forced a quick reply. "How did you know I had refused?"

Her cheeks colored the deep red of a pomegranate before her eyes fastened on his again, her dark brows drawn together.

"My prince, it is difficult to talk with you, when you insist on answering one question with another."

Her sedate tone belied the angry flush of her skin. Tension radiated in her fists curled into the folds of her garment and her rigid stance. He sensed deep emotion coursing through her, though held in reserve. It stunned and fascinated him in equal measure. She could likely teach him a lesson or two about natural composure.

The words rushed out of him. "Fatima, I have never dealt with so many questions before. At least, not from a... wife."

When he hesitated before speaking the last words, her gaze widened. His head and shoulders slumped, and he avoided her insistent stare for a moment. How could he make her understand?

"Fatima, you must recognize that our... situation is unique. We hardly know each other and I wish to avoid offending you. I am simply unaccustomed to such determined inquiry into my welfare."

She swallowed so loudly that he heard it. "It is the duty of a wife to care for her husband's welfare. Although our circumstances are unique, as you say, in that we do not live together, I cannot forget my responsibilities."

He sighed and nodded, as the sensation of a heavy weight settled in his stomach. "I thank you for your concern, Fatima."

"It was prompted by your answer. I was with the Sultan when it arrived, just before my lesson."

"Are you close to him?"

"He's my grandfather. I love him best in the world, as much as my own father and my brother and sisters."

He did not share the same sentiments about his own family. His father had treated him like his treasured heir, but duties to Malaka and the governorship had occupied his short existence until death. Faraj had three sisters, whom he had not seen for years since each of them married. He and his half-brother loathed each other.

"Aren't you close to your family, my prince?"

"I've never been." He tamped down a natural inclination toward asking why she wanted to know, but his admission left him embittered and unwilling to delve further into the topic. Had she asked the question, intent on belittling him for it, or just as a demonstration of her knowledge about his circumstances? Had she asked for another unexpected reason? Did she care for him?

She said, "It's unfortunate, as you were all orphaned in your youth. Yes, Father told me about your past. Your eyes betray your surprise. Yet, who should you have clung to except each other?"

Her knowledge astonished him, in particular her pertinent observations. His gaze slid away under her scrutiny. The intent warmth of her expression unnerved him, though he sensed her stare held no pity, only curiosity. He worried about what else might she have learned of him.

After a time, he inhaled deeply. "My half-brother has no love for me. I share the same views of him. There was always a little rivalry between us. My younger sisters are married. I suppose their duties as wives and mothers keep them to their respective homes. Not every family can be as fortunate to be close, like yours."

"Have you ever tried to know your family better?"

He shrugged. "They'll never have a high opinion of me, so it's useless."

She nodded. "I may not know you as well as I should like, but my instincts tell me you don't avoid a challenge, if you really want something."

He drew back, flabbergasted. Damned girl, how did she perceive the worst and best of him? She edged too close to the truth, one he could not confront. Not yet.

He forced a smile. "For the moment, I'm focused on improving your opinion of me."

Her blush returned. "Why do you say that?"

"You have made many assumptions, some true, but most of them unfair. If I don't take the trouble to correct you, we shall never have a companionable relationship."

"Is that what you want from me, a companionable relationship?"

She awaited his answer in silence, her gaze stark, piercing to his very soul.

He sucked in a harsh breath and looked at her companions, who had intently followed the conversation. The women exchanged abrupt, wary glances with him and each other, before they looked away. The eunuch's black eyes darted to Faraj's face before he studied the blackened sky.

Faraj nodded to Fatima. "My parents married according to the wishes of the Sultan, as we did. They shared a delicate peace. If we are fortunate to have a small measure of the happiness they did, it would suit me."

She lowered her eyelids. "Only a small measure would suffice, humph? If that is what you wish, then it is what you shall have."

Those sparkling eyes that had intrigued and invited a moment ago closed him out. A chill rippled through his body that had nothing to do with the soaking rain.

He looked down at his muddied, sandaled feet. No words passed between them, but thoughts swirled in his head, all revolving around her. How had she stirred his anger, curiosity, and now, regret, in such a short span of time?

He began, "Fatima, I...."

"I believe the rain has stopped, my prince. Please, allow me to return to my father's harem."

At the sound of her voice, he looked heavenward. As suddenly as the rain had started, it tapered off.

She curtsied before him. "The peace and blessings of Allah, the Compassionate, the Merciful, be with you."

Her servants bowed, before they all turned away and left him.

He hung his head and kicked a pebble in his path. Snagging the reins of his sodden, snorting horse, he glanced over his shoulder. Fatima's silken *jubba* grew fainter in the distance, the thin material of her robe clinging to her smooth hips.

He arrived at his house just before another abrupt downpour started. He bellowed for Marzuq and gave him terse instructions. The steward bowed and departed.

Faraj handed his wet cloak to a waiting slave and went to his bedchamber. There, he undressed hastily and changed into a woolen caftan and trousers. Dim light illuminated his way as he crossed the corridor.

Entering the cavernous chamber where his women resided in the harem, Faraj beheld a delectable sight. His *jawari* waited in the center of the room in various stages of undress, their sheer, pastel silk garments betraying and hiding sensuous curves at the same time.

"Master, Marzuq said you were unsettled. Surely we can improve your mood." Samara looked up at him beneath hooded eyelids painted with malachite.

The trio smiled invitingly, snaking toward him. Yet, even as Baraka nibbled the curve of his ear and pressed the softness of her pale breast to him, and Hayfa and Samara's hands undid his garments, he stilled the roving hands and stepped back.

"I... I should not have come. I shall return to my room, unaccompanied."

Baraka frowned and slipped her supple limbs about him. The tips of her rouged nipples grazed his chest.

He removed her arms and shook his head. "I said, not now, Baraka."

***

On the following day, the Sultan summoned him. Tortured by rampant dreams and irritable for lack of restful sleep, he performed the minor ablution before leaving his house. He joined his uncle, just as the Sultan's servants set the morning meal of dry flatbread, cheese, sliced pomegranates and cinnamon-flavored tisane on the table.

"Ah, here's my nephew at last. Sit with me."

When he did, Faraj could not help noticing how the Sultan had aged. His eyes were still clear and alert, but other signs betrayed his years. Deep crinkles mired his eyes and lines furrowed his olive-skinned brow. His body had shriveled. The gnarled hands lifting the ceramic cup to his lips shook unsteadily.

"You study me as my wives do when they are concerned for my health," the Sultan commented over the rim of the cup.

Faraj smiled and shook his head, but the Sultan continued, "You need not deny it and I wish you would not. It is not often I see such a candid expression on your face. You look pale. Are you unwell?"

"No, my noble uncle, I did not sleep well last night. The tisane is helping."

"Eat and drink your fill." The Sultan set down his cup. "You met with Fatima yesterday."

Faraj drained his cup. Too many spies in Gharnatah watched his movements. "It was raining. We took shelter under the Gate of the Merchants."

His almost rueful reply irritated him. He did not have to explain seeing his wife to anyone. She was his. A warm, lovely feeling settled in his stomach at the thought.

"Was your meeting altogether agreeable?"

Though he nodded, it was not entirely true. Afterward, Fatima had robbed him of his desire for his concubines. When he had seen the women, in truth, he thought only of her.

He shook his head. He could not allow her such influence over his mind. "She's still very young."

"Much too young to interest you, eh? Still, I am glad you spoke to her. It is my hope you and she shall become better acquainted. It is unfortunate then that despite my wish, I must now send you away from her, on a diplomatic mission."

"Send me away, my Sultan?"

"Yes, I would have you be a part of the peace delegation that goes to al-Maghrib el-Aska next week. I seek the Marinids as Gharnatah's allies again, so I send emissaries to Sultan Abu Yusuf Ya'qub. I expect you may be gone for a few months."

"A few months?"

"You object to my request?"

"No, but you have said you wish me to become better acquainted with Fatima. I can hardly know her better, if I am gone."

"What are a few months compared to the lifetime which you shall have with her? You both can bear the separation. It's not as if you are in love with her, are you?"

Faraj stared down at his hands. A vision of her hair gliding through his fingertips assailed him. He shook his head and jerked his gaze to the Sultan, who watched him steadily.

"I shall go al-Maghrib el-Aska as you command, master."

***

Faraj requested a meeting with Fatima the next day. He did not want to leave Gharnatah without an amicable parting. The prospect of his departure nagged him, but he refused to consider the source of his disquiet.

He arranged to meet her in the center of the extensive gardens separating the households of the Sultan and his heir. A package in hand, he walked toward the precincts of the Sultan's palace. Admitted through the sentry gate, he crossed cobblestone streets bustling with courtiers seeking the relaxing comfort of the baths in the royal *madina*. He walked eastward, finally arriving at the outskirts of the garden park. Then he turned north, strolling along an avenue of juniper trees. When he rounded a row of hedges at the center of the garden, she appeared, with a group of slaves waiting on her attentively.

Silver bracelets jangled on her limbs, as she paced under an octagonal pavilion. A string of opals fell to her hips, paired with a shorter necklace of amethysts. Her long purple *jubba* and the lavender trousers underneath outlined a slender body, which showed promise of becoming womanly. She was no longer a child, but not quite a woman worthy of his interest. Surely not.

Her dignity and composure took him aback. In a clear and confident voice, she spoke to her slaves with an unquestionable level of authority. Spying him, she spoke with the pale man at her right. He turned to the slender dark-skinned woman seated beside him. They led the group of slaves away, all except for three others, one of whom Faraj recognized as the eunuch who always shadowed Fatima.

She sat on a large green cushion, while her eunuch bowed before him.

"Princess Fatima shall see you now, my prince."

Two delicate brown-skinned slave girls bowed. They were identical in feature and dress and moved with precise synchronization. After addressing them, Fatima dismissed her slaves. She and Faraj were alone.

"*Eid mubarak* and the peace of God be with you, my prince."

Clearing his throat, he answered, "Uh... yes, and to you, as well and the peace of God be with you and your house."

She gestured toward a red cushion beside her. He set down his package at his feet. Her dark eyes remained on him. He shrank under her scrutiny. She stared unabashedly without emotion. Her inscrutable expression concealed her thoughts.

He reached for the parcel and placed it before her. "I brought a gift for the passing of Ramadan."

Her delicate eyebrows arched. "Such things are usually for children. Is that how you think of me still, as a child?"

When he stammered, she laughed, surprising him. Something about her drew him near, but he closed his fingers into tight fists until they dug into his palms.

"I don't want to seem ungrateful, my prince. Thank you for your consideration."

"Yes, well... it's appropriate for me to consider you. You're my wife."

She removed the cotton covering and revealed a golden gilded cage. Inside, a bird folded its black wings. Its small white head bobbed as golden-brown eyes darted everywhere.

He said, "The seller assured me this kite is gentle enough to eat from your hand. I named her Fatima in your honor."

She looked at him askance. "Do I remind you of a bird now?" Before he could answer, she continued, "I had a bird like this, once. My brother shot a sparrow and I helped to heal her broken wing. She died a year ago. I never thought I would have my own for a pet."

"Then, you like the gift?"

"I do, very much. I thank you for her."

Her face flushed with happiness. Her mouth curved in a delectable smile. A surge of elation filled him at the thought of making her happy.

"I believe I could be content for the remainder of my life, if only you would always smile at me."

When her eyes widened, he chided himself for his thoughtless slip of tongue. He was not some lovesick fool for her.

They sat in silence until he said, "I must leave Gharnatah in a few days, at the Sultan's request. I do not know how long I shall be gone."

"Grandfather relies on you. What do you do for him when you're away?"

"I follow his commands and do what he wishes of me."

She scowled. "If you do not wish to tell me, I won't pry."

Sighing, he said, "Your grandfather gives me different responsibilities. I have served as his interpreter and as a secretary, commissioned to write his letters of state."

"Grandfather can write his own letters. Why does he ask you to do it?"

"You object to his choice of me as his emissary and scribe?"

"I wonder why he chooses you for such missions."

Often, he wondered the same. The men who usually undertook such duties were learned ministers, or preparing for administrative office. He had no interest in, or prospect of, either possibility. The sole responsibility he desired in life remained elusive, as in the days after his father's death.

Chapter 12
The Raiders

Prince Faraj

Al-Andalus: Jumada al-Thani 671 AH (Andalusia: January AD 1273)

The rocky promontory at Jabal Tarik pierced the morning mist, welcoming Faraj home to al-Andalus after a nine-month absence. He returned with the Sultan's retinue of emissaries by trade ship from al-Maghrib el-Aska. They had left the Marinid ruler without assurances of an alliance. Just before departing the capital city at Fés el-Bali, Faraj wrote his master about the apparent failure of the negotiations.

Except for the crew, he stood on deck alone while the ship crossed the White Sea that Christians called the Mediterranean. Salt spray thickened the crisp, wintry wind. The boat rounded the western portion of Jabal Tarik and proceeded along the coastline of al-Andalus. They neared the port of disembarkation at Munakkab, one of the few seaside towns the Ashqilula family did not control.

On dry land again, Faraj commandeered one of several mounts the Sultan had sent from Gharnatah. A groom, who held the reins of his horse, proffered a rolled parchment bearing the Sultan's seal. Faraj scanned it and mounted the gray stallion. He considered the instructions in the letter and sensed Gharnatah's fortunes were once again about to change.

He parted from the others, who would return to Gharnatah directly, and circumvented the hillside base of Munakkab's citadel. At the outskirts of the city, bare mulberry trees covered the plains, evidence of the flourishing silk trade within the Sultanate. The sun glittered against the pale brick and rubble masonry of the city's walls. In the citadel's courtyard, a detachment of Moorish soldiers barred his entry. He dismounted, looking for the crown prince. Within minutes, the heir of Gharnatah emerged from the citadel and he was not alone. The Castillan commander Doñ Nuño Gonzalez de Lara strode beside him.

Faraj's fists tightened at his side. Nearly six years after his secret encounter with the commander, his parents' blood cried out for revenge against the Ashqilula traitors and all those who had helped them.

The crown prince spoke in animated tones and smiled at his cohorts, before he approached.

Faraj bowed. "I came as your noble father ordered. I trust all goes well in Gharnatah," He nodded to the crown prince's companions standing a few feet away.

The heir favored him with a cautious smile. "We shall speak in a moment of Gharnatah's affairs. Tell me instead of your sojourn in al-Maghrib el-Aska and of Sultan Abu Yusuf Ya'qub's words."

Glancing at the Lara men who waited and observed, Faraj shook his head. "The Marinids cannot commit to an alliance with Gharnatah now."

The crown prince stroked his dark, pointed beard and nodded, before looking over his shoulder to where his guests awaited him. He smiled at them and then whispered, "It's just as well. My father anticipated such a decision from our brothers of the Faith. His greatest disappointment may be that the Marinids cannot yet rid him of my sister Maryam. We shall know the Sultan's true feelings soon enough, when we arrive at Gharnatah."

"Do we depart soon?"

"Yes, in the company of those whom you see here. In the time that you were away in al-Maghrib el-Aska, the Lara men approached my noble father with entreaties, seeking another agreement. Against ardent objections, particularly from me, the Sultan does as he wills. Thus, we are to host the family of Lara and their companions for a time. My father has provided a large estate in al-Bayazin for his new allies."

"I must ask, is this the wisest choice? Your father has committed the Sultanate to a course of action that has unforeseeable consequences for us all. How can we be assured the Castillan rebels shall remain steadfast, when in the past, they...?"

"We must trust in the Sultan to do what is right for Gharnatah's future. Come, let us dine with these fools here, and enjoy the entertainment their presence may provide."

***

Weeks passed, in which the Sultanate of Gharnatah existed in a state of uncertainty. Minor skirmishes at the border with Castilla-León and near the territories under Ashqilula control resulted in a handful of injuries, but few deaths. In fearful whispers, courtiers predicted that either King Alfonso or the Ashqilula or both would besiege *al-Qal'at al-Hamra*. Yet, neither declared open warfare. Faraj did not know which situation the Sultan found more intolerant; the lack of a decisive victory over his enemies, or their pragmatic positions.

Then, Gharnatah's soldiers and the Castillan rebels raided at border towns, which Doñ Nuño Gonzalez de Lara had identified as weak targets. Buoyed by their successes, the Sultan joined his compatriots in the raids, taking plunder and slaves.

Faraj had accompanied them in the last two successful raids into Castillan territory, but he would not do so today, in the attack on the town of Martus. Instead, he waited in the precincts of *al-Quasaba*, with the royal family and the courtiers who wished the Sultan success.

He stood beside Princess Fatima in the cold balm of morning. Since his return to Gharnatah, they had seen little of each other. His repeated requests for an audience, at first, seemed ill timed. The crown prince's chief eunuch always offered the excuse that she was too busy or indisposed. Faraj was not a fool. He knew she was avoiding him and he suspected the reason, however foolish. He had not corresponded with her during his sojourn in al-Maghrib el-Aska, but surely, she did not care about that.

Even now, her apathy annoyed him, as she stared straight ahead. Though she wore the veil, like other married women around her, he would have known his wife among all others, for only she displayed the coldest indifference to him.

Now, he almost wished he had joined the raiding party, for Fatima's silence was maddening. He suspected she would have preferred him gone, too. Her sister Muna showed some sympathy, or at least her eyes said as much, whenever she regarded Fatima and him.

The Sultan called the raiders to attention. He rode the length of the entire column of men with a brusque charge. In that moment, he looked nothing like an octogenarian. The energy he displayed enthralled everyone. His family cheered him loudly and lustily in, what must have been for him, a heady reminder of his youthful days.

He accepted the acclaim with a broad, charming grin and spurred his horse toward his family and retainers, who awaited him. Three women approached his horse. His wives and honored concubines wore white silk. Opaque veils covered their hair and faces. The women took hold of the Arabian's reins without fear, though the horse snorted and tossed his head. The Sultan spoke with each of his women. In turn, they kissed his hands and bid him farewell.

The women moved aside when the crown prince approached and bent on one knee at his father's side. The Sultan dismounted. Words passed between the men beyond the hearing of anyone else. The Sultan clasped his son by the shoulders. They exchanged the kiss of peace. Then the Sultan mounted his horse and raised his hand in salute. He ordered the raiders out of the western gate of *al-Qal'at al-Hamra.*

Fatima whispered a soft, fervent prayer. When Faraj glanced at her, moisture glistened in her eyes. He laid a hand upon her arm. "He always returns, you know."

She stiffened at his touch. "If such is the Will of God." She glared at his hand on the white sleeve of her *jubba.* A silent command flared in her gaze.

When he withdrew his hand, she turned away without another word.

Without forethought, his fingers closed on her forearm, none too gently.

She stared at him, wide-eyed. "My tutor awaits me."

"Surely, he can bear the demands of your husband."

She looked over her shoulder. The princesses Muna and Alimah lingered, with anxious gazes. She waved them away. They hesitated, briefly. When the royal family and courtiers finally dispersed, some with curious glances at him, Faraj released Fatima's forearm, which she rubbed gingerly.

He began, "I am sorry if I have hurt you."

Her soothing gesture stopped. "I'm not fragile and do not bruise easily. Yet, I must warn you. Do not touch me again with so little care. I am a princess and by that title alone, I am worthy of your respect. Because I'm your wife, I also deserve to be treated with gentle care."

"As your husband, princess, I expect to be treated with the same respect and care you desire. Why then do I feel slighted by you?"

"I do not know what you mean."

"Then let me make my meaning plain. You have ignored me in polite silence and abused me with determined indifference since my return. How have I offended you? I expect a truthful answer from you. I demand it as your husband."

She frowned and set her hands on her hips. "Very well, I shall tell you how you have offended me. You are a riddle, impossible to understand. Your words and actions are always at odds. You leave for nine months without a word of greeting whilst you are gone. I am your wife. When you treat me with so little interest, you can't ask for more than the same from me."

He drew back under her harsh words, but she pressed on. "I want to respect and admire my husband. Yet how can I, when in every instance of our years of marriage, you have shown you don't care for my thoughts or feelings?"

Faraj shook his head. She was angry because the Sultan had sent him to al-Maghrib el-Aska. If anything, she should have been annoyed with her grandfather. Besides, why did she care about his absence?

He bowed. "I'm sorry to be found so wanting in your eyes."

Fatima sighed and shook her head, before her angry gaze returned to his.

"Mock me, if you like. You shall have those things of me, which I must give, because they are your due. But, you shall never have my respect, until you can give the same with an open heart."

***

Princess Fatima

After her lessons, Fatima returned to the harem and slunk into the *hammam*. Absentmindedly, she lingered in the water until her skin reddened. Alone in her room, she brushed her hair before a long silver gilt mirror, while Amoda laundered the clothes and Leeta oversaw the preparation of the evening meal.

The bristles whipped through her hair, tugging strands from the scalp. Her anger lingered. Faraj had ignored her for nine months and then expected her joyous welcome at his return. His arrogance embittered her. He wasn't worth her attentions. Yet, she had thought of him so often during his absence and even more now since his return. With a sigh, the brush hung in her hands.

Terror suddenly implanted itself in her mind. At first, she did not understand what it meant, but it squeezed at her heart like a mist of dread that enshrouded her. Grandfather. The reality of his fading mortality struck her.

Her reflection in the mirror became unclear as a chill shuddered through her. The brush slipped from her loose hold and clattered on the tiles. It cracked in half.

"What has you so pensive, Fatima?"

The unexpected sound of her brother's voice forced her from her reverie. Startled, she slid from the wooden stool where she sat, and landed on her buttocks with a sharp thud. The wool robe she wore fell around her shoulders. She clutched it tight. Muhammad's bemused expression infuriated her even more than Faraj's arrogance.

"What are you doing here?"

"I called for you. One of your slaves told me you were within."

Holding the robe closed, she stood. "This is my bedchamber and you shouldn't be here. It's unseemly."

"You're my sister, how can it be unseemly that I should visit you here?"

"I'm wearing only a robe, Muhammad."

His eyes glittered with a widening smile. "Your maidenly modesty isn't necessary. What you have under that robe is the same as every one of my *jawari*."

"I'm not one of your concubines. I'm your sister. Please wait outside."

Muhammad laughed and sketched a mocking bow. "As you wish."

Alone again, she cast off the robe and threw it on the floor. Dressing with haste in the garments Leeta had arranged on the bed, she shoved her feet into leather slippers and went to Muhammad. He stood in the central chamber, trailing his long fingers through the water fountain in the midst of the room. She gestured toward the cushions arranged around the square-shaped room and joined him.

Over the years, she and her brother had grown further apart. The estrangement pained her deeply. Try as she might, in her heart, she could not forgive him for his harsh words spoken at their mother's death, seven years before.

Muhammad grasped her slim hands in his larger ones. She fought against her instinct to pull away and returned his intent, probing gaze.

"I'm sorry if I embarrassed you earlier, sister."

"The moment is past, but please do not do it again."

He sighed. "I've missed you, Fatima, the friendship we used to share, in which we confided everything to each other."

"I did not end our friendship, Muhammad, you did."

"Yes, I know it was my fault. Please believe that I am sorry. I wish that we would be friends again. I have missed you very much."

He laid his head against her shoulder. When she flinched, he rushed on. "Forgive me, Fatima, be my sister again." His voice was a low murmur. "Let this anger end between us."

He drew back and looked at her again, with eyes so like her own. She turned away, but Muhammad persisted. "You must forgive me and let us be brother and sister again."

Her heart and head warred inside her. He had treated her cruelly for so long, but he was her only brother, the beloved heir of their father. She couldn't hate him forever.

"Yes... we are brother and sister."

"Good! Now, let us seal our pledge with the kiss of peace."

Words trapped in her throat, she turned her cheek to him. Muhammad's warm, wide mouth pressed against hers, lingered on her lips. She pulled back and stared at him, her heart pounding with uncertainty and fear. Something about his fervent embrace troubled her.

He smiled and kissed her hands. "You've made me so happy, Fatima. I'm glad you have forgiven me."

She stammered, "I haven't said I forgive you...," but Muhammad interrupted.

"No, say no more. I know you need time, but at least you may try. For that, I shall always be grateful. I have so much to tell you, but I must share the most important thing now. I have told no one yet, not even our father, because I wanted you to be the first to hear the good news. I am to have a son."

She stared in silence while Muhammad continued. "In less than seven months, I shall hold my firstborn son in my arms, at sixteen years of age! Imagine our father's surprise when he learns he is to be a grandfather so soon."

"But, how do you know it may be a boy?"

"It must be a boy. That is what I wish for and that is what shall be."

"Muhammad, our father has six daughters and only one son. God willed it. No man may ask for more than God gives him."

"I'm not Father. Why should I be cursed with daughters? I must have sons, Fatima, strong sons worthy of our family name."

She withdrew her hands from his grip. "I do not think our father considers himself cursed for having more daughters than sons."

Muhammad laughed and traced a line across her brow with his fingertip. "You're still so easily offended. I didn't mean Father regrets you or my sisters. But, as his heir, I must have sons to succeed the throne of Gharnatah. No female could ever rule al-Andalus. The Traditions of the Prophet, may peace be upon him, forbid it. I must have a son, I cannot accept a daughter."

"What of your *jarya*, the mother of your child? What are her sentiments?"

"Zuleika wants what I want. She knows the value of a son to me."

"Surely, she has thoughts and opinions of her own. What is she like?"

"She is beautiful, with dark, honey-brown skin and eyes like a cat's own. That is all that matters to me. Her thoughts and opinions don't concern me. She is a pleasure slave. Her sole duty is to entertain me, in and out of my bed. If I had tired of her before this pregnancy, she would have been sold, like others in the past."

"She carries your heir, and needs your gentleness and care. A midwife has already confirmed her condition?"

"Zuleika has had no show of blood since I first bedded her, three months ago."

"Allow me to send for a midwife to confirm her pregnancy."

He nodded and continued speaking. He was not the childhood playmate of their days in the harem. The same dangerous undercurrent of emotion in him, as at the time of their mother's death, still existed. Something ugly had festered inside him over the years - as plain to the eye as the winsome smile on his lips.

"Grandfather would not let me go on his raid," he said, sulking. "He's old and one day soon, he shall die. Then Father would be Sultan and I would be the crown prince of Gharnatah."

She recoiled from him. "Don't talk about Grandfather dying."

"Why? We must all die someday. One day, I shall be Sultan in Father's stead. I'll raid the Castillan border towns and make their people my slaves."

"But Muhammad, each time we fight them, many of our soldiers die. When you are Sultan, you should strive for peace with the Christians. Gharnatah cannot survive without peace."

He rolled his eyes heavenward. "Peace is boring, Fatima. When I'm Sultan, my enemies shall never know peace."

She believed him and the thought frightened her.

"To think, you were married first, so long ago," Muhammad said, "but I shall be the one to give our father his first grandchild. You must be capable of bearing children by now."

"That is not your concern. I shall be a mother when God chooses...."

Another sudden, but painful sense of her grandfather filled her mind and heart. She gasped and her brother shuddered, clutching his chest, his eyes faraway. His reaction didn't frighten her. She knew, at once, the source of their shared premonition. She whispered a soft prayer and rubbed her arms against a deathly chill.

His expression was bewildered. "Fatima... what is it? You feel it, too?"

"Yes. Our mother once told me our maternal grandmother Saliha was like this."

"Then it is true, what I sense."

"Yes, I believe the Sultan is dead. I don't understand how or why I know."

Her brother nodded. "I felt such emotions when... the Princess Aisha died, perhaps at the very moment of her passing."

She nodded and waited in silence with him.

The great brass bell high atop the watchtower of *al-Quasaba* pealed a sonorous, mournful tone. Rain battered the roof of the harem.

Her brother clutched her hand. While she did not welcome the contact, she soothed him. The tremors coursing through his body passed through her like waves of sorrow.

She whispered, "Be at ease, they shall come to us soon." Niranjan entered with his clothes sodden and his expression somber. As he sagged on one knee, he looked older than his twenty-one years.

"With regret, I announce the death of our master, the Sultan," he said. He stood at Fatima's gesture. "Are the other princesses in the harem, my princess? Your father has asked all the family to convene in the throne room at once."

Fatima nodded. "Muhammad, go to our father. Your place is at his side. My sisters and I shall come."

When Niranjan and Muhammad left, she undid the first two strings of her *qamis*, fingering the blue prayer beads she wore underneath the cotton shirt. She woke this morning with the sense of the precariousness of her grandfather's life on earth, but the foreknowledge didn't alarm her. She had accepted it calmly, for who could go against the Will of God?

Arrayed in veils and a hooded leather cloak, she fetched her sisters. Together, they walked through the rain to the throne room, where the family gathered. The wives and children of her uncles and their aunt Maryam sat together, wailing and rocking back and forth. Muhammad stood at Father's side. To the left sat the Sultanas Hamda and Qamar. Beside them, the Sultan's beloved honored concubines wept. Their cries echoed in the room. Then Faraj entered, his mouth pressed into a thin line. He preceded several courtiers. Fatima spared him a glance, before she hugged and comforted her youngest sister, Nadira.

Darkness covered al-Andalus. Silent servants set torches sputtering to life, illuminating multicolored tiles and incised decorations along the walls.

The bells of the neighborhood of al-Bayazin pealed in competition with the unrepentant pounding of the rain. It seemed as if the very heavens wept for the passing of Gharnatah's leader. The great bell of *al-Quasaba* had ceased, which signaled the return of the Sultan's body to his beloved city. Hooves clattered on the cobblestones.

Fatima looked at her father. He stood silent before a square patchwork of tiles inscribed with the blessed ninety-names of God, set a few steps before the throne.

The echo of heavy hooves on cobblestones and marble faded. When the cortege arrived, the Sultan's three younger sons led the way, while Gharnatah's soldiers carried a still, silent shape on a wooden bier. When they set the body down, Fatima studied her grandfather's form. He was Muhammad ibn Yusuf ibn Nasr, the only Sultan of Gharnatah she had ever known. His arms crisscrossed his chest. His eyes were closed in death. His head had been positioned to face the *Qiblah*, the direction for prayer

Her father stood in the midst of his brothers. Words passed between them that could not be overheard. Then he prayed in a whisper.

Tears pricked at the corner of Fatima's eyes. Across the expanse of the throne room, her gaze sought Faraj. He watched her in silence. His lower lip quivered. She had lost her grandfather. He had lost the man who raised him from childhood like a father. Bound by grief, they offered each other silent comfort in the union of their stares.

Chapter 13
Deeds

Prince Faraj

Gharnatah, al-Andalus: Rajab 671 AH (Granada, Andalusia: January AD 1273)

The princes of Gharnatah buried the old Sultan on a bleak, gray day, the second in the month of Rajab. The body shrouded in white linen, his bodyguards placed it in a grave at the heart of the *rawda* and covered the pit with earth. Afterward, the courtiers dispersed in anticipation of his son's coronation. Faraj waited beside the crown prince.

"Master, the full court awaits you."

The crown prince stood beside his father's grave with the Sultan's bodyguards, now his to command. With a weary sigh, he knelt in silence. Faraj did not wonder at the thoughts whirling in his mind. The enormity of the destiny that awaited him would have overwhelmed any man, even one whom the old Sultan had prepared for his new role.

Then the crown prince stood. "I'm ready."

The men walked through a copse of trees. In silence, they approached the palace. Faraj contemplated many things on the quiet journey, for it seemed the loneliest he had ever taken. It paled only in comparison to the moment he had arrived in Gharnatah as a child, after the murder of his parents.

The crown prince entered from the back of the throne room. The cacophony of sound in the city had faded. Faraj trailed at the end of his retinue. In a small, windowless chamber adjoining the throne room, the imam of the Great Mosque awaited them.

A fountain inscribed with one of the Traditions of the Prophet stood in the center. A dull brass lantern hung on the wall. In this sacred place, reserved for the minor ablution, the crown prince prepared his ritual wash before entering the court. Water bubbled up and filled the shallow basin.

Faraj studied the words inscribed around the circumference of the bowl. "God does not judge you according to your bodies and appearances, but He looks into your hearts and observes your deeds."

He wondered what God might perceive in his actions. Would He look into his heart and see the worth of his desires? Were all Faraj's hopes a sin of pride and vanity?

The crown prince removed his garments and spoke the traditional words of the washing ritual. "In the name of God, I intend to perform the *wudu.*"

At the fountain, he washed his face and arms up to the elbows. Then he smoothed beads of water over his head and lastly, washed his feet up to the ankles. He raised his palms heavenward, touching the sides of his head and spoke the declaration of faith. "There is no god but God and Muhammad is the messenger of God. *Amin.*"

He put on undergarments and then took the robe of state the imam offered. The *khil'a* was the same his father had worn at his coronation. Three decades later, it remained in pristine condition; a red silk garment sewn together with gold thread, ermine lining the hem and cuffs and *tiraz* bands sewn on the wide, full sleeves.

He donned a pair of red leather traveling boots and faced the imam again. The religious leader bowed low, touching his forehead to the ground. At the Sultan's gesture, his companions entered the throne room behind the latticed *purdah* where the women of the court waited. During the old Sultan's reign, his wives had attended daily court proceedings, sometimes with his *kadin.* Now, the newest generation of Sultanas joined them, Fatima and her sisters.

The girls greeted their father. Fatima stood closest to him, resplendent in a gold brocade *khil'a*, her warm smile discernible through the gauzy yellow veil covering her face. Faraj drank in the sight of her.

"May God be with you this day and forever, Father," she whispered.

"May he be with us all, my child," her father replied.

The royal women took their seats on plump cushions. A lull descended in the room. Sultana Qamar tugged at Sultana Hamda, who regarded her with a narrowed gaze.

"Hamda, you must remove yourself from the forefront. The position of honor belongs to Sultana Fatima, since she is the eldest female of the current Sultan's harem."

Sultana Hamda frowned and in a huff, she left her seat with obvious reluctance and took up her opium pipe again. She faded in a haze of sickly sweet smoke. Fatima hesitated, but took her place, her head held high. Pride in her grace and beauty suffused Faraj.

The court herald Ibn Ali recited the profession of faith. Then he listed the new Sultan's titles and praised him to the heavens, in much the same manner as he used to do for the old Sultan. Faraj could not help but chuckle, when his master yawned at the end of the oration - it was just what his father would have done.

The new ruler entered the throne room. At his gesture, Faraj joined his counselors on the left of the room. The guards fanned out. Conversations among the courtiers, who were dressed in their finest robes of state, ended abruptly. The Castillan lords were among them, Doñ Nuño Gonzalez de Lara at the forefront. As the herald proclaimed him, the crown prince surrendered his given name of Abu Abdallah Muhammad and claimed the regal title of Sultan Muhammad II of Gharnatah evermore.

Despite the happy moment, filled with cheers and merriment, Faraj could not wholeheartedly enjoy it. The Castillan presence at such a grand occasion infuriated him. He could never forget that Doñ Nuño's family had aided the Ashqilula, which resulted in tragic deaths and painful losses for him. He silently vowed, one day, Doñ Nuño would pay the debts incurred by his father's treachery with his blood. Faraj would have his revenge against all who had conspired to rob him of the bright future he once envisioned, first Doñ Nuño and then, Abu Muhammad of Ashqilula.

***

Later in the evening, Faraj dined with the Sultan, while he and the chief eunuch, Hasan, discussed the old ruler's plans for the women belonging to the old ruler.

Hasan hefted his bovine bulk off the floor where he had been prostrate. At the Sultan's gesture, he unrolled a sheet of parchment from which he read. "There are thirty *jawari* who were the slaves of your late father, my Sultan. The women are from Abyssinia and Nubia, Ionia and Salonica, Genoa and Corsica, Provençal France, Castilla-León and Galicia. The eldest is in her mid-forties approximately and the youngest is perhaps nineteen, at most. The senior women, of whom there are nine, might make suitable rewards for loyal chieftains, my Sultan."

Muhammad II scratched his dark beard. "What do you suggest I do with the others?"

Hasan's moon-shaped, pale face colored pink. "Sell them, my Sultan. You would gain favorably, for they are well-trained concubines, skilled in the arts of pleasure. The least among them would fetch a minimum of a thousand *dinars*, more if sold through an exclusive slave broker."

The Sultan mulled over the suggestion, a finger tapping at his temple. "Very well, arrange for the sale of the older ones. Of the others, decide which ones would be best suited to private or public auction."

Hasan bandied the names of prospective merchants and counted their number on his beefy fingers, before his master suddenly interrupted. "You mentioned there are women from Galicia among the slaves. Is there a *jarya* with a heart-shaped face, unblemished skin and pale eyes?"

Faraj frowned. How had the Sultan ever seen any of his late father's women to describe one so perfectly? It was unlawful for one man to see another's women unveiled.

Hasan replied, "Yes, master, that's the youngest. Her name is Nur al-Sabah."

The name sounded familiar, but Faraj could not place where he had first heard it.

Hasan added, "Since Umar of the clan Mahalli gave this girl to your father, she has become the most highly prized among your father's slaves. Not only shall she fetch the largest sum, for her beauty, musical talent and intelligence are exquisite assets, but also she remains a virgin. Your late father never bedded her."

Faraj nodded, understanding Hasan referred to the girl the Sultan had coveted seven years ago, when he was crown prince. Had he truly remembered her after all this time? Could one woman be so remarkable that after many years, thoughts of her lingered in a man's thoughts? Suddenly, an image of Fatima at her father's coronation flashed in his mind. He shook his head and cleared his thoughts, concentrating on the moment.

Muhammad II said, "I want the Galician for myself. Arrange this before you consider the sale of other concubines."

Hasan protested, "But, she belonged to your late father."

The Sultan silenced him with a look. "She is mine. Bring her to me tonight, after *Salat al-Isha*."

***

Princess Fatima

In the glimmer of midday, Fatima dressed in a cloak trimmed with ermine to turn back the cold. She strolled through the grounds between the palace complexes. Her father had started several building projects in the first week of his reign, repairing the roofs and porticos of Grandfather's palace, which had suffered from years of rain damage. Her father planned to enlarge his residence, with additional apartments for future use. As the widowed monarch of the last bastion of Islam in the peninsula, surely other Muslim rulers would look to him with an eye for a political match, offering their daughters to seal an alliance.

Even knowing this, Fatima was unprepared for the sight of workers demolishing the façade of the western wing, part of which included her mother's oratory. Masons wielded crowbars and hammers against the stucco walls. They attacked the stylized foliage motifs incised in the early days of her grandfather's reign. Red, black, and green glazed tiles crumbled into shards. Dust billowed and covered everything with a thin film, even the blue and violet flowers of the rosemary bushes.

Hasan emerged from a nearby building, which was still intact. The chief eunuch spoke with one of the workers, likely the supervisor. Fatima ran to them, interrupting their conversation.

"Why are they destroying my mother's sanctuary?" She pointed to the workers.

Hasan shouted above the din, wheezing with the effort. "My Sultana, you shouldn't be here in this noisy, dirty place."

"I don't care! Tell me what's happening here."

"Your father has ordered the destruction of the entire western wing of the palace, my Sultana. Surely you were aware of his plan?"

"I know about the remodeling, but I did not know it would occur at the expense of the rooms here! Hasan, the west wing contains Princess Aisha's oratory and her private baths. Father cannot tear down the prayer room... it was her sanctuary."

"He is Sultan, he can do anything."

Fatima shook her head. Tears blurred her vision as she ran away. How could he do such a thing?

Returning to the harem, she stumbled between rows of myrtle trees at the entrance, and rounded a pool filled with fish. The olive wood doors of her father's apartments loomed across the garden courtyard.

She approached the entryway. "Open this door."

The guard nearest to her shook his head and bent on one knee, mumbling something about not disturbing the Sultan and a plea for forgiveness.

She pounded against the heavy wood. "Open the door. Father! Open the door!"

With each passing minute, determination and anger grew until she struck the door in a fury. She nearly fell forward when the portal opened suddenly. Her father stood in the doorway, his *qamis* wrinkled and barely tucked into his trousers.

"Fatima, what is the matter?"

She stared beyond him into the room. An exquisite woman sat in the center of his bed, a damask cover hiding most of her form, but for her shoulders and one bare leg draped over the edge of the bed. Golden hair cascaded down her back, shimmering against the crimson coverlet.

"For her... for her you are destroying my mother's sanctuary?"

"Fatima, I do not understand your behavior, but I demand an explanation."

"I demand one as well! Do you destroy my mother's sanctuary for a slave?"

He grabbed her wrists, jerked her inside the room, and closed the door firmly.

She wrenched from his grasp. "Does she bring you so much pleasure that she has made you forget my mother? I knew when you became Sultan, part of you would be lost to us, but I did not expect my siblings and me would have to share you with some... with this whore!"

He gripped Fatima's arms. "Do not dare speak of Nur al-Sabah that way!"

Wrapped in the coverlet, the concubine came to his side and placed a hand on his forearm. With this simple gesture, she compelled his full attention.

"Please let her go," she whispered. "She is your daughter and you love her. Do not do something you shall regret."

Fatima turned on her as soon as he released her. "I don't want your help, you...."

"Fatima, get out of my sight before you say more to anger me!" Her father's voice thundered through the room. "I've had enough of your tantrums today. You're a disgrace."

"But Father, she...."

"I said leave now, Fatima! Go, or I shall order my guards to put you out!"

He drew the woman to his side and cocooned her in his embrace. Heart hammering in her chest, Fatima opened the olive doors and stumbled into the courtyard. Tears blinded her and she broke into a run, leaving the harem behind. Suddenly, she slammed into hard, lean muscles. She collapsed on to cool marble stone.

"By the Prophet... Fatima, what is the matter?"

Faraj hovered over her. Without another word, he lifted and carried her trembling form. She buried her face in his garments, turning away from those who milled about the precincts, pointing and whispering. Then a wooden door creaked and warmth enveloped her. He sat down and kept his grip on her. She laid her head on his shoulder. His hand massaged her back.

"Relax, draw deep breaths. It's over. You're safe now."

His soothing voice calmed her. When she regained her composure and tried to rise, his grip did not ease. Embarrassed, she struggled against his hold.

"Fatima, stop. I would never hurt you."

"It is unseemly for you to hold me in this manner. Someone might see us."

"You are my wife. I may hold you as I please. Besides, we are in my house."

She stared at him, incredulous. "You brought me to your house? Why?"

"I was on my way to meet your father. I did not think. I acted out of concern for you."

The intimacy of his embrace startled her, but also brought a sense of safety. Only her father had ever made her feel so secure. Her eyes watered again, but Faraj cradled her close. She cried without restraint, her face buried in the curve of his neck. He said nothing until she stopped shaking.

Then he tugged aside her veil and wiped at her cheeks with a white cotton kerchief. "Tell me what happened."

Her words tumbled free at his gentle coaxing. She fought against the tightness in her throat. When she finished, he heaved a long sigh.

"In my youth, my father Ismail had a favored concubine, Butayna. She was a Christian captured at Ishbiliya when the Castillans took the city from its Hud masters. She was the mother of my half-brother, Muhammad. My father loved my mother Leila, but he also loved the *kadin*. It was a love I could not understand or accept and because of it, I grew to resent her place in my father's life and my father's love for my brother. Then came the night when my brother and I lost our mothers, mine to a suicide and his to the mercenaries who destroyed our home at Malaka. When I think of that time, I remember the fear in Butayna's eyes most."

Fatima cleared her throat. "I know the story of your family's betrayal. I never thought you would talk about it with me."

His plaintive gaze met hers. "I've never spoken of that time to anyone. I don't know why I should speak of it now except...."

"Except you understand what it is like to see your father care for another, besides the woman who bore you. It is another thing which we share."

At his quizzical glance, she continued, "We both lost our mothers as children."

He rested his forehead against hers. "Your father is still alive, but mine is not. I wish he were, so I could let him know how much I honor him still. You have the chance to do so with your father. He deserves your love and loyalty."

"I know and he has it, until my death... but, he loves the *kadin*. I saw it in his eyes, his tenderness toward her."

He leaned back, his eyes meeting hers again. "You begrudge him happiness? Did you think he would pine for your mother forever?"

She shook her head, but mumbled, "In some ways, I had hoped he would."

"If he has found love again, rejoice in his happiness. Love is so fleeting in this world. Each of us must take our happiness where we can find it."

She said nothing, staring into his dark eyes. They had never been this close before in their years of marriage. His almond-eyed gaze remained level with hers for a time. Then he leaned closer, his lips hovering close to hers. She drew in a breath. Her heart pounded so loudly, he must surely have heard it.

"What is this?"

A high-pitched screech echoed from a woman who stood in the archway. Her gauzy garments revealed more skin than they covered. Cosmetics enhanced her curvy lips and alabaster cheeks.

She tossed her head, sending dark chestnut waves tumbling off her shoulders. She pinned Faraj with her gaze. "I have been waiting for your return, master. You promised you would summon me when you arrived. Now, I find you with this woman. Who is she?"

Through gritted teeth, Faraj said, "You'll speak with respect about my wife, Baraka. She is the Sultana Fatima. Remember that you're only a concubine."

The *jarya*'s hard green eyes glittered. "Yet it is my body which pleasures you every night. You cannot favor her over me. Why is she here?"

Faraj set Fatima aside. When he dumped her on the floor in his fury, she gasped. He glared at the woman, having forgotten all about Fatima. "She's none of your concern. Get back to the harem!"

The concubine's eyes narrowed. She disappeared into the adjoining chamber. He raked his hand through his heavy, silken hair and turned to Fatima.

"I am sorry she interrupted us."

Fatima clasped her hands together and eyed him. "Do not apologize, my prince."

He frowned and reached for her. She drew back from his grasp. "I should leave now. I promised to read to my sisters."

"Very well... but before you go, I wish to say... I hope you understand about Baraka."

She shook her head. Bitter bile filled her throat. She swallowed past a choking sensation and ground out an answer. "I do not want to hear about your *kadin*. My father's lover is enough."

Faraj rubbed his temples. "She is not my *kadin*. She's been with me for years, but she is not my favorite."

"Is there another who is the favorite then? When we first married, Father told me you had three concubines. Surely, one of them has endeared herself to you. It's no wonder you can defend my father. You're just like him."

"I cannot believe it. I bring you into my home to offer you comfort and this is my thanks. A jealous tirade!"

She cast him an icy glare, and then left him, slamming the door in her wake.

Chapter 14

The Heart of al-Andalus

Prince Faraj

Gharnatah, al-Andalus: Muharram 672 AH (Granada, Andalusia: July AD 1273)

On the first day of a New Year, Faraj hurried to the Sultan's throne room. When he passed through the great doors of the marble room, its occupants fell silent, regarding him with expectant eyes.

He strode toward Muhammad II and bowed, before whispering. "Our spies have confirmed the report. We are ready."

The Sultan rubbed his hands together. "We march for Madinah Antaqirah."

Faraj sighed to disguise the thrill of anticipation coursing through him, though others were not so cautious.

Only the Sultan remained silent. For a moment, he stared straight ahead, almost blindly. His lips thinned in a grim line. Then he dismissed the assembly. He rose with a gesture toward Faraj, who followed him to the audience chamber.

The Sultan asked over his shoulder, "Do the commanders believe the Ashqilula have been forewarned of our intent, cousin?"

Faraj replied, "No, the commanders do not believe so."

"Our plans are secure for the moment. We must make haste if we are to catch the Ashqilula by surprise, as we were surprised today."

Faraj kept his silence, as they entered the vast room where the Gharnati and Marinid commanders awaited them. The Castillan, Doñ Nuño Gonzalez de Lara, and his sons stood alongside the Moorish soldiers.

The Marinids Umar and his brother Talha had come to Gharnatah nearly eight years before. The Sultan had recently appointed Umar to the post of *al-Shaykh al-Ghuzat*, commander of the Volunteers of the Faith, the Berber and expatriate Andalusi warriors who served in Gharnatah. Umar remained loyal to his master in Fés el-Bali, but Muhammad II believed he aided Andalusi interests, unless they threatened Marinid interests. Faraj did not envy Umar for serving two masters.

The commanders spoke with the Sultan. Their plans were for a swift and surreptitious deployment of men to Madinah Antaqirah. The old Sultan once called the city 'the heart of al-Andalus' thought it occupied the coastal region. Faraj would join the campaign, as part of the detachment of cavalry under Talha's command.

When Muhammad II dismissed the commanders, Faraj left too.

Soon, at an impulse, he stood at the entrance to the Sultan's harem. Yet he couldn't enter without permission, not even to see his own wife. Shaking his head at his foolishness, he turned to go. Just then, one of the princesses entered the precincts, accompanied by a wiry eunuch. Dark red hair spilled from the confines of her light-colored gauzy veils. Her dark eyes sparkled with recognition and she approached him.

"The peace of our God be with you, Prince Faraj. I am the Sultana Muna, Fatima's sister. Are you waiting for her?"

Faraj recalled Princess Muna, who her father had betrothed to a prince of the Zayyanids, the rulers of al-Jaza'ir.

He bowed before her. "I made no formal request to speak with your sister." When she frowned, he paused and looked around. "Perhaps then, you wonder why I am here at all. I hadn't planned on it. I walked without direction and found myself at these doors, I suppose."

"Fatima told us what happened." The princess's eyes offered pity, but he wasn't sure whether she meant it for him, her sister, or both. "I believe she is still within. I shall fetch her."

Faraj lingered at the base of the steps until Fatima appeared. She hesitated, frozen on the spot, her brow furrowed. She wore a tunic and skirt, her hair a billowing mass curled at her shoulders. When he gestured to the stone bench adjacent the northern wall, she slowly descended the steps. Her gaze averted, she slunk past him and sank on the marble, her hands balled into fists on her lap. Small sandaled feet peeked out under her skirt.

Faraj sat beside her on the cold bench. She flinched. Her face paled.

"Do you think I would harm you, Fatima?"

"I don't know what you'll do." She gave him a furtive glance. "But I won't let you hurt me."

His heart soared in esteem. Pride suited her well. He wouldn't have her any other way.

"Though it seems hard to believe, we've been wed for eight years this month." At her sigh, he continued, "Yet, we still know so little of each other's moods. You're hardly the child I married, even if you still do childish things."

He met her stare, just as a spasm of irritation rippled across her face. Her fingers clenched so tightly, he wondered that the nails did not draw blood.

Her mouth crimped in a determined line. "What do you mean by childish things?"

"You understand me well, I think. When you endanger yourself in intrigues and letters between you and an Ashqilula slave, you risk your safety and disregard the concerns of those who care for you. That is childishness."

"I'm sorry to disappoint you." She shrank away from him. "I thought my actions showed how much I care for and love my father."

His hand covered hers. "He's not the only person who cares for you."

Her eyes widened. "Are you saying you care for me as well?"

"You are my wife."

"That's not an answer!"

"It's the only answer I can give!"

She withdrew from his touch, her face drawn and pinched.

He sighed and raked his hands through his hair. "Tell me, as you told the Sultan this morning, how you learned about the defenses at Madinah Antaqirah. I expect full candor. Do you understand me?"

He waited for her to speak.

She looked away. "I know a slave in the house of the Ashqilula. Her name is Ulayyah. When Ibrahim tried to kidnap me as a child, she and the Jewish trader the Sitt al-Tujjar aided my return. Since then, Ulayyah has sent me news of the Ashqilula's treachery, whenever she can."

He shook his head. "You were but eight years old when you escaped from Ibrahim. Yet you couldn't allow your family to deal with the aftermath. Instead, you recruited a spy among his household. Don't you see how you risked your own life?"

She wrung her hands. "I would do anything for my family. Isn't that my duty as a princess of Gharnatah?"

He grasped her by the shoulders. Though she winced and pulled away, he jerked her toward him. "Your first duty is to your husband, to my interests. I knew you had your father's pride, but this is beyond my expectations. You are my wife. I won't let you come to harm."

"You want a simpering wife who'll do as she's told?"

"I want a wife who considers the consequences of her actions before she undertakes them. What do you think the Ashqilula would do to you if they ever discovered your arrangement? Your father hasn't weeded out all their spies. They can still attack us. How would your father react if you were hurt? Did you weigh his fears when you plotted with this slave? What of my feelings? Does my concern mean so little to you?"

He released her and buried his face in his hands, shaking his head.

When she touched his arm, he shrugged her off, massaging his temples. "You haven't finished."

"When Sitt al-Tujjar travels between Gharnatah and the other cities of al-Andalus, she carries payments for Ulayyah to Naricha. She returns to Gharnatah with Ulayyah's letters sewn between silk. I last received a letter from Ulayyah yesterday. The governor of Madinah Antaqirah has dispersed most of his household guards and half of the province's guards to quell a rebellion against him at the town of Arsiduna. By Ulayyah's account, he has left Madinah Antaqirah almost defenseless. This is all I know from her. I swear it by the blessed ninety-nine names of our God."

"Do you understand why your father is disturbed by your knowledge of his enemies' doings?"

"I know he was very angry with me," Fatima murmured. "I disobeyed him with my continued exchange of letters from Ulayyah. He thought our communication had ceased."

"Fatima, I don't believe the Sultan is angry with you. Your audacity shocks him. It frightens me. But his greater concern is for your well-being. Your involvement in these intrigues must stop."

"What are you saying?"

"Can I speak more plainly? You must cease all contact with the slave Ulayyah. Your father's wishes are clear, as are mine. You belong to me. It's my duty to protect you from all mischief, including that of your own making. Heed my words and do as I ask."

Fatima nodded, her eyes averted. Faraj raised her face for his inspection. A glimmer of rebelliousness shone in her gaze and in the thrust of her narrow chin.

He shook his head. "You intend to defy me and your father? You won't stop?"

"You must try to understand."

He stood and towered over her. "I'm your husband. I won't accept your insolence!"

She sank to the ground and clutched his legs, her eyes brimming with tears. "Our family is very important to me. I cannot do what you ask if I can somehow prevent the destruction of my family, even if I risk Father's censure... and your wrath."

Exasperated, he grasped her shoulders and brought her to her feet. "You risk more than my wrath and your father's censure."

"Tell me, what would you do if you had the knowledge to help rid Gharnatah of its enemies? Wouldn't you do the same as me?"

"You're the daughter of the Sultan, a mere female."

"A mere female? How dare you? But for the endurance of some 'mere female' as you say, neither you nor my father would exist. You think because I'm a princess, I should feel less loyalty to my family than you? I cannot accept such an argument."

"You cannot ask me to condone your actions, to accept the risks you undertake. I'm going with your father to Madinah Antaqirah. When I return, we'll talk again. I hope by then you'll have stopped this childish behavior. I won't let you continue this way."

Tears spilled from her eyes. She settled on the bench with soft sobs. He longed to soothe her, but clenched his fists at his sides. She had to understand the seriousness of her actions.

He bowed stiffly in farewell. Then Fatima clutched at his hand and kissed the skin. Her tears tracked across his hand. Tears, which he knew now, would always rend his heart.

"If I disobey you?"

Her faltering voice quivered with so many emotions that he renewed his struggle not to enfold her in his arms and never leave her side.

"Then you go against the clear wishes of your father and my own. If you defy me, I'll end your lessons with the royal tutor. I'll ask the Sultan to keep you confined to your rooms. All your correspondence shall cease to be private."

She shrank away from him, but he grasped her hand.

"I care for you, perhaps more than I first believed possible when we wed. Don't force my hand in this, I beg you. When I return from Madinah Antaqirah, I pray you'll have made the right choice. Until then, may the peace of God be with you."

***

The next day, Faraj departed for Madinah Antaqirah at the side of Muhammad II, along with the Sultan's brothers and others of his retinue. They traveled southwest in the wake of the commanders who led the Andalusi army and the Maghribi and Castillan mercenaries.

The Sultan slowed his horse to a canter beside Faraj. "You've spoken with my daughter?"

Faraj stiffened. Had the Sultan guessed he had been thinking of Fatima since midmorning when they rode out? How had she managed to beguile him, so that he would do anything to keep her from harm? It was dangerous to care so much for the Sultan's daughter, but he couldn't deny his feelings any longer.

"We talked yesterday."

"She's very spirited like her mother. Indeed, she is even more like Aisha than I knew. You know she shall defy both of us in this?"

Faraj clamped his jaw tight. "I'm aware of the possibility."

"I won't allow it. Neither can you."

"I'm also aware of that."

"Then, what shall you do when she defies us both?"

He scrutinized his father in-law's features for clues as to the Sultan's thoughts. "You're deferring her punishment to me?"

"You're her husband." The Sultan's hooded eyes and guarded smile belied his smooth reply.

Faraj wondered if he merely didn't want to deal with his daughter's resentment. Despite chiding himself for such base thoughts, he recalled that this wouldn't be the first time a Sultan rejected responsibility for his own actions. If the father of Muhammad II had not conspired against the Ashqilula, they would never have tried to kidnap Fatima. She might have never encountered the slave Ulayyah or started her dangerous correspondence.

"Master, do you allow me to decide her punishment, without your interference?"

"She's your wife, but she is also my daughter. You won't harm her, I trust?"

"I could never hurt her."

"I don't envy your lot. I trust your judgment where my daughter is concerned."

The Sultan kicked his horse into a canter. Faraj's thoughts returned to Fatima. More than her actions and their argument, he regretted leaving Gharnatah without bidding her farewell. She had not appeared among their family and courtiers this morning. He feared what might happen when they saw each other again. If she did not submit to his wishes, he would have to punish her. He could not bear the thought of causing her pain.

***

At Madinah Antaqirah, Gharnatah's army poured into the poorly defended city. In a mindless frenzy, they cut down all those who raised a weapon. The hacking and slashing of swords vied with horrific screams and pleas for mercy. The massacre spilled across the alleyways of the city. Rivulets of blood surged along the channels between the cobblestones.

Over the fray, Faraj shouted to the Sultan, "What of the people of Madinah Antaqirah? Surely you shall spare them?"

The Sultan bellowed, "Do you want me to go amongst my enemies to determine who my friends are? I shall not give them my own *khanjar* to slit my throat."

He ordered his commanders, "Cut down every male of an age to bear a sword!"

Outraged, Faraj shouted, "We came to capture the governor, not decimate the town!"

"You don't have to like my orders. Just obey them." The Sultan urged his horse forward, his sword swinging wildly. He plunged it into the chest of a spearman who rushed him. His attacker screamed as if in surprise and fell backward. His helmet rolled away, revealing a youthful boyish face. Faraj shook his head in disgust.

Fifteen days later, the Sultan's entourage returned to Gharnatah. Despite strict orders to the contrary, a great deal of rapine and looting had occurred. Most, if not all, the accused were Muslim soldiers, not the Castillan mercenaries among the Gharnati companies.

While on the journey home, Faraj blotted out images of starving, orphaned children and the disgraced women picking among their men's corpses littering the earth. Gharnatah and his return to Fatima beckoned.

Muhammad II entered his capital city in triumph. People lined the streets and acclaimed him, as they had done for his father. Trailing the edge of the royal retinue, Faraj rode his wearied mount up the Sabika hill and into *al-Quasaba*. He searched for Fatima's face among those who thronged to greet the victors. Disappointment at her absence crowded his heart. He welcomed the prospect of seeing her again. Yet he also dreaded their reunion.

When he dismounted, the Sultan beckoned him. The pair had barely spoken in the aftermath of Madinah Antaqirah.

After they held each other's gazes for a moment, the Sultan averted his eyes. "I celebrate the victory with the rest of our family tonight in my palace garden." A sheepish grin spread across his face. "You must attend. Fatima shall be there."

Faraj nodded and returned to his house. Marzuq and his concubines greeted him. After a brief exchange, he withdrew to his room alone.

Later in the evening, he joined the revelry. There was nothing to celebrate after the carnage and destruction at Madinah Antaqirah, but he longed to see Fatima. She spied him first and ran toward him. With just a few paces separating them, they both halted.

He admired her elegant appearance. She wore a black *jubba* embroidered with silver threads. A gossamer veil matched the robe. Trousers peeked from beneath, nearly covering her leather sandals. She hesitated for a moment before approaching. He took her slim hands in his.

She smiled. "You're not hurt. I was worried. Forgive me, but I could not see you off before you left, when I feared the worse."

"You weren't avoiding me?"

Under hooded eyelids, she snuck a furtive glance. "Why would I have done that?"

"Don't dissemble. Please, I must have your answer on the issue we discussed before I left. Tell me the truth now. Can you leave it to your father to deal with our enemies? Do I have your promise I won't hear of your letters to Ulayyah anymore?"

She sighed. "I promise you'll never hear of the letters again."

He studied her angular features. She met his gaze without wavering. Then she smiled demurely and drew closer. "Trust me, husband."

Chapter 15
A King in His Own Land

Prince Faraj

Gharnatah, al-Andalus: Jumada al-Ula 672 AH (Granada, Andalusia: November - December AD 1273)

Some months after the victory at Madinah Antaqirah, a frigid winter descended, during which King Alfonso of Castilla-León sent an emissary with entreaties of peace to the court of Muhammad II.

Faraj attended the Sultan's meeting with his counselors and the Castillans in the throne room on a blustery afternoon after *Salat al-Asr*, the third daily prayer. Standing in the northern recesses of the shadowy tower, with the guards flanking him, he grinned at the incredulous looks on the Castillan faces. With good reason, he had never trusted them. Now, the Sultan seemed ready to get rid of them, too.

Doñ Nuño Gonzalez abased himself on both knees. "Great Sultan, I beg permission to address your court."

When the Sultan nodded, Doñ Nuño continued, "Your army decimated the Ashqilula and their allies, with your glorious victory at Madinah Antaqirah. King Alfonso recognizes the folly of supporting the Ashqilula. He knows you are the stronger adversary, with my loyal aid. This is why he presses for my return and an end to our alliance. He bargains from a position of powerlessness. Why would you parlay for peace with him now?"

154

The Sultan groaned softly. Faraj stood close enough to hear it, but perhaps Doñ Nuño did not for he continued, "You are the master of this domain, the prince of the Faithful. Our alliance has proved fortuitous, has it not? Do not turn from my cause now. With my support, you have strengthened your position and mine. We won at Martus. We vanquished the Ashqilula at Madinah Antaqirah."

The Sultan pounded the samite-covered arms of the throne. "Doñ Nuño, don't take me for a fool. Do you think I don't perceive the real threat? The Ashqilula are but flies upon a festering wound. The real threat remains in Castilla-León. The Castillans can't be beaten back forever, one little town at a time. Martus and Madinah Antaqirah are nothing compared to the entire Sultanate! It doesn't matter if we control one border town. Your King Alfonso intends to pierce the very heart of Gharnatah, by supporting his Ashqilula allies.

"If Castilla-León offers the boon of peace, I'll accept it for the sake of my people, who tire of war. You read the king's promises. You'll return to your homeland, with all honors and rights restored to you. We'll never forget your service to us."

Doñ Nuño shook his head. "If you wish me gone, I'll leave with your blessing. But I still believe, given your victories, it is you and not King Alfonso, who has the right to demand peace on your own terms. You have seen the Castillan approach to peace before. Broken promises and half-truths."

The Sultan leaned forward. "Tread carefully, Doñ Nuño, lest you slander yourself along with your king. I remember well your broken promises to my father. It cost the Sultanate many lives at a useless siege of Malaka."

Doñ Nuño showed no reaction to this insult. His face never colored, he barely raised a yellow eyebrow.

"But it's humiliating to submit to the dictates of Alfonso's treaty," he continued. "Would you have Castilla-León trample on your pride?"

The Sultan rested his chin on his hand. "My pride can bear it well, Don Nuño, as can yours. I hope you do not suggest your pride is worth more than mine."

His face blanched, Don Nuño shook his grizzled head and stood, sketching a stiff bow. The Sultan waved him off. "It is the hour of prayer. We'll re-convene in the afternoon."

Muhammad II invited Faraj to join him and his family at *Salat al-Zuhr*. After the noon prayer, Faraj stayed with them for an early lunch. Fatima seemed surprised and then delighted in turn, by Faraj's appearance. She sat beside him. He struggled with his concentration while the Sultan explained the day's events to his children. Faraj found himself surprised at how the Sultan kept his daughters so well informed. They asked thoughtful questions in response. They were a remarkable family, unlike any he had ever known.

Fatima proved the distraction. More often than not, a glimpse of her profile, the curve of her soft cheek, or the tinkling melody of her voice as she addressed her father, held him entranced.

After they finished the meal, slaves removed the platters and plates, replacing them with enticing desserts. He did not indulge, having barely touched the spicy chicken served with fresh greens and herbs. Fatima didn't eat much, either.

She asked, "You didn't like the food?"

He turned to her. "It was good, but I wasn't very hungry."

Just then, his belly rumbled and belied his words. She chuckled and smiled at him.

In the midst of their easy rapport, a message arrived from the chief eunuch Hasan.

"What is the matter?" Fatima asked, looking at her father's ashen face.

Faraj immediately worried whether some tragedy had befallen them. Worse, had the Castillan king already rescinded his invitation to the Christian rebels?

The Sultan said, "Nur al-Sabah's child shall be born today."

Fatima plunked her spoon in the center of the dessert. After a while, she pushed it away. Faraj reached for her hand beneath the low table. When their fingers touched, a warm jolt rippled through him. He barely noticed when the Sultan left. Only Fatima mattered now. Their gazes wound together as tightly as their hands. His heart pounded in a fierce rhythm. Her eyes, now wide and expressive, betrayed deep emotion that robbed him of his speech. Had she always been so beautiful, he wondered. When had the unremarkable child given way to the enthralling woman at his side?

***

Ishbiliya, al-Andalus: Jumada al-Ula 672 AH (Sevilla, Kingdom of Castilla-León: December AD 1273)

Shortly after the Christian Yuletide season began, the Sultan, his bodyguards, Umar the *Shaykh al-Ghuzat* and the Castillan mercenaries rode to Sevilla, to parlay with King Alfonso. Faraj joined the Sultan's retinue.

The riders skirted north of Ashqilula territories. After a three-day journey, they arrived at the outskirts of their destination. Sevilla straddled the Wadi al-Kabir, or Guadalquivir River. Trade thrived along the riverbank, with vessels plying its depths to reach the southern marketplace.

Faraj viewed the city sprawling across the plains. Two years after his birth, the Castillans had defeated the Hud family and conquered Muslim Ishbiliya, with the help of his uncle the old Sultan, who often spoke with regret of his role in the re-birth of Christian Sevilla.

King Alfonso's guards met the riders at the city gates. Heading northeast, they forded the Guadalquivir. They entered under the watchful eyes of the city's residents. Many new arrivals had repopulated the town after the king's father, Fernando, expelled its former Moorish and Jewish inhabitants.

A towering remnant of Seville's Moorish past under *al-Muwahhidun* princes loomed on the eastern bank of the Guadalquivir. In the glory days of Ishbiliya, gilded tiles had covered the dome of this twelve-sided crenellated tower, earning it the name 'Golden Tower' but the Castillans stripped the precious tiles away during the conquest. The Hud had once incorporated the stone tower into their defenses, which once ranged from their palace to the river's edge.

Faraj's heart sank at the sight of Ishbiliya's Great Mosque, which stood nearby the Golden Tower. Workers toiled within its precincts to remove all traces of its Islamic past. The Moorish observatory rose at the pinnacle of the former mosque.

Umar spat upon the ground. "They convert our scared spaces for yet another of their cathedrals."

They arrived at the Moorish palace, also built during the reign of *al-Muwahhidun* rulers. The old King Fernando had captured it during the conquest. Faraj studied the remains of the thick, ancient walls as they rode through the gateway. Pages met and led them to spacious quarters, where they remained for an hour. The tapestries hanging along the wall could not ward off the chill seeping through the stucco walls. From his window, Faraj spied an ornate rectangular courtyard brimming with flowers and rosemary bushes. A marble walkway led from one end of the yard to the other. Peaceful stillness overwhelmed the space, but he knew such tranquility could not last.

Then, ushered into the presence of King Alfonso of Castilla-León and the Castillan parliament, Faraj began the exchange of formal greetings between the Christian ruler and the Sultan, serving as his master's official interpreter. The negotiations began soon afterward.

The Sultan presented terms of peace favorable to Gharnatah. The Castillans appeared amenable to everything he suggested.

Faraj frowned at this. He hadn't expected the Castillans might be so eager for peace. For his pledges, the Sultan submitted the requisite offer of tribute. The Castillans readily agreed to his first offer of three hundred thousand of their gold coins, maravedies.

Something troubled Faraj about their easy acquiescence. Muhammad II had vowed he would only make one offer, but they could not have known that, could they?

Then the Sultan presented terms for the end of the Lara rebellion against Castilla-León. When he renounced the formal alliance between the Sultanate and the rebels, King Alfonso heaved a loud sigh of relief. The entire court erupted into cheers. The king welcomed his favorite and forgave the rebels. Doñ Nuño moved to the forefront. On bended knee beside the Sultan, he offered his obeisance before his master Alfonso.

Faraj sighed with contentment. Muhammad II had accomplished his goal. The Castillan mercenaries would no longer enjoy a comfortable refuge in al-Andalus. Gharnatah and its people would have peace for the duration of a year.

King Alfonso stood and scratched at his sparse brown beard, interspersed with gray hairs. Through his official interpreter, he said, "In your honor and for your pledges, my lord of Granada, the Royal Consort has prepared a great feast for tonight. A week of festivities will mark this occasion of your first visit to Sevilla. We ask that you remain here, where you and yours are to be our honored guests. This shall be a sign of the understanding between our two kingdoms."

The Sultan looked over his shoulder at Faraj, who cursed beneath his breath. He should have known matters between Castilla-León and Gharnatah could never be easily resolved.

The Sultan murmured, "We would be honored to accept your gracious invitation."

He and his retinue followed Alfonso into a large hall. The Sultan sat at the high table with the Castillan ruler, his family, and Doñ Nuño Gonzalez. Heavy silver platters were set on the table, along with pewter cups and spoons. The highest-ranking resident clergyman, whom the king referred to as Archbishop of Toledo Doñ Sancho de Aragón, blessed the meal.

Seated below the dais on the left, Faraj avoided the open, rude stares and whisperings of the nobles. An array of dishes covered the tables. Of fowl, there were several varieties, baked swans, roasted peacocks, boiled capons, and chickens. There was salmon as well as eel, the latter of which he politely refused, in addition to the roasted boar, but the venison stew was passable. He recognized onions, peas, and beans among the vegetables. The only drink offered was wine, which he also declined for religious reasons. The desserts were sliced apples, pears and oranges, as well as many varieties of cheeses, cakes, cookies, pastries, and meat pies.

Alfonso offered a food taster, but the Sultan had brought his own. If he had offended the king, Alfonso's features never betrayed it.

The hot mulled wine the nobles imbibed smelled sour, though they seemed to enjoy it. Faraj sampled almost everything, except for what he could not eat for religious reasons. He did better than Umar, who sat below the dais directly opposite him. The *Shaykh al-Ghuzat* stared with dismay at the food piled high on his plate. Faraj caught the Sultan's eye, winked, and nodded, calling his attention to the discomfort of the acclaimed defender of the Faith. The Sultan chuckled low.

Faraj wiped his hands on a towel, which a page offered. Some of the Castillan women still stared at him, most in mute horror at the Moors among them. But others took him aback with their open appreciation and curiosity. One among them smiled coquettishly and fluttered her eyelashes, preening in a stiff, wrinkled garment.

He ducked his head and sopped up the stew with a portion of crusty loaf. He recalled Fatima walking though the autumn rain, soft, silken material flowing like water around her swaying hips. Her modesty enticed him more than the boldness of any other woman. Perhaps her allure accounted for his lack of interest in his concubines of late. How could he desire the practiced nuances of trained pleasure slaves, when Fatima's innocence tempted him?

King Alfonso called for silence in the room. All conversation ceased. Every eye turned to view the Castillan monarch.

"We have extended the hospitality of our court to our worthy vassal, the king of Granada. By the grace of our God, we have demonstrated our peaceful intent to all. Let us now show the esteem with which we regard our vassal. We shall knight the king of Granada, bestowing upon him all the honors implied."

Everyone watched the Sultan with expectant eyes.

After a tense silence, the Sultan said, "Surely, I could ask for no more than the esteem you have shown."

"That is nonsense, my lord," King Alfonso insisted. "You are our vassal. We would honor you as we please. Stand forth and be knighted."

Every moment the Sultan remained in his chair, he jeopardized all he had just won. Many of the Castillans murmured disapprovingly. Alfonso eyed him with suspicion.

Stiff-backed, he stood and stepped away from the table. He rounded it and stood before King Alfonso. A page placed a cushion at his feet and fled from the Sultan's deepening scowl.

King Alfonso drew his sword. "Kneel before us, my lord, as a vassal should kneel before his sovereign."

A low buzz of voices rose to the rafters again, accusations of disrespect and contempt for the court. Faraj leaned forward in rapt attention, fear, and worry crowding his heart. Didn't Alfonso recognize the problematic course he now pursued? The Sultan could never acquiesce to his demand and once made, Alfonso could not withdraw it, without looking like the fool he was.

The *Shaykh al-Ghuzat* Umar pushed back the bench from the table, startling the other occupant who shared the seating. The Sultan's bodyguards looked around them, studying the room. Faraj assessed their tense mood. Twenty men were no match for the king's nobles, but they would give their lives for their leader, if necessary. Did they deem it a suitable time to show their resolve?

Doñ Nuño Gonzalez stood. "Great king, may your humble vassal, who only wishes to be of assistance in this grave affair, be allowed to speak?"

Both King Alfonso and the Sultan turned and regarded him with stern stares.

He ignored the warning echoes in their mutual gazes. "Your Majesty, in my time in Andalusia, I came to know the king of Granada as a proud and brave man. He is your vassal and you are his sovereign. Yet, he is a powerful and mighty king in his own land. If you would esteem him as a worthy vassal, I pray, let the king of Granada bow his head as he stands before you, rather than kneel in subjugation. By this action, great king, you would demonstrate that you deem him worthy to stand in your presence; a great ally to your kingdom and the legitimate ruler of his own."

While Alfonso considered his advisor's words, the Sultan locked eyes with Doñ Nuño. His steady gaze communicated volumes. Faraj relaxed when Doñ Nuño nodded and sat. The old man had done his last service for Gharnatah.

"We have too long been without the worthy counsel of Doñ Nuño Gonzalez. His words are good and just," King Alfonso proclaimed. "The king of Granada shall stand before us with his head bowed to receive the knighthood."

When the Castillan King tapped the Sultan's shoulders with his heavy sword and uttered some obtuse language about the honor of knighthood, the courtiers cheered.

Faraj rubbed his temples and prayed to get through the rest of the evening.

During the next days, the Castillan court feted them. They also attended two sessions of the king's council, the Cortes. Faraj joined the nobles in tournaments of the sword and lance. Some ladies offered him tokens of their favor. He hesitated, but Doñ Nuño insisted that refusal would have been impolite. The Sultan laughed and promised he would not tell Fatima, for fear of rousing her jealousy.

The final day of their sojourn arrived. When one of the queen's pages arrived with a summons, Faraj was playing a game of chess with his master.

He read the note over the Sultan's shoulder. "Do you worry she desires an assignation? The queen seemed captivated by your win against her councilor in the contest of arms yesterday."

The Sultan crumpled the note. "Come and let us see what this queen wants."

When they left the room, the pageboy waited at the end of the hall. He escorted them to a dimly lit chamber where the Castillan queen, Violante de Aragón waited.

The daughter of King Jaime called the Conqueror and his Hungarian consort, the Castillan queen appeared plain and unremarkable. Of an average height, she wore a gown of wool in a deep blue color. Her brown hair coiled on either side of her head and bound in a thick gold net, she sought to convey the appearance of royalty in her mantle lined with thick ermine and embroidered by gold thread. Recalling Fatima, Faraj thought his wife possessed a more regal bearing than this queen, surrounded by her ladies.

Faraj translated the conversation between her and his father in-law. The Sultan said, "The peace of God be with you, my lady."

"I pray that the peace of God be with you also, my lord. Thank you for coming."

"I could not ignore the gracious invitation, my lady."

"We have enjoyed your presence. Your charm and dignity impressed me. You must understand if I say I did not know Moors were as civilized as Christians."

"Moors do not often believe Christians can be as civilized as we are."

Violante sniffed haughtily and gestured to an array of dishes on a table behind her.

The Sultan shook his head. "We have eaten this morning and so, must refuse. We are eager to return home."

The queen flashed a grin, exposing her yellowed teeth. "I have heard of the splendor of your capital city, great Sultan. You must miss your family, your wife and children, my lord?"

Muhammad II replied, "I am not married, my lady. My wife passed away some time ago. As for my children, I do miss them. I have a son and six daughters... no, I have seven daughters now, the last born but a few days before my arrival at Sevilla. All but the last are the children of my late wife."

"Ah... I see." By her reddened cheeks, it seemed the queen understood the role of concubines in Moorish society. "I won't keep you from them any longer. Permit me to explain the purpose of my request to see you. I speak for my husband the king."

"If I might ask, why did the king not speak with me himself?"

Violante's eyes narrowed. "Does it offend you to discuss matters of state between our two kingdoms with a woman?"

"No, though such a thing is hardly done in my land."

"We have many differences, my lord, but some of our goals and desires are the same, such as a peaceful and secure future for our children, perhaps?"

"I would agree with such an observation, my lady."

The queen raised her chin a notch. "Understand then, in keeping with such desires, my lord the king wants your treaty with Castilla-León amended. The treaty must resolve the disagreement between you and your former allies, at least for a time. Your conflict affects the entire peninsula. He is aware the Marinids look upon this land with covetous eyes like the Almohade and Almoravid Empires did. If the Marinids try to emulate the glory of their predecessors, Granada, fractured by a civil war, cannot hold out. Peace with the enemy is the best deterrent against future aggression."

After Faraj had translated her words, the Sultan stared, the corners of his mouth twitching. But this was not time for levity.

Queen Violante continued. "It would not be a betrayal of my husband's confidence to tell you that before your arrival, he had considered an alliance with the Marinids to keep them out of the peninsula. The king would do anything to contain any threat from... the south."

The Sultan shifted his stance. "By that, your husband means to contain all threats from the south, including Granada."

The queen made no reply.

"If I were to refuse to offer my enemies a truce," the Sultan paused and tapped his chin with his forefinger, "what would happen then, my lady?"

Turning suddenly cold gray eyes upon him, Violante replied, "My husband would consider you to be in violation of the peace treaty you have signed here, for by your recklessness you would imperil the security of the entire peninsula. Such an action could not be ignored."

***

A few hours later, the Sultan and his retinue departed for Gharnatah. Faraj reviewed the addendum to the peace treaty he had signed.

Muhammad II said, "Never mind the nonsense about a truce with the Ashqilula. The year shall pass. I have two new tasks for you when we arrive in Gharnatah. First, you shall convene with my counselors and share with them all you saw of the court of the Castillan king. I found the ministers' functions to be quite interesting. I think a

165

similar formation would benefit me. Indeed, of my counselors, some have no interest in statesmanship and think only of the riches to be won through their intrigues."

Faraj frowned. "You want to convene a *Diwan*, a formal council of ministers?"

"Yes and you shall assist in its formation, modeled upon the Castillan king's court, with our own functions."

"As you wish. What is your second task?"

"You'll enjoy that part much more, for it requires your... unique skills. And, it shall hasten our vengeance against the Ashqilula."

Faraj looked over his shoulder to the walls of Christian Sevilla. The Ashqilula were not the only ones responsible for the pain he had suffered as a child. Though he and Doñ Nuño had parted cordially, he wondered when he might see the old man again, under different circumstances.

Chapter 16

The Assassin

Princess Fatima

Gharnatah, al-Andalus: Rajab 672 AH (Granada, Andalusia: January AD 1274)

Fatima felt the eyes of her servant, Amoda, upon her as she paced the length of her bedchamber. She had to act. Whatever decision she made would have consequences for her marriage. Either, Faraj would hate her forever, or he would die. In the gilded cage on the table, the kite interrupted her worries with loud chirping. She smiled with the memory of the day Faraj gave her the pet bird. If he survived this, he might never forgive her. She could bear his displeasure, but she could not bear to lose him forever.

She gripped the slip of parchment in her hand. Fighting against a heavy lump in her throat, she willed courage into her voice. "This letter damns me for a liar, but I won't let fear keep me from acting. I cannot let the Ashqilula assassinate my husband, while I do nothing to save him. Bring your brother, Amoda, I need him now, more than ever."

"Yes, my Sultana, at once."

Amoda hurried away in a flurry of yellow silk.

Fatima returned to her bed and wrapped her shoulders in the multicolored silk coverlet.

Outside, a wintry chill descended on Gharnatah. Frigid morning air intruded through the lattice windows, despite the metal braziers at two corners of the room.

Her nails tapped on the bedpost. She studied Ulayyah's script on the parchment, barely legible. Where was Niranjan?

When Amoda returned with Niranjan in tow, he bowed.

Fatima gestured to a stool beside the bed. "Please sit and let us talk." She then asked Amoda to go to the kitchens for food.

When Amoda left the room, Fatima spoke to Niranjan. "I need your help. A message must reach my husband in al-Maghrib el-Aska. I cannot write to him. You must memorize my words. Can you do this?"

"You know I shall."

"I'm more grateful to you than you may ever understand. You know for many years that Ulayyah has spied for me among the Ashqilula?" When he nodded, she continued, "Now I have received news, which if true, affects my husband. After the battle at Madinah Antaqirah last summer, when my husband returned, he wanted my promise that I would not correspond with Ulayyah again. I have lied to him."

She looked down at her feet for a moment, embarrassed by her admission. Niranjan nodded. "The Ashqilula are dangerous. I understand your husband's concerns, but you are loyal to your family. I know you'll do anything to protect them."

Her heart swelled with emotion. "Ever loyal... I do not know what I would do without your steadfastness."

"You shall always have it, my princess. Please, continue."

Euphoric, she confessed all in a rush of words. "Six weeks after he left Ishbiliya, Faraj departed from Gharnatah for al-Maghrib el-Aska to meet with the Marinid Sultan. Ulayyah reports the Ashqilula have sent an assassin to intercept him. Despite a peace treaty between the Sultan and Castilla-León, there have been raids at the border again. Marauders killed the Muslim governor at Martus last week and took hostages for ransom. King Alfonso claims he does not support these raids, but Father cannot allow the Castillans to make a fool of him. He needs a strong ally, like the Marinids. He has sent my husband to their Sultan with entreaties and the promise of the strategic ports at al-Jazirah al-Khadra and Tarif. Somehow, the Ashqilula learned of Faraj's intent. They have dispatched someone to the Marinid capital to kill him.

"He must know of the danger he faces. You shall go to Fés el-Bali and warn my husband of the assassin. Ulayyah said the Ashqilula man left the port at Malaka one day before the date of the letter, so he must be in al-Maghrib el-Aska already. You must leave today."

Amoda arrived with the food. Niranjan ate, while Fatima struggled to soothe the erratic thoughts swirling through her head into a precise message for her husband. When Niranjan finished his meal, she settled on what she would say. He rehearsed her words until he could repeat the speech verbatim.

Then he asked, "Others, in particular your father, shall want to know where I have gone. How can you explain my absence to the Sultan?"

She paced, dragging her coverlet behind her. "Father plans the celebration of the birth of his new daughter. I want a very special gift for him."

She halted and stared at Niranjan. "What do you think of my father's choices in women?"

He cocked his head. "I see the Sultan ranks beauty, intelligence, and wit as high ideals in his women. Although he acknowledges beauty fades with time, I suspect he prefers it to wit. Beauty and intelligence in equal measure seem to please him with the *kadin*."

Fatima's face grew hot at the mention of the woman. "In al-Maghrib el-Aska, you shall procure a *jarya* of exotic beauty and worthy intellect. If anyone, including my father, should inquire about your departure, speak only of this part of your journey."

Niranjan shifted on the stool. "It shall be done, my Sultana. However, I must say your father is faithful to Nur al-Sabah al-Muhammad. He did not want another woman in the long months before she birthed her daughter. I believe your father is in love with the *kadin*, my Sultana."

"It is unworthy of him to show devotion to a slave!" She threw the coverlet off her shoulders, breath coming raw in her throat.

He stared, his eyes wide. She knelt beside him and patted his hand.

"If the Marinids accept Father's offer, they may want a political marriage. No Sultana should rank second best to a slave. The *kadin* is no different from any other *jarya* who has ever infatuated Father. When another woman tempts him, he shall forget her."

She met his potent stare. "Find me a *jarya* to seduce Father's heart and mind."

***

Prince Faraj

Fés el-Bali, al-Maghrib el-Aska: Rajab 672 AH (Fez, Morocco: January AD 1274)

Faraj strolled through the royal *madina* of Fés el-Bali, capital city of the Marinids, at a leisurely pace. The city was a chaotic jumble of spectacular new monuments, interposed among decayed palaces and fortifications from the previous dynasties that had ruled al-Maghrib el-Aska. The great fortresses and mosques of the empire of *al-Murabitun* vied with the ornate palace complexes and lush baths built by *al-Muwahhidun* rulers long ago. Marinid mosques, hospitals, mental asylums, hospitals, and religious schools dotted the landscape. Faraj made mental notes about everything he saw, intending to provide

Fatima with a full account of the city when he returned home to her. Perhaps, when he'd had enough of her father's intrigues, he would return to this land and bring her with him. He sighed with longing for such a day when he might know peace with her at his side.

Since his arrival two weeks earlier, he had enjoyed the comfort of a guesthouse on the palace grounds. The Marinid Sultan's chief minister, *al-Shaykh* Abu Bakr Ibn Yala assured him the delay should not offend. His master knew the purpose of Faraj's journey and intended to see him soon.

In the meantime, Faraj could not complain for the treatment he had received. Each night, Ibn Yala's slaves prepared dishes that displayed the variety and excellence of Maghribi cuisine. He often enjoyed excellent *harrira* soup, made of mutton and spices and couscous - the mutton, vegetables and semolina being the only ingredients he could identify.

The Marinid capital at Fés el-Bali was an intricate maze, in which he would have been lost without the knock-kneed young boy who always led him through the streets. His host, Ibn Yala, had provided the boy's services. This morning, Faraj attended the Great Mosque of *al-Qarawiyyin* and its *madrasa*, one of the oldest sites in al-Maghrib el-Aska. The mosque's tiled courtyard afforded an interesting view of the city and its myriad people.

Now, he and his guide rested in the shadow of the courtyard. Faraj marked the progress of the faithful to and from the mosque, while he contemplated home and Fatima. She had endeared herself to him and never strayed far from his thoughts. Powerful emotion filled his heart, feelings he had never expected.

The ancient battlements surrounding Fés el-Bali loomed over the green-tiled rooftop of the mosque and *madrasa*. The city stood on the banks of the Wadi Fés and was more than five hundred years old. Despite its narrow winding streets and the buildings that were a jumble of confusion for any non-Fezi, surely this ancient city remained one of the most beautiful in al-Maghrib. In the distance, dust clouds rose, as did the sounds of men giving orders to each other. Faraj wondered at the daily toil and cacophony that reached him. He supposed the Marinid Sultan must be on another building project across the Wadi Fés.

When he left *al-Qarawiyyin* a moment later, he became absorbed in the chaotic, aromatic splendor around him. Easily distracted, a sudden grip on his shoulder startled him. He drew his scimitar and whirled, prepared to strike a deathblow.

"No, master, it's me, Niranjan!"

The hooded figure pulled back his head covering hastily. Faraj beckoned the bewildered guide to remain nearby and confronted the trembling servant of his wife.

"Fool! I could have killed you. What are you doing in Fés el-Bali?"

"I have been searching for you. I first saw you here two days ago, then yesterday again. I realized you must come every day at the same time."

"What would you have done if I had not come today?"

With a sheepish grin, Niranjan replied, "I would have waited until you came."

"Again, why are you here? Did something happen to Fatima, is she hurt?"

"No, the Sultana is quite well. Yet, I have come because of her." Niranjan looked beyond him to his guide. "I must speak to you in private. When can I meet with you, alone?"

"I shall come again to Qarawiyn this afternoon for prayer."

"Without the boy?"

Faraj looked over his shoulder. "I have memorized the route. Why don't you want me to come with the boy? Are you certain nothing has happened to Fatima?"

"Master, I promise you, the Sultana is well. Though, I believe she misses you terribly."

"Surely, you cannot have come all the way here just to tell me that? If you are lying, if she is hurt, I swear...."

"Do not be forsworn, master. It may bring you bad luck. I vow upon my soul, your wife is as you left her."

"You just told me not to swear!"

"I never have bad luck, master. I must go. Tomorrow, I shall meet you in the white courtyard, just after *Salat al-'Asr* has ended."

Niranjan disappeared into the crowd before Faraj could think to say another word. The dense throng hid the escape route, despite all of Faraj's efforts to find the exasperating eunuch again.

Faraj resumed walking to the palace behind his guide. Worry shadowed his footfalls. What had Fatima deemed of such importance that she sent Niranjan, with such urgency and secrecy?

When Faraj arrived at the guesthouse, his apprehension subsided. Stalwart guards allowed him past the iron gates. Ibn Yala stood at the entryway, between two shady, argan trees growing out of the semi-desert soil. Ibn Yala gave him a gap-toothed smile from thin, nearly black lips that barely stood out from the rest of his coal-colored appearance. The minister was pigeon-toed, which gave him an odd gait. His paunch, jutting beneath loose-fitting robes, seemed out of place on an otherwise scrawny body with bony shoulders and claw-like hands.

"May the peace of God be with you, Prince Faraj. I bring good news. The Sultan shall see you tomorrow evening. One hour after the prayers of *Salat al-Maghrib*, you shall dine with the Sultan and enjoy his entertainment. Then you may speak the concerns of your master, the Sultan of Gharnatah."

The minister bowed before he went on his way. Faraj went to the *hammam*. A massage with rich argan oil should have soothed him, but his mind remained preoccupied. Niranjan's startling arrival perplexed him. It also worried him. The servant would never have come to al-Maghrib el-Aska except at the behest of his mistress.

Such a clandestine visit couldn't bode well for Gharnatah. Niranjan's arrival also warned of his wife's activities during his absence. As expected, she kept to her intrigues with the Ashqilula spy. He gritted his teeth at the thought of her continued defiance.

"Master, you're not relaxed," the masseuse purred at his back. The willow-thin, naked, slave girl rubbed his shoulders, brushing her pert nipples across his skin. He might have responded to her bold invitation, but only one woman swayed his desires and emotions now.

At the designated hour of prayer, he returned to *al-Qarawiyyin*. He dismissed his guide, despite the boy's protest and stood in the shadows of its white courtyard. Though convinced the child reported his activities to Ibn Yala, at least Faraj could be certain he would enjoy privacy.

Desert wind spiraled through the city. Niranjan appeared as if out of the whirlwind. Faraj blinked fast. How had the eunuch avoided being seen before now? Niranjan beckoned him to a more secluded spot, apart from those who idled about the mosque's courtyard.

"May the peace of God be with you, master. You came alone?"

"You said I should. Now what is this all about, why this secrecy?"

"I come bearing a message from your noble wife."

Faraj held out his hand for the anticipated missive. "Well, give me the letter."

"I cannot, for the Sultana made me memorize the message. She bid me say, 'Husband, your life is in danger. Even as you meet with the Marinid Sultan, the enemies of Gharnatah seek your death. The governor of Malaka has sent an assassin to kill you. You must alert the Marinid Sultan to the danger and ensure the Ashqilula fail.' That is the entire message, master."

Faraj retreated among the shadows below the wall. He watched the crowd for a menacing face or gleaming eyes, full of purpose. If Fatima's servant found him within two days of his arrival, surely nothing should stop a trained assassin from doing the same.

"Master, what shall we do?" Niranjan asked in a hoarse whisper.

"Come back with me to the palace!"

They returned to the guesthouse in silence. Faraj maintained a brisk walk. His heart thumped so loud, it seemed ready to burst from his chest before they reached the grounds.

Within the safety of the palace complex and the guesthouse, Niranjan gasped and leaned against a wall to catch his breath. Faraj called for a slave with water. Drinking greedily, he asked Niranjan to remain and eat, but the servant shook his head.

"We risked enough being seen together today, master."

"If the assassin followed me to Fés el-Bali, why has he hesitated to strike? He's had many opportunities at *al-Qarawiyyin* with only the boy at my side."

"My mistress knows only of his intent, not his plans."

"Did she tell you how she learned about this plot?"

"Yes."

Faraj frowned at the one-word reply. His wife anticipated his displeasure, but her servant's loyalty protected her.

"Your mistress has your trust and devotion?"

"The Sultana trusts me."

"Yet, you owe your accountability, indeed, your very life to the Sultan of Gharnatah. Doesn't he deserve your unfettered loyalty?"

"The Sultan has my loyalty. Every duty I perform on his daughter's behalf is based on her loyalty and love for her father."

Faraj shook his head. Niranjan's skill with words could rival any diplomat in Gharnatah or al-Maghrib.

"Does the Sultan know you are here in al-Maghrib el-Aska?"

"Yes, I asked his permission before I left Gharnatah. Only the Sultana Fatima knew the full purpose of my coming here. Others, including the Sultan, were misled. They believed my sole purpose was to visit the great slave market of Fés el-Bali, in search of a rare and special gift from Sultana Fatima for her father."

"Who concocted the lie, you, or her?"

"Such a thing is not a lie. My mistress charged me to find a new pleasure slave for her father. I have found the girl, a most exquisite slave of noble birth, with hair as black as the *Kaaba* in the Holy City. I have fulfilled the dual responsibilities with which my mistress charged me. I merely omitted half of my purpose from everyone else."

"I understand. Are you returning to al-Andalus now?"

"I'll fetch the slave from the marketplace and make my way homeward. Is there a message for my mistress?"

Faraj considered his words. "Tell her we shall talk when I return to Gharnatah."

Niranjan bowed and left him.

***

Later, when dressed for dinner, Faraj followed the escort Ibn Yala provided. The Sultan's minister met him at the entrance of the palace.

A group of men exited the ornate horseshoe gateway, chattering loudly. Recognizing their language as the vernacular spoken in the Christian kingdom of Aragón, Faraj asked Ibn Yala about them.

The chief minister answered, "Those are the ambassadors of the king of Aragón, my prince. We have signed a peace treaty with them."

Faraj asked, "Is this the reason your honorable master delayed our meeting?"

"Yes. Understand if I could not tell you so beforehand, but now you know."

"This is interesting. I wonder what Castilla-León shall think of this treaty, since it is Aragón's neighbor and the Castillan king is married to a daughter of Aragón."

Ibn Yala raised his eyebrows. "I expect the Castillans might not be pleased by our new alliance. The treaty forbids Aragón from aiding its neighbors in aggression against other Muslim lands, including wars in Gharnatah."

Faraj smiled. "It is remarkable you were able to effect such terms."

Ibn Yala nodded. "The world is remarkable, made even more so by money and greed."

The pair bypassed the gate and entered a spacious courtyard with a murmuring fountain at its center, surrounded by palm trees, acanthus leaves, and the pale yellow of the narcissus flower. The setting sun threw long shadows against buildings ornamented with glazed tiles, each entryway bordered by carved and painted wooden arches, cornices, and marble columns. The harsh desert climate sharply contrasted against the lushness of al-Andalus.

Guards lined a long, intricately carved wall. Ibn Yala gestured to the doors ahead.

Faraj had prepared his arguments with the Marinid Sultan against the Ashqilula. They wanted to kill him, as they did when he was a child. He would not allow them to do what they had done to his father.

"Prince Faraj!" Ibn Yala pushed him to the ground and drew his dagger.

So, the chief minister was the assassin. There was no Ashqilula plot to murder him, just Marinid treachery. Faraj faced the prospect of the violent death he had escaped as a child. But he would not submit to fate. If he died today, the Sultan's devious minister would fall with him.

Then, he realized the guards had surged forward and restrained one of their own. One of the soldiers tore the lance from the man's murderous grasp.

Ibn Yala's expression betrayed shock, fierce anger, and relief in turns. "Are you unharmed, Prince Faraj? I'm sorry I was so rough, but he was prepared to kill you."

When Faraj nodded, Ibn Yala sheathed his dagger and faced the would-be murderer. "Who is this traitor who would attack a guest?"

The captain of the guardsmen answered, "He arrived nearly two weeks ago from the fort at Sebta. The commander wrote that he is a cousin of his and fit to join the royal corps."

"I know the commander at Sebta," Ibn Yala snarled. "He's an orphan with no relations. Bring the letters of assignment to me. I'll prove they are forgeries. Take our prisoner to the dungeon. I want him unharmed, but prepared to talk. The Sultan and, I believe our guest, shall wish to speak with him before he's executed."

Ibn Yala helped Faraj to his feet. "Someone wanted to prevent our meeting."

Faraj nodded. "Yes and I know exactly who's responsible."

Chapter 17

Homecoming

Princess Fatima

Gharnatah, al-Andalus: Sha'ban 672 AH (Granada, Andalusia: February AD 1274)

A month passed once Niranjan returned to Gharnatah. Fatima waited for word of her husband. Each messenger who arrived at court every day filled her heart with terror. Fearful imagining of Faraj's brutal death at the hands of some unknown assassin haunted her nights.

Dreading sleep, she stood in her father's garden in the late evening. A wintry chill swept down from the mountains, scattering dried leaves and wilted petals. The sky glowed in ominous hues of orange, red, and purple, as though fire had set the heavens ablaze.

Leeta bowed beside her.

She sighed. "Yes, Leeta, I know it's time for dinner with Father and my sisters. Can you tell them that I won't come tonight?"

"The invitation to dine came from your husband."

The breath caught in her throat. "He's... home?"

Leeta smiled. "The message just arrived from your husband's house. He wants to dine with you this evening. Isn't that wonderful news?"

A chill swept up her spine. She clasped and unclasped her icy fingers.

Leeta patted her shoulder. "Don't be nervous, you've longed for his return. Now he's here and we must find some lovely attire for the evening. Perhaps the black *jubba* with the braid embroidery? Let's consider it in the *hammam.*"

Leeta ushered her from the garden into the small alcove at the entrance to the bath. Beautiful turquoise and beige pigments covered the walls of the room. *Nashki* calligraphy incised at the top of each wall extolled the virtues of cleanliness. The colors and artistry transformed the otherwise utilitarian area into a place of beauty. In one corner, a marble water fountain stood at the center of a low pool. A carved stool sat before the fountain, while a tray of implements lay on a smaller stool next to the wall. Two thick wool towels hung on a brass rod.

"Sit and I shall tend to you, my Sultana."

Fatima relaxed as Leeta pinned her hair up, before inspecting the bathing tools. Fatima gestured to a thick scrub, made of ground apricot seeds mixed with milk and almond oil in a copper jar. Leeta smoothed it from her neck downward. Then she took a bronze scraper from the tray and removed the sticky mixture, occasionally rinsing the scraper in the fountain. Fatima sighed as Leeta dipped a thick sponge in the water and lightly wiped the contours of flesh.

When Leeta finished the ritual, she reached under the stool where Fatima sat. Removing two pairs of bath sandals made of cork. Fatima stepped into the smaller pair. Fatima led the way into the next chamber, while Leeta followed with towels draped over her arm.

Three times the size of the first room, the harsh glare of sunset sent light streaming into the bathing area through rounded glass windows near the ceiling. Torches in the corners reflected light toward a large square pool at the center. Four columns at each corner of the room supported the roof.

Fatima sat at the edge of the pool, while her servant scrubbed her skin with olive oil, alkali, and natron. Then she dove under the water and washed.

Later, perfumed and massaged, she returned to her bedchamber where Leeta and Amoda dressed her. The women wrapped her in a black silk robe. Slippers, a beautiful full-length wrap, and gossamer black veils completed her attire.

She frowned at the number of jewelry pieces on the bed; a long necklace of opals and rings, bracelets and anklets. "This is not a state occasion, Leeta."

"But my Sultana, this is your first occasion to dine in private with your husband. Show him that you value your bridal trousseau."

While Amoda affixed the necklace, its pendant the size of an egg, Fatima replied, "I doubt my husband shall be concerned about whether I am wearing anything among the gifts he has given me. He's probably deciding whether to beat me or have me locked in my rooms."

Amoda applied light cosmetics to her face. "My Sultana, surely he's not cruel."

"Neither of you have husbands yet, so you wouldn't know."

Behind Fatima, her pet kite twittered loudly, perched on the bow of her cage. She patted the cage. The bird was the only present from Faraj that she truly treasured.

Niranjan entered the room. "You look enchanting, my Sultana. By your permission, may I escort you to dinner with your husband?"

She glared at her servants, who blushed and tittered behind their hands. "Does everyone in the palace know I'm to dine with Faraj?"

Bundling her wrap around her shoulders, she murmured, "But perhaps it's for the best. He'll be less inclined to kill me if more people are aware of my evening with him."

In silence, she followed Niranjan to Faraj's house at the southwest limits of the *madina*. The red brick residence with its walled gate looked sinister in the dim light. She recalled her first visit, which had been pleasant until

Faraj's slave appeared. Now, a household servant waited outside the horseshoe-arched door.

Niranjan stopped under the shade of a juniper tree. "I await you here, my Sultana."

She drew in a deep breath and crossed the smooth cobblestones to meet the prince's servant.

"My Sultana, I pray the peace of God be with you. I am the steward of the house, Marzuq. I welcome you in your husband's name."

"Thank you for your gracious welcome."

The steward led her inside. She remembered the small antechamber strewn with cushions. They emerged at an indoor courtyard with a lonely fountain, which led to a small dining hall, where Faraj waited.

After so many weeks apart, she took in the full measure of him, her heart swelling with pride, which dampened all her fears. He looked very handsome, dressed in black and gold robes.

"I bid you welcome." He gestured to the cushion at her feet.

Fatima stopped staring and sat down. The servant bowed and left.

Puzzled, she turned to her husband, "If he goes, who shall serve us?"

Faraj chuckled. "You've never been without servants for even one night?"

"I'm a princess."

"Indeed. Allow me to attend you."

He lifted the covers of the platters and she gasped.

"I asked your father about your food preferences when I returned to Gharnatah this morning. He said lamb kebabs and rice with carrot, onion, garlic, and scallion were your favorites, but 'tharid was also something you enjoyed. He also said my cook should not flavor the dessert pudding with too many almonds or too much sugar. Was he right?"

Their conversation throughout the meal began on a light, entertaining note, but soon Fatima dug her fingernails into her palms, stifling a scream of exasperation. After her husband praised the Marinids for saving him from the assassin and shared the success of his meeting with their Sultan, now he spoke of the architectural wonders and cuisine of Fés el-Bali.

"You're not really listening to me, are you?" His voice intruded on her internal ramblings.

"What? I am listening. You just said the people of Fés el-Bali eat too much camel meat, which they sell within the sacred confines of *al-Qarawiyyin* Mosque."

"Indeed. What is the matter?"

"Can you truly ask that? Have you no idea what might be bothering me?"

"It is obvious I do not know, so please tell me."

She threw up her hands. "I'm awaiting your judgment, your punishment! Yet, you relate ridiculous stories of the people of Fés el-Bali and their camel meat. I wish you would simply shout at me and be done with it."

Faraj smiled. "You'd prefer my anger to my hospitality? It's a strange choice."

She crossed her arms over her chest, fuming.

He tugged her hands away. "If you await punishment, Fatima, you wait in vain. I knew you would disobey me when you promised never to be involved with the Ashqilula slave again. I've always known how you value the safety of your family above all else."

"I didn't send Niranjan just to protect our family. I sent him for you."

"It was very loyal of you."

"You're my husband. You should have my loyalty."

"I am grateful for it. As to future letters from this slave, you shall deliver them to me. I shall commend them to the Sultan. Do you understand me, Fatima? I want to see every letter. No more secrets between us."

She stared at him, perplexed by his easy resolve. "I understand and I swear upon the blessed ninety-nine names of God, you shall have every letter."

"You have sworn by our God and such is a sacred oath."

"I know, you needn't caution me. Why did you send for me if not to punish me?"

"I wished to enjoy the company of my wife whom I have not seen for nearly two months. Is it not right that I should wish to be with you?"

His candid expression made her heart soar. "May I ask something?"

"What is it that you wish to know?"

She cleared her throat. "In the years we have been married, you've never tried to kiss me. Don't you want to kiss me? I'm not a child anymore."

He stared wide-eyed and laughed, an uproarious sound filling the room.

Her face grew hot. "I do not understand what is so amusing about my question."

He wiped the corner of his eyes. "There shall never be a dull moment in this marriage."

"I do not understand your reaction to a simple question."

"Oh, Fatima, nothing with you is ever simple."

She threw up her hands again in disgusted resignation. "You make sport of me and I shall not tolerate it. By your leave, I bid you goodnight."

When she stood, he grasped her hand. "I did not give you leave. Please sit and let me talk with you." He tugged her down to the cushions. "Take off your *hijab*."

"What? Why should I remove my veil?"

"Please indulge me and take it off. I haven't seen you unveiled since the day of our first meeting."

He reached for the sheer cloth covering her hair. She slapped his hands away and removed the pins holding the veil in place. Seemingly impatient, he helped, though his touch was as gentle as Amoda's own. He smoothed back the locks from her brow. One curly strand slipped through his fingertips.

"Do you remember the first time I brought you to this house? When you confided in me in one instance and then railed at me in another?"

She ducked her head, but he grasped her chin and leaned closer. "I see by the blush on your cheeks that you do."

"How could I forget? You were very disagreeable that afternoon."

"Is that why you blush so prettily?"

She shook her head.

"Fatima, since that evening and many times afterward, I've wanted to kiss you."

She swallowed. "You have?"

He loomed closer, stroking the length of her hair. "How would you like me to kiss you, exactly?"

His mouth met hers and her eyes closed of their own volition. She became aware of different things - the tangy taste of apricot juice, the tender stroke of his thumb across her cheek.

Abruptly the kiss ended.

"Well, was that to your satisfaction, Fatima?"

"I've never been kissed before. I would have to try several more kisses to be sure." She pursed her lips again.

"Well, it's true you've never been kissed before. Our kiss confirmed it."

Suddenly downcast, she reached for the *hijab* to cover her hair again. "The hour grows very late. This has been a pleasant evening, but I think I should leave."

Deep lines furrowed his brow. "Why, are we not having a pleasant time here together? Stay, we might practice some more of the kissing."

"I'm tired. Please permit me to take my leave."

He stood when she did, his hands on her shoulders. "You're annoyed with me."

"Please let me go."

"At least, let me escort you to the harem gates."

She headed for the door across the courtyard.

"You need not. My Niranjan can protect me," she said over her shoulder, but his footsteps followed.

At the entrance, she bid him farewell. Niranjan stood under the juniper tree, his gaze seemingly on the star-filled sky.

Faraj grimaced. "Indeed, your faithful bodyguard awaits you. His loyalty appears boundless. I... bid you good night."

"You also, my prince."

Chapter 18

The Rivals

Princess Fatima

Gharnatah, al-Andalus: Sha'ban 672 AH (Granada, Andalusia: February AD 1274)

Faraj's return from al-Maghrib el-Aska preceded a landmark ceremony three days later; the investiture of the Sultan's chancery, the *Diwan al-Insha*. Fatima joined her aunt Maryam and her grandfather's widows for the occasion. Behind the latticed *purdah*, the sweet odor of the poppy seed in Sultana Hamda's water pipe suffused the air.

Suddenly, she started, her eyes widening with fury. "What are you doing here? You are not welcome!"

Fatima turned and found the Sultana Faridah, mother of the Ashqilula governor of Malaka, standing in the shadows. Her once fair skin was sallow and gray hair peeked beneath her veil. Her large eyes were rheumy. In her youth, they had been a vibrant, sparkling sea-green color.

"There is no reason Faridah should be unwelcome among us," Sultana Qamar said in a conciliatory attempt, "after all, she is sister to our late husband, Hamda."

"She is an Ashqilula spy. Her son is the governor of Malaka," Sultana Maryam said, casting a cold emerald-eyed gaze at Faridah, who drew back under her harsh scrutiny, her pallid face marred with misery. Her eyes glistened with moisture.

Before a tear could fall, Fatima moved from the forefront. She took Faridah's hand and addressed the other Sultanas.

"You should be ashamed of yourselves. How dare you heap scorn on her? She shares Father's blood and mine. She is a Sultana and shall always be welcome here."

Aunt Maryam colored with indignation. "My father did not want her here and neither shall my brother. She is a traitor to our family. Call the guards."

Fatima pulled Faridah closer. "How dare you? Sultana Maryam, we both bear Ashqilula blood, through our mothers. If there are any among us with questionable loyalties, it should be you and me."

"I have no idea what you accuse me of," Sultana Maryam said, her eyes narrow with disdain, "but I tell you, girl, I shall not stand for it."

Fatima frowned at the odd choice of words on her aunt's part. "I accuse you of nothing, but you have no right to judge Sultana Faridah. More than blood ties still bind us to the Ashqilula."

She continued glaring at the room's occupants. "Can you tell me, the Sultan's daughter, to go as well?"

Sultana Maryam rolled her eyes in disgust and faced the stucco wall, while Hamda focused with renewed interest on the water pipe.

Fatima squeezed Sultana Faridah's hand affectionately. "Sit with me."

The wounded look in her dark eyes disappeared. They shone with gratitude. "I could not. The place of honor belongs to the women of the current Sultan's harem. But, I do wish to stay."

"Then I pray you shall sit beside me," Sultana Qamar said, indicating space beside her.

With her aunt ensconced beside her grandfather's widow, Fatima took her seat again and witnessed her father appointing his foremost minister of the council. For more than thirty years, her tutor Ibn Ali had served the Sultans of Gharnatah. He taught her father and his brothers and her generation of royal children. He deserved this greatest of honors.

Now he knelt on aged knees with a slight groan, while the Sultan poured a drop of rosemary oil on his high forehead and proclaimed, "Arise, Ibn Ali, *Hajib* of the *Diwan al-Insha*, Prime Minister of my court and leader of my chancery. By the blessings of God, long may you serve this esteemed council and the people of Gharnatah."

Ibn Ali stood on spindly legs and flashed a crooked smile. The gesture softened his liver-spotted, careworn face, with its fleshy wattle beneath the chin. The Sultan bestowed the kiss of peace on his former tutor. The room erupted in applause. Fatima's heart soared, as she joined the acclaim.

***

Fatima and her aunt Faridah strolled arm-in-arm, between rows of myrtle trees along the garden path outside the throne room.

"I wish you had told me of your intention to visit Gharnatah, Aunt."

The elderly woman sighed. "I feared I might not be welcome. At first, the guards refused to allow me up through the tower from the garden entry. One among them had to convince his fellows that only a Sultana of Gharnatah would know the secret passages into the throne room."

"Does your son Abu Muhammad know you're here?"

"I don't share everything with him. A woman must have her own secrets."

Fatima nodded in understanding. "Can you stay with me?"

"I'll return to Malaka this evening with the camel caravans. I came only for the day to witness the proceedings. Ibn Ali was a favorite of my brother's."

Fatima halted and touched Faridah's cheek. "You must miss Grandfather so."

"I cried alone when I heard of his passing, while my son and his compatriots cheered. To think, I raised Abu

Muhammad upon my brother's knee. There was a time when he loved his uncle. Now, I only wish I might die rather than endure this conflict between our two families."

The women resumed walking, passing through her father's courtyard.

Fatima said, "I wish you would stay a little longer. Tonight, my father hosts a feast to celebrate the birth of his daughter."

"He has sired another girl. So, the rumors of the *kadin* who's stolen his heart are true?"

Fatima drew apart from her aunt and halted beside the fishpond. The mid-afternoon sun shimmered like molten gold across the surface. A distorted image of herself reflected in the depths of the water, lips slashing across her face in a thin angry line.

She forced a smile for Faridah. "I have a present for Father. Would you like to offer your opinion?"

Faridah raised an eyebrow. "Is this someone to tempt him away from the *kadin*?"

"Someone to remind him there are other women in the world."

"Your father is very devoted to his lovers. For a time, he only loved your mother."

"She was a princess, not a lowly slave. This new attachment is beneath him."

Faridah shook her head. "That is your opinion alone. You are a Sultana, his eldest daughter. A mere slave can hardly be considered worth your attention." She paused and bent beside the fishpond, scooping up some liquid in her gnarled hands. "Water is water. No matter how you contain it or change its form, water remains the same."

She stood and took Fatima's fingers in her grasp. "But I'll see this gift, for which you've wasted precious coin."

They went to the harem. Amoda greeted them. "Niranjan has come, my Sultana."

Fatima asked, "Is there anyone else with him?"

"A slave girl also awaits you in your receiving room."

Fatima struggled to suppress her smile. "Excellent, we'll see them."

A frown marred Faridah's brow, but she said nothing.

They walked into the windowless room at the heart of the harem. Red cushions trimmed with gold brocade lined the walls. Niranjan rose and bowed. The petite woman beside him mimicked his actions. In her long opaque robe and damask veils, the folds of cloth hid her features.

Niranjan said, "I have brought the slave Ayesha, by your command, my Sultana."

Fatima avoided Faridah's scrutiny and gestured for her aunt to sit on one of the cushions. Then she joined her. "Niranjan, I wish to inspect her now. Instruct her to remove the veils."

After the slave followed Niranjan's command, Fatima studied her face. She looked to her aunt, who clutched her prayer beads against her chest.

Faridah shook her head. "What sorcery is this?"

"None, I assure you, Aunt."

"What have you done, child?"

"Then you see the resemblance, too?"

"It is uncanny, as if Princess Aisha stood before us again. Do not do this, my lamb."

Fatima stood. "Why do you caution me, Aunt? If Father loved Aisha so much, he shall welcome this new woman in his life." She approached Niranjan. "You told me her hair was black."

"It was, but I asked Leeta to dye it with the henna. The effect is compelling."

In closer quarters, she scrutinized the slave. The woman's honey-brown skin complemented dark brows and lashes, and a pert mouth and nose, framed by wavy hair now dyed a dark red. Her luminous gaze held Fatima's own, with eyes the mirror of Princess Aisha's own.

"The resemblance is remarkable, Niranjan. It is unfortunate we cannot dye her hair to match a chestnut color. If I did not know better, I would swear the Princess stood before me."

"Yes, my Sultana. It is likely your father shall have the same reaction when he sees Ayesha for the first time."

"A midwife has examined her?"

"She declares the *jarya* is fit and of child-bearing age. I am sure she shall please your father greatly. Should she undress now?"

"If this girl is to be the *kadin*'s rival, I want to ensure she is pleasing in all aspects."

Fatima returned to her seat, by which time the slave had removed her robe for her inspection.

Fatima considered the various concubines she had seen in her father's harem, their images a silhouette in the steamy *hammam*. Under the ministration of attendants, who washed, massaged, and perfumed their skin, they prepared daily to court her father's desire. However, she had never seen anyone who looked like this woman.

Her petite form and compacted curves would stir the desire of any man. A slender neck met graceful shoulders, tapering into willowy arms and long fingers. Her breasts were small and round, the nipples budding, pink peaks. Her belly, a taut length of sinew flared into generous hips and thighs. By custom, every hair on her body, except that adorning her head, was gone. She stood flawless, the image of the *houri* in Paradise.

Fatima nodded. "You've done well, Niranjan."

"I am glad she meets with your expectations, my Sultana."

"Does she speak Arabic?"

"Yes, her first owner tutored her. She was a gift for a prince of the Zayyanids. When he died in a border skirmish with the Marinids, her owner brought her to al-Maghrib el-Aska, hoping she might catch Abu Yusuf Ya'qub's eye."

Faridah stood. "Leave us, eunuch."

He bowed and departed.

Faridah turned on Fatima. "Your mother is dead. How dare you pain your father with this mockery of her memory?"

"He's forgotten her."

"Aisha is dead, child. Accept it. Your father did. Allow him a measure of happiness with his *kadin*."

"I cannot."

Faridah turned away. "You've been too long in this harem of your father's. It is high time you took an interest in your husband's life. You are a married woman, yet you behave as a spoiled child would. You hardly deserve the honors accorded to you as the Sultan's eldest daughter. I won't stay here and indulge you in this pettiness."

She swept from the room without looking back, head held high.

Fatima crossed her arms over her chest. Yet when her aunt's footfalls faded, a tiny doubt nagged at her.

The slave girl coughed. She glanced at her, suddenly remembering the girl stood there.

"You may put on your garment and sit beside me."

"Yes, my Sultana." Her voice was throaty, almost a cat's purr. Not like Princess Aisha's tone. She padded on slender feet across the floor, sat, and folded her hands on her lap. Again, she met Fatima's level stare.

"Where were you born, Ayesha?"

"In a town called Palermo, it is on the northwestern coast of an island called...."

"... Sicily. I know of it. Moors ruled your country until nearly two centuries ago. Niranjan said you are a nobleman's daughter. Are you descended from the Franks?"

"Yes, my name is... it was Maria."

Fatima nodded. The woman had accepted her lot in life. "Do you know why you're here?"

"I am to serve the Sultan of Gharnatah. He is my master now."

"You shall dance for the Sultan tonight, Ayesha, and entertain him with song if he wishes. I am sure you shall please him, so do not be nervous." When she remained silent, Fatima inquired, "Are you nervous?"

"I heard you and the eunuch talking. You said there is a rival."

"Do you fear her?"

The slave's hazel eyes shone like amber. "No. She's nothing to me."

***

Later in the evening, Fatima attended her father's banquet in his upper-level apartments. Some of her sisters stood with their father, while he introduced them to his new daughter and the *kadin*. Alimah took the golden-haired child in her arms. She and Azahra cooed at the squirming bundle. Their father looked on adoringly with his arm draped on his slave's hip, holding her close to him.

Fatima cursed beneath her breath and approached.

When she bowed, her father beckoned her. "You look beautiful, my dear."

"Thank you." She fingered the gold brocade of her *jubba*.

The *kadin* smiled and curtsied. Fatima turned away, just as her grandfather's queens and *kadin* arrived. Her brother Muhammad appeared in the company of the *jarya* Zuleika who, it seemed, was with child again, after suffering a miscarriage. Then, Fatima's younger sisters, the Sultanas Tarub and Nadira came.

At a large table, the family dined together. Fatima sat next to Muhammad, who took his place at their father's left. The *kadin* sat on his right.

Beneath the ivory and gold tablecloth, Fatima dug her nails into her palm. Since Princess Aisha's death, she had occupied the place of honor beside her father. Now a slave displaced her. She ate with little appreciation for the cuisine, among them her favorite 'tharid with mint-flavored lamb. Noisy chatter swirled around her, while she kept her silence.

From time to time, the *kadin* looked down the table. Each time she did so, Fatima frowned in her direction.

194

Then, another slave interrupted to take the newborn to her cradle.

Fatima muttered below her breath, "Ridiculous! One slave does the bidding of another."

Muhammad coughed loudly. Their father patted his back. "Are you well, son?"

"Too much pepper on the lamb," Muhammad murmured. He glanced sideways at her, the corners of his mouth crinkling.

She ignored him, certain he had overheard her remark, but she did not care what he or anyone else thought. The *kadin*'s influence was infuriating.

After the meal, the guests presented as many gifts, if not more, for the woman than her child. At the climax of the reception, the Sultan presented Nur al-Sabah with a necklace of finely cut stones; opals, jade and sapphires gleaming in gold.

Fatima turned away to the window behind her. Niranjan crossed the patio on the lower level. The Sultan had arranged for an evening's entertainment with female musicians.

He signaled to them where they sat in a corner of the room. Then Ayesha appeared at the top of the steps. She wore a short black tunic, closely fitted to her torso, fastened in a low V-neck just above her waist. Her skirt comprised a thick silk waistband, slung low over her curvaceous hips, and sheer strips of red silk sewn to it. Her attire bared her midriff and the skirt revealed her shapely legs with every movement.

"What's this, daughter?" Her father leaned forward, favoring Fatima with a bemused smile.

"She is my gift for you, honored father." She looked past him to the *kadin*, who also smiled.

Ayesha slowly began a sensuous sway of her hips in rhythm to the music and captivated all the guests. Lust fired Muhammad's candid gaze. At least, he had stopped staring at their father's *kadin*.

Smiling in triumph, Fatima looked at her father, who whispered something in the *kadin*'s ear. She laughed and covered his hand with hers, before they turned their attention to the dance. Occasionally, he leaned and nuzzled her, or kissed her hand. She chuckled low, and always pointed to the dancer at the center of the room.

Fatima shook her head. He acted like a lovesick fool with a mere slave, according her the affection he should have reserved for a wife. In a pique of annoyance, Fatima missed the conclusion of Ayesha's performance. Uproarious applause followed.

When the new slave bowed in the center of the room, Fatima stood. "My noble father, this is the slave, Ayesha. She is my gift to you, in celebration of the birth of your new daughter."

"She is a most beautiful, wondrous gift, for which I thank you, my daughter." He beckoned Ayesha forward. When she stood before the table, he said, "Beautiful dancing, you gave an excellent performance."

"Thank you," the slave replied, her eyes fixed on the floor.

He continued, "What gift would you have of me for your display tonight?"

Now, she raised her head slightly. "You have a gift, for me?"

"Such skill must always be rewarded. What do you desire most? Speak whatever is in your heart and within my power, I shall grant it. Surely, there must be something you want."

She glanced at Fatima and then met his stare. "I only wish to serve you."

Fatima turned away. The slave was a fool! Her answer was too insincere and well-crafted to please the Sultan. She could have had anything she desired, perhaps even her freedom. Fatima had seen enough of her father's behavior with women to know that the concubines who seemed too acquiescent or clinging never held his attention. He desired someone with his wife's spiritedness. Had he found that with the *kadin*?

At the conclusion of the festivities, Fatima waited to say goodnight to the Sultan. Though the *kadin* hovered nearby, she ignored her.

Her father clutched her hands. "I wish you to know I truly did enjoy your gift, but the girl shall only languish unattended in my harem. I have no desire to see her talents wasted there. Before your brother retired left, I told him that he might have Ayesha. I pray you are not too disappointed?"

Fatima whispered, "You are Sultan, Father."

She bowed at his side and swept past the *kadin*, who curtsied and murmured her farewell. Fatima's heart raged inside her, but she could not deny the truth. The *kadin* had won.

Chapter 19
An Uneasy Alliance

Prince Faraj

Gharnatah, al-Andalus: Muharram - Rajab 673 AH
(Granada, Andalusia: July AD 1274 - January AD 1275)

Five months after Faraj had presented the Sultan's request for an alliance with the Marinids, the Marinid ruler sent a reply to his counterpart.

Summoned to the royal chamber, Faraj read the missive and looked at his master in disbelief. The Marinid Sultan had promised to send his son Prince Abu Zayyan, who he acclaimed one of their greatest commanders, to campaign against the Castillans.

"Abu Zayyan rides in command of five thousand Marinid cavalry. You may anticipate his arrival soon. I offer my esteemed son as a husband for your honorable sister, the widowed Sultana Maryam. In addition, I further secure this alliance by the offer of my own daughter, the princess Shams ed-Duna, as a bride for you. All this shall occur if you, the appointed of God, hold to your pledge to cede the ports of Tarif and al-Jazirah al-Khadra, as well as Jabal Tarik....' He expects us to give him Jabal Tarik too?"

At the Sultan's nod, Faraj growled, "That was not a part of our original bargain! He asks us to cede the only ports the Ashqilula do not control, to embroil ourselves in *jihad* against Castilla-León and we are to acquiesce without complaint?"

"We always knew this would be an uneasy alliance."

In disgust, Faraj tossed the letter on the low table between the Sultan and him. He snatched the water pipe at the center of the olive wood surface. Though neither man had ever used the pipe, they commiserated and drowned their concerns in a haze of smoke.

When Faraj passed the pipe to him, Muhammad II inhaled deeply. "Control of the ports serves Marinid interests and allows them a foothold for entry into the peninsula. That is why I made the offer, even knowing the risk that I might lose cities almost as valuable as Malaka. There can be no debate among my ministers. We must hold to the bargain. Castillan dogs nip at our heels and continue the border skirmishes unchecked. This cannot be entirely without the knowledge or sanction of King Alfonso."

"Have you told the Sultana Maryam of the offer of marriage?"

"Yes, unfortunately, I was dining with her and my brothers last night when the messenger arrived. Her reaction was strange. She refused to leave Gharnatah but she'll do as I say."

"And you shall tell your family you are to re-marry soon?"

"I shall speak with my children, after I have met with the *Diwan*. I want to tell the girls, but I must reassure my *kadin* first. No royal wife shall ever take her place in my heart. Perhaps after I am wed, she might consent... but that is for another time."

Faraj did not wonder at what the Sultan might have said. He worried only for Fatima who remained fiercely loyal to her mother's memory.

***

For nearly six months afterward, the court awaited the arrival of the Marinid Prince Abu Zayyan. When he arrived, just before winter approached, the Sultan met him at the port of al-Jazirah al-Khadra, now under Marinid control and brought him northwestward to the border. From there, the army of the Maghribi prince

199

carried out devastating raids against the Christian populations, killing as many as they enslaved.

Faraj remained in Gharnatah, where the court received weekly dispatches concerning each success. The marketplaces of Gharnatah and Fés el-Bali were soon flooded with human booty bound for distant Islamic lands, slaves who would not see their homes again.

In the midst of the conflict, Prince Abu Zayyan and Muhammad II withdrew from their encampment and returned to Gharnatah. For nearly a month since the Prince's arrival, the populace had celebrated the impending nuptials of the Sultana Maryam.

In a brief ceremony, the Sultan officiated while the *Shaykh al-Ghuzat* Umar and Faraj witnessed all requisite documents. The tall, burly prince of the Marinids and the petite princess of the Nasrids must have thought well of each other, for when he returned to the frontier one week afterward, she accompanied him.

Nearly six weeks later, Muhammad II summoned Faraj to the throne room. The Sultan stood alone in its recesses, leaning against a stucco wall carved with a hunting motif. Faraj closed the door behind him. Dim light from dulled lanterns gave the chamber a haunting, gloomy effect.

Grim-faced, Muhammad II held up a weathered parchment in his hand, the ink glowing blood red against the pages.

Faraj swallowed loudly, certain of the contents of the letter even before the Sultan spoke.

"The Castillans have declared war against Gharnatah and its southern neighbor. King Alfonso's army numbers in the thousands. We shall meet them with the combined Gharnati and Maghribi forces at the outskirts of Istija, the domain of the Castillan king's advisor, Doñ Nuño."

***

On the eve of the conflict with Castilla-León, Faraj exchanged letters with the Marinid court minister Ibn Yala in Fés el-Bali, renewing Gharnatah's pledges. The Marinids welcomed the news. Within two weeks, Faraj received confirmed sightings of their ships ready to sail from the ports at Sebta and Chella.

He went to the Sultan with the news. A bitter chill preceded his entry into the throne room. Muhammad II sat with Fatima at his feet.

"Then you'll let me accompany the court to the frontier? I cannot stay here, Father. Worry shall kill me if I don't know how you and Faraj fare."

"Daily dispatches shall not suffice?"

"He's my husband. You are my father. Please, don't ask me to remain behind."

"You've harassed me for weeks about this. Very well, I permit it."

She clutched his hand and kissed it.

Faraj stood in awe at the doorway, hardly comprehending what he had overheard.

"Fatima, I forbid it!" He crossed the throne room in quick strides. "In the past, I have indulged your whims and fancies, but I cannot accept your willfulness now."

She rose and turned to him. "Faraj, you cannot forbid me from going with you, when the Sultan has given his consent. His authority supplants even the will of my husband."

"It must be very convenient for you that your father is master of Gharnatah. As usual, you use your position as his daughter to defy me. I shall tolerate it no longer!"

"It is only you who sees my action as defiance! I care not how you bluster and rage. You can't keep me from going with you to Istija."

The Sultan sat silent between them, his chin on his hand.

A muscle twitched along Faraj's jaw line. "Fatima, by the Prophet's beard, I wish you would see reason! A battlefield is no place for a woman, it has never been."

"Do not lecture me on a woman's place!" Fury strained her voice. Her angular features flushed with indignation. "If a battlefield is no place for a woman, why then did Ayesha, beloved of the Prophet, gird herself for battle against her husband's enemies? I am not asking to fight at your side. I won't remain here in Gharnatah, awaiting news of the outcome."

Faraj turned to the Sultan with an exasperated groan. "Your daughter's stubbornness tries my patience. Won't you counsel her to listen to reason?"

Fatima screeched, "Do not speak of me as if I am not here!"

Muhammad II shrugged. "You know no power on earth, or very likely in the heavens, can alter my daughter's course when she has her mind set upon a thing. I see no danger in this, not when part of my personal guard shall protect her. Your wife has my consent. I cannot rescind it. Now, she desires your approval."

Faraj crossed his arms over his chest. "She shall never have it."

"This debate is useless," she concluded. "By your leave, I bid you good day, Father."

She kissed the hem of the Sultan's *jubba*, before her sharp gaze stabbed at Faraj. Then she stalked from the room. He turned away, shaking his head in disgust.

Behind him, the Sultan inquired, "Have you told my daughter the truth yet?"

Hard-pressed to hide his annoyance, especially when the Sultan had caused all the trouble in the first place, Faraj asked, "Have I told her the truth of what?"

"That you love her."

Faraj shook his head, but he could not deny the truth.

The Sultan continued. "Have you told her how your concern for her safety is nothing compared to the love you feel for her?"

Faraj questioned, "Why should I speak of love? Why speak of what is obvious?"

"You should tell my daughter of your feelings. Perhaps then she shall understand your fears."

"She understands. She simply does not care."

"Oh, she cares, cousin. If she did not care for your feelings or desire your approval, she would not press this issue. Go to her and see that I am right."

Faraj sighed. Fatima was as much a part of him as the heart beating inside his chest.

"Do I have your consent to enter your harem, my Sultan?"

"You do not go to the harem to seek my daughter at this hour. Fatima is most likely with her brother. He is training her to use the bow, should she find herself under attack."

"I cannot believe he aids her in this folly."

Muhammad II smiled. "Admittedly, when she first approached him to learn, my son dismissed her. She convinced him by taking up his bow and trying to learn on her own. Finally, he took pity on her rather vain efforts, and taught her to use the weapon properly. He believes that if no one can dissuade Fatima, she should at least know enough to safeguard her own life. I'm inclined to agree."

"Dare I ask if she is skilled enough?"

"Go to her at my son's house and you shall see for yourself."

***

Faraj went in search of Fatima at her brother's brick abode to the southeast. A slave escorted him to the indoor patio of the house.

She stood at the center of the courtyard in the open air, her veils discarded. Her hair, bound loosely in one braid, trailed down the length of her back and curiously, she wore a blindfold. Her brother stood at her side, adjusting the manner in which she gripped a wickedly curved bow. The head of the arrow glinted in the sunlight, the promise of a swift death gleaming at its edge.

"Loose!" he instructed.

The arrow struck just shy of the center of the target.

Faraj rolled his eyes heavenward. He leaned against the wall behind him, arms crossed over his chest. "My wife's become addle-brained, but I never thought you would lose your sensibilities as well, Your Highness."

Muhammad turned with a scowl. Fatima removed her blindfold.

Her brother said, "My sister can be persuasive, as you must know, being her husband."

Faraj ignored him and held out his hand to her. "Come with me."

She had another arrow nocked in the bow and pointed at him, before he could say another word. Her hand trembled.

Her brother laughed – great, belly-quaking, cackles that made him collapse on the ground, howling with delirious mirth.

Faraj ignored him. "Fatima, are you aware our marital contract states I am within my rights to beat you now for threatening me?"

"As you have seen, I know what to do with this weapon, so please, try." Her grip tightened on the bowstring, her face a dark mask.

Her brother's incessant laughter grew annoying. She must have felt the same way, for she kicked his leg. "Be quiet, you braying ass! Go away, you are of no help."

Still holding his belly, Muhammad sketched a clumsy bow and left.

Faraj moved a step closer to Fatima. The arrow tip indented his silk caftan. "If you must shoot, then do so. I shall not leave without you. This is madness."

"It's madness that I want to be with you, to ensure you don't come to harm?"

His emotions too frayed to acknowledge her tender feelings, he insisted, "Stop pointing that thing at me, please? You're ruining one of my favorite garments."

"I'm sure you have more than enough *dinars* to buy other clothes."

"Why would you risk your life and safety?"

"Don't you know why? This one conflict may determine the future of Gharnatah." She paused with a sigh. "You men with your wars, you never think of those whom you leave behind. I waited after Madinah Antaqirah, wondering if you had survived the fight. I shall not linger here, not knowing if you have suffered an injury. What if you died at Istija? I could not bear it if something happened to you."

He shook his head. Her emotions tugged at his heart. Could she possibly feel the same way as he did? If so, he was doubly committed to ensuring she remained in Gharnatah. He would die if anything happened to her, his beloved.

"Fatima, put that thing down, so I can say what I must without fear of a wound or death."

She hesitated, before she lowered the bow to the ground. He took the weapon and tossed it aside, before capturing her in his arms. She stood stiff and unyielding for a moment, but after a time, she surrendered.

They remained silent, his chin resting on her head. Then, he framed her face in both hands. Tears glimmered in her eyes. As always, they unmanned him.

"I could not bear it if you were harmed at Istija. Fatima, you are my life and my love. I do not say such words just because I want to keep you away from the battle."

Her gaze softened and her tears flowed freely. "I believe you."

He traced the glistening moisture on her cheek. "I love you too much to expose you to any danger."

She stared at him blankly, as if she had not heard what he said. Then she smiled, though tears still shimmered in her eyes.

"Faraj, if I go to Istija, I shall be even safer than you, for I'll have the guards Father assigns to me. And there shall be a retinue of Gharnati and Marinid warriors to protect my aunt Maryam."

When he drew back, she continued, "Aunt Maryam is going to Istija, as well. She must love her husband, because she shall not leave his side. Faraj, please do not ask me to remain here. Whatever danger you encounter, I want to be with you when you face it."

He groaned at her dogged refusal. "You may not be afraid, but I am. I cannot allow you to travel with me and the army to Istija. The Sultan has given you his consent, but I shall not. You must respect my opinion and believe it is born of the love I feel."

"Just as my love demands I must be with you! Why would I argue so with you, risking your displeasure yet again, if I did not love you, did not fear losing you? Why would I risk my safety, if not for love of you?"

He stared, incredulous. She placed her hand over his heart, which thumped loudly with the emotions churning inside him.

"You are my life, Faraj, and my love. If you should die... must I wait here to receive your body, cold and stiff? Don't ask me to do that."

Her voice dissolved on a whimper. He wanted to spare her pain, especially at this moment, when they had admitted their feelings to each other for the first time. However, he could not pretend he wanted her with him in the coming conflict.

"Then we are at an impasse, Fatima. You want the one thing from me that I cannot give. If you leave Gharnatah with the army, you do so without my approval."

Chapter 20
Jihad

Prince Faraj

Gharnatah, al-Andalus: Sha'ban 673 AH (Granada, Andalusia: February AD 1275)

During the month of Sha'ban, the first Marinid contingents arrived at the port of Munakkab, under the banner of their leader, Sultan Abu Yusuf Ya'qub. The Marinids numbered twelve thousand cavalry and infantrymen with siege weapons. Their ships swarmed the White Sea and remained anchored just off the coast of Munakkab, until the Sultan gave permission for them to go ashore. Faraj waited to welcome his master's new allies to al-Andalus.

The Marinid Sultan refused to embark, insisting the success of the coming battle would require yet another truce between the Nasrids and Ashqilula. Weary, Faraj returned to Gharnatah.

He had never seen Muhammad II so angry in all his life. He raged, cursed, and bellowed as a man possessed.

"By the Prophet's beard I swear... that camel-eating sot thinks he can interfere in the internal matters of the Sultanate!"

He stalked back and forth across the width of the room, rage emboldening his steps. The members of the *Diwan*, who had stood at his side earlier, scrambled out of his way. Faraj remained where he stood, awaiting the end of the Sultan's tirade.

The Sultan demanded, "By what right does he press such a claim against me? I am the master of Gharnatah! How dare any outsider impose his will upon me?"

Faraj cleared his throat. "Lest you lose perspective completely, my master, he is right."

The Sultan turned to him with murderous rage, daring him to repeat those words.

Though Faraj's heart rebelled against peace with the Ashqilula, who had helped kill his father, he said, "If we want to win this campaign, you must have peace with the Ashqilula. While we fight the Castillans, would you risk the Ashqilula attacking our cities? Worse, that they should join forces together with the Castillans? Do not let your pride sway your judgment. Only further delay and the possible withdrawal of the Marinids shall result."

Muhammad II shook his head in frustration, but Faraj pressed him further. "My Sultan, in days of old, your noble father taught you to place the survival of Gharnatah above all else. Since you ascended the throne, you have lived by his words in every decision and action you have undertaken. Let us enter into a truce with one enemy, so we may fight the other, for we would face an even greater foe, if the armies of Castilla-León and the Ashqilula united against us."

***

The next day, Faraj readied for the journey with Muhammad II, the Sultan's brothers and heir, to meet the Marinids and the Ashqilula. The army would follow in a day, led by Umar, the *Shaykh al-Ghuzat*.

Faraj had tried to speak with Fatima beforehand. Her eunuch-guard Niranjan replied she was indisposed, but Faraj guessed she remained angry at his refusal to let her go to Istija. Annoyed at his wife's childish behavior, he left his house in a huff. Marzuq waited at the side of his horse. The Sultan's retinue had already mounted in the courtyard of the *madina*. He snatched the reins and barely acknowledged the steward's farewell with a grunt, before he spurred his horse to join the group.

A rider swathed in black drew his attention at once. His spine tingled a warning. The rider turned to him. Dark eyes glittered between the slits of a blue-black veil.

He urged the dun-brown Arabian stallion closer to Fatima's gray Andalusi mare. She wore masculine attire, despite her concession to modesty with the veil. A wickedly curved dagger was in a sheath at her waist and over her shoulder, she had slung a bow and quiver of arrows.

"If you delay us in any manner, I shall send you home."

Though his voice barely rose above a whisper, she drew back as if the fury in his tone were a slashing whip. Then she stuck out her chin defiantly. "I can ride a horse well. You'll hear no complaints from me or my servants."

Then he noticed the two other riders in black at her side and Fatima's constant shadow, her eunuch guard. He groaned, realizing she intended to bring her damnable servants too. He shook his head at their foolery and jerked his mount away before joining the Sultan.

At the Sultan's signal, they rode out in a flurry of rapid movement, leaving behind the confines of the Sabika hill. They covered ground swiftly and moved out on to the dun-brown plains surrounding the city. They sighted the encampment of their new allies and the Ashqilula in the distance. The flags of the Marinids floated in a sea of other banners.

Awed for a moment, Faraj angrily recalled his wife's presence. Didn't she recognize the danger in all this?

He slowed and drew his mount beside hers near the middle of the column. Her brother Muhammad also hung back to ride at her right side. Muhammad leaned forward in the saddle and nodded to him. He returned the gesture, pleased to see they were of the same mind about his sister's safety. Fatima's gaze darted between him and her brother, but she said nothing.

Muhammad II stopped short of the outer edge of the camp, and waited. His horse snorted, stamped, and tossed his head. Faraj wondered whether the stallion could feel his master's obvious tension. Then Abu Yusuf Ya'qub rode toward him, flanked by the governor of Malaka, Abu Muhammad.

Faraj could hardly fathom it, but the truth overwhelmed him. When he had come to Gharnatah years ago, just before that bright morning of the Ashqilula's triumph, he had looked on the face of the man who murdered his parents. Abu Muhammad bore responsibility for everything he had lost that night. The blood of his parents demanded justice, but he only wanted retribution. He imagined thick globs of blood pouring from Abu Muhammad's throat, ripped from ear to ear, as his father had suffered.

His belly tightened in a heavy knot. He had not seen the man who conspired to murder his family in years. Yet again, circumstances forced him to put aside his vengeance for the good of Gharnatah. He vowed Abu Muhammad's death would come, but not this day.

Fatima whispered. "He's here."

Her brother asked, "The Marinid Sultan impresses you so much?"

"Not him. I meant Abu Muhammad of Malaka. He once wanted to marry our mother. He was there when she stole me away to the house of her brother Abdallah."

Faraj clenched his jaw tightly. "Did he hurt you?" He waited expectantly, but in truth, the prospect would just be yet another reason to murder the man.

Fatima answered, "No, but he let my mother die."

"Then I have one more reason to hate him."

"You hate him, too? What has he ever done to you?"

He made no reply, despite her puzzled stare. He was not ready to reveal the depths of his hatred, even to his beloved. Still, the burden of the secret weighed upon him.

The Marinid Sultan and his companions met Fatima's father, who greeted his ally with the kiss of peace. Then the sovereigns drew apart and seemed to assess each other.

Faraj judged Abu Yusuf Ya'qub and Muhammad II to be very much alike, though physically they could not have been more different. Where his master stood lean and tall, with olive skin and in the prime of life, the Marinid ruler was small and swarthy. His hair had gone completely gray since Faraj saw him at Fés el-Bali, just over a year ago.

"It is good that you have come, my brother of the Faith." Abu Yusuf Ya'qub's voice boomed across the plains.

Muhammad II replied, "I wish our alliance to remain strong. I would not have it threatened by what is, at least for me, an internal matter for Gharnatah."

Abu Yusuf Ya'qub chuckled and stroked his gray beard. "You are a man of plain speech, which is good, for I am the same. You resent my interference. Yet, you cannot deny the Ashqilula proved worthy allies in the early reign of your father. They can do so again and help us inflict a resounding defeat upon our common enemy in this *jihad*, Castilla-León."

Muhammad II said, "The Ashqilula clan doesn't view the Castillans as the enemy."

Abu Yusuf Ya'qub offered him a shrewd smile, "The same could be said of your father. At times, he counted the Castillans as enemies, but sometimes he was not so certain."

"Circumstances often change." Muhammad II paused and glared at the other Ashqilula chieftains gathered behind Abu Muhammad. "And they can again. What do the Ashqilula pledge by way of this truce?"

"They shall provide three thousand cavalry, archers, infantry, and siege weapons."

"At what cost to me?"

"The one who leads them, Abu Muhammad of Malaka, shall speak the terms, when your envoy negotiates with him on the morrow."

Faraj blanched. The Sultan had compelled him to be Gharnatah's envoy in the negotiations. How could he endure bargaining with his father's murderer?

Fatima interrupted his reverie. "I don't understand. Where is the chieftain Ibrahim? Why doesn't he lead the Ashqilula today?"

Faraj ignored her question, intent on the ensuing discussion, though he had wondered the same.

Muhammad II asked, "If I refuse to bargain with the Ashqilula? What shall you do then, my brother of the Faith?"

The Marinid ruler considered his reply before he answered, "Let us hope, by the Will of God, that our negotiations do not reach such a conclusion."

Muhammad II nodded and turned his horse away. He rode directly toward Faraj.

Scowling heavily, he whispered, "Bargain with them. Offer them Paradise if you must, but know this: I shall not hold to this treaty one moment longer than it takes to defeat Alfonso."

***

Princess Fatima

Fatima spoke with Leeta inside their tent while Faraj met with her father and his counselors. "I think I'll visit with my aunt Maryam. Since our arrival, the talk has turned to war. Maryam may be glad for the company, since Prince Abu Zayyan has joined his fellow commanders to plan strategy."

Leeta brewed a tisane of crushed mint leaves, lemon peels, and cinnamon. "Soon Sultana Maryam won't be so lonely. I heard her body slave talking in the *hammam* last week. The Sultana is pregnant, three or four months now."

"Are you certain? You should know better than to believe gossip, Leeta."

"The slave was arguing with another servant about whether their mistress should travel to al-Maghrib el-Aska before the baby is born. The Marinid prince believes she should give birth at his home. It seems the Sultana refuses to leave."

"Aunt Maryam must want her baby born in Gharnatah."

Amoda entered the tent with breakfast. While her servants chattered, Fatima thought of Aunt Maryam's probable pregnancy. She pressed her palms to her belly. What would it be like to have Faraj's baby growing inside her? Would their child favor her or Faraj?

Fatima looked up and found Leeta grinning at her. She dropped her hands to her sides. "I'm visiting the Sultana Maryam. If Faraj is successful in his negotiations, war shall come soon."

Amoda protested, "But Prince Faraj may not like it if you go alone to visit the princess. Her tent is pitched at the outskirts of the encampment."

"Niranjan shall protect me, I'll be fine."

When she stepped outside the tent, he stood beside the flap, silently scanning the encampment although there was a detachment of her father's personal bodyguards ringing the shelter. She shook her head. "Do you expect an attack here? The Ashqilula would never be so bold."

Niranjan glanced at her. "They were bold enough to move against your husband, though he was an honored guest of the Marinids. Never forget that Ibrahim of Ashqilula wanted you for himself. We must remain vigilant, my Sultana."

His subtle scolding reminded her of the gravity of the situation. She nodded and said, "Accompany me to my aunt's tent."

She strolled toward the green and white striped tent the Sultana shared with her husband. Covered in discreet garb, she kept her eyes averted from the soldiers who milled around the campsite.

Again, her mind swirled with thoughts of Faraj's child inside her. One day, their beautiful daughters and fine sons might play in the gardens where she and her siblings had whiled away the hours as children.

One of her mother's last wishes for her echoed in her thoughts. *Be happy in your marriage to Faraj.*

She stopped for a moment, and looked up at the sky with a smile. Her mother's wish had blossomed. Faraj loved her, as she loved him.

She continued to Sultana Maryam's tent. There were no guards posted. Perhaps the Sultana had gone elsewhere – but then raised voices of a man and woman escaped the folds of the tent. Certain it was the Sultana and her husband, Fatima turned away. "We'll come later, Niranjan, when the Sultana is perhaps alone...."

"Stop, Abu Muhammad! You're hurting me."

Fatima halted. The man in her aunt's tent was not Prince Abu Zayyan. Sultana Maryam's voice had never sounded so high and hysterical before.

Niranjan drew a short dagger from the belt of his tunic. Fatima jerked in surprise, never having seen her slave handle such a sharp blade. She was also unaware that he carried it in violation of the Sultan's rule that no slave should possess a weapon. When she stared pointedly at the dagger, he shrugged. "How else can I protect you?"

She gestured for his silence and edged closer to the tent. When he followed, she whispered, "No! I am also armed. Wait here. I shall call if you are needed." She cut off his ready protestation with a curt wave of her hand. However, he did not return the weapon to its sheath.

Fatima ducked inside, her hand on the dagger concealed at her waist. "Aunt, are you unwell? I heard you cry out."

Sultana Maryam sat on a wooden chair. Her coloring faded into a deathly pale shadow of her usual healthy glow. A man hovered over her. He shook her roughly and then released her, before he turned to Fatima. Luminous hazel eyes, hooded under heavy brows, met her stare. She drew back, stunned into silence, looking from one face to another, one full of anger, the other a mask of terror.

Abu Muhammad of Malaka glared at Aunt Maryam and tossed a bag to her. Her eyes widened with alarm.

"Find a way, damn you," he muttered.

Before Fatima could raise an alarm, he dashed from the tent. Maryam stared after him. Her talon-like hands gripped the arms of the chair until her knuckles turned white. Then, the haunted look in her eyes dissipated. She gripped the leather pouch on her lap.

"Fatima, why did you come to me unannounced?"

"There are no guards outside your tent, but you know about their absence, don't you, Aunt Maryam?"

Though she seemed distressed a moment ago, Maryam's features became remarkably composed now. "What are you saying? I knew they were gone. I dismissed them, after all. What I meant was why didn't you warn me that you were coming? I could have...."

"... Told Abu Muhammad to come later? What was he doing inside your tent? What does he demand of you? What must you 'find a way' to do?"

The Sultana's thin lips crimped with annoyance. Fire smoldered in her green eyes. "I do not stand for questions from you, child!"

Fatima moved closer. "Perhaps you can answer my father. You can explain why his enemy was here with you! Your husband might like the explanation too, of why another man was alone in his tent with his wife. Shall I call him?"

Blood drained from Maryam's face. "Your petty accusations," her voice broke. "I have done nothing for you to treat me so poorly."

"Your voice is your undoing. The pitch goes higher when you lie. Tell me that you are not a spy for the Ashqilula, that you have not betrayed our family to the enemy. I shall know the truth when I hear you speak."

"How dare you accuse me? Get out of my tent, at once."

Indignant, Maryam stood. The leather pouch on her lap fell, spilling an array of precious gemstones. A ruby, the size of an egg and the color of blood, rolled across the carpet and stopped at Fatima's feet. She bent and clutched the precious stone in a tight fist.

"For jewels... for jewels you destroy our family?"

Maryam knelt on the floor, gulping air furiously. She shoved the gems into the bag. "You don't understand, Fatima, you're... mistaken."

"I am not mistaken! For the first time, I see you more clearly than I ever have. At the installation of the *Diwan* last year, you accused our aunt Faridah of spying for her son. When I told you that you and I were the only ones with suspect loyalties, I did not understand why you said I had tried to accuse you of something. You thought I had discovered your secret, didn't you? Now, I have."

Maryam dropped the leather bag. "What can you do, take me to your father? Whom do you think he shall believe? I'm his sister!"

"I'm his beloved daughter and he trusts me. He'll know I am telling the truth."

Maryam rose from the floor and sank into the chair, her face ashen.

Fatima asked, "How long have you been spying for them. Was it before or after your first husband died?"

Her aunt responded with only cold silence, but Fatima pressed on, "My husband went to al-Maghrib el-Aska last winter. Did you warn your Ashqilula masters of his journey?"

Fatima lunged at her aunt when she refused to speak, nails pressed against the large vein at the side of her throat. Maryam let out a strangled cry.

"I swear, Fatima... I swear I did not know what they meant to do!"

"You told them, didn't you? That is how they knew of Faraj's journey. They tried to kill him. Do you understand me? My husband could have died because of you!"

"You're hurting me! If I die, you shall kill my baby too! Stop! I am pregnant with the Marinid Sultan's grandchild."

Fatima drew back. Maryam clutched at her throat, where nail marks gouged the flesh.

"Do you know how many have perished in this civil war?" Fatima paced the floor. "How can you carry a child in your belly, knowing how your treachery has robbed so many mothers of their children and wives of their husbands?"

"Why should I care? I lost a husband because of a Sultan of Gharnatah!"

"What are you talking about?"

"My first husband!" Maryam's voice exploded in a piercing screech. "He was one of the Ashqilula. He died because of my father! The Hud family assassinated him during a banquet at our home, because of his loyalty to the Sultan. My father refused to help the Ashqilula avenge his death. He said the time was not right to move against the Hud family. He did nothing. I hurt him in the only way I could, by siding with others who eventually found reason to betray him, too! What was I supposed to do?"

Her ugly words ended on a pitiful sob. Though Fatima realized there had been equal acts of betrayal on both sides, she refused to summon a shred of pity for her aunt, not when her treasonous behavior had almost ended Faraj's life.

"I'll tell you what you shall do. Leave Gharnatah, Sultana Maryam. You shall beg your husband today to send you to al-Maghrib el-Aska, to have his child there. You shall never return to al-Andalus. Beg his favor, or I shall tell him and my father the things you have done. No traitor can escape the Sultan's justice, not even his sister."

Fatima returned to her tent. Leeta offered her the tisane. "Did you have a pleasant visit, my Sultana? How is your aunt? Did she tell you her news?"

Fatima sank on a low stool. "She told me everything I needed to hear, Leeta."

***

Prince Faraj

Faraj arrived at Fatima's tent in the early evening. She stood with her back to him, dressed in a midnight blue *jubba*.

He sensed the tension in her. "I want you to stay here, while I dine with the Marinids this evening. If there is treachery, you shall be safe."

She nodded.

Suspicious of her easy acquiescence, he grasped her arm and turned her to him. "Why do you yield? You have made it clear you shall defy me whenever you wish."

Great pools of tears welled in her eyes. "I am fearful for you. What if something should happen tonight?"

Cursing his mistrustful nature, he took her in his arms and kissed her brow. "Do not be troubled. We'll be safe in the company of your father's guards."

He could not resist the temptation of a kiss from her trembling lips. Her eager response thrilled him from head to toe. The embrace lingered longer than he intended. The velvet softness of her lips intoxicated him. She seemed almost disappointed when he pulled away.

"Stay here, Fatima. I trust that I don't have to post a guard outside."

The evening passed without incident and he retired early, intent on checking on Fatima. He called out at the entrance to her tent, but no one replied. Light glowed from within, but he feared something was wrong and pushed the flap aside.

Fatima's slaves gasped. She ducked behind the women who blocked his view, but not before he had spied her perfect form. With her wavy hair pinned up, she revealed the pale olive skin of her back and the smooth contour of her hips.

"Forgive me. I worried when you did not immediately respond after I called out. I wanted to ensure you were well. When I did not hear a reply, uh, I, well...."

His voice trailed off. He remained rooted to the spot in silence.

Fatima said, "Do not apologize, Faraj. You are my husband and may see me in a state of undress." As if to prove the truth of her words, she allowed her servants to continue rinsing her.

He stepped inside the tent and closed the flap. Before now, he could not have guessed at her flawlessness. Two candles cast eerie shadows in the recesses of the tent, but mainly served as illumination for the perfect view of his wife's body. Her slim hips flared in delicate, rounded curves. Her legs were taut, slightly dimpled at the backs of her knees. She showed no coyness or abashment. She appeared completely at ease in his presence, though he was not the same. A throaty groan escaped him when water trickled across her skin, gliding along her spine down to the twin globes of her rounded buttocks. A harsh intake of breath whistled through his teeth. His hands closed into tight fists.

She said, "This evening must have been very hard for you."

"Uh... what? Oh, you must mean the dinner. I left early. As I said, I only wanted to ensure you were well. I should go now."

"Don't leave."

He swallowed, not trusting himself to speak just yet.

"Faraj, I know you share a smaller tent than this with my brother and my uncle Yusuf. Remain here with us tonight, where you might be more comfortable. Amoda and Leeta may wash you, if you like."

"I... I have no garments here for the morning. There is only one pallet."

"Then fetch your clothes and pallet. The twins shall attend you when you come back."

Folly made Faraj enter the tent the first time. Surely, madness inspired his swift return.

When he tugged the flap a second time, Fatima stood with her arms outstretched, her back to him. One of her slaves massaged her entire body with fragrant oil, a blend of cassia and ambergris. Her skin, already glowing with the health and vigor of youth, glistened in the lamplight under the ministrations of her slave. By the time she slipped into her sleeping garments, Faraj did not trust himself to be alone with her.

"Thank you both. Please tend to my husband now," she instructed her slaves.

He cleared his throat. "How... how can you tell them apart? They are dressed identically and each is a mirror of the other's features."

She smiled. "With one difference. Amoda always wears her hair parted on the left and Leeta prefers to part her hair on the right."

He stared at the slave girls. "That is all?"

"It's enough for me. Leeta and Amoda shall tend to you with care."

She turned away and lay down on her pallet, the slender curves of her form hidden under her blanket. Her slaves approached him. They were almost methodical in the removal of his garments. They put fresh water into a bucket, washed, and dressed him in silence. He thanked them both, before he moved to the tent's entrance.

"You won't remain here?" Fatima asked, as she rolled to face him.

He shook his head. He thought she had fallen asleep. "I'll sleep outside to protect you."

"The air is chilly tonight. If you must protect me, sleep inside at the entrance of our tent, where the brazier may still warm you."

Unable to fault her reasoning, he unrolled the bedding and lay down. The slaves damped down the lanterns and took their rest.

He looked toward where Fatima lay. "Good night."

She rustled underneath her coverlet in the dimness. "Good night, Faraj."

***

In the morning, Faraj rose early to continue the negotiations with the Ashqilula. He stared at Fatima, who still slept. He washed, trying to make as little sound as possible. Dressed for the day, he knelt beside her pallet. The angular contours of her face enthralled him, the delicate arch of her eyebrows and her dark lashes like soot against the pale olive skin of her cheek. The sweet curve of her mouth invited a kiss. Instead, with a lingering glance, he left the tent.

Chapter 21

Union

Prince Faraj

Gharnatah, al-Andalus: Sha'ban 673 AH (Granada, Andalusia: February AD 1275)

When Faraj left the tent, Fatima opened her eyes. She had woken almost at the instant he did. In silence, she listened to the swirl of water for his morning wash and the rustle of the fabrics while he dressed. As he had knelt at her side, her heart wrung with pity. When his heart must be so heavy with emotion, she did not know how to comfort him. Her father asked much of him, to negotiate a treaty and fight alongside those who had tried to kill him in al-Maghrib el-Aska.

Light filtered through the slight opening at the tent's entrance. Amoda and Leeta stirred and rolled up their pallets. She greeted them.

Amoda said, "Your husband is gone, my Sultana."

"Yes, he left a short time ago."

Leeta knelt beside her. "God be with him."

She forced a smile. "I pray He is with us all today."

In the afternoon, they learned Faraj had struck a peace accord with the Ashqilula. When Fatima's father visited after the meeting, he informed her of it. He drew her outside the tent, where they strolled together.

"I yield the glory to the Marinid Sultan. I shall await the news of the coming battle at home. For now, we'll withdraw to Gharnatah and seal our alliance with the Marinids."

She laid a hand on his shoulder. "You mean with a royal wedding?"

He halted and took her hand. "I have hesitated to speak of the possibility for months. I feared your reaction most of all. You anticipated me."

Fatima nodded. "The Marinids shall strengthen us. I am sure your new wife shall be happy in our home. My sisters and I shall welcome her. We've been without a mother for too long."

He kissed her brow. "You please me greatly, daughter. You looked so gloomy when I arrived, my dear. Is it because you shall miss your aunt Maryam?"

"Miss her?"

"Yes, she came to me before I met Abu Yusuf Ya'qub this morning. After the wedding, her husband's retainers shall escort her to the Marinid capital. I thought you might have known her intentions. She is carrying Prince Abu Zayyan's child and wants the baby born in his father's capital. She surprises me, though. When I first told her of the betrothal, she swore she would never leave Gharnatah. Love can make people do extraordinary things, don't you agree?"

Fatima nodded again. "Yes, love can do that."

She returned to the tent alone.

Faraj arrived within a moment. Her heart thrummed at the sight of him.

He clasped her hands and drew her to him. "You have heard?"

"Father told me. I know how you must hate the Ashqilula for what they tried to do to you in al-Maghrib el-Aska."

"Don't worry for that, now. I want to discuss the future. I wondered what you plan to do when we go home and your father marries the Marinid princess."

"I don't understand."

"Well, she'll take your role as the mistress of your father's harem. It is time for a change in your living arrangements. That is, I would like you to consider it. I want you to live with me in... our house."

His gaze, so expectant and full of hope, tugged at her heart.

"I want that too, Faraj. I shall live with you when we return home."

***

Festivities in celebration of the Sultan's nuptials began within the following week. The princess Shams ed-Duna was the daughter of Sultan Abu Yusuf Ya'qub and a beloved Nubian concubine. Like Fatima and her sisters, Shams ed-Duna's mother had died when she was young. Though barely aged twenty-four years, the Sultana was twice a widow.

The Marinid Sultan arranged for the delivery of his daughter from her ship docked at the port of Munakkab. Beforehand, Fatima met with the chief eunuch Hasan and her old governess Halah, and told them that she intended to leave the harem, ceding all authority to the Sultan's new wife.

"Be good to your new mistress as you have been to me."

At noon, with her sisters and Halah, Fatima waited to greet the Sultana Shams ed-Duna at the entrance of the harem. Her father would escort his new bride in advance of the wedding ceremony later in the evening. Fatima and her sisters stood resplendent in silks and gold brocade, in honor of their father and new stepmother.

The Sultan's distinctive footfalls echoed against the marble floor. Fatima hushed Nadira, who trilled a silly song. Their father walked with his head held high. He held aloft the hand of a beautiful woman, radiant in gold jewelry and yellow silk. Her smooth, dark skin and the column of her graceful throat evoked the epitome of beauty, pride, and nobility. Long narrow feet peeked out under her garments. Her eyes were obsidian, set in a heart-shaped face with a short nose and a full mouth, framed by jet-black hair elaborately braided into twisting locks. She was somewhat plump and shorter than their father was. As they drew closer, Fatima realized she and the princess were the same height.

Their father halted and the princesses bowed, as did the new Sultana of Gharnatah.

The Sultan said, "My children, I present the princess Shams ed-Duna bint Abu Yusuf Ya'qub of the Marinids. I bid you welcome her to our home."

"The peace of God be with you," Fatima and her sisters intoned.

Their father turned to his prospective bride. "Before you stands my eldest, the princess Fatima and beside her, my daughters the princesses Nadira, Tarub, Azahra and Alimah. My second daughter, the princess Muna, resides in al-Jaza'ir with her husband. My other daughter, the princess Zaynab, is with her mother, my *kadin* Nur al-Sabah al-Muhammad."

Fatima thought his mention of his slave woman and her child seemed callous, however, no discernible change altered his new wife's pleasant expression.

Shams ed-Duna bowed again. "I greet all of you with the peace of God."

He continued, "Sultana Fatima has had charge of the harem since the death of my first wife, authority which shall become yours when our union is made official tonight. She shall show you to your apartments that you might rest."

Fatima bowed before the Maghribi princess and introduced Halah as the governess of the royal children. They led the Sultana to the newly constructed apartments, rooms fit for the Sultan's queen. The rooms were four times the size Fatima had ever seen in any part of the palace, with *Nashki* calligraphy and foliage incised on the walls. Multicolored carpets covered the marble floors and a frosty winter breeze unfurled damasks and silk curtains hanging before latticed windows. Fatima dismissed Halah, who bowed and left them.

Sultana Shams ed-Duna said in a quavering voice, "These chambers should give anyone pleasure... but I have no entourage to require such a large domain. All my life, I have relied upon one slave from birth, my governess. I do not even have her now. She died of fever on the journey here."

"I'm sorry for the loss of your honored servant. Know that the slaves here are at your disposal. You are mistress of this harem now."

Shams ed-Duna admired the striking vista to the south. "Your father told me that you were a child bride, but you shall be living in your husband's house now. Do you like your husband?"

"Yes, I love him very much. I did not always love him, but now it is different."

Shams ed-Duna's eyes shone with pleasure. "Then you are fortunate. I have never cared for any of my husbands. The first was nearly eighty years old when we married. He could not give me children. The second was a commander of my father's armies. Though he was young and vigorous, he refused to believe he could not sire children. He beat me and his other three wives every day for what he saw as our failures. He died two years ago. Now, I marry again."

Curiosity filled her face. "What of my new husband's *kadin*? How long has she been the Sultan's lover?"

Fatima frowned. "Truly, my Sultana, this slave is of no concern to you."

The Sultana put her small, dark hand on Fatima's forearm. "No, you misunderstand me. I do not care how your father feels about her. I wish to meet her, for if she has held the Sultan's attentions and borne him a child, she must know how to please him. Will you arrange for me to speak with her?"

Fatima hesitated. "Yes... if that is what you wish, my Sultana."

"Please, let us not be so formal. Do call me Shams."

"I shall, if you would call me Fatima."

In the evening, the Sultan wed his new bride. The guests celebrated their marriage afterward at the traditional feast. All the queens, princesses, and honored concubines of *al-Qal'at al-Hamra* attended, except for Maryam Sultana.

During the wedding feast, Fatima observed the easy rapport developing between her new stepmother and her father's *kadin*. Shaking her head, she vowed not to worry for her father's domestic situation anymore.

Throughout the previous week, slaves had removed her belongings to Faraj's home. At the conclusion of the wedding feast, while Hasan escorted Shams ed-Duna to his bedchamber, Fatima led Niranjan, Leeta, and Amoda from the palace under a brilliant full moon, which marked their progress. Up ahead, her husband's steward stood outside the door.

"Good evening, my Sultana, the peace of God be with you."

"Thank you for your gracious hail, Marzuq."

They followed him into the house. Faraj waited, leaning against the doorway that led to his inner courtyard. Fatima interlaced her fingers with his. He kissed her hand.

"Welcome home, Fatima."

A surge of elation filled her. Tucking her arm under his, Faraj led her forward.

They dined with Marzuq and Fatima's twin servants attending them. Niranjan stood at the entryway with his back to them, scanning the shadowy patio. Faraj eyed her quizzically, but she shook her head.

"My eunuch is ever vigilant. He does not doubt that you can protect me in our home. I have learned to trust and rely upon him, as my mother once did."

Niranjan glanced over his shoulder briefly. She nodded to him.

At the end of the meal, Faraj went to the *hammam*, while Marzuq led Fatima to her room. He opened the door to a spacious chamber with a carved wooden bed at the center, draped in a silken coverlet. Two windows, covered by lavender damask curtains, faced east and opened on to a garden of fragrant bougainvillea. Between the windows, an inlaid stool stood on legs carved in the shape of a lion's feet. Fatima's chests and wooden jewelry boxes occupied the southern wall. Small torches glowed in brackets at the corners.

A shadow fell over her shoulder. "A message has arrived from the Marinid Sultan for your father. Sultan Abu Yusuf Ya'qub must return home. One of his sons has rebelled against him. We cannot continue without the Marinids."

Fatima turned to Faraj. The frustration at further delay gave an edge of impatience to his voice. His lower half wrapped in a long linen towel, he stood with a parchment crumpled in his hand. It must have been the message about the Marinids. The obvious tension inside him stirred other emotions within her.

Soft wisps of dark hair curled on his chest and forearms. His lean muscled form glistened with water and smelled of rosemary. Though unprepared for the sight of him, she admired his form. Her heart pulsed in a steady rhythm.

Behind him, Amoda asked, "Will you also bathe, Sultana Fatima?"

Dragging her gaze from Faraj, Fatima said, "After we've talked. You may go."

Amoda nodded, and she and Marzuq left.

Faraj said, "I have dismissed your eunuch. He stood stationed at the door. I shall not have him listening while we... are together tonight."

His words made her imaginings run rampant, already stirred by the sight of him undressed except for the towel. Her fingers itched to remove it and reveal him for her appreciation.

He closed the door behind them. "Fatima, we must talk about something else. I need to tell you about the night my parents died."

New tension twisted in her belly. She breathed in a rippling sigh and gestured to the bed. He sank on it, while she sat beside him.

"I've never spoken of this night to another. None of my sisters or half-brother knows the full truth of what I must tell you. I ask that you keep it a secret, for now."

She touched his chest, just above his heart. "Trust me, Faraj."

He grasped her hand for a moment and pressed it against his heated skin. "I do."

One of her satchels rested against the southern wall. She crossed the room, grabbed a towel and a vial, clambered onto the bed, and patted his skin dry. He leaned back against her while she smoothed argan oil on his flesh.

He said, "On that last night at Malaka, my mother came to my room after I had a bad dream. Before she left, she kissed me goodbye. At the door, she turned to favor me with another beautiful smile. I shall never forget how resplendent she looked in her *jubba*, the black and red silk robe trailing gracefully at her feet. A diadem of garnet stones held her *hijab* in place. Gleaming gold and garnet jewels completed her finery. This was how I always wanted to remember the Princess Leila of Ashqilula.

"After my mother closed the door behind her, I listened for the tinkling melody of her bracelets as she left the harem to join my father in the dining hall. Eventually, weariness overcame me and I drifted again, only to experience another nightmare. Rough hands tugged me from my pallet. Bleary-eyed, I watched without comprehending, while my mother helped my younger sisters to dress. My half-brother stood at the side of his mother, the *kadin* Butayna. The sheer terror in her ice-blue eyes drew me to full understanding. The citadel was under attack.

"My mother herded us before her, the *kadin*, and her son following, to an upper floor where the steward kept provisions. My mother and Butayna hid us carefully between the crates. Then the women took each other's hands and moved to the door. Their sudden cries frightened us, but I cautioned my siblings to remain silent. We heard the women scream again. I peeked out behind the crates where we hid. Two men held my mother down, while another man rutted between her legs. One of the marauders entered the room. He said the Hud clan paid them to kill my father and his children, not rape a woman. They let my mother go and left with Butayna, whom they had also ravaged. When my mother was certain they were gone, she called to me.

"I hesitated before taking her hand. She rose, commanding my siblings to remain where they were. I walked in silence behind our mother, stepping over the lifeless bodies of faithful servants; our steward, the cook, even our aged governess. My mother had been quiet while we moved through our ruined home, but she cried out when she entered the dining hall. I followed her gaze, to where they had slit my father's throat. She killed herself after that. I vowed I would never be like her or my father, never surrender to the will and whim of fate. That is why I always tried to control my destiny afterward."

He bowed his head with a shudder. Her heart cleaved for him. She could only guess at how difficult it must have been for him to unburden himself. His naked pain and sadness overwhelmed her. He reached for her, pulled her onto his lap. She could hardly breathe. His arm snaked around her waist. Fatima kissed his brow, his cheek.

He continued, "I needed to tell you this, so you might understand the sort of man you married. My lust for revenge has ruled me. For so long, I have lived only regain everything I lost that night, though I know I cannot. Not truly. Yet, for the first time, I want something more than vengeance. I want a life with you, to be always at your side. I want you to bear my children, to raise them in love and comfort. They must never know the pain I endured as a boy. Give me sons and daughters, Fatima, to heal my wounded heart. Love me and be my wife, always."

The first touch of his lips against her forehead made the breath catch in her throat. The second made her sigh. He trailed light kisses on her brow, his hand caressing the curve of her cheek. She closed her eyes. Their breaths melded together. She met the demand of his lips with fervent desire of her own, returning each kiss and caress with the same eagerness. Urgent hands smoothed down the column of her throat and went to the strings of her *qamis*, setting her blood aflame everywhere he touched. Her shirt slid down. She shrugged her arms free of it.

Cool air stung her skin, before the warm wetness of Faraj's kisses replaced the sharp tingle. A deep ache coursed through her belly. Her hands drifted between their bodies.

"Oh, my Sultana! Oh, a thousand pardons, I beg you."

Fatima opened her eyes, glimpsing the edge of Leeta's skirt, before she darted outside.

Forehead against Faraj's shoulder, she breathed a rippling sigh. She raised her head and looked at him. His gaze held steady. Desire fired his stare. Her body shook in response. He kissed her brow and held her close.

"It's your first night in our house. I'm sorry I ruined it with talk of death and betrayal."

She stroked his skin. "Don't be. I know now how much you trust me, to have spoken with such candor about the past. My heart grieves for you, beloved."

He exhaled a harsh breath. "There's something more I must tell you about the night my parents died. You heard what I said about the Hud rivals of our family?"

She nodded. "Yes, they killed your parents. I know why. They were Grandfather's enemies. He rebelled against them and seized power."

"They aren't the only ones responsible. Others bear the guilt of my parents' deaths." He set her aside and stood, wrapping the loose towel around his waist. "When the Castillan rebels came to Gharnatah eight years ago, I met with Doñ Nuño Gonzalez de Lara in private. He wanted me to press your grandfather's support of his rebellion. He claimed to know something of my parents' deaths."

He paused and turned away. "He told me his father brokered an alliance between the Hud clan and Abu Muhammad of Malaka, who took the governorship when my father died. The Hud family had reason to hate your grandfather. They lost Ishbiliya to the Castillans because of his help and saw their capital city reborn as Christian Sevilla. The Ashqilula wanted my father dead, because he was the governor of the richest territory in the Sultanate by virtue of the Sultan's love for his brother. The Hud and the Ashqilula conspired to kill my family."

Fatima gasped and covered her mouth. "By the Prophet's beard! Then it is true."

Faraj whirled toward her. "What are you talking about?"

"After my mother died, I heard the chieftains Ibrahim and Abu Muhammad talking. Ibrahim said that if he had not helped Abu Muhammad, the old governor of Malaka would still have been alive. I realized later he meant your father."

When he reddened, she rushed on, "Forgive me, I should have told you, but I did not remember it until you spoke now."

"I understand. You had just lost your mother. You had your pain and loss to accept. What could you have known of mine?"

She crossed the room and wrapped her arms around him, her cheek against him. "I know it now and it hurts me as much as my own loss. Your pains are my pains to bear. Your heart has been so burdened."

"It still cries out for vengeance. I have had no one with whom I could share this pain. I've buried it inside me." He grasped her chin and raised it until their gazes met. "Now, you're here."

"And I'll always be by your side, loving you as you are."

His fingers trailed through the mass of curls spilling free down her back. She stood on tiptoe to kiss him again.

She sought only to soothe him with caresses, soft and lingering. He returned her embrace with a silent plea, but she pulled back.

"Fatima...."

Her slim fingers trembled slightly, while she loosened the cord belting her trousers. Stepping out of them and her leather kid slippers, she interlaced her fingers with his. His eyes glowed in the lamplight, his expression candid.

He cupped her cheek. "Are you ready?"

In answer, she removed his towel and drew him to her bed.

In his arms, her heart thrummed with so many emotions. Though inexperienced, she became the aggressor. Her tiny hands roamed over his skin, sharp nails scoring his back while he trailed a line of kisses down the column of her throat. She pushed him on his back, draped her fleshy thigh over his hip, and sought his lips again. He stayed her eager hands.

"You understand because you are a virgin, this first time may be... difficult for you. I would be gentle with you... but I do not think I can be."

"Then do not. I won't turn from you."

His eyes raked over her form, possessive. He kissed her again, as if he could not bear to be apart. His heart thumped steadily beneath hers while he caressed her pale breast. A ragged sigh escaped her throat. His fingers palmed her belly, taut with her burgeoning desire. When his dark, olive-skinned hand settled against her pale flesh, she marveled at the beautiful contrast in their complexions.

"I want to have many beautiful sons and daughters with you, to see your belly filled with our children."

She drew him to her again.

"Touch me," he whispered against her mouth. "Do not be afraid."

Her hands skimmed the bunching muscles of his shoulders and torso, and trailed lower, then up to his arms again. He repeated the motion along the silken smoothness of her pale body. She trembled against him. She scored her nails across the planes of his chest. His fingers swept again to her breast, lingering there when she gasped. They caressed each other in kind. With each slow stroke of his hand, she grew feverish with yearning, marveling at the instinctive passion she possessed. She raised her leg higher along his hip. Her name was a whisper of pleasure on his lips.

Her senses amplified, Fatima became aware of many things all at once – the erratic beating of her heart, Faraj's short panting breaths. Beads of moisture glided down her back. The silken feel of Faraj's lips as they shared long, drugging kisses that seemed to flow together, one after another. The hair on his forearms tickled her thighs.

His brow deeply furrowed, he rolled with her on the bed. She surged against him, but he soothed her with light kisses on her neck and shoulders. Her arms wound about his neck. When he joined their bodies at last, her eyes widened. He stared down at her, her image reflected in his eyes, which glowed like liquid pools of amber. Pleasure-pain filled her when he buried his face in her neck, teeth nipping at her skin. In his throes of their mutual desire, she surrendered.

Chapter 22

A Warrior's Death

Prince Faraj

Gharnatah, al-Andalus: Rabi al-Awwal 674 AH (Granada, Andalusia: September AD 1275)

The Marinid Sultan returned to Gharnatah at the end of summer, the rebellion against him quelled after five months. He declared the *jihad* against Castilla-León with renewed fervor.

On the evening before Faraj left to join the army, he stood alone at the center of the indoor courtyard of his house. A luminous, full, moon shimmered between wispy cloud cover. In a small antechamber just off the courtyard, Fatima busied herself helping Amoda and Leeta make bandages and poultices.

In the week since Fatima's father had announced his army would join the ensuing battle at Istija, she had become subdued. She hardly spoke unless addressed. Faraj woke every morning to find her eyes puffy and swollen. He understood her sentiments and shared them. He did not wish to leave her behind either, but he did not speak of it.

Through the arched entryway of the antechamber, he watched the twins washing their hands in a basin. They also whispered to each other, casting poorly concealed frowns of concern at his wife. Faraj approached and dismissed them with a wave. Fatima averted her gaze as she reached for the basin. He grabbed her, but she smacked his hands away. "Would you prefer to smell like saffron and mint?"

Despite her protestation, he dragged her closer. "I would rather we talked, beloved. I'll be gone in the morning."

"Don't you think I know that?"

He lifted her face for his inspection. Her tears tore at his heart, as they usually did. He pulled her tighter against him. She buried her face in his neck.

His fingers caressed the length of her back along her spine. "You must not fear, beloved. Trust in God."

"I know I cannot go with you." Her voice muffled against his skin, she clung to him. "I won't make that old argument again."

He chuckled. "I thank you. I'd hate for us to quarrel on the eve of my departure."

"And I know you must go. I'll worry for you, but I pray God shall return you to me."

"Then believe it."

"It is my second most important wish."

"What is the first?"

"I hope, upon your happy return, that I may greet you with the news that I carry your child."

"God shall give us children when the time is right."

At night, in their bed, she clung to him in her passion, but a little sadness tainted her desire. He kissed her tears and held her throughout the night, stroking small circles on her pale skin. While she snored lightly, he never slept. He considered the events to come.

Istija belonged to Doñ Nuño Gonzalez, the man whose father conspired with the Ashqilula to destroy Faraj's legacy. Now he would join the Marinids and the Ashqilula, to destroy the Castillans and Doñ Nuño Gonzalez. He recalled how Fatima's father once rightly said that circumstances often changed. How else could Faraj explain that he now allied with a former enemy to fight another?

In the morning when Fatima awoke, she forced a smile. Her effort pleased him, but he knew her true feelings and shared them. They ate dried figs and pomegranates, and drank mint-flavored tisane in his bedroom. Dawn filtered through the lattice windows, heralding the new day.

He said, "I must ready myself for today."

Fatima nodded. She called for Leeta to remove the remnants of their meal and went to her prayer room, a small chamber directly next to her bedroom.

Amoda helped Faraj dress. He put on a long shirt of black chain mail over his *qamis*, followed by a quilted leather tunic. When a link snagged the cotton material, she tugged and salvaged it. A sword belt studded with gold encircled his waist, from which a red leather scabbard hung, gilded along the hilt with diamond-shaped studs. Leather leggings bound the bottoms of his trousers. Tall leather boots replaced the sandals he had used during the summer. He slid a gleaming Damascus steel sword into its scabbard and put on his mittens, chain mail stitched on to the leather gloves.

He said to Amoda, "Hand me the helmet on the stool."

His wife reappeared in the doorway, sniffling. Leeta bowed and left them.

Fatima picked up the helmet, tracing the ornate swirling designs carved into the brass. A chain link covering hung from metal rivets. She tugged at it. "Does this offer enough protection for your head and neck?"

He laughed. "I shall know very soon."

She did not share his levity. Her eyes watered as she gripped the helmet under her arms and breathed a ragged sigh.

He opened his arms. She threw herself into his embrace, despite the chain mail covering him from his neck to his hips.

He kissed her brow and lips. "I must leave. To delay further would anger your father."

She nodded and he took the helmet.

When he exited the room, their household attendants lined the hallway leading out to the courtyard. He passed between them, acknowledging their bows and well wishes with nods.

Marzuq waited at the center of the patio, holding a javelin and green-painted round shield decorated with tassels. "God be with you this day, master."

"May he be with us all today."

Fatima and her twin servants followed him to the entrance. A slave held the reins of his dun-brown Arabian stallion. He mounted the horse. A gelding followed the senior mount.

Fatima stood framed in the horseshoe-shaped doorway, a veil covering the lower half of her face.

Faraj gazed at her for a long time before he spoke. "You are in my heart, beloved, wherever I am."

She said nothing, but her eyes glittered with unshed tears. He kicked his horse into a canter and rode toward the company assembled in the courtyard of *al-Quasaba*.

***

Istija, al-Andalus: Rabi al-Awwal 674 AH (Ecija, Castilla-León: September AD 1275)

The Marinid Sultan, along with Abu Muhammad of Malaka and Crown Prince Muhammad, led the company that covered the plains in four days. As representative of the Sultan's interests in the campaign, Muhammad had command of the entire Gharnati army.

Faraj had charge of a detachment of cavalry. On the first morning of the battle, horns blared through the camp. He led his cavalrymen, riding the same stallion he had brought down the slopes of the hillside at Istija. The gelding remained with other horses at camp in case he needed a second mount. Eyes shielded with his hand, he scanned the scene. Behind the infantry, cavalry prepared to engage Gharnatah. The banners of military orders from the cities of Calatrava, Santiago, and Alcantara fluttered above the valley floor. To counter the enemy's armored knights and infantry, cohorts of Marinid and Gharnati units stood ready. Moorish infantrymen deployed at the front, crossbowmen in the rear, supported on three sides by the cavalry. The Marinids in their padded armor wielded two short spears, compared to the sole javelin or spear each mounted horseman of Gharnatah carried.

Faraj's horse nickered, restless in the lingering summer heat. He patted the beast's head. Green, gold, white, and red pennons and flags flapped loudly in the breeze. Tension reverberated through the ranks.

Sultan Abu Yusuf Ya'qub rode to the forefront of the Marinid cavalry, with his son Prince Abu Zayyan and his advisors at his side. His black stallion, festooned with gold, snorted loudly and other animals shied from the horse. Sunlight glinted off the gold pommel of the Sultan's sword in its scabbard. He scratched at his heavy gray beard, while surveying the valley. He spoke often with his son and the commanders.

Then Fatima's brother appeared with his commanders on the battlefield. Abu Omar, a minister of the *Diwan al-Insha* of Gharnatah rode with them. He looked a few years older than the crown prince did and though he wore simple brown robes and a *shashiya* covering his cropped brown hair, he rode tall and arrow-straight in the saddle. He looked down at the soldiers whom he rode past with narrowed, black eyes and sneered at those who did not bow in acknowledgement of him. A youth bearing a slave collar trailed behind the prideful Abu Omar.

The minister dismounted gingerly with the aid of the slave and then brushed the boy aside with a claw-like hand. Abu Omar steadied himself on his clubfeet and bowed reverently before the Marinid Sultan and Muhammad, before offering his address.

"Here lies the path. Is there one willing to enter it? Who dreads *Jahannam*'s flames, the torments of the damned and longs for the eternal bliss of Paradise, where cooling shades and fountains await? All you who are eager for victory in this our struggle for the Faith, obey the impulse of your heart! Go, armed with hope and confidence to meet salvation and since your cause is noble, there shall be success. Do not delay, for who can assure you of life tomorrow? We never know the time of death, but rest assured, none shall escape the payment of the debt from which no mortals are exempt. If not today, you yet must soon expect to leave this place. The journey before you is difficult and one from which there may be no return. Be up then and ease the hardship of the road! And recollect, the first and most important of pious works is this *jihad*; our sacred war for the maintenance of our Faith. Go at once to defend the soil of al-Andalus. For God loves and rewards all who dedicate themselves to such a fight!"

Cheers erupted throughout the camp. Faraj wondered whether the men praised the orator or the fact that his verbose speech was over. Abu Omar bowed again and withdrew from the battlefield. Faraj did not regret seeing the last of him.

He clutched blue-black prayer beads to his chest in a firm grip and whispered a prayer. "By the blessing of God, I beseech the Prophet, may peace be upon him, to guide my actions on this day. Let the Will of God and not my vengeance, determine this fight for the Faith. And if I should fall, may I greet my forefathers in Paradise."

***

Hours later in the heat of battle, one of the Castillan knights bore down on Faraj, his long sword held high. Faraj's mount sidestepped the charge. He drove his sword deep into the enemy's chest, while a Marinid infantryman impaled the horse with his spear. The beast's hooves kicked out in a reflex move as it fell, catching Faraj's mount, which tumbled and pinned him beneath it.

A frisson of heat swept up his spine. He raised his shield in time to deflect a sword attack. The double-edged weapon cut deep into the leather. Its owner had a hard time withdrawing it. Faraj pushed back against him with his shield arm. The man stumbled backward with a grunt. Faraj scrambled from under the weight of his felled horse and struggled regain his footing without putting too much weight on his battered left leg.

His adversary carried a kite-shaped shield half the length of his body. Familiar heraldic devices covered the red leather hide. The man's eyes glittered like hard emeralds beneath his helmet, which partially obscured his face. With a guttural cry, he leapt on Faraj. They rolled together on the ground. Knocking him aside, Faraj sprang to his feet at the same time the other man did. His agility startled Faraj, for when they tussled on the ground, his adversary's brass helmet came off, and revealed thick, graying hair and a weather-beaten face Faraj recognized.

Doñ Nuño Gonzalez said, "I'll not be so easy to kill as the others you have fought. I have more to fight for than most, prince of Gharnatah."

The old Castillan threw the ball of dirt hidden in the palm of his right hand at Faraj's face, while stabbing with his left hand. In a shower of dust, his blade bit deep into Faraj's shoulder. Cursing, Faraj pivoted on his right leg, crying outside as the muscles in his left quivered. Then Doñ Nuño's sword sliced across his back and Faraj screamed like a man possessed. The old man laughed and circled him, tossing his weapon from one hand to the other.

Faraj rubbed his eyes and steadied himself. "Fight me fairly!"

"Why should I do that?"

With that, his enemy lunged forward again, but this time their steel swords clanged together. Doñ Nuño looked surprised for a moment, but continued his attack. He lunged to the right. Faraj blocked him. For an old man, he proved cunning and quick. In the clash of their swords, his blows had the power to shatter the arms of a much younger man. He drove Faraj back into the fray.

"Is this enough for you, whelp?" he taunted.

"Hardly," Faraj muttered. Teeth gritting together, he dove at Doñ Nuño again. Driven backward, the Castillan did not see the dead body of a foot soldier lying prone behind him. He tumbled over, reeling backward in a crumpled heap, his sword knocked loose by the jarring motion. Faraj ripped off his helmet, towering over the warrior who glared at him.

"I have waited for this day, when you would pay the price of your father's folly. Now I dread it."

Don Nuño cursed and spat. "What you want does not matter. Our destiny was preordained when my father aided others in the killing of your family. We are enemies."

"We were not always so, my lord de Lara."

Don Nuño lunged for his discarded blade and held the sword high above his head. "The past is the past. Defend yourself, Prince Faraj. I shall not hesitate to kill you."

Faraj donned his helmet again. He and Don Nuño circled each other once more in a dance of death. Many emotions warred inside him. He faced a man with whom he had shared the kiss of peace in the past, yet whose father had procured an arrangement with the Ashqilula that resulted in his parents' death. He kept the latter thought in mind, as he defended himself against Don Nuño's powerful blows, delivered with the strength of a man Faraj's age.

Steel clashed together, but the Castillan weapon wobbled slightly. Within minutes, Don Nuño tired, his breath coming in short, shallow pants.

Faraj shouted, "Stop this now! I don't want to kill an old man!"

Don Nuño seemed past caring, while he rained down blows. Faraj's sword arm grew weary in his defense. Don Nuño had the dexterity that allowed him to fight with both hands. He wielded his weapon in powerful strokes. A wheezing breath escaped his lips.

Faraj drove him back, slashing at his arms. Bloodied, Don Nuño wore no mail underneath his tunic, just padding. Awed, Faraj marveled at the bravery of the old warrior he must kill.

Don Nuño's labored breathing continued. When Faraj brought his scimitar down in a ferocious movement, Don

Nuño's blade met the thrust, but his weapon warbled and bent. The old warrior threw down his shield.

He sagged on his knees, crumpled hair falling over his eyes. "Do... not hesitate. I would not. Give me a warrior's death. I have earned it."

One last time, Faraj swung his weapon in an arcing swoop. The blade sliced through bone and sinew. Doñ Nuño tumbled forward, his severed, grizzled head landing at Faraj's feet.

***

Sultan Abu Yusuf Ya'qub retired from the bloodied battlefield outside Istija at midday. His son Abu Zayyan ordered the heads of the Castillan dead cut off and counted.

Faraj withdrew to his tent alone. He stabbed his sword into the ground, sank to the floor, and wept. Doñ Nuño's father had escaped punishment for his part in the murder of his parents, but Faraj took no pleasure in the death of the son.

The call to prayer resounded through the camp. He roused himself from his torpor, completed his ablutions, and performed the act of worship. He mumbled the words. For the first time, they did not comfort his wearied heart and head.

In the evening, Crown Prince Muhammad summoned him to dine with the Gharnati commanders. Beforehand, Faraj saw the camp physician, who cleaned and bandaged his wounds as a barrier against infection. When Faraj arrived for dinner and stepped inside the tent, Fatima's brother sat in the midst of his men. He grinned at Faraj and beckoned him forward. He pointed to a wooden box. "It is a present for the Sultan."

"What is it?"

Muhammad laughed and threw back his leonine head. "Open it and see."

Faraj lifted the cloth cover. Heady camphor, saffron, and pepper assailed him. Doñ Nuño's sightless eyes came into view. He dropped the box, provoking more laughter from Muhammad, as the grayed head rolled out. Stumbling outside, Faraj held his belly and vomited.

Chapter 23

The Breach

Prince Faraj

Gharnatah, al-Andalus: Shawwal 676 AH (Granada, Andalusia: March AD 1278)

The crackle and hiss of steam emanated from the brazier in Faraj's bedchamber. The acrid scent from hot coals drifted through the room. Dim lanterns cast long shadows on the walls.

In the darkness of the room, he stroked soft circles on his wife's silken shoulder. Her arm encircled his chest. A mass of her curly hair blanketed him. Her sighs warned she was not asleep, though the water clock indicated it would be dawn in two hours.

"You are deep in thought tonight, Fatima. Is something wrong, my beloved?"

"No, husband."

He found her face in the gloom and cupped her chin. "If you mean to convince me, you do a poor job."

For weeks now, she appeared pensive and withdrawn. Whenever he questioned her moods, she dismissed his concerns.

Now she rolled away from him. "For nearly three years, I have shared this bed with you. We have known every joy as husband and wife, except that of children. What if there is something wrong with me, which makes it impossible for me to have a baby? I am twenty years old now. My sister Muna in al-Jaza'ir is already a mother of twins and she's younger than me."

Her words ended on a sob. He snuggled against her, somewhat relieved by the source of her disquiet. "We cannot despair, beloved. There is no reason to think we cannot have children. We must have faith that when the time is right, we shall have the child we both desire."

"Something must be wrong." She turned in the circle of his arms. "I asked Marzuq why your concubines don't have children. He said they drink a special cup of tisane in the morning, but I do not. What explanation can there be for me?"

He held her face in his hands, smoothing the moisture on her cheeks away. "Fatima, if you truly fear something prevents you from conceiving, let us consult a midwife."

"If she should find something is wrong, what shall we do?"

"We shall try again. I want a baby born of our love, too. I believe when the time is right, God shall give us the children we want."

He kissed her soothingly, but she responded with passion. Later when she finally dozed, a knock at the door stirred him. Fatima shifted when Faraj rose from the bed. Marzuq greeted him with an urgent summons from the Sultan.

Faraj washed, dressed, and went to the council chambers of the *Diwan al-Insha*, the *mashwar*, which was west of the throne room. In a stark chamber with two windows, a quarter of the size of the throne room, the ministers gathered in a tight circle around the Sultan. The men argued while their leader, the *Hajib* Ibn Ali, struggled for a voice above the fray. Umar, the *Shaykh al-Ghuzat*, entered the already crowded space along with some of the commanders of the Marinid regiments, the Volunteers of the Faith. He abased himself before Muhammad II.

The Sultan waved him off. "No time for such nonsense, Umar. Now stand up, meet my eyes, and tell me that you knew nothing about this breach at Malaka."

Faraj's heart pounded. Who had invaded Malaka?

Umar addressed Fatima's father. "I swear upon the blessed ninety-nine names of our God, Sultan Abu Yusuf Ya'qub sent me no warning of his intention to take Malaka. Let me help you resolve this crisis."

Muhammad II said, "Then ride to Malaka. If the Marinid warriors there accept only your authority, I charge you with the task of entering that city and securing it for the Nasrids. By your actions, you shall prove whether my sentiments about you are misplaced. Those are my orders."

Umar sketched a stiff bow and departed with his officers.

After he left the chamber, Ibn Ali said to his master. "The *Shaykh al-Ghuzat* is in an unenviable position. It is certain no man may serve two masters with faith. Do you trust Umar to secure Malaka in your name?"

Muhammad II replied, "You and my honored father taught me to trust in no one, but our God."

While the Sultan spoke with his ministers, Faraj garnered an understanding of the events that had transpired from several, separate conversations occurring in the room. The governor of Malaka had suddenly fallen ill a month ago, which led to the suspicion that someone had poisoned him. By the Will of God, he had recovered. Fearing for the security of his city, Abu Muhammad had begged Marinid assistance to defend Malaka against Muhammad II. The Marinids agreed and intervened on behalf of the Ashqilula against the Sultan, their ally.

The Sultan looked at Ibn Ali. "I wish to know two things. One - did we arrange the assassination of Abu Muhammad of Malaka?"

Ibn Ali shook his head. "If he was poisoned, it is unlikely that any of our agents carried out the deed. Not one of them has been able to get close to him for years. The Ashqilula family has enjoyed success in rooting out our spies and agents, as we have theirs."

Thinking of Fatima's role in these intrigues, Faraj knew that was not entirely true.

Muhammad II frowned. "Regrettable. Now tell me this - what would we need to take Malaka? Have you and the minister of war assessed the men, the armaments, the weapons of siege we need?"

Ibn Ali struggled with his speech. He offered the Sultan only a blank stare. The other ministers murmured among themselves or averted their eyes.

Muhammad II pounded his fists on the chair. "As old women you are, cowering at the thought of such a venture when you should be planning my victory! Malaka has its weaknesses. We have but to find and exploit them. Assemble my commanders. We go to make war on the Ashqilula!"

Faraj struggled to keep his face impassive. The governorship of Malaka, which had eluded him for so long – he did not dare finish the thought. His uncle the old Sultan had enjoyed no success in his half-hearted attempt to take the city. Why should his son fare any better? Especially when the Marinids had involved themselves and taken the side of the Ashqilula.

Muhammad II dismissed his *Diwan* and gestured for Faraj to walk with him. "It is dangerous business we are about, cousin. In his youth, my late father preferred the solution of the sword, but in his later years, he used diplomacy to achieve his conquests. I rely on both the sword and words evenhandedly. Today, you shall serve as my diplomat, but later, I may call upon your sword. I am sending you and my heir in advance of the army."

Faraj replied, "I am your man, in whatever you may ask of me."

"Yes, I do not doubt that."

The Sultan's cheeks reddened before he continued. "We have not always agreed upon my course of action, but your loyalty has remained steadfast throughout all our travails."

He referred to their argument during the conquest of Madinah Antaqirah. Smiling at him, Faraj said, "You shall always have my loyalty."

They adjourned to the Sultan's chamber. Fatima awaited them in the ethereal glow of pre-dawn with her father's Sultana at her side.

Shams ed-Duna bowed before the Sultan. "Nur al-Sabah told me what has happened at Malaka. Is it for certain, husband? Is it truly my father who has done this thing?"

Muhammad II answered, "It is certain, for who else could order Maghribi warriors to annex Andalusi soil, except your father? We have not heard of a coup in his capital. He remains in control of his government and the actions of his warriors."

The Sultana replied, "I don't doubt you, but I cannot accept that my father would do such a thing. How could he jeopardize the future of his own grandson and our happy union?"

The Sultan took his wife's slim dark hands in his olive-skinned, larger ones. "Nothing that your father or anyone else could do would alter our happiness, or the love I feel for our son."

While the Sultan spoke with his wife, Faraj embraced Fatima. "Why did you wake so early?"

"I missed you beside me. Marzuq told me of my father's summons. Then the Sultana Shams came to our house, seeking reassurances. She explained what she had heard."

Fatima's father hugged his wife and kissed her hands.

Faraj said, "It's obvious the Sultana need not worry. Your father's regard for her is secure."

Fatima nodded. "Yes, but he does not love her. She does not love him either. She has confided in me. They enjoy each other, yet he remains in love with the *kadin*."

Kissing her brow, Faraj murmured, "Return to our home, we shall talk later."

Fatima nodded and took Sultana Shams ed-Duna's hand. They bid the Sultan farewell and retreated across the harem courtyard.

Faraj observed, "Your wife seems a worthy woman."

Muhammad II nodded. "Shams ed-Duna ranks high among the best of women."

***

Princess Fatima

In the midmorning, Fatima returned to her house. The screeching voices of her husband's concubines echoed from the harem on the other side of the residence. Not an odd occurrence, but she could not recall when she had ever heard any of the women up before noon.

She stood in the central courtyard, suffused in sunlight. With two years of hard work, she had transformed the large open space, which formerly held only a fountain at its center, into a replica of her father's garden. Pale blue flowers, rosemary bushes, rows of crown daisies, star thistles, honeysuckle, and spiny broom grew. In the center, a tiny pavilion replaced the old fountain. She hoped someday her children would take delight in playing in this place.

Under the pavilion, she leaned against a marble column with a sigh. Children. The word filled her with such angst and fear. She palmed her belly, still as maiden-flat as when she had first made love to Faraj. Tears welled up in her eyes.

The screams from the harem reached a crescendo, louder than before, if that were possible. She found the Nubian Hayfa and her counterpart, the little mouse named Samara tolerable. The concubine Baraka was not. Her eyes were like emeralds, green and hard.

Fatima returned to her room. Leeta knelt, looking under the heavy bed frame and the multicolored carpet covering the floor, muttering to herself.

Bemused, Fatima tapped her on the shoulder. "What are you doing, clucking like a worried mother hen?"

"Remember your necklace of black opals? It is so long it reaches your hips," Leeta replied in a voice strained with exasperation. "You wore it last week when you and the master dined with the Sultan and his wife. I saw it on your pile of clothing the next morning. I remembered telling my sister not to mix it in with the clothes she laundered for that day. Now, I cannot find it. I have looked under every fixture of this room. Your cedar closet, under the chest where you keep the other valuables from your bridal trousseau... everywhere, my Sultana."

Fatima tapped the gilded cage, where the kite trilled noisily. "Perhaps this fat bird swallowed it. She has been rather plump lately."

Leeta's groans and sighs showed no appreciation for her levity.

Fatima took her hand and helped her stand. "It's only a necklace, one among several other pieces of mine. Do stop making yourself so frantic. The loss of a trinket doesn't concern me."

She went to the window directly across the room. A cool breeze filtered through the lattice, stirring the lavender curtains. "I have greater concerns now."

Leeta joined her at the window. "What is it, my Sultana?"

She unburdened her worries to the loyal servant who had been at her side for more than ten years. Her sympathy was palpable, but Leeta had doubts about her theories.

"My Sultana, there is no reason to think you cannot conceive. Your menses are regular each month. There has been no change in your cycle since you began it five years ago."

"How would you know that?"

"Amoda records the days of your cycle. It is how she ensures we always have enough cotton bands for you to wear each month. In addition, Marzuq insists upon a

251

strict accounting of all household linen since it is so expensive, including the purpose of ordering such materials. Amoda estimates how much cotton she needs for the use of harem women, including you, the concubines, and all female servants."

Fatima blinked rapidly, somewhat embarrassed that her husband's steward knew so much about her menstrual cycle. She said, "Faraj suggested we seek the help of a midwife."

"If you wish it, my Sultana. I shall make inquiries on your behalf, discreetly."

Fatima dismissed Leeta. Alone, she leaned against the adjoining wall, but someone knocked at her door.

When she opened the door, Marzuq bowed. "Forgive the intrusion, my Sultana, but I thought perhaps... my master's women, they have been fighting for most of the morning."

She patted the steward's arm. "I shall see to them."

His pale face lit up with grateful appreciation.

The concubines lived in opulent accommodations with silken cushions lining the walls and brightly colored pillows strewn about the central chamber. Four separate apartments branched off from the main room, affording each *jarya* some privacy in her own sleeping space. Musk and sandalwood drifted through the open doorway.

Baraka hurled a gilded tray across the room. Her aim was poor or she would have hit an outraged Hayfa square in the face. Samara cowered behind a cushion in the corner. The tray clattered to the ground.

Fatima clasped her hands together. "Ladies, why disturb the peace of my husband's house so early in the morning?"

"I did not start this!" Hayfa's voice thickened with insinuation.

"Then who did?" Fatima looked between two alabaster faces and a dark one. All the women refused to answer her query. Baraka's expression reddened with hauteur and menace.

Then the Nubian shouted, "You should banish Baraka. She is nothing but a troublemaker!"

Fatima turned to Hayfa. "Why do you suggest that? She is my husband's property."

When none of the slaves replied, Fatima turned on Baraka. "Perhaps, I should tell my husband to sell you. Of his concubines, you are the most disagreeable."

"He shall never let me go! I am still the favorite."

"Truly? When was the last time he called you to his bed?"

A small thrill of satisfaction settled in Fatima's stomach. The murderous gleam in Baraka's hard eyes bolstered her suspicion that Faraj no longer slept with any of them. He was often at Fatima's side, even on the nights of her cycle when he simply held her and rubbed her back, easing her slight cramping.

The little mouse hiding in the corner said, "Baraka is a jealous fool, jealous of you. That is why she stole your jewelry!"

Fatima gasped, but Samara did not stop there. "She knows the master loves you and always shares your bed at night. She took a necklace from your room last week. She said you would not miss it, but we told her to put it back."

"Bitch! I'll kill you for betraying me." Baraka advanced on her counterpart with outstretched hands.

Fatima grabbed her and whirled her around.

She struggled like a maniac. "Let me go. Barren cow! If you don't quicken with his child soon, Faraj shall tire of you."

Fatima slapped her hard across the face. Baraka reeled from the blow and she cupped her reddened cheek.

Fatima commanded, "Samara, fetch my necklace, you have nothing to fear."

When Samara returned with the black opals dangling between her fingertips, Fatima took the jewels and looked at Baraka. The concubine swallowed audibly.

Fatima whispered, "There is a penalty for theft in Gharnatah. Under Sharia law, a thief's hand is cut off."

A spasm of fear crossed Baraka's face, though her chin jutted defiantly. Just then, Leeta's voice resonated through the harem. "My Sultana, where are you?"

"I'm here, with the *jawari*," Fatima called over her shoulder, her gaze still on Baraka.

Leeta entered the chamber. "Marzuq told me that you had come here, but I couldn't believe it. Oh, you've found your necklace! Where was it?"

Fatima turned to her. "The only place you did not look – inside the chest with the other jewels. I have so many pieces, you could not have seen it buried among the others."

Leeta gaped pop-eyed, but Fatima dismissed the question in her gaze and held the piece up to the light. "In truth, I don't like this very much. I brought it here in the hopes one of the women might like it. Baraka does. I believe she should have it."

Collective expressions of shock glazed over the concubines' faces.

Fatima continued. "It would be unfair to give Baraka something and not the other two. Leeta, bring the chest and I shall look for two more necklaces."

Leeta's quizzical frown slowly faded as she bowed and left the room. Fatima held out the opals to Baraka.

After some time, the *jarya*'s fingers closed on the necklace. "This changes nothing between us, Sultana."

Fatima clasped her hands together again. "I didn't expect it would. I'll keep the peace of my husband's house by any means." She paused and eyed each of the concubines in turn. "However, you should never mistake my kindness for weakness. You would not live long enough to regret it."

Chapter 24
Stalemate

Prince Faraj

Gharnatah, al-Andalus: Dhu al-Hijja 676 AH - Muharram 677 AH (Granada, Andalusia: May AD 1278)

The latest siege of Malaka had ended in a stalemate after only two months. On the seventh day of the month of *Hajj* to Makkah, the wearied and bloodied Sultan's army walked and rode into Gharnatah, and up the Sabika hill. From the battlements of *al-Quasaba*, Fatima and her father watched their progress.

Near the end of the cortege, two soldiers guided a horse-drawn cart. Inside, Faraj's body lay prone under a white cloth.

Fatima clutched her father's hand. He squeezed hers in return. "My physician shall examine him. Do not fear for his life. He shall survive."

The Gharnati warriors brought the cart into the citadel. Fatima followed her father from the battlements down winding steps into the open-air courtyard. Panting, the team of horses slowed on command, their gray coats gleaming with sweat. They drew abreast just when she reached the last step.

She reached over the side of the cart and touched her husband's face. He was pale and beads of perspiration dotted his brow and cheeks. New growth sprouted from his unkempt beard. He moaned in a stupor, head lolling, the only signs that he still lived.

255

Her father's bodyguards hefted Faraj's lean frame on the bier in the cart and carried him to the palace. At the Sultan's command, the men laid him on their master's bed. Her father's personal physician waited to examine him. The doctor washed his hands in a ceramic bowl, the scent of rosemary rising up from the hot water. He lifted the sheet and revealed a yellow-tinged, putrid-smelling area near the groin. The flesh cracked at the edges. An Ashqilula swordsman had stabbed Faraj during the siege of Malaka. Fatima's eyes misted, but she held back a shuddering sob. Her father placed a comforting hand on her shoulder.

The physician turned to them. "I'll inspect the wound, clean and dress it. The pus has set in, because he did not receive treatment immediately. He burns with fever, another mark of the infection. Bloodletting may reduce it. The wound is close to the groin, but not life threatening. With care and medicine for the infection, he shall live."

Fatima asked, "What about poison? Is there a risk the blade that wounded him carried poison? The Ashqilula use such tactics in battle."

"Most poisons applied to a sword or an arrow act fast. He would have died. Now, I must tend to him without delay."

Her father drew her away. "Trust my physician."

Fatima nodded and followed him to the throne room, where the *Diwan* awaited him. She sat behind the latticed *purdah* with Shams ed-Duna and watched while her father gestured toward his *Hajib*, Ibn Ali.

The prime minister said, "We have made contact with al-Hakam pirates at Mayurqa, my Sultan. Their representative shall meet with us in ten days' time."

Fatima turned with a puzzled frown to Shams, who put a finger over her lips in a bid for quiet.

Ibn Ali continued, "Forgive me, my Sultan, but we are uncertain about your intentions. How can the clan of al-Hakam, the rulers of a tiny island in the White Sea aid us in a war against the Marinids?"

The Sultan answered. "I do not intend to declare war against them."

Muttering and grumbling rose to fill the room. He called for silence.

He continued, "The Marinids are powerful. I cannot risk open warfare against them. Along the frontier of their eastern border with al-Tunisiyah, they have adopted a defensive posture to counter Hafsid raids for nearly a year now. Most of their army is concentrated there, with other regiments in the capital and on the coast. I need to convince Sultan Abu Yusuf Ya'qub that he cannot hold the ports of al-Andalus when his own domestic situation requires attention."

Understanding filled Ibn Ali's gaze. "That is why you enlist the clan of Hakam, my Sultan? You shall use the pirates to harass the Marinids at their home bases."

The Sultan nodded. "The pirates of Mayurqa have plagued the coasts for years. Abu Yusuf Ya'qub's treaty with Aragón nearly ended their raids, as he could rely upon his allies in Aragón with their ships to defend the White Sea coast. Now the treaty is over and the pirates have returned. They do not care who they raid. They fight for anyone who pays them the most. If they attack the Marinid Sultan in force, he must recall his warriors to defend his port cities. He cannot risk leaving the capital undefended. He cannot pull back his warriors from the borders of al-Tunisiyah. Instead, he must recall the Marinid forces he has garrisoned at Malaka."

Ibn Ali said, "The pirates are ruthless turncoats. What can stop them from eventually attacking us?"

The Sultan smiled wryly. "God has truly blessed me with many daughters. I shall offer the chieftain of al-Hakam my third daughter Alimah for his bride. I shall gain a pirate for my son in-law, but also ensure the protection of my country."

The council members murmured their approval.

After he dismissed the *Diwan*, the Sultan crossed the chamber and went behind the latticed *purdah.* He helped his Sultana and Fatima stand.

Shams ed-Duna said, "My father has agents in Gharnatah. You must move your forces with discretion and speed if you hope to surprise the Marinid warriors."

The Sultan kissed her brow. "Everything shall happen according to our plan. You must believe, whatever happens, you and our son shall be safe. Your father shall never know it is your dower that finances the pirates at Mayurqa."

Shams ed-Duna nodded. "It matters little to me. You are my husband. A wife owes her duty to her husband, not to a father who would break oaths with his sworn ally or endanger his family through his treachery. You have my loyalty, my Sultan."

He raised her hand to his lips. "Truly, you are the best among wives."

Fatima smiled at their easy accord. Linked arm in arm with Shams ed-Duna, they followed the Sultan from the throne room.

***

In the following three weeks, Faraj recovered from his wound. When Fatima insisted he keep to his room and rest, he resented it. He chafed at taking sponge baths, rather than relaxing in the warmth of the *hammam* and complained about how much he missed riding his horse through the gorges and valleys of the capital every day.

When her father's physician visited, he seemed pleased with Faraj's progress. The doctor told Fatima her husband was well enough to resume most of his normal activities that did not require great exertion. Though he walked with some stiffness on his left side, Faraj healed. Laughter and passion filled Fatima's bedchamber at night, as she took the lead in their lovemaking.

Towards the end of the month, Amoda came to Fatima with a wide smile. "You're late."

A giddy chortle escaped her lips. She held out a series of bound parchments. Turning to the last page, she said, "See the notations for the previous month of Dhu al-Qa`da? Here was the first day of your last menses. I have been tracking your cycle for five years. For the first time, you're three days late."

Understanding dawned. Fatima palmed her belly. "Do you think it is possible? I could be pregnant?"

Amoda nodded and laughed as Fatima hugged her.

Five days passed where she spun fantasies of what her baby would look like. Would it be a boy or a girl? She nursed her tiny secret, offering silent prayers to God. If Faraj noticed her improved mood, he did not comment. He seemed very happy to have her smiles by day and caresses at night. Her secret remained hidden.

At the end of the week, she awoke and leaned on one elbow to watch dawn's light play on Faraj's face while he slept. He opened his eyes and caught her staring.

He nuzzled her cheek. "Was I snoring like you do?"

"You were snoring, but that's not why I was staring. Do you know how handsome you are?"

"You're in a playful mood this morning. You have been for days now. I should stay here with you all day instead of meeting with your father and brother."

"You told me Father wanted to discuss the recent Castillan naval movements off the coast. You should see him. I'll be waiting for you when you come back."

His warm kiss entreated her consideration, but she gave him a light push out of the bed.

Leaning back into the familiar comfort of her pillow, she admired his lean, hairy legs as he walked away. Yet, she could not linger in the bed any more than Faraj could. She had arranged yesterday to meet with Marzuq for a weekly review of household accounts. She stood, stretched her arms above her head, and then froze as a familiar dull ache tugged at her back. Instantly she knew there would be no child.

"My Sultana, are you awake?"

Leeta's voice drifted beyond the doorway. Fatima blinked back tears and composed herself. "Enter."

"Good morning, my Sultana, I hope you slept well." Leeta's voice trailed off.

"I did. Thank you." Fatima's hand on her empty belly shook. Her mind screamed denial. A tiny frown marred Leeta's face, but Fatima did not have the heart to share her disappointment with anyone. She had harbored so much hope for such a fleeting thing.

How could losing something she never had cause so much pain?

***

On the first of Muharram, Fatima attended her father's gathering in the palace gardens, Music and children's laughter filled the air. Mothers chided rambunctious older children and soothed fussy, younger ones. Shams ed-Duna and the *kadin*'s children played together, laughing with their plump baby arms held out to their mothers. Shams ed-Duna balanced her son on her hip, twirling around while he giggled. The *kadin* stood next to Shams ed-Duna, helping her eldest daughter Zaynab on to a child-sized, wooden horse, festooned with a silken, padded saddle. Zaynab kept sliding backward on the colorful material whenever Nur al-Sabah left her unattended.

When Shams ed-Duna set her little prince down, on pudgy legs, he ambled to where the *kadin*'s second daughter Fayha sat with Fatima's youngest sister, Nadira. She spun a brightly colored metal top for the younger children's amusement. Nur al-Sabah looked on, stroking the rounded bump underneath her robe. Her two daughters, Zaynab and Faridah, were the mirror image of their mother with wavy blonde hair and her eye color.

Pain knifed through Fatima's heart. After consultation with many midwives, none could find the cause for her failure. She stared at the children, wishing desperately for one of her own.

Faridah took hesitant first steps, moving very unsteadily toward Fatima. She tugged at her skirts and stared, two fingers in her mouth. The *kadin* reached for her.

Fatima said, "Truly, I don't mind. She is very beautiful. She does not look like Father. Only his children with my mother resemble him."

The *kadin* sat nearby with her daughter on her lap. "I believe, Sultana Fatima, this is the first time you have acknowledged my daughter."

Fatima nodded. "She's a sister to me, Zaynab, too. At first, I resented them. How could I feel that way about any child? Especially, my own sisters."

She turned to Nur al-Sabah. "May I hold her?"

The *kadin* placed Fayha in Fatima's lap. The child gingerly pressed her fingertips to Fatima's nose and then her lips. Fatima playfully nipped at her chubby fingers and her little sister chortled, showing two budding upper teeth. Then Fayha poked at Fatima's eye. Nur al-Sabah snatched her away. "Naughty girl!"

Pools of tears welled up in the child's eyes. Nur al-Sabah summoned her body slave, who took a whimpering Fayha away. Fatima swiped at her eyes.

The *kadin* said, "I'm sorry, my Sultana."

Fatima sniffled and patted Nur al-Sabah's left hand. "Please, she's just a child, she didn't know better. You are very lucky to have her and her sister."

Nur al-Sabah slid her fingers from under her grasp and covered Fatima's hand instead. "Motherhood is a great joy, my Sultana. One day you shall come to know it. Believe, for God hears and answers all prayers."

A tear trickled down Fatima's cheek. "What if His answer is no?"

***

Fatima and Faraj returned to their house in the late evening. While he bathed, Amoda prepared her for bed. A shawl around her shoulders, Fatima walked to her bedroom window, overlooking the garden. She flung the lattice open.

Behind her, Faraj said, "Beloved, please close that window. The torches die down too early in the wind."

His arms slipped around her waist, his fingers interlaced with hers, pressed against her empty belly. "Your hands are icy. Come to bed and let me warm you tonight."

When she turned around, the smile on his lips faded. "Beloved, what troubles you?"

"We cannot remain married any longer."

He paled and stared without blinking.

She pushed at him. "Did you hear me? I want our marriage dissolved. It is finished."

His arms dropped to his side.

"I love you too much to consign you to a childless union with me." She crossed her arms over her chest. "Our marital contract states if you take another wife, I can divorce you and reclaim my dowry. You should not suffer because of me. If you tell Father you're divorcing me because I am barren, you can keep the dowry and find a wife to give you the sons and daughters you want."

He gripped her arms and shook her. "What are you saying? You think I would let you go because of your foolish fears?"

"You refuse to accept the truth. I cannot give you children and if I cannot do so, my heart shall break along with yours. Who would know you lived if you have no sons, no children to inherit? I won't condemn you to that fate."

He released her, panting with exertion. "So, you would leave me instead?"

She took his hand. "No, I give you a chance at happiness."

He pulled away. "Who says I am unhappy? That is your claim! In your usual manner, you make a decision that affects both our lives and expect me to follow it. Well, I won't, not this time."

"I won't change my mind. I want a divorce!"

His dark eyes bored into hers. "You must be mad to think I would ever let you go!"

He crossed the room. The bedroom door slammed shut behind him.

She sank on the carpet and buried her head in her hands.

Chapter 25
A Great Divide

Prince Faraj

Gharnatah, al-Andalus: Muharram 677 AH (Granada, Andalusia: May AD 1278)

Faraj avoided Fatima until the next evening, when the moon rode high in the moonlit heavens. Jasmine flowers scented the air as the sentries called the hour of midnight. He returned to his house, carrying a rolled parchment bearing the Sultan's seal, the red wax thick like congealed blood.

The Castillan navy had attacked the port city of al-Jazirah al-Khadra. The *Shaykh al-Ghuzat* Umar defended the city and needed reinforcements. The Sultan gave Faraj command of three cavalry detachments. The men were to ride at dawn and re-take the port.

Marzuq greeted him at the door. Weary, he decided to forgo the *hammam* and went to his bedchamber. He plodded across the darkened room. In the bed, he rolled on his side.

"Faraj, what happened? You've been gone all day."

Fatima's voice filled the chamber. Her hand alighted on his arm. "I feared you would not come to me again. I waited for you."

Groaning, he rolled away. "If you wish to speak the same nonsense, I refuse to listen to more foolishness."

When she sighed, he continued. "Go back to sleep. We'll talk in the morning."

"No, tell me what's happened. I know you were... upset with me last night. Then, Marzuq said my father called you to his side this morning. Please, talk to me."

Sighing, he swung his legs to the floor. When he told her of his orders, she moaned as if in pain. "Must we be apart again?"

He sucked in a breath at her familiar touch. "You ask that when you wanted a divorce just last night?"

She sobbed. "I'm afraid."

He shook his head, wishing himself immune to her moods. "You must not fear, Fatima. I shall be safe. Umar defends the citadel along the beachhead against the Castillan siege. With reinforcements, al-Jazirah al-Khadra shall hold."

Her head drooped on his shoulder, her fingers threading in the wiry wisps of hair on his chest.

He closed his eyes and inhaled the fragrant jasmine that infused her hair. "You should go to your chamber."

"Don't send me away now, not when we need each other. I only want to be with you tonight." Her fingers curled at his waistband.

"You think making love can solve the problems between us?"

"Faraj, please do not do this. Don't turn from me now."

"Me, reject you?" His reply echoed in the darkness of the room. "You come to me demanding a divorce last night and now, accuse me of rejecting you? You have hurt me more deeply than anyone could. Still, my love for you burns brighter than the sun. You cannot stay here tonight, you should not have come."

"Would you ride out in anger, not knowing when we shall see each other again?"

He turned and hauled her up against him, shaking her. Her anguished cry stopped him. "I love you, Faraj. I have only ever loved you. Can't you see that I'd do anything for love of you, even leave you, so you might have your heart's desire?"

"You are my heart's desire!"

He kissed her wildly, a need to punish her spurring him on. She encouraged his savagery. When his teeth nipped at her jaw line, her moans reverberated through the room. When he pinned her beneath him, she welcomed him. Her limbs held him prisoner and her nails raked his back and arms, demanding. Their joining was a fiery death, both of them consumed.

In the morning, he went to the *hammam*. He winced when the fragrant water stung tiny cuts on his arms and back. Fatima had drawn blood in her passion. When he returned to the chamber, she was awake and helped him with his garments. He kissed the hands that had tortured and wounded him the night before, while she stared in silence.

He whispered, "Too often we've stood upon this point already. I leave you to wonder what shall become of me. Keep the peace of my house. Know that I love you and believe that I shall return to you, always."

Fatima nodded and embraced him, her soft sobs muffled in his padded tunic. He kissed her with all the love inside his heart and let her go. He did not look back, lest courage fail him.

***

Princess Fatima

Gharnatah, al-Andalus: Safar 677 AH (Granada, Andalusia: July AD 1278)

Fatima endured seven weeks of bitter silence, during which she received no word from Faraj. Her father shared the daily dispatches on the reclamation of the port at al-Jazirah al-Khadra and the defense against the Castillans. Still, no word arrived of her husband's fate. She retreated into a shell of suffering, filled with self-recrimination. The remembrance of his final words offered little comfort in the emptiness of her bedchamber at night.

On the first cool day of the summer, Sultana Shams ed-Duna insisted she accompany her and the *kadin* Nur al-Sabah to the souk of Gharnatah. Her stepmother refused Fatima's initial rebuff.

After prayers, the trio, in the company of Niranjan, the palace guard and some servants, took the route down the Sabika hill and across the bridge of the *Hadarro* River. The *Qaysariyya* marketplace spread across the dun-brown plain at the south of the city, extending from the foot of the Sabika hill to the red brick walls of Gharnatah. Jewish and Christian merchants plied their trade alongside their Moorish counterparts, the local goldsmiths, armories, shoemakers, blacksmiths, and textile makers.

The Sultan's guards jostled everyone and made a clear path for the women. Fatima shrank from the resentful gazes of those displaced by the guards' rough handling. She kept close to Shams ed-Duna and Nur al-Sabah, who doggedly haggled with the market sellers, while their slaves idled alongside the narrow streets and alleyways. Merchants offered slaves from faraway lands, bartering away their lives as easily as the silk, leather goods, brocades, ivory, and olive oil sold in the souk.

The stench of piss and offal in the streets vied with ambergris, musk, and incense from a nearby stall. Fatima gripped her stomach, as a wave of dizziness overcame her.

The *kadin* frowned at her. "Are you unwell?"

"I hadn't expected it to be so crowded, or smell so bad."

"Look, it's a symbol of the *Nauar*." Shams pointed to a burnished copper wheel dangling from a tent post under a faded, blue awning. "I have not seen one since I left Fés el-Bali."

Nur al-Sabah peered over her shoulder. "Hmm, the Gypsies. Is it true they foretell the future?"

Fatima shook her head. "What nonsense they must teach in Christian households. The *Nauar* speak only in riddles to confuse and delude the mind."

Shams asked, "How can you be so certain? Have you ever been to one?"

Fatima replied, "I wouldn't dare. Sorcery and divination is the work of the court astrologer. Ask him anything you would like. I'm sure Father wouldn't object."

Then, a heavily veiled woman followed by two eunuchs exited the shop. One of the slaves pressed two silver *dirhams* into the olive brown hand of a little girl with bulging, black eyes. She took the coins and disappeared into the tent. The other eunuch handed his mistress a silken kerchief. She dabbed at the corners of her eyes, before bustling through the marketplace, her slaves following.

"I'd like to go in." Nur al-Sabah cupped the roundness of her belly jutting beneath the green silk robe. "The court astrologer has promised another girl, but I know the Sultan wants a son. Perhaps the *Nauar* might know for certain."

Fatima sniffed at this and looked away. She did not resent Nur al-Sabah's desire anymore. Still, her father did not need more sons. He already had her brother Muhammad and now Shams ed-Duna's boy.

Shams ed-Duna tugged at her hand. "What harm could there be if you came with us, Fatima?"

She pulled away. "I forbid it!"

Shams ed-Duna chuckled and Nur al-Sabah rolled her eyes.

Fatima gritted her teeth together and then expelled a sighing breath. "Very well, I'll indulge you both in this foolishness. Come, let us see this fraud."

They crossed the street, avoiding refuse and excrement, while a cadre of the guards and their servants surrounded the stall. Niranjan held aside the low curtain hanging over the entryway. Fatima glanced at him briefly, but he averted his eyes from her. She entered first and asked the little girl with black eyes for the fortune-teller. She led them behind a cloth curtain and gestured to the lone seat at a table.

Behind it, a shriveled figure with lips drawn tight over her teeth peered at them in silence. A ring of seashells, all oddly shaped, dotted the edge of the table, with one black pebble in the center. Fatima grinned at this poor mockery of mystic symbolism, but Shams ed-Duna urged her forward.

The gypsy woman bowed her head. "Peace be with you."

Fatima asked, "And with you. Are you the one who speaks of the future?"

"Do you wish to know the future, noble one?"

Ignoring Nur al-Sabah's gasp, Fatima leaned forward. "Why do you call me 'noble one' when you do not know me?"

"It is what you are." The woman turned to the girl hovering at her side. Whispering in some language other than Arabic, she waved the girl away. The child soon returned with a cup of fragrant tisane, which the woman offered to Fatima. "It cannot harm you."

Fatima glared at her companions, both of whom nodded. She drank the brew, bitter to the tongue at first, but sweeter as she continued. She finished and handed the cup to the woman, who said, "If you could swirl the cup, noble one?"

Fatima ground her teeth together, but complied. She set the vessel down with an abrupt clank. A few of the leaves clung to the sides and bottom. Her gaze fixed on the woman who nodded. "We must wait for the leaves to settle."

When Fatima groaned, Shams pressed a hand against her arm. "Be patient."

After an interim, the gypsy asked, "What is it that you wish to know, noble one?"

Fatima countered, "Tell me what you see."

The woman stared into the cup and after a brief interval, she pronounced, "The future of Gharnatah lies within you."

Fatima smiled at her companions. "You see? An answer, if I can call it such, without any meaning. Just as I expected." She stood and looked down her nose at the gypsy. "Can your leaves tell you anything about me?"

The woman stated, "Nothing you would believe, princess of Gharnatah."

Nur al-Sabah pecked at her arm and whispered something, but Fatima stilled her and leaned toward the gypsy. "Why do you call me a princess?"

"It is what you are. As I have said, the future of Gharnatah lies within you. Already, you carry one of its heirs in your womb, your son, who shall become the Sultan of Gharnatah."

Shams ed-Duna pressed her hand against Fatima's shoulder, but she shrugged her stepmother off. "If you knew anything of me, you would know that no child of mine could ever be Sultan. It is treason to suggest it, when the Sultan already has an heir. Besides, I would know if I am with child."

"I speak only of what I see, noble one. You are a princess of Gharnatah. You carry a son. One day, he shall become the Sultan. Such is the fate that awaits you, whether you would wish it or not."

***

When the women returned to *al-Qal'at al-Hamra* in the early evening, Fatima sagged from exhaustion. The *kadin* and her stepmother stayed with her in her house. Shams ed-Duna remained so unnerved by the gypsy woman, she insisted on summoning a midwife from the Jewish quarter, whom all the mothers at court respected and had relied upon.

Fatima dismissed the musings of the gypsy, until Amoda remarked that her monthly flow had not arrived.

Fatima asked, "Why didn't you say something sooner?"

Amoda shook her head. "I did not want to watch you suffer again. I was wrong before."

Fatima smiled and patted her hand. "Fetch the midwife."

She remembered her last night with Faraj. In their angry passion, had they created a child?

When the midwife and her assistant arrived, Amoda remained with her. Shams ed-Duna and the *kadin* hovered nearby. The midwife asked the last date of her link with the moon, which Amoda knew. Then in her bedchamber, the woman examined her. She probed her breasts. Fatima sucked in her breath at the dull ache her touch caused, while the midwife commented to her assistant, about the darkening around the nipples. She palmed the pelvis, while her assistant asked questions.

"Have you felt sick at all, at morning or in the night, my Sultana?"

When Fatima shook her head, she continued, "Do you feel ill-tempered in any way?"

Fatima glanced at Amoda before answering. She and her sister had endured Fatima's sporadic bouts of irritability for the past few weeks.

Amoda said, "My Sultana has not been herself."

Grateful that Amoda had not resented her too much, Fatima added, "I assumed it was all worry for my husband. He defends the citadel at al-Jazirah al-Khadra."

The midwife's assistant nodded. "Have you experienced any pain?"

"Sometimes in my lower back at times when I use the chamber pot, which I have been using more than normal."

The midwife and her assistant looked at each other. Then the midwife said, "You are with child, my Sultana, I am certain of it. I congratulate you."

Shams ed-Duna let out an excited squeal. Fatima pressed a hand against her lower abdomen. It did not feel any different. So many thoughts coursed through her mind, which she struggled to form into cohesive sentences.

"I've wanted a baby for so long. Why now?"

The midwife asked, "Tell me, has your husband changed his daily pattern lately?"

"Months ago, he suffered an injury at the siege of Malaka. When he was healing, he took shorter walks and did not visit the *hammam* for a period." She paused in midsentence. "Do you think Faraj is responsible for why we've had no children?"

The midwife nodded. "I've consulted with other women. One in particular could not have a child until her husband stopped frequenting the public baths in the summer. Within a month of his change in behavior, his wife conceived. Admittedly, I serve the wives of many men who frequent the *hammam* daily and have no problem impregnating their women, but perhaps for some men, repeated use of the hot baths affects their potency. I have no proof, only the changes in the males' behavior, then the pregnancies."

Fatima palmed her stomach again, scarce believing the miracle could have come about so easily. "Does this mean my husband has to stop bathing altogether? I could bear many things for love of him, but not his stench if he stopped visiting the *hammam.*"

The midwife's laughter rumbled through the room. Fatima joined her, a buoyant feeling overwhelming her heart. At last, she would become a mother.

Lisa J. Yarde

Chapter 26
Honeyed Pleasures

Princess Fatima

Gharnatah, al-Andalus: Ramadan 677 AH (Granada, Andalusia: January AD 1279)

"Shams, I can't believe you would betray me in this way!"

Fatima exploded in frustration, coupled with fear and the burgeoning panic of the last six months. Her raw emotions now channeled themselves into a bitter confrontation with her stepmother.

She continued, "How could you do it, betray my confidence in this way? Why did you tell my father about my husband's *jawari*? I shared how they resent me because I wanted your advice. I never expected you would tell my father. Now he insists I return to the palace! I want my child born at home in his father's house."

From her position near the latticed window of her receiving chamber, Shams ed-Duna rolled her eyes. "I didn't betray your confidence, but if you won't acknowledge the danger your husband's concubines pose, I cannot allow it to be on my conscience."

"I am not in danger in my own house!" Fatima ground the words out between clenched teeth. "I have my Niranjan, Leeta, and Amoda."

Shams interrupted. "Accidents can happen even with your servants to protect you. You are heavy with child. At

273

least you'll be away from that nest of vipers. You may not like it, but you shall do as your father commands."

Fraught with annoyance, Fatima threw up her hands in disgusted resignation. She sank on one of the multicolored cushions lining the wall.

Nur al-Sabah sat between them on a damask cushion while nursing her newborn baby, Princess Battah. She said, "Fatima, your father and your stepmother are right to feel concern. You have told Shams how Prince Faraj's women resent you, how the Genoese slave hates you in particular. What if one of them tried to hurt you? You must be cautious with the Sultan's grandchild."

Betrayal stabbed at Fatima's heart. "You side with her against me?"

Nur al-Sabah lifted Battah from her breast to her narrow shoulder, patting her daughter's back with a slim hand. "I side with no one. I do not want to see you hurt. I know how important this child is to you."

Shams ed-Duna sat at Fatima's feet. Her warm brown eyes compelled Fatima to look at her. "We care for you. When you told me of how the *jawari* treated you, I felt sorry. I've never experienced any rivalry in my husband's house."

Shams ed-Duna's gaze drifted to her friend, settling her daughter in the hand-carved cradle. Nur al-Sabah returned the smile she offered.

Her gaze flitting back to Fatima, Shams continued. "I don't want to worry that one of your husband's women may try to hurt you. That is why I shared your concerns with your father. He agrees with me. Your safety is important to us. It is the sole reason he insists you return to this harem, with your servants, until your husband returns."

Fatima refused to give in just yet. "Samara and Hayfa are tolerable."

Shams said, "Yet the slave Baraka thinks you are a threat. Would you risk your safety and the health of your baby just to prove your father and me wrong?"

Sighing, Fatima shook her head. "I suppose you're right. It seems so long since Faraj left Gharnatah. Sometimes, I think I hear his footsteps at night, but when I wake, I am in the bed alone. Being in our house is a comfort for me. Yet, it is also painful when I think of how long he has been gone. I am so big now. I doubt he would even recognize me. That is, if he ever returns home to see me before our child is born."

Of a sudden, she burst into tears, great shuddering sobs. Her stepmother and Nur al-Sabah consoled her, but a long time passed before she stopped crying.

Shams ed-Duna cupped her cheeks. Fatima sighed. "I have no idea where that came from."

Nur al-Sabah said, "You suffer a tremendous strain. You find yourself with child when the father is absent. Gone to war no less, facing dangers women cannot know."

Shams ed-Duna urged, "Won't you reconsider and write to your husband of the child you carry? You should make him come home."

When Fatima first learned of the pregnancy, she insisted anyone who might communicate with Faraj should send no word of the child. It seemed an arbitrary reason to her father, but she wanted to reveal the news in person. However, as time went on, she began to wonder about the wisdom of her decision. Was he ever going to return?

She said, "I know he would come, I do not doubt it. How can I think of my own desire to have him near when he, and every husband or father is needed at al-Jazirah al-Khadra to withstand the Castillan siege?"

Nur al-Sabah said, "The Sultan has demanded Marinid aid to lift the siege, in exchange for their bid to have the ports back. Now that they have suffered under al-Hakam pirates, and entreated your father's forgiveness and a renewal of the old alliance, your father shall ensure he gains as well. I do not think he expected the siege would last so many months. If the Marinid navy sails from Sebta soon, your husband and other husbands may come home."

Fatima frowned. "How do you know of my father's request for Marinid aid? He only told me last night when he dined with me and my sisters."

Nur al-Sabah replied, "Your father shares much with me. He may not ask my advice, but he confides in me. Does that bother you?"

She drew away, her palms flat in her lap. Fatima grasped her hand and Sham ed-Duna's own. "I'm glad my father has both of you in his life. My father loved my mother, but she never gave him the affection and tenderness he has found now. I never imagined he would experience the complete love of a woman. Our God has doubly blessed him with a devoted wife and *kadin*. I feel blessed also, to have such companions in my wearisome days. You must both promise we shall always come together like this, as friends, until the end of our days."

Nur al-Sabah's eyes misted over and Shams ed-Duna smiled, blinking back tears.

Fatima returned to her house in the evening. While Leeta brushed her hair, she explained what Shams ed-Duna had done.

Behind her, Leeta said, "She's right, my princess. You didn't think a few trinkets would make your husband's women accept you?"

"No, but I could have hoped it would," Fatima murmured. Did everyone think her behavior idiotic, even her servants?

After a time, Leeta added, "It was not foolish hope my Sultana, but truly, returning to the Sultan's harem may be best. Surely, the siege shall lift and the master may return soon. Oh, I almost forgot. The crown prince sent an invitation for you to dine with him tomorrow evening."

Fatima frowned. "Why would he do that? Muhammad has avoided me for months, ever since Father announced my pregnancy. Whenever I see him, my brother has little to say."

"His Highness has a mercurial temper, as you would know, my Sultana."

"Too mercurial, but I suppose it would be wrong to refuse him. I'll dine with him."

***

Just after sunset on the next day, Marzuq escorted Fatima to her brother's residence.

The steward said, "I'll take good care of the house while you're in your father's harem, my Sultana."

"My husband trusts you and I trust you, Marzuq. This move is temporary. I shall come back when Faraj returns. When I am gone, send word when you want to discuss accounts."

"Please do not trouble yourself, my mistress, I shall come to you."

"I'm pregnant, Marzuq, not sickly. Keep the peace of my husband's house, please. I know the concubines can be tiresome."

Marzuq nodded, his face drawn, possibly at the prospect of being alone with the harpies.

At the entrance to the house, a slave announced Fatima's arrival. She followed him into the dining area, where Muhammad stood. He was the image of their father with his lustrous, dark hair and the hooked nose as all men in their family possessed. Despite his handsomeness, she took no pleasure in the sight of him.

He smiled and bowed. "Welcome, sister."

She forced a reply. "I thank you. Your invitation surprised me."

"I am glad you came."

He helped lower her clumsy bulk to the floor cushions. She settled herself in an ungainly manner, which must have looked ridiculous, but he said nothing.

He sat beside her. "The child thrives within you. I envy your happiness."

She did not doubt it, as she removed her veils. "I'm content."

Slaves arrived with the first courses of the meal.

Muhammad said, "If you would allow it, perhaps we might wait a bit for Zuleika. I asked her to join us. She has been sad of late since the loss of her third child. I thought female company would cheer her disappointment at yet another failure."

Though she bristled at his choice of words about Zuleika's troubles, Fatima said, "These misfortunes are a temporary delay to your happiness. Wait another six months and try again for a baby."

Zuleika arrived. Fatima greeted the *jarya* amiably. She was beautiful with delicate features and a serene nature. Despite her tragedies, she remained pleasant and engaging.

After dinner, slaves introduced wonderful desserts, yogurt scented infused with jasmine and vanilla, cheese-filled pastries and cakes slathered with fragrant honey. Muhammad filled Zuleika and Fatima's plates, but ate none of the desserts. Craving somewhat sour foods, Fatima enjoyed the yogurt and a few of the cheese pastries.

Her brother said, "Sister, you are eating for two, yet you have not tried the cakes."

She replied, "I am too full of your cook's delicious *'tharid* to have even one honey cake, so I leave them to Zuleika's enjoyment."

He shrugged and smiled at Zuleika, as she licked honey from her fingertips.

Fatima asked, "Have you had news of the siege at al-Jazirah al-Khadra?"

"Nothing more than the dispatch we received yesterday. I do not understand what Father thinks your husband can accomplish in his stead. Besides, the Marinids are traitors at their core. I don't know why Father would rely on them again."

Ready to defend both of the men she loved, Fatima said, "Faraj is a brave warrior. You fought with him at Istija. Father is Sultan, we must trust his judgment."

"Indeed. I only meant I would have acted another way if I ruled."

Fatima realized she dreaded that day. The thought of Muhammad on their father's throne only soured her belly, when it should have given her great joy. She did not trust him.

The slaves cleared the table and brought Muhammad his water pipe, which he declined. "Take it away. The smoke is bad for my sister's health."

Fatima smiled with appreciation and rubbed her belly. Zuleika's wistful look made her stop. Then, the slave girl swayed a little.

Fatima drew back at the sight of Zuleika's flushed skin. She asked, "What's the matter?"

"Suddenly... I am very hot." The concubine removed her hair veil, the silky black curls underneath damp and clinging to her temples.

Muhammad said, "You look unwell, my dear. Perhaps you should rest."

"Yes, master... I shall go," Zuleika murmured, gripping the edge of the table while she tried to stand. Fatima screamed when she lunged forward, spewing the contents of her belly. She groaned, clutching her stomach.

Recovering from the shock, Fatima grasped her brother's arm. "She's very ill. Call for a physician. Muhammad? Why are you just sitting there? Do something to help."

He stared at the *jarya*, transfixed for a moment. Then he turned to Fatima. "You should leave."

"But, Zuleika... there is blood in her vomit."

"Don't worry for her. Come away, now, Fatima."

She could not turn from the sight of Zuleika's horrid pain. Her brother hauled her up and deftly maneuvered her to the doorway, bellowing for his steward.

Zuleika's screams echoed from the dining room.

Fatima insisted, "You must call for a doctor now, Muhammad!"

He handed her off to his steward. "Take her."

A slave brought her cloak. "Please, brother, let me know how she fares on the morrow."

Muhammad disappeared into the dining area again.

***

Fatima hardly slept. Each time she closed her eyes, she relived the horror of Zuleika's expression contorted in agony. In the morning, she heard the awful news of the *jarya*'s death from Niranjan. He kissed her hands and sat across from her on one of a pair of carved stools.

Fatima asked, "Does anyone know why she died?"

"It is uncertain." He took a cup of mint tisane his sister Leeta offered.

"I don't understand. Zuleika was fine throughout the meal. When she became ill, my brother, he seemed so shocked, he could not help her. No, it was not shock. It was like he waited to see what would happen."

Leeta muttered something under her breath before she turned to leave the room.

Fatima called her back. "What did you say?"

Leeta's toes curled on the carpet. "He probably poisoned her, I said."

Fatima clutched her prayer beads. "What? Why would you say that? Zuleika was his favorite. She might have been his *kadin* if she'd ever borne him children."

"Maybe he got tired of waiting for her to do that."

"Leeta, stop! He may be a difficult man, but my brother is no murderer! Besides, why poison a slave who could be sold away at profit?"

Leeta said nothing further. Fatima looked to Niranjan, who sipped from the cup with his eyes averted. "Come now, you don't also believe my brother would murder anyone. He could not. I was there, too."

When he said nothing, Fatima waved Leeta away. "Niranjan, you told me long ago that your father concocted poisons for his master, to kill his enemies."

"It's true, my Sultana."

"If my brother poisoned Zuleika, how would he have done it?"

He set the empty cup at his feet. "Most poisons have a bitter taste on the tongue. You need something sweet to hide them."

She gasped. "Like honey?"

"Yes, like honey, but sometimes it can also be used as a poison on its own."

"What do you mean?"

"My father used to keep bees and grow oleander. When the bees pollinated on the flowers, their honey became very toxic. If someone ate large quantities of this honey, they would die. First, the victim starts to sweat and vomit. It causes great pain in the belly. There is some respite, but that means the end is near. Then the victim thrashes around and dies."

While he spoke, she envisioned Zuleika's distress.

"If he did poison her, then my brother intended two victims that night. Zuleika started to feel ill after she ate those honey cakes. I remember now, Muhammad didn't have any of them, but he urged me to try some."

Niranjan gaped openly. "Do you think he wanted to kill you, too?"

Fatima gripped the *khamsa* charm dangling from her necklace. "He nearly succeeded. He tried to kill me and my baby!"

Niranjan shook his head. "Calm yourself. Your agitation endangers the child."

"I have greater concerns." Fatima sighed. "Don't you see? I must tell Father. It would destroy him if he thought my brother capable of such crimes. I must ensure Muhammad never harms anyone else. Why would he have done such a thing?"

"Does he need a reason to be cruel, my Sultana?"

"No, but I cannot think that... could he have done it because I shall have a child and despite all his efforts, his women have borne him none? Could he be jealous of me?"

"You shall never know, my Sultana."

***

The next day, Fatima went to her father's apartments across the harem. Niranjan trailed a discreet distance at her back. Rows of myrtle trees bounded the olive wood doors. The Sultan's bodyguards lined the walls around the courtyard. Fatima's father and Muhammad stood beneath the shade of one tree.

Fatima halted. Niranjan peered over his shoulder, his breathing rapt. "He's come to spin his web of lies for your father. You're too late."

Fatima shook her head. She would not allow him to get away with it. "Stay here, Niranjan."

"But, my Sultana...."

"Do as I command! I must confront Muhammad."

She steeled herself for their encounter, her fingers closed into tight fists. As she approached, her brother glanced at her first. Their gazes held. A lazy smile slowly spread across his lips before the Sultan turned from him and looked at her, too. Their father crossed the distance between Fatima and him. He hugged her tightly.

"God be praised, you are safe and well. Your brother told me you dined with him last night, when his slave was poisoned."

Fatima looked over his shoulder, her eyes still on Muhammad. He returned her stark gaze with a bemused expression.

She drew back from their father and took his hands in hers. "How has it been determined that Zuleika died of poisoning?"

Muhammad said, "Ayesha, a jealous slave girl, conspired with my cook to rid me of Zuleika. They tainted the honey cakes."

Fatima clutched her stomach. "Not the same Ayesha that Father gave to you? Not the dancing girl from Sicily?"

Their father nodded. "It is a regrettable end for any life. She brought it on herself."

Fatima glared at Muhammad. "What have you done to Ayesha and your cook, brother?"

He dared to laugh. "What else happens to traitors, Fatima?"

Her stomach soured. She had not brought the slave Ayesha to al-Andalus only to have her die at Muhammad's cruel hands. She could not believe his guile or savagery. She truly did not recognize the man who stood before her. He was no longer her brother.

Their father said, "Do not let Muhammad's casual tone fool you. The loss pains him although he pretends otherwise. Stay and comfort him, Fatima, as only a beloved sister can. I must attend a meeting with the *Diwan.*"

He kissed her brow and patted her rounded belly. With a nod to Muhammad, he left them. His bodyguards followed him.

Fatima watched them go before she turned to Muhammad. "You may have fooled Father. I remain unconvinced."

Muhammad crossed his arms and leaned against the tree. A forelock of his dark hair fell over his glittering eyes. "Of what, sister?"

"That you are not a murderer and a liar. You killed Zuleika, Ayesha and your cook to cover your own treachery. How could you have done it?"

Muhammad shook his head. "Your pregnancy has addled your mind."

"Wretch! I can only thank God I have wits about me, wits enough to escape your plans for me last night. You intended to kill me, too, didn't you? Are you so jealous that I shall give our father his next grandchild?"

He came to attention. His mocking smile evaporated so swiftly, she might have imagined it had been there. "Careful, sister."

"Or, what? You'll do to me what you did to Zuleika?"

He sighed and left her.

Her voice dogged him. "I know you, Muhammad, I see you for what you are. You can't hide the truth forever!"

Chapter 27
A Prince of the Royal House

Prince Faraj

Gharnatah, al-Andalus: Shawwal 677 AH (Granada, Andalusia: February AD 1279)

Faraj traveled with the camel caravan to Gharnatah and arrived at the capital in the morning. Sunlight filtered through a wispy cloud cover. The sure-footed beast that bore him climbed the steep slope of the Sabika hill and entered the precincts of *al-Quasaba*, just after dawn. The camel's knees buckled and Faraj slid down from the animal's back.

He went to the Sultan's harem, knowing his master to be an early riser. A bleary-eyed eunuch escorted him to the inner courtyard. Muhammad II stood beside a myrtle tree in the shade of the buildings. He smiled and beckoned Faraj, who then knelt before him with his head bowed.

The Sultan said, "It has been long months that you have been away. I have missed your wise counsel."

"Master, the siege at al-Jazirah al-Khadra continues. I do not understand why you called me away. I've held the city as you commanded."

"Indeed, you have done so and I'm grateful. The city is the concern of others, for now. I summoned you home because you have concerns that lie here."

Faraj's heart sank. On the journey home, he had feared the worst. Now, the Sultan confirmed it. In his absence, Fatima had gone to her father and insisted on a divorce.

Even after their last night together, she still meant to abandon him. Obviously, her father had taken her side.

He began, "Master, if you would let me explain."

Muhammad II shook his head. "There's nothing to explain. Walk with me."

They stopped beside the pond in the courtyard. The Sultan took pieces of dried bread from a small silk satchel, throwing the crumbs to the waiting fish. "We have enjoyed mild weather in the capital this season, but I look forward to the coming months."

Faraj shook his head at the Sultan's casual conversation. How could his father in-law be so nonchalant, if he meant to allow the divorce? How could Fatima do this? Did their love mean nothing to her?

"You seem worried, Faraj. What is the matter? You have yet to ask after your wife."

"Is Fatima still my wife?"

Muhammad II frowned. "Why would she be otherwise?"

Faraj stared in silence, hardly comprehending his father in-law.

The Sultan tossed the last of the breadcrumbs to the fish. "She mentioned yesterday, she would be speaking with your chief steward early this morning. Perhaps she's awake already."

"Yes. She's an early riser, just like you," Faraj murmured. "But I don't understand something. Didn't she talk to you about us?"

"She's told me how much she's missed you every day. She needs you here, not at al-Jazirah al-Khadra. She does not know that I summoned you, so she shall be surprised to see you. Go to her, I'm sure she's longed for this day."

Faraj scrambled to his house. The Sultan's rumbling laughter echoed behind him. At the inner courtyard, he slammed into a startled Marzuq, who fell backward.

Faraj helped his steward up. "Where is she?"

"Who, master?"

"My wife!"

"She is in the oratory, master," Marzuq replied, a puzzled frown crinkling his brow.

Faraj opened the door to the prayer room and stood just outside the threshold. Fatima knelt on the floor facing the window, a lavender and silver veil blanketing her. When she stood slowly, he crossed the room and touched her shoulder. Ignoring her shocked gasp, he hugged her. Then, he realized why he could not hold her close as usual. Her swollen belly jutted out.

"You're... pregnant." The words seemed a foolish statement for what was so obvious, but he did not know what else to say.

"I wanted to tell you, I swear I did, but I couldn't do it in a letter. Then I feared you would never come home, because of what I said about wanting a divorce. I never wanted to leave you. I thought it was the only way you might have children."

He knelt before her, awed. His hands caressed the firm roundness of her belly. He kissed her stomach where the child lay quiet under his hands.

She said, "I believe it must be a boy, I feel surer every day. He kicks so hard at times that I cannot sleep. But I love him already, as I love his father."

He stood and kissed her. "You understand if I choose not to divorce you now?"

When she made no reply, he drew back. Her tears flowed freely.

She pleaded, "Can you forgive me, my heart?"

He traced a thumb across her quavering lips and kissed her tears away.

***

Two weeks after his homecoming, at the wedding of the Sultana Alimah and the pirate chieftain from Maqurya, Faraj recalled his own marital ceremony. A Sultan officiated again, but this time Fatima's father took the lead role. The chieftain, Abu Umar of al-Hakam clan, fidgeted in his white robe and looked like a frightened youth instead of a grown man, the same age as the Sultan.

Faraj smiled at Abu Umar's obvious nervousness and anticipation. In thirteen long years of his own marriage, he had known contention and contentment with Fatima. The arguments and misunderstandings paled in comparison to their mutual happiness, now soon to be complete with the arrival of their first child. He looked down at his hands, imagining them holding his son or daughter aloft.

At the end of the wedding ceremony, the male guests wished the chieftain well. Immediately afterward, the marital feast began, as did the teasing about the impending nuptial night. Muhammad II introduced Abu Umar to his new family by marriage.

A eunuch who hovered at the Sultan's elbow interrupted the wedding and whispered in his master's ear.

The Sultan thumped Faraj's shoulder. "Fatima has likely started her labor. Shams ed-Duna and my *kadin* have taken her to the birthing room in my harem. They have summoned the midwife. These things take time. The women can let us know how her labor progresses. You must not worry for her. The midwife shall arrive soon and Fatima is in the care of Shams ed-Duna, my *kadin,* and my father's wives."

"But what if she needs me?"

"You cannot attend the birthing. No man should see such things. Be at ease, she and the child shall be well."

Faraj sat among the other guests and tried to appear jovial as before. The celebration lasted well into the afternoon. After he ate, musicians and dancing girls paraded between the tables, but he paid them scant attention. The Sultan nodded to him and together they left the reception, while an enticing Syrian belly dancer held Abu Umar enraptured.

As they walked, the Sultan said over his shoulder, "I am concerned that none of the women have sent word, as I know you must be."

Several of the royal women waited in the courtyard, including the bride Sultana Alimah, a vision of beauty in her gleaming, gold garments.

Faraj asked her, "Has there been no word of Fatima or the child?" Alimah shook her head.

Muhammad II spoke with a female slave who entered the courtyard. After she disappeared into the women's quarters, the Sultan's *kadin* came out and bowed.

"Your daughter fares as best she can, my Sultan, but... there is a problem with the baby. The midwife says the child is not in the correct birth position. When the midwife visited Fatima last week, she palpated her stomach. Then, the baby's head was where it should have been. The child can be born with its legs and bottom first, but the midwife says it shall be difficult for Fatima."

Faraj's heart fluttered inside his chest. "I don't want Fatima to suffer. What's this midwife going to do?"

The Sultan and his favorite turned to him, wide-eyed. Nur replied, "Calm yourself. The child cannot be born without help. The midwife is very experienced. Fatima trusts her."

Faraj nodded. "With your permission, my Sultan, I want to see my wife."

Gasps of outrage and dismay echoed among the women, but he continued, "I cannot wait here, not knowing how she fares!"

Muhammad II said, "Nur al-Sabah has told us what we need to know, Faraj."

"Still, I want to see Fatima."

The Sultan shook his head, but his *kadin* put her lily-white hand on his arm. "If my master would allow it, the princess might be happy to see her husband, for a moment. She tries to be brave, but she is concerned for the child's safety. She's frightened."

Muhammad II mulled her words. "Faraj, if you promise not to upset my daughter, you may see her. When the midwife asks you to leave, do so without delay."

The *kadin* beckoned Faraj. Narrow steps led to the upper chamber. The occupants met his arrival with open-mouthed expressions.

Nur explained, "Prince Faraj has the Sultan's permission to be here."

"Then bid him see his wife and be gone," barked the old midwife, who knelt at Fatima's side.

Fatima's stepmother hovered, patting her brow with a cloth. The widows of the former Sultan watched from the corners, as Faraj knelt and took Fatima's hand. It trembled in his grip.

Her voice wavered when she spoke. "Faraj... our son." Tears cascaded down her cheeks and her lips trembled.

He kissed her slim fingers. "He shall be well by the grace of our God. Do not be fearful, love, trust only in God."

The midwife removed the sheet and revealed Fatima's engorged belly. Her palm flat on Fatima's stomach, she studied the water clock across the room. Droplets fell in a steady interval, before Fatima gasped. Her abdomen tightened and rippled.

"Yes, the pain is more intense now, which means your time draws nearer," the midwife whispered. "This prince of the Nasrids shall be born soon."

She glanced at Faraj. "My husband is a physician. He has shown me how to help birth a breech baby. This shall not be easy for your wife. It may not go as I intend. If one or both lives are imperiled, I may have to make a choice between the mother and the child."

He shook his head. "There's one choice for me. I can have other children, but I shall only have this woman for my wife."

The midwife nodded and patted Fatima's hand.

Sultana Sháms ed-Duna said, "This is truly no place for a man, my prince. You should leave now. You would not want to remain."

Fatima squeezed his hand. "Please... stay with me. Don't go."

He did not ask if she was sure, only glared at the other occupants of the room.

The midwife nodded. "If she wishes you to stay then you must help her."

Fatima groaned as her abdomen tightened rapidly, signaling more intense pains. The midwife brought forward an ornately carved chair, with a large hole in the base. She examined Fatima again.

"My Sultana, you must prepare yourself. The head of a baby normally comes first. It is easier for the womb to expel the rest. The birth canal opens wide enough to allow the head to pass through, but a breech birth is different. It shall be painful, but you and the child shall live."

Fatima nodded, licking her cracked lips. The Sultan's *kadin* appeared at her side with an earthenware cup of water, from which she drank greedily.

Faraj kissed her hand again. "Know that I am here with you and our child."

"Our son, remember? I promised you a son."

"Yes, a son."

Fatima's lips trembled as she tried to smile through her tears. The midwife massaged her abdomen. She groaned and shuddered while the woman worked, but her gaze did not waver from Faraj. Each grimace and stifled cry stabbed at his heart.

Time passed slowly, the hours never-ending. The midwife warned birth was imminent. "We must move her before she becomes too weary to push."

Faraj lifted Fatima to the stool at the room's center. The midwife instructed him to kneel and support her with his arms. Her eyes closed, her head lolled against his shoulder. The *kadin* and Sultana Shams ed-Duna hovered beside them.

He whispered against his wife's damp curls, "Love, you must ready yourself. Now is the time for our son to be born, our Ismail."

"Ismail... for your honored father? Yes, that is... a good name," Fatima replied in a hoarse whisper.

She labored tirelessly, while everyone urged her to push. The midwife aided her efforts and eased the child's passage. Fatima looked weary and bloodied. Though delirious with pain, she kept up the struggle.

"Where is he? Why do I not hear him cry yet?" Fatima groaned weakly.

The Sultan's *kadin* urged, "You're not done. Push again with the next contraction."

As Fatima expelled the contents of her womb, the baby's loud echoing cry erupted.

The midwife proclaimed, "Here's a fine son for you and the Sultana, Prince Faraj."

Many emotions filled Faraj as his and Fatima's child entered the world in a gush of fluids, just as sunset bathed the room in a fiery glow. When the midwife held the newborn up by the legs and cradled his head, Fatima laughed and cried all at once. A thin line of fluid streamed down his body. White paste covered his tiny form. The midwife tied a piece of red twine around the birth cord and severed it.

Moments later, the midwife laid the child on his mother's belly. Fatima touched his head and Faraj covered her hand with his. The midwife took the newborn away for a moment, before she bathed and swaddled him.

She returned to Fatima's side and gestured to Faraj. "Would you like to hold your son, my prince?"

The tiny bundle in his arms, Faraj stared in wonder at his son's face. Tears pricked at the corners of his eyes, but he did not care that the women of the Sultan's court saw. Then he remembered his duty. Love for the miracle of his and Fatima's creation overwhelmed his heart, as he bent to whisper the Profession of the Faith and the Muslim call to prayer to the child.

Dressed in a new robe, Fatima rested on another pallet. He brought their child to her.

She opened her eyes at the same time her son did. Easing herself into a sitting position, she cradled him in the nook of her arm and kissed his fuzzy, dark-red hair.

Faraj smiled at their tiny family. "He is beautiful, just as you are."

She took his hand and placed it on their tiny son's chest. "He has your spirit inside him."

"Ismail shall be like you, not me. I pray he may have all your good traits and none of my faults."

She nuzzled their son gently, adoration glowing in her eyes. The midwife showed her how to nurse. "Hold your breast, with the thumb and index finger. Bring the baby up now."

The midwife tickled the baby's pink lips and he opened his mouth to close on the nipple.

Faraj sat behind them and kissed Fatima's shoulder. "I have one regret about his birth."

Fatima whispered, "What is that, my love?"

"I wish he had been born in our home, instead of the Sultan's harem."

"Why should that matter?"

"Only heirs to the throne have ever been born in a Sultan's harem."

Fatima gasped and clutched their child closer. "That can never be our Ismail's fate. I'll never allow it."

Enraptured in the sight of their newborn, Faraj did not question the solemnity of her vow.

Chapter 28
The Victors

Prince Faraj

Gharnatah, al-Andalus: Rabi al-Awwal – Jumada al-Ula 678 AH (Granada, Andalusia: August – September AD 1279)

Six months after the birth of their son, Faraj and Fatima settled into their roles as parents of a healthy and bright baby, blessed with auburn hair and his grandfather's eyes. They celebrated everything their son did as a major accomplishment. Neither of them could bear to be apart from him for too long.

On a late summer morning, they enjoyed the delicate beauty and the fragrance of jasmine and honeysuckle in the garden courtyard. Amoda, whom Fatima appointed as governess, brought their son. "The little prince has something to show you!"

Fatima became alert, rising from where she languished with her head in Faraj's lap. "Is he well?"

Amoda set Ismail, with his dimples and creased legs, on the marble. She left a distance of several paces between them. At her urging, he crawled across the floor.

Faraj scooped him up. "Crawling already! Soon, you shall walk. Then, you shall ride your first pony."

"I think not," Fatima said, deftly reaching for Ismail. "You and Father would have him defending the Sultanate and riding off into battle before he is a man. I want him safe at home with me, always."

293

She kissed the squirming baby and held him close.

Then, the Sultan entered the garden with his the crown prince. "It is a blessed morning."

Faraj replied, "Indeed. I trust you're well and you also, Crown Prince Muhammad."

The Sultan patted Ismail's head and tickled his chin. "How is my fine grandson today?"

Fatima smiled. "He's well, Father. He started crawling."

The Sultan grinned. "We shall have him walking and then riding his first horse soon."

Faraj looked at Fatima with a sheepish grin. She rolled her eyes.

Her brother scowled. "You're feeding him too much, Fatima. Isn't he getting fat?"

She said, "My son is not too fat, he's in excellent health."

Faraj frowned at her icy tone and the cold contempt in her eyes. What could have provoked such a reaction to her brother?

Muhammad held out his arms. "Let me hold my nephew."

Fatima clutched Ismail closer. "It's time for his nap. Please, excuse us."

She bowed and took the baby with her, Amoda in tow.

Faraj gaped in her wake long after she had gone. Then he faced Muhammad. "I'm sure she didn't mean to offend you."

"There's no need for an apology." Muhammad yawned, as if already bored. "New mothers are always overprotective of their children."

The Sultan patted Faraj's shoulder. "I've received a missive this morning of great importance. Let us talk in private."

They went to the small antechamber. Faraj gestured for them to sit on the green damask cushions and summoned a slave to bring fruit and water.

While they waited, Muhammad II said, "Abdallah of Ashqilula, the brother of my late wife, has gone into a self-imposed exile. He fled to Jumhuriyat Misr this month, the land of the pharaohs and the pyramids."

While Faraj reeled in astonishment, he continued, "More importantly, Abdallah took over fifteen hundred Ashqilula warriors with him, half of the men at-arms that supported the family. The loss of such a sizable force leaves our enemy vulnerable. Now, I intend to disperse my army and navy to attack every domain under Ashqilula control, save for one."

Faraj waited for him to speak.

"We shall save the prize for last. Malaka."

***

In the six weeks that followed, the Ashqilula defensive bastion of Wadi-Ash, close to the capital, fell first. Further south, Arsiduna capitulated and shortly afterward, the town of Lawsa surrendered. Within two weeks, the denizens of the cities of al-Hamma, al-Mariyah, and even Qumarich revolted against their Ashqilula masters, who could not provide food or water with the Sultan's siege engines battering at the gates. As the Sultan's enemies ceded each territory, his army arrested and transported the chieftains and their families to Gharnatah, to hear the judgment of Muhammad II.

Faraj awaited their arrival in the throne room. He stood beside the Sultan. The chieftain of the Ashqilula, an aged Ibrahim with his eight sons in tow, led the defeated Ashqilula family. Where Ibrahim had once stood tall and proud, age had been unkind to him. He was a dried up husk of his former self, hunched and rickety with rheumy eyes and parchment-thin skin stretched over his skull. Thinning hanks of hair clung to his balding pate. Deep lines still scoured his complexion, mostly around the hollows beneath his eyes. He reminded Faraj of an old, beaten leather saddle.

Without preliminaries the Sultan stated, "Abu Ishaq Ibrahim ibn Abu'l-Hasan Ali of Ashqilula, you have been declared an enemy of Gharnatah, by your acts of treason against the Sultanate. I owe you a debt of blood for the loss of one I loved, Ibrahim, but justice constrains me. As Sultan of Gharnatah, I am not above the reach of the laws I have decreed. Your blood shall not taint my hands. It is my command that you, all your relations, and your supporters shall endure permanent exile from al-jazirat al-Andalus. Your sentence begins immediately upon the arrival of the rest of your supporters. Until such time, you and all your relations shall remain in the dungeons of *al-Quasaba* to await your transport to al-Maghrib el-Aska."

***

Princess Fatima

Fatima sat behind the latticed *purdah* with Shams ed-Duna and Nur al-Sabah while her father pronounced his judgment. While she understood the rule of law, Ibrahim deserved death. She vowed he would not enjoy a comfortable exile outside of al-Andalus. Fourteen years later, her mother's blood demanded justice and vengeance.

After guards led the Ashqilula family away, she left the throne room with little Ismail balanced on her hip and returned to her house.

"Fatima? Where are you, beloved?"

Faraj's voice echoed across the expanse of the courtyard garden. As she approached, he strode through the evergreen leaves of the rosemary bushes. In the custom of men who had fathered children, he now wore a full beard, which he kept neatly trimmed. When he kissed her, the dark hairs on his chin tickled her cheek.

His almond-shaped eyes regarded her with open fondness. "You have a visitor."

She shook her head. "I don't want to see anyone. Did you know my father was going to do that?"

His gaze faltered. "You mean the exile of the Ashqilula?"

"Yes! Although Ibrahim killed my mother, Father set him free! Father knows what she suffered at Ibrahim's hands and he let him live!"

"Fatima, I did discuss the matter with your father before today's proceedings. The Marinids offered asylum for the Ashqilula if your father promised not to harm any of them, even Ibrahim. The Sultan swore a sacred oath. Your father is the Lawgiver. He is rightly guided...."

"How can you say that? Would you let your father's murderers escape? Would you?"

Ismail whimpered at her harsh tone and she hushed him.

Faraj sighed. "I would not, Fatima."

"Then I have your permission to pursue my own course? You shall not hinder me?"

"Do as you must. Ibrahim deserves death. I caution you only to wait until after he has left al-Andalus. The Sultan would suspect too much if Ibrahim met his end here."

Mollified, she kissed his cheek and he returned the gesture on her forehead. Ismail wriggled between the crush of his parents.

"Fatima, you must come with me to see your visitor." When she protested, Faraj pressed his forefinger to her lips. "For once in our marriage, I would love the pleasure of my wife obeying me. Is that so much to ask?"

A playful gleam returned to his dark brown eyes. He beckoned her across the garden, opened the door to the antechamber, and motioned her inside.

Two sets of twin girls and a boy sat on the gold-striped cushions lining the base of the pale yellow stucco walls, their tiny toes barely skimming the plush multicolored carpet. A woman stood beside them, in a blue hooded cloak with a yellow circle sewn at the shoulder.

When she removed the hood, Fatima exclaimed, "Sitt al-Tujjar? Why are you here?"

Sitt al-Tujjar laughed. "When the Ashqilula surrendered, they sold off all their possessions. My agents descended on every marketplace in al-Andalus. I was fortunate enough to be at Qumarich to find Ulayyah's children."

Faraj added, "As before, she came to me first."

"Your handsome prince is also very wise," Sitt al-Tujjar interjected. "I remembered your, ah, history with the mother of these children, my Sultana. When I approached him, your husband offered to purchase the freedom of the little ones. He assured me that you would desire it."

"These are Ulayyah's children?" Fatima asked. "But where is she?"

The boy turned his face away. One of his sisters sobbed against his shoulder.

Faraj clasped Fatima's arm. "She's gone."

"Gone? We must get her back, husband. It would mean so much to Halah."

"Beloved, you misunderstand me."

Sitt al-Tujjar drew closer. "After Abdallah turned traitor, Ibrahim took over his household. Ulayyah's boy Faisal told me she tried to buy her children's freedom. She had saved her money over the years for this one chance. Ibrahim strangled her. She is dead, my Sultana. The children saw it before they were sold away."

Tears blurred Fatima's vision. "It's my fault she's dead. Don't you see? The money she had, it came from me. If I hadn't paid her to spy on the Ashqilula, she would have never come to this fate."

Faraj pulled her close and kissed her hair. "Don't blame yourself. You could not have foreseen Ibrahim's madness. It's over now."

Ulayyah's son Faisal met her gaze with sad, wide eyes. She buried her face in her husband's shoulder. Guilt tore at her heart.

Faraj said, "Let's take them to your governess."

Fatima nodded and knelt before the children. "You are safe. You are free. No one shall ever mistreat you or hurt you again. I know someone who shall be happy to see you."

Chapter 29
Bittersweet

Princess Fatima

Gharnatah, al-Andalus: Rajab 678 AH (Granada, Andalusia: November AD 1279)

As the coolness of autumn winds swirled around them, Fatima stood with Amoda at the entrance of the house. Faraj cantered his horse in a circle with his son on his lap. Ismail chortled and waved his chubby arms in the air. When they came around again, Faraj slowed the horse and handed down the baby to his governess.

Fatima asked. "Is he not too young for horses?"

Faraj slid from the gelding's back easily, since his legs nearly dangled to the ground. "It's never too early for a prince of the Nasrids to study his horsemanship."

Amoda said, "I shall take Prince Ismail in now, my master."

Before Amoda left, Fatima kissed her son's little hands covered in woolen mittens. When he giggled, she could not resist another kiss on his pink cheeks. Amoda disappeared into the house with him on her hip.

Faraj took Fatima's hand. "I met with your father. We leave tomorrow for Malaka."

She nodded. He led her to a marble bench beneath a swaying date palm. "There's something I must tell you, beloved. It is something I have never spoken of to anyone else."

They sat together. After a weary sigh, he asked, "You remember the story of my parents' deaths?"

"Yes, I have always remembered what you told me."

Her heart ached for him, that he must now confront the ghosts of his past in Malaka. She sensed his thoughts were far away, as he stared at the ground.

"I've told you of the night they died, but never fully shared how I felt, my emotions on that night, how their deaths changed me forever. I became a different person, unfeeling, conniving. Vengeance ruled my heart. All I ever wanted was to reclaim my birthright. I did not care about anything or anyone else. Not my half-brother or my sisters, not even myself."

She touched a finger to his trembling lips. "My heart, anyone can understand how hard it must have been for you, barely ten years old. To have seen what you saw... it would have altered a man, much less a young boy."

"I remember how it was before, when we were happy. I used to ride along the shore with my father once a week. He trained my half-brother and me to use the sword and the bow."

She sighed while he spoke of the happy life he had at Malaka, even with the rivalry between he and his half-brother.

"I was so ashamed of my parents," he whispered, pausing to draw breath before he continued, "ashamed of them for dying as they did. I decided, right there in our ruined home that I would never be like them. I would never submit to fate. For many years, I could not forgive them for what they had let happen to them. The guilt I have felt has burdened me. My parents' blood cries out for justice, Fatima. When I killed Doñ Nuño, I thought the pain would have lessened. His death was a hollow victory, bittersweet. I won't feel I've honored my parents until the real culprit is dead."

Fatima's heart wrung with pity at the sight of his face, twisted now in anguish.

He knelt before her and cupped her pale hands in his dark olive ones. "Your father has offered exile to the Ashqilula. Abu Muhammad cannot join them. He must pay for what he did to my family. Then, I shall feel as though I have truly avenged my family and our losses."

"Please, Faraj, the Sultan's justice awaits him. I know your heart rebels against it, but you must accept and let justice prevail. I want Abu Muhammad dead too, but do not risk your life to kill him. We must wait for another opportunity."

"How can you say so? You have told me nothing further, but I know you and your eunuch are plotting the demise of Ibrahim. Why should he suffer alone? Abu Muhammad shall join him in death, at my hand."

"The life of Abu Muhammad is meaningless compared to yours." She lifted his fingers and kissed them. "Do not risk it for vengeance's sake. Would you see your son orphaned and your wife made a widow? My father shall surely kill you if you disobey him. Do not do it, please. Let my father's soldiers take him. We shall deal with him afterward."

***

The next morning, Fatima held her son in the garden courtyard while they awaited Faraj. The household servants gathered behind them. The Sultan's army prepared to leave Gharnatah for Malaka.

Faraj approached in his long shirt of black chain mail and his brass helmet, the nose-guard obscuring his features. Ismail whimpered at the sight of him and turned away, bawling.

"He doesn't recognize you," Fatima said. "He's never seen you in armor."

He removed the helmet and kissed their son's dark auburn hair. Ismail fussed and Amoda took him on her hip. Fatima drew her husband away.

He hugged her. "I've asked you too many times to wait here for my return."

"It's no more than the burden you bear. I shall pray for your safekeeping. Please, remember what I have said about Abu Muhammad. You cannot go against my father's will. The exile of the Ashqilula chieftains must be enough for both of us now. When the time is right, we shall each have true justice for our parents."

He embraced her again in silence. With a kiss on her brow, he left her.

Fatima stared long after he had gone. "God be with him. God be with them all this day."

***

Prince Faraj

The army of Gharnatah rode across the craggy, rocky headland of al-Andalus, its wide brown plains, and the dried remnants of orchards. A strong morning breeze from the sea came ashore. Malaka rose above the landscape in the distance. Restless, Faraj's mount pranced beneath him.

Under the shade of a fig tree, he reached up for a shriveled lump, peeled back the skin, and bit into it. As a child, he once played with his father's pages among the fig groves planted around the citadel. He wondered whether the Ashqilula had maintained the grounds as he remembered. He wondered whether his half-brother thought Malaka looked the same as in their childhood. He glanced at him furtively.

His half-brother led a cavalry detachment today. Surprised to see him, Faraj had questioned his presence. In response, his half-brother shrugged.

The crown prince ordered the sounding of the battle horns. "They've expected us for weeks, enough time to mount a resistance against our siege."

Faraj turned from glaring at his half-brother. "Why not sue for the terms of a peaceful surrender first? Abu

302

Muhammad has no more support. He can't hope to defend the city against siege weapons."

The crown prince shook his head. "Who knows what he may expect? Besides, what is the fun in a peaceful surrender? There would be no glory for us, eh?"

Some of the commanders around him yelled their assent and rattled their weapons, but Faraj did not join them. "If you attack Malaka with siege weapons, you'll destroy *al-Jabal Faro*. It is an important bastion on the coast. Your father wants those defenses maintained."

The crown prince's scowl descended. "Father's not here yet you think only of his commands. Fine. Send a herald to sue for this damnable peace."

Flying the white flag of peace, their courier rode across the plains toward Malaka. When he returned, his face seemed glazed in shock. "They've surrendered."

The crown prince raised his hand, ready to direct the commanders and their regiments forward.

"No! I have seen Ashqilula treachery at Madinah Antaqirah," Faraj cautioned. "They pretended to surrender to the Sultan and then tried to cut him down. No, if the Ashqilula have surrendered, they should send out Abu Muhammad."

"Faraj is full of advice today," his half-brother commented dryly. Faraj scowled at him, but vowed one day to settle the discord between his half-brother and him.

The crown prince sent the herald to the gates again. The messenger returned an hour later. "Great prince, they say they are ready to admit defeat, but they cannot surrender the governor to you. They say he is gone. No one saw him leave, not even his own family, but he is nowhere in the citadel or the governor's castle."

Faraj cursed and slapped his thigh. "Gone? Abu Muhammad would never just leave the city like that! It must be a trick."

"We take the city," the crown prince said. "Faraj, you were born here. You know Malaka best. Find that rat, Abu Muhammad and root him out!"

Faraj glanced at his half-brother, who colored and looked away, reddening with vexation.

The gates of the city creaked open. The army rode into a desolate scene. A lone dog ambled down the deserted street, nosing for scraps. Two shopkeepers peeked out from behind their stalls before hiding again. The battlements were empty, masonry crumbled at the foot of the walls. A few guardsmen idled at the gatehouse.

Faraj took a portion of the cavalry in his command with him. In the center of town, they rode up a steep slope, passing into the inner sanctum of the city. Whitewashed homes with thatched roofs perched on the sides of road, the domiciles of Malaka's poorer residents. Cobblestone streets led them further up the summit, to the marble homes of the city's *khassa*, whose noble estates dotted the hillside. There were hardly any people around. Those few they saw fled indoors and bolted their gates or doorways.

He approached the first of the military fortifications built at Malaka, at *al-Jabal Faro*. Its rectangular towers flanked massive, protective walls. The guards at the site surrendered quickly. The governor's castle loomed behind towering palms. He ordered the Ashqilula guards jailed in its depths and moved on to the estate where he was born.

Under the shade of dense pine and eucalyptus trees, he rode through the double bent entrance that existed since his childhood. Beyond that, the gates gave access to beautiful, if somewhat overgrown, gardens that surrounded the estate. Worn bricks glinted golden-brown as the sun beat down upon them. Two men guarded the entrance.

One of them said, "Our mistress Sultana Faridah bids you welcome."

Faraj cut him off with a dismissive wave. "Arrest them also."

Dismounting, he drew his sword. Sultana Faridah, mother of Abu Muhammad, waited under the archway. Her gray hair, unveiled, billowed in the sea wind. Her once clear sea green eyes met his, the opaque orbs murky and filled with tears.

"You've come to kill me, Prince Faraj?" she asked in a wavering voice.

He shook his head and dropped the tip of the sword into the sand.

She continued, "It is only me here now, the rest of my family has fled."

"Where is your son?"

The aged princess shrugged. "I do not know. I have not seen him for days. He did not leave with my daughters by marriage or my grandchildren. I believe he is hiding, in this place."

Over his shoulder, he said to the guards, "Search this place. He is here."

Dried leaves blew around the windswept courtyard. He struggled to recall this barren place as it once was.

Suddenly, Sultana Faridah approached him. "How does Fatima fare? Is she happy?"

Puzzled by her attempt at polite conversation, he replied, "She's at home with our son."

"Good. Tell her that I said goodbye."

She disappeared in a flurry of black garments. He followed, but she kept ahead of him in the maze of the house. Her laughter beckoned. He surged forward and emerged in daylight again, out on to a belvedere overlooking the sea. He looked up the heights of the wall. The windows of his childhood nursery faced on the belvedere. More than twenty years ago, he had last seen his father alive here with his *kadin* Butayna.

The Sultana stood precariously on the ledge. The sharp drop below came to an abrupt end. Rocks and the battering waves of the sea met the belvedere.

Faraj extended his hand. "Sultana Faridah, come with me to Gharnatah. You can stay with Fatima and me."

She shook her head. "No, I do not think so. My days are at an end, as is my son's reign over Malaka. What reason do I have to remain in this land?"

She stepped back and plunged over the ledge. Waves crashed and broke against the sharp stones below.

***

The guards had searched the governor's castle, finding no trace of Abu Muhammad. Clenching his fists, Faraj demanded they keep looking. He leaned against the wall behind him, still in shock at the Sultana's suicide. Then he looked up again, past the windows of the old nursery to the upper stories. He remembered the storeroom above the nursery where he had hidden as a child.

Gripping his sword, he entered the castle again. He took the steps slowly. Yet his lungs felt as though they were on fire. He emerged at the uppermost story, an open space where his father's steward once kept provisions. Crates lined the walls. Here, his mother had hidden him and his siblings for protection on that terrible night. He crept forward, drawing the dagger from his belt and raising his sword.

"Come out, you murderer. I know you're hiding here like the coward you are."

Abu Muhammad, the last of the Ashqilula governors, scrambled from behind a tall stack of crates with a crossbow in hand. He stood the same height as Faraj, though much older with his graying hair. His fiery, golden brown gaze marked him as a predator. Like an old lynx sensing the end, he would never surrender without a fight.

"Come to die, whelp?" His deep baritone resonated throughout the room.

Faraj gripped his dagger tighter. "Haven't you learned yet, in all your attempts at treachery that I do not die easily?"

Abu Muhammad's gaze narrowed. "I'll take care of that now."

"You should have dealt with it twenty-one years ago! You put a nine-year old boy and his siblings through a night of terror, by your treacherous dealings with the Hud and Lara families. You should have killed me then, along with my father and mother. I know it all now!"

"I had no hand in Leila's death! She was my kin."

"After your henchmen raped my mother, she didn't want to live. You killed her, as surely as if you had plunged the knife into her heart!"

Emboldened, he advanced. Abu Muhammad sent a bolt whistling past his ear. Faraj's dagger sailed across the room, plunging into his enemy's chest. The chieftain tumbled backward with the force of it, sprawled with his hands outstretched.

Faraj towered over his adversary. Disappointment filled him at the positioning of the dagger. He had not delivered a mortal wound against Abu Muhammad. Blood congealed and trickled from the man's mouth.

Abu Muhammad mocked him. "You're right, whelp. They should have killed you when they had the chance, when you were a feeble, defenseless child. You are still weak, just like your father. I have seen you in battle. I know you shall show mercy. You shall take me back to Gharnatah, for the Sultan's justice. You could end it right now, but you have no courage for cold-blooded killing."

Faraj drew back the sword, the tip poised at Abu Muhammad's exposed neck. "You think I don't?"

Three guards entered the room, followed by others. "Come quickly. He found him! Prince Faraj found him."

Faraj wrenched his weapon away from Abu Muhammad in frustrated fury.

Abu Muhammad leered at him with a hoarse laugh. "It seems you do not have the courage after all, whelp. You won't kill me this day."

Faraj drew a harsh breath, his chest paining him. He ordered the soldiers, "Take him... back to Gharnatah."

Chapter 30
The Prize

Princess Fatima

Gharnatah, al-Andalus: Sha`ban 678 AH (Granada, Andalusia: December AD 1279)

Just two weeks after the siege at Malaka, Fatima stood beside her father on the battlements of *al-Quasaba*. They braved the bitter cold and welcomed the Sultan's victorious army home. Fatima had bundled Ismail up in furs and perched him on her shoulders. He gabbled happily, his gums watering, and pointed at the soldiers. When his fat fingertips began reddening with cold, she held his squirming form against her hip although he loudly protested. Her rapt gaze scanned the lines of cavalry for the only face she yearned to see.

Her heart skipped a beat. She whispered a silent prayer of thanks before kissing Ismail's cheek. "Oh, he's here, he's come home at last. It's your father!"

She waved toward Faraj as he emerged beneath the northern barbican of the citadel. He stared straight ahead and never noticed her.

Disappointed, she nuzzled her son's pink cheek. "He didn't see us, but he shall come to us soon."

Her father asked, "Are you sure it is not too cool for my grandson?"

"Ismail is hearty, strong, like his father and grandfather."

308

"Still, I don't like him outdoors for so long. You should return to your home."

She patted his forearm. "There's no need to dissemble with me. I know you want to meet with my husband and the commanders in private."

The Sultan grinned and kissed Ismail's cheek. "Sweet boy, I won't keep your father for long."

Fatima and her son returned to the house. Amoda emerged and took Ismail. Baraka darted from behind a column at the southern edge. Fatima rounded the corner with her head held high, ignoring her.

"Your husband's come back alive?"

Fatima turned at the tremulous waver in Baraka's voice. "He's returned victorious."

The concubine pursed her full lips. "I hoped he would die." Amoda's shocked gasp almost drowned out the rest of Baraka's words. "He deserves death for how he treats me."

Fatima gestured to Amoda. "Leave us. Take my son to his nursery."

Alone with the concubine, Fatima slapped Baraka hard across the cheek with all the force she could muster. The concubine staggered and nearly fell.

Fatima's emerald ring cut a slashing, bloody line across her cheek. She looked down at her adversary. "When Faraj dies, do you think I shall suffer you one moment longer than necessary? He tolerates you, despite your arrogance. Be thankful for his mercy. If it were my choice, you would've been sold long ago or worse."

She withdrew to her room. Her annoyance at Baraka grew into agitation, when Faraj did not return as soon as she expected, or as her father had promised. The sun cast long shadows along the walls before dipping below the horizon. Still she waited for him. In the early evening, she ate alone with Ismail and put him to bed. When the moon rode high above her head, she retired from the solitary vigil in the garden courtyard. Leeta readied her for bed. Fatima pulled the silken covers up to her shoulders.

Sometime during the night, the familiar scent and warmth of Faraj woke her. With a groggy sigh, she curled an arm around his chest and nestled her head on his shoulder. His feathery kiss rustled her hair. "I'm sorry, beloved. I know you must've been worried for me."

"I was. I waited for you. I think Ismail waited for you too. What hour is it?"

"It shall be midnight soon."

"Father kept you for so long at his side?"

He pulled her tight against him. His sigh rippled through the air. "Go to sleep, we'll talk in the morning."

After dawn, she awoke and found him smiling at her. He tweaked her nose. "You were snoring again."

"I've told you before, princesses don't snore."

"Perhaps not, but you did last night."

She hit him across the chest with her pillow. He grabbed his. In the ensuing mock fight, she forgot all the worries of the past few weeks and delighted in having him home again. A particularly good wallop sent him sprawling. However, he grabbed her ankles and yanked her off the bed. She tumbled beside him. His warm, wide mouth covered hers. Her bubbling laughter faded and she clung to him, while his hands roamed her body. A heavy knock at the door shattered their burgeoning intimacy.

Between each long, drugging kiss, she said, "Most likely... our son... is awake and... screaming... for his milk."

"Then, we should have heard him by now." His fingers pulled at the strings of her tunic. "He has the loud, lusty cry of his father."

"Is that what his father is, lusty?"

He grabbed her hand and drew it between their bodies. "Can't you tell?"

The knocking came again. Her fingers curled around the bulging beneath his trousers. He groaned and kissed her shoulder blades.

She threaded her fingers through his dark, silky hair. "We can't ignore our son, you know. What sort of parents would we be?"

"I wouldn't dare ignore Ismail, but I wish I could stay here with you forever."

His wistful look made her sigh.

She kissed his brow. "You can, my love, always, except when our son demands to be fed."

The incessant pounding continued. He released her and stood, stamping to the door. She admired the lean muscles of his back.

He opened the door to admit Marzuq, who sketched a stiff bow. "I'm sorry, my prince, to wake you and the Sultana, but the Sultan's guard is here."

Fatima adjusted the folds of her tunic and approached them. "Why are they here, Marzuq?"

The steward averted his gaze. "They have come... to arrest the master, on the charge of high treason against the Sultanate."

She stared at him for a moment, barely comprehending anything he had said, except for the word treason. "My husband arrived in triumph yesterday and now my father's arresting him for treason? This cannot be! Wake Leeta and Amoda at once. I'll see my father about this."

Faraj's hand closed on her arm. "Fatima, stop."

"I won't let them take you to *al-Quasaba*. There must be some mistake. What could you have possibly done to warrant such treatment? My father must have lost his senses. Where are the men who have come to arrest you? I'll speak to them."

Despite her indecent attire, she went to the entrance of the house, Faraj and Marzuq trailing her. Twelve guards stood fanned out beneath the porticoes. All but one had the grace to avert his gaze when she appeared unveiled. She glared at him, a squat, rounded man with a pair of manacles dangling between his fingers. "Explain yourself."

He handed her a summons bearing her father's wax seal. She read it and looked at Faraj. "This is incredible...

it says you murdered Abu Muhammad sometime last night in his jail cell at *al-Quasaba*! But that's ridiculous, you came to our bed."

She shoved the parchment at the guard. "This is a mistake."

Faraj touched her shoulder. "Let them take me."

"I shall not! High treason is a capital offense. Don't you understand? I won't lose you now, not after all we have suffered together."

He brushed past her and held out his hands. "I'm ready."

Even as the soldier chained his hands and feet, she clutched Faraj's arm. "What are you doing? Why are you letting them do this?"

He said nothing, only shook his head, and staggered as the guards led him away.

"Faraj? Faraj!"

Her screams died in sobs as Marzuq held her steady.

***

Fatima stood in the midst of the Sultan's quarters less than an hour later. "Father, you can't believe my husband is a murderer!"

He sat at his writing desk eyeing her, his gaze speculative.

"Fatima, I know you love him. I would have spared you this pain. You cannot deny he had the chance and, more importantly, a compelling reason to kill Abu Muhammad. Faraj has confessed all that he had been keeping secret about the Ashqilula's role in the death of his father. He told me Abu Muhammad ordered my uncle Ismail's death. Faraj has all but admitted to killing Abu Muhammad."

"Abu Muhammad deserved to die. All the Ashqilula do! That doesn't mean my husband killed him."

Her heart and head warred. Faraj deserved the right of vengeance, but they had talked about this and made alternative plans. Would he have moved without her? Would he have risked everything they could have accomplished together?

"Fatima, I believe Faraj has the right of revenge, but it must give way to the Sultan's justice. No one may disobey the laws of the Sultanate, or the oaths I have made. I gave my sacred promise regarding the safety of the Ashqilula. Now, I have a dead Ashqilula governor, hanging by his bed linen in his jail cell with a stab wound to his heart. The jailer says your husband was the only person who requested to see him. Abu Muhammad was alive until late last night. I can only assume your husband returned to finish the work he had started in Malaka. Did you know Faraj tried to kill Abu Muhammad? Three of my guards stopped him. Are you aware of that?"

"I don't care what happened in Malaka. Abu Muhammad could have hung himself."

"Did he stab himself, too?"

"Father, Faraj would never disobey you!"

"Do I know that? It seems I do not know him at all, when he has kept secrets about the Ashqilula for years. I notice you showed no surprise at hearing his claims. That means he has told you beforehand. When did you both become so comfortable keeping secrets from me?"

She gasped, incredulous at the doubt in his eyes. "He didn't do it. I know him. He would not risk our futures."

Her father sighed. "Show me the proof that Faraj is innocent, Fatima, and he shall live. Otherwise, he dies by the executioner's blade. I am sorrier than I can say. I love Faraj, too. He is my cousin, raised in my father's household. I do not want to see him die. Yet, he can no more escape his fate than I can deny my duty. I am Sultan. I can't allow anyone to defy me, even among my own family."

***

Later, Fatima sat on the steps leading down into her garden, head buried in her hands. Thoughts roiled inside her mind. He could not have done it. Faraj would never defy the Sultan. He knew the consequences. She had warned him. He would not risk his life, their lives together, for vengeance's sake.

Ismail's cries echoed from the house. Fatima swiped at her eyes, burning after a day spent in weeping. Amoda brought the baby out. "I think he misses the master."

Fatima took her son and kissed his auburn hair, as he whimpered, fat tears rolling down his cheeks. Cuddling him close under his blanket, she whispered, "I miss him, too."

She spent the rest of the evening in terror, hardly eating. Ismail fussed and cried for her, even though he loved Amoda. Only his mother's rocking soothed him. He fell asleep just before midnight in her arms, but she never slumbered.

Her heart ached with the desire to have her husband alive, safe and back in her arms again. Faraj's fate weighed heavily on her. The council's verdict the next morning would decide his future. Islamic law required witnesses before the Sultan could lay a charge of high treason. Anyone could testify on behalf of the accused, even a woman. Sharia law had a strict requirement that two women must testify, whereas one man's testimony was enough to exonerate the accused.

She refused to let that requirement stop her from offering testimony on her husband's behalf. He was her beloved, as much a part of her as the heart beating inside her chest. He could not die. His son would not be an orphan, or his wife, a widow.

***

After the first prayer hour, the *Diwan al-Insha* convened in the throne room and considered the charges against Faraj. Fatima struggled through the gathering crowd. The council did not usually allow courtiers into the chamber, but the news of Faraj's arrest had spread in the royal *madina* and throughout Gharnatah. The *Diwan* also did not usually permit women to attend or interfere in the proceedings in public, unless they appeared as witnesses. After she persisted in her repeated requests for admission, the guards allowed her entry.

"... We have ample witnesses who say this man was the last person to see the Ashqilula governor. He sought to kill him at Malaka!" Abu Omar, one among the Sultan's ministers who had not hidden his resentment of Ibn Ali's appointment as *Hajib*, now addressed the Sultan. "What more proof does justice demand? Prince Faraj has broken the Sultan's oath and our laws. The penalty is death. He has forfeited his life."

Bathed in the sunlight streaming through the lattice windows, Faraj knelt in the center, his head bowed. Manacles shackled his hands behind him. Fatima stifled a cry at the dirt and muck soiling his clothing, after only one day in a cell at *al-Quasaba*.

When Abu Omar finished speaking and the Sultan waved him off, Fatima approached. "May I be allowed to speak?"

Her voice wavered and echoed in the cavernous space. Faraj's tortured gaze flew to her face. She sidestepped him and bowed. "Please, my Sultan?"

Her father rose from his chair with a grave expression. "Fatima, you should not be here."

She sank on her knees at her husband's side. Unshed tears stung her eyes. "I have no other place to go. I am his wife." A few murmurs arose, but she continued. "I beg for his life. He is a good man. He has served Gharnatah faithfully all his days. You know him, Father, and you know his nature. He could never have done this."

Her father reached for her hand, pulling her up.

She refused, clasping her fingers in supplication. "My husband has honored you all the days of his life. He would never betray your sacred trust."

"Fatima, don't dishonor yourself by pleading for my life." Faraj's voice sounded wooden and hollow.

She shook her head. "You are my life. If you die, I shall be dead to the world, as well."

His lower lip trembled. She touched a grimy mark on his cheek.

"The Sultana Fatima speaks the truth." A familiar, shrill voice filled the council chamber. "Her husband couldn't have killed the Ashqilula governor last night."

Though heavy veils partially muffled her voice, Baraka spoke out clearly. "I know master. He is good, kind and loyal to those he loves. He could not have done this."

Abu Omar barked, "Who is this woman?"

Fatima replied, "She is my husband's concubine."

Abu Omar stomped his clubfoot. "Bah! A concubine and a wife, they would say anything."

Baraka continued, "I speak the truth. I know my master could not have done this. He was with me in my bed last night. He returned to the house two hours after sunset, after he had dined with the Sultan and his officers."

Fatima gasped. Foolish jealousy ripped at her heart. So, that was why Faraj had taken so long to come to their bed? Why had he gone to Baraka, instead of waking her?

Her father beckoned the slave girl forward. "I can account for his presence in my chamber until such time. Was he with you all the hours after that?"

"He was, except when he went to the Sultana just before midnight. Master returned to his house and desired her. She was already abed. Then, he remembered me. For many years, master has remained faithful to his wife. He did not want her to know I had tempted him to my bed. It would seem a betrayal. I can't keep silent and watch him die, even though the truth may hurt her."

Another wave of jealousy overwhelmed Fatima. She could not help it. She wished Faraj had woken her instead of going to Baraka's bed. Even so, she welcomed the news. It made the possibility that he had murdered Abu Muhammad in the night less certain.

Her father grasped her hand and helped her stand. He cupped her face in his. "Is this true, daughter, what this slave has said?"

She swallowed before answering. "Faraj came to my bed just before midnight. I awoke and asked him the hour."

316

"Do you believe he had been with his slave before he came to you?"

She drew back. "How can you ask me that? What woman wants to admit her husband chose a slave over her?"

Her father nodded and turned away.

Abu Omar insisted, "We cannot accept the word of a slave, great Sultan."

Muhammad II glared at him. "But we can accept the word of a Sultana, which is beyond contestation. Do you suggest we have the concubine detail her activities with my kinsman last night? Is that the proof you require? Do you want to see my daughter hurt further? Can't you see how she feels about it already? It's no wonder the slave hesitated to speak."

"But they're both women, my Sultan."

"And Sharia law permits evidence to be brought by two women. Can we deny the circumstances of Abu Muhammad's death remain unclear? Treason is a grievous offense and requires grave proofs. Shall I kill Prince Faraj without incontestable evidence of his guilt? I am the Lawgiver. The laws of the Sultanate bind me, as they govern all of Gharnatah's citizens."

The Sultan summoned his jailer, who stood in the recesses of the room.

"Release him," he said with a gesture toward Faraj.

The jailer removed the manacles. Faraj rubbed his bruised wrists. When he stood, her father drew his sword.

Fatima gasped and stepped between them. "What are you doing, my Sultan?"

He gave her a wry smile. "This may be my last opportunity, my child, but I ask you to be quiet."

She sidestepped Faraj. Her father raised his sword over her husband's head. "Our enemies killed your father. The governorship, which should have gone to you, went to Abu Muhammad. He is gone now, but I can find no absolute proof that his death came at your hands. I release you. Today, I right a wrong done to you, one your family

317

suffered for more than twenty years past. Therefore, rise and stand before me, the new governor of Malaka. Long may you and your heirs hold the city in the name of the Sultan of Gharnatah."

When he stood, Faraj's legs wobbled slightly. The Sultan sheathed his sword and embraced him.

Afterward, Fatima fell into step beside Faraj, as they left the council chamber together. When they emerged in the daylight, loud cheers erupted. Well-wishers thronged them, jostling Fatima aside as they cheered her husband.

She spied Baraka on her solitary walk. She called out twice. The concubine ignored her. Pressing through the crowd, she reached Baraka and grabbed her arm.

"Did Faraj come to your chamber last night and make love to you? I can forgive him anything, but I must know the truth."

Baraka stopped and looked at where Faraj stood, swallowed up in the crowd.

"Do you have to ask, Sultana? Don't you know how much he loves you, or how I envy you? You know the truth. I don't have to speak of it."

Fatima sighed and nodded. "I don't understand. You hate him. Why did you lie, just to save him?"

Baraka's emerald eyes swam with tears. "Why else does a woman lie? She would do anything if she loves someone, even if he doesn't love her."

The concubine fled, her loud sobs echoing across the courtyard.

Fatima did not know what to say.

She waited until mid-morning when Faraj finally cleared the crowd. Despite the onlookers, he tugged her veil aside and tipped her face up for a kiss. She returned his embrace, their arms enfolding each other.

When they drew apart, he sighed against her hair. "You saved my life."

She shook her head. "Baraka did it with her lie about being with you."

He hugged her close again. "She didn't lie. I did go to her that night."

She pulled away and peered up at his dark olive face, speechless.

He said, "Baraka met me at the door to our house. She helped me wash Abu Muhammad's blood from my hands. She burned my bloodied clothes and attended me in the *hammam*. She flung my dagger into the river Hadarro. Your father allows Ibrahim to depart in exile, but I could not do the same for the one who killed my father. I could not risk that he might escape my justice in al-Maghrib el-Aska.

"Now, you know the truth. It is enough to damn me for a liar and a murderer. Most importantly, I have lied to you. If you can ever forgive me, I promise it shall be the first and last time I ever tell you such a falsehood again."

She sighed. At last, he had avenged his losses. Although her father's justice had robbed her of immediate recompense for her mother's death, at least one among Ashqilula had already received a fitting end.

"Let us return home. Ismail slept poorly. He missed that song your father taught you, the one you sing to our son at night."

She resumed walking ahead of him. He pulled her back, a lingering question in his eyes.

She cupped his cheek. "Don't you know I shall always love you as you are?"

He kissed her palm. "I could want for no better ally but you, my beloved."

***

Before the week concluded, Faraj and Fatima prepared to leave Gharnatah for his birthplace at Malaka. Most of her family and former retainers came to say farewell on that final morning. She hugged Shams ed-Duna, Nur al-Sabah, and her remaining sisters, and promised to write often. After exchanging goodbyes with her beloved family, she bowed before her father and kissed the hem of his silk *jubba*. He helped her rise and held her by the shoulders.

She whispered, "I'm fearful, Father. Gharnatah is my home and Malaka...."

"... Is where you shall build a new home, where you shall raise my many grandchildren in love and wisdom, as you and your siblings were raised."

His forehead pressed against hers for a moment. Then he kissed her brow. "Go with God always, my beloved daughter."

"May He guide your thoughts and deeds forever, noble father."

Fatima took a squirming Ismail from Faraj. She walked to a waiting camel. Niranjan stood at her side.

She touched his shoulder. "I await you at Malaka. Come to us soon, when your task is complete."

He nodded. "I shall not tarry for long. I promise, my Sultana, Ibrahim shall have a short and painful exile, before the end."

Faraj eyed them for a moment before he gave the order for the caravan to depart. Leeta and Amoda, accompanied by Basma and Haniya, the first set of Ulayyah's twins, rode on horses behind them. Fatima would raise the girls in her household as her personal servants. Other household slaves at the rear guided the pack animals.

They stopped often for the sake of their child. To his credit, Faraj was an indulgent father, despite his eagerness to reach home. After nearly six days' ride, with Malaka only a few hours away, Fatima asked Faraj to allow her a horse.

She said, "Beloved, I want the people of your new city to see you with your family; your wife, the daughter of the reigning Sultan and your son, the grandson of the Sultan and the heir of Malaka. It would affirm the faith my father has placed in you."

Niranjan brought a gray mare. Faraj set her astride it and then handed Ismail up to her. She rode beside him, while their son sat on her lap, alternately tugging the reins from her grasp, or waving his chubby hands.

His father laughed at his antics and then sent a herald on ahead for the announcement of their arrival later that evening.

Fatima leaned toward him. "You're ready to see your birthplace, where your parents died? You've endured so many painful memories."

He touched her cheek. "With you and my son at my side, we shall erase the terrible past. We and our children shall never be touched by it."

***

When they entered the city, the people of Malaka greeted their new governor with cheers and well wishes. Fatima doubted many of them had ever seen him, or remembered his father, but the welcome was effusive. They climbed to the top of the promontory, site of the governor's castle.

While Faraj directed his steward, Fatima took their son to a point halfway between their new home and *al-Jabal Faro*. The entire city spread across the plains in a semicircle. Lamps and lanterns set it aglow with brilliant colors in the evening. Ismail babbled happily, while she pointed out various parts of the wide, remarkable vista.

Faraj joined them. "Dearest, there's more to see."

Fatima took his hand. "Let's stay here a little longer."

They stood side by side with Ismail between them.

Faraj sighed. "It's a remarkable view, an evening in Malaka, much as I remember it."

"It is a beautiful sight. One, which I hope, may greet us for many evenings to come."

"So, beloved, you can be happy here?"

"I intend to be happy here, my love."

Fatima kissed their son's hair and whispered in his ear, "Behold, the city of your future."

THE END

Author's Note

I wrote *Sultana* after many years of research into the lives of the last dynasty to rule the southern half of the country, the Moorish family of Banu'l-Ahmar, alternatively known as the Nasrids in a later period.

The Moors

The Moors were Islamic people of Arabian and Negro descent, who invaded the Iberian Peninsula, which encompasses modern-day Portugal and Spain, beginning in the Christian eighth century. They called the conquered land al-jazirat al-Andalus, but in later years, the term referred only to the south of Spain and became Andalusia in modern times.

The Moors penetrated the interior and brought three-fifths of the peninsula under their control. They gave their unique culture, rich language, and the religion of Islam to a land that welcomed them at first, for the valuable riches and social order they brought. Where superstition and ignorance once pervaded all elements of life, the Moors brought intellectual pursuit and reasoning. Their blood mingled with that of the Visigoths and produced a mixed race of individuals.

By Islamic law, Muslim men could marry or have relations with non-Muslim women. Periods of zealous anti-Christian and anti-Jewish views occurred and resulted in forced conversion, but mostly, Christians and Jews enjoyed religious tolerance under Moorish rule. Some families chose to convert willingly, for all the requisite benefits including as the avoidance of certain taxes and the gains of political and social advancement, while others practiced their former religion in secret.

Spurred on by religious fanaticism, bigotry, and jealousy of the Moorish achievements, the people of the northern half of the peninsula began the Reconquista, a determined struggle against the Moors. Beginning in the Christian tenth century, the rebellion spread slowly southward, until only one Moorish kingdom remained, Granada, nestled within the Sierra Nevada Mountains. The various ruling houses of Christian Spain employed capricious strategies against this last bastion of Islam in the peninsula.

The Hud Dynasty

At the dawn of the thirteenth century, others vied for control of Andalusia before the rise of the Nasrids. The Hud family, which originated in northern Spain, controlled the southeastern portion of the country from the 1100's onward. In AD 1228, an alliance between the Nasrids and the Ashqilula threatened Hud control over the region. With their new allies, the Nasrids encroached on the domain of their enemies, and aided the Castilian kings in wresting control of the last significant Hud stronghold at Seville.

The Ashqilula Family

The Ashqilula family formed an alliance with the Nasrids against their mutual enemy, the Hud, but their allegiance lasted nearly thirty years. The two families had inter-married for several generations, beginning with the marriage of Fatima, the daughter of the chieftain Abu'l-Hasan Ali of Ashqilula, who married Yusuf ibn

Muhammad, the father of Sultan Muhammad I of the Nasrids. In later years, Muhammad I's daughter Mumina would wed Abu'l-Hasan Ali's son Ibrahim and Mumina's sister would marry another son of Abu'l-Hasan Ali of Ashqilula, Abdallah. When Muhammad I wedded his granddaughter Princess Fatima to her cousin Prince Abu Said Faraj, orphaned son of the Sultan's brother Ismail, the Nasrids and Ashqilula warred over the balance of power for the next decade.

The Nasrid Dynasty

The Nasrid family allegedly arrived in the peninsula during the early stages of the establishment of Moorish rule. They claimed descent from Sa'd ibn Ubadah, a chieftain of the Khazraj tribe in Arabia, a contemporary of the Prophet Muhammad. Ibn Ubadah's descendants settled in the Arjuno region and served in the army of the Umayyad Caliphate, distinguishing themselves in their military leadership as officers and generals.

Sultan Muhammad I

The first ruler of the Nasrid Dynasty was Muhammad ibn Yusuf ibn Nasr ibn al-Ahmar and his people hailed him as Muhammad, "victorious through God" (al-Ghalib bi-llah). Sultan Muhammad I was born in Arjuno, part of the Andalusian province of Jaén during the Muslim year 587 AH, equivalent to AD 1191. He was a son of Yusuf ibn Nasr ibn al-Ahmar and his wife, Fatima. Muhammad's brothers included Ismail, Yusuf, and Faraj.

At the time of Muhammad's birth, the territory of Islamic Spain encompassed the lower half of the peninsula. A loose confederation of emirates, known as the Tai'fa states, had evolved after the collapse of the Almohade Empire. Abu Abdallah Muhammad ibn Yusuf of Hud controlled the province of Gharnatah.

Muhammad became governor of his home region of Arjuno (628 AH or AD 1231). Later, Muhammad revolted against Abu Abdallah Muhammad of Hud and began his quest for political dominance in al-Andalus, beginning with his base in Arjuno (27 Ramadan 629 AH or July 16, AD 1232). He extended his influence only as far as Cordoba after its political and spiritual leaders rejected his claim.

Focusing on other areas under Muslim control, Muhammad soon conquered the following principal cities: Guadix (630 AH or AD 1232), Granada (634 AH or AD 1237), Almeria (635 AH or AD 1238), and Malaga (637 AH or AD 1239). With the aid of his allies among the family of Ashqilula, other Islamic leaders in the provinces recognized Muhammad as ruler. Muhammad maintained his expanding territory by ceding nominal control to Ashqilula governors and members of his own family. He appointed his brother Ismail as the governor of Malaga. Ismail retained that post until his death (655 AH or AD 1257). However, early attacks on Muhammad's power base eroded his jurisdiction over portions of Andalusia. Christian armies reclaimed the following territories: Murcia (642-643 AH or AD 1243-1244), Arjuno (643 AH or AD 1244) and Jaén (644 AH or AD 1245).

Muhammad began construction on his palace in Granada, over the foundations of an Islamic fort from the Zirid period in Spain (635 AH or AD 1238). It would become one of the finest examples of Islamic architecture in the West, the Alhambra or "the red fortress" named for its red, brick walls.

At various periods throughout the majority of his reign, Muhammad paid tribute to the kings of Castile (Castilla-León), who considered the Nasrid kingdom a vassal state (beginning in 645 AH or AD 1246). The estimated tribute was forty thousand *dinars* or gold coins. Although Muhammad submitted to the Castilian demand for aid, particularly in the conquest of Muslim Seville (Ramadan 646 AH or December AD 1248), he did not always accept the terms of vassalage. The initial period of vassalage only lasted approximately 20 years. Muhammad began openly inciting or aiding the Mudejar populations of the Jerez and Murcia regions to revolt against Castile's rule (beginning 662 AH or AD 1264).

After his brother Ismail's death, Muhammad I gave dominion over Malaga to Abu Muhammad of Ashqilula, who was likely also his nephew by marriage; despite this possibility, none of the brothers of Muhammad I are noted as having married Ashqilula women nor are any of the sisters of Muhammad I named. Muhammad I raised his orphaned nephews Abu Said Faraj and Muhammad, sons of the former governor Ismail, at the Alhambra. The wife of Muhammad I, Aisha, was the daughter of his paternal uncle, Muhammad ibn Muhammad ibn Nasr. Muhammad I had at least four sons of his own: Nasr, Yusuf, Faraj, and Muhammad. The latter would reign as the Sultan Muhammad II, with his full name as Abu Abdallah Muhammad; he and his brother Faraj were likely the sons of Aisha. Another unnamed partner of Muhammad I became mother to his daughters Mumina, who married Ibrahim ibn Abu'l-Hasan Ali of Ashqilula, and Shams, who married Ibrahim's brother Abdallah ibn Abu'l-Hasan Ali of Ashqilula.

The first Sultan died after he accidentally fell from his horse while raiding the frontier town of Martos (1 Rajab 671 AH or January 22, AD 1273). Muhammad I was approximately 78 years old at his death.

Sultan Muhammad II

The second Nasrid Sultan, Muhammad II was born in the Arjuno region shortly after his father declared his suzerainty (634 AH or AD 1237). His people called Muhammad II al-Fakih, "the jurist" or "Lawgiver" for his swift justice. During his reign, he added to his father's work at the Alhambra. Feuds with the Castilians, the Marinid rulers of Morocco, and an enduring civil war with the Ashqilula plagued his reign. His young cousin, Abu Said Faraj ibn Ismail, became a trusted and loyal advisor. Abu Said Faraj also married the Sultana Fatima, the daughter of Muhammad II (664 AH or AD 1265).

Muhammad II accomplished the overthrow and exile of the Ashqilula. Under pressure from the Sultan and his allies, the majority of the Ashqilula clan fled to Morocco (678 AH or AD 1279). The date is not fixed; some historical records indicate the exile occurred ten years later. The earlier date seems correct, given that the Ashqilula fought on the losing side with the Castilians against the Nasrids in two subsequent battles (11 Muharram 679 AH or May 12, AD 1280 and 2 Muharram 680 AH or April 22, AD 1281). It seems unlikely that the Nasrids would have tolerated their presence in Spain after these defeats. Muhammad II claimed the city of Malaga and installed his cousin and son-in-law, Abu Said Faraj as the new governor (677 AH or AD 1278).

Muhammad II had two known companions in life. His wife Nuzha was a paternal cousin, the daughter of Ahmad, uncle of Muhammad II. Nuzha became the mother of Muhammad II's children, a boy also named Muhammad who would succeed his father and Fatima, the heroine of *Sultana*. Muhammad II also had a relationship with a woman named Shams al-Duha, a Christian concubine, who was the mother of his daughters Aisha, Shams, Mumina and another unnamed daughter who married Sultan Abu'l-Rabi Sulayman ibn Yusuf of the Marinid Dynasty (reigned 1308). Muhammad II and Shams al-Duha also had two sons, Faraj and Nasr, who would also gain the throne in future years.

Prince Abu Said Faraj

Faraj was the son of the governor of Malaga, named Ismail, a brother to Sultan. The exact date of Faraj's birth remains uncertain, but it occurred at some point in 1248. When Faraj's father died when the boy was just nine years old in 1257, Sultan Muhammad I raised him, alongside Faraj's brother Muhammad and presumably an unnamed sister. On his father's side, Faraj was a first cousin and son-in-law of Sultan Muhammad II, cousin and brother in-law of the Sultans Muhammad III and Abu'l-Juyush Nasr and cousin to his own wife, Fatima. The governorship of Malaga came under the control of Abu Muhammad of the Ashqilula clan, named as a nephew of Muhammad I. Since none of the details about Muhammad I's sisters are certain, no one knows the exact nature of Abu Muhammad's relationship to the Sultan and Faraj's family.

Faraj apparently enjoyed a strong and loyal relationship with his cousin Muhammad II, enough to wed the man's daughter Fatima in 1265 when Faraj would have been eighteen years old. His bride might have six or ten years younger at the time of their marriage. When Muhammad II ascended the throne, Faraj became an advisor to Muhammad II, although I can't find any reference to him having served among the Sultan's chancery. After the defeat and banishment of the

Ashqilula, Faraj became the governor of his birthplace at Malaga, where he retired with his wife Fatima and their young son Ismail.

Sultana Fatima

Fatima, the daughter of Sultan Muhammad II and his paternal cousin Nuzha, was a remarkable historical figure, so it seemed only right for her to serve as the heroine of Sultana. I don't know her date of birth; the most common speculation makes her between eight and twelve when she married in 1265 by the dictate of her grandfather Sultan Muhammad I; if so she was born as early as 1257 or 1253. I have even seen recent sources placing her birth in 1260 or 1261. No matter the date, she was a child bride by modern standards when she married. Islamic law allowed such union, as it also permitted weddings between close family members. Fatima's father Muhammad II was the paternal first cousin of her husband Faraj. Fatima's youth at the time of her marriage is also hinted by the fact that her first known child, Ismail, was not born until 1279.

All the primary and secondary sources describe Fatima as a cultured princess. She studied the repertory of the names of teachers and disciples devoted to religious matters. As I have come to a better understanding of Islam in the Moorish period, I wonder if this study shows evidence of Fatima's interest in Sufism, which involves masters and disciples in the mysticism of Islam. Her awareness gives an indication of Fatima's educational upbringing, likely on par with that of her brothers the royal princes. She had one full blood brother from her mother Nuzha, named Muhammad, and two brothers of the half-blood, born of a Christian concubine, Nasr and

Faraj, as well as sisters Aisha, Shams, Mumina and another who remains unnamed.

I chose to end this novel at the moment of the Ashqilula defeat and the rise of Abu Said Faraj as the governor of his birthplace, because it was a pivotal moment for the historical figures. The latter half of Fatima and Faraj's adventures continues in *Sultana's Legacy*, the sequel to *Sultana*.

Thank you for purchasing and reading this book. I hope you found the period and characters fascinating. Please consider leaving feedback where you purchased this book. Your opinion is helpful, both to me and to other potential readers.

If you would like to learn more about the Alhambra and Moorish Spain during the Nasrid period, visit Alhambra.org. You may also email me at lisa@lisajyarde.com or join my mailing list for more information on upcoming releases at http://eepurl.com/un8on. I love to hear from readers.

Islamic Regions and Modern Equivalents

Al-Bayazin: Albaicin
Al-Hamma: Alhama de Granada
Al-Jaza'ir: Algieria
Al-Jazirah al-Khadra: Algeciras
Al-Jazirat al-Andalus: Spain
Al-Maghrib: Northern Africa
Al-Maghrib el-Aska: Morocco
Al-Mariyah: Almeria
Al-Qal'at ibn Zaide: Alcala la Real
Arsiduna: Archidona
Aryuna: Arjuno
Chella: Salé
Fés el-Bali: Fez
Gharnatah: Granada
Ishbiliya: Seville
Jabal Tarik: Gibraltar
Jumhuriyat Misr: Egypt
Lawsa: Loja
Madinah Antaqirah: Antequera
Makkah: Mecca
Malaka: Malaga
Mayurqa: Majorca
Munakkab: Almunecar
Naricha: Nerja
Qumarich: Comares
Sabta: Ceuta
Tarif: Tarifa
Wadi-Ash: Guadix

Glossary

Abu: father of

Al-Andalus: the southern half of Spain

Al-Ghuzat: the Volunteers of the Faith, the Moroccan soldiers billeted in Granada

Al-Hisn: fortress

Al-Jabal Faro: Gibralfaro citadel, which protected Malaga

Al-laylat al-henna: traditional henna night for brides, where their guests gather to feast and decorate their bodies with henna

Al-Murabitun: the Almoravid Empire, which ruled North Africa and southern Spain, AD 1062 - 1150

Al-Muwahhidun: the Almohade Empire, which ruled North Africa and southern Spain, AD 1145-1269

Al-Qal'at al-Hamra: the Alhambra, a complex of palaces, residences, shops, mosques, etc. that served as the royal residence in Granada. Captured in AD 1237 by Sultan Muhammad I, each of his successors made improvements, especially Muhammad III, Isma`il I, Yusuf I, Muhammad V and Yusuf III

Al-Quasaba: the citadel within the royal residence in Granada

Al-Shaykh al-Ghuzat: commander of the Volunteers of the Faith

Amin: Amen

Ashqilula: one time allies of the Nasrids until AD 1266, known as the Escayola among Christian states

Bint: daughter of

Cortes: the rudimentary Castilian parliament

Dinar: coin bearing a religious verse, commonly made of gold or silver, or rarely, copper. They were minted in Granada with the Sultans' motto, "none victorious but God" and could be round or square shaped. Gold *dinars* weighed 2 grams, contained 22 carats of gold and were widely used for internal and external trade. Their value fluctuated over the centuries. Silver *dinars* were square and had a fixed value. Copper *dinars* were used for internal trade in the Sultanate and had a fixed value

Dirham: coin bearing a religious verse, commonly made of silver or other base metal. In Granada, they were minted with the Sultans' motto, "none victorious but God" and weighed 2-3 grams

Diwan al-Insha: the Sultan's chancery of state

Eid mubarak: traditional greeting celebrating the end of Ramadan

Hadarro: modern-day river Darro that flows through Granada

Hajib: Prime Minister

Hammam: bathhouse

Harrira: a Moroccan soup of mutton, couscous, and spices

Hijab: a veil

Houri: virgins in Paradise

Hud: enemies of the Nasrids

Ibn: son of

Jahannam: Hell

Jarya: concubine, plural *jawari*

Jihad: the struggle; to personally maintain the Islamic faith, to improve Islamic society and to defend Islam and an Islamic way of life against its enemies

Jubba: floor-length robe with wide sleeves, opening at the neck, worn by both sexes of the nobility

Kaaba: the most sacred site of the Islamic religion in Mecca, which Muslims circumnavigate during pilgrimage

Kadin: favored concubine, who has also had children for her master

Kāsatān: wooden, bowl-shaped percussion instruments

Khamsa: the Hand of Fatima, an amulet in the shape of a hand, meant to convey patience, abundance, and faithfulness to the wearer, attributed to the daughter of Prophet Muhammad

Khanjar: dagger

Khassa: collective Moorish nobility

Khil'a: ceremonial floor-length robe with wide sleeves, opening at the neck, decorated with *tiraz* bands, worn by courtiers on special occasions

Kohl: black eyeliner

Madina: a city

Madrasa: school of higher education

Maravedies: Castilian gold coinage, originating with the Islamic conquest. When the Castilians incorporated the coinage in their use, it eventually fell in value from silver to copper coinage. The Castilian government stopped issuing *maravedies* in the 1850's when the Spanish currency changed to the decimal system

Marinids: rulers of modern day Morocco AD 1248-1548

Mashwar: the council chambers of the Sultan's chancery

Nashki: a cursive form of Arabic writing

Nasrids: rulers of Granada AD 1232-1492

Nauar: a Gypsy

Purdah: room divider or screen

Qamis: long shirt of white cotton or linen, worn as an undergarment by both sexes, in all social classes
Qaysariyya: the central marketplace in Granada
Qiblah: the wall of a mosque facing the city of Mecca, Saudi Arabia

Raïs: provincial governor
Rawda: cemetery

Sabika: the hill where the Alhambra was built
Salat al-Asr: third prayer time, obligatory at afternoon
Salat al-Fajr: first prayer time, obligatory at sunrise
Salat al-Isha: fifth prayer time, obligatory at nighttime
Salat al-Maghrib: fourth prayer time, obligatory after sunset
Salat al-Zuhr: second prayer time, obligatory at noon
Shashiya: skullcap

'Tharid: dish of crumbled pieces of bread served in a meat or vegetable broth
Tiraz: richly brocaded bands of cloth decorating the upper sleeves of a ceremonial garment, often bearing symbols, geometric motifs or script

Ummi: my mother

Wadi al-Kabir: modern-day Guadalquivir River that flows through

Wadi Fés: modern-day river that flows through Fez

Wudu: partial ablution

Xenil: modern-day Genil River

Zaggats: brass, finger cymbals

About the Author

Lisa J. Yarde writes fiction inspired by the Middle Ages in Europe. She is the author of two historical novels set in medieval England and Normandy, _The Burning Candle_, based on the life of one of the first countesses of Leicester and Surrey, Isabel de Vermandois, and _On Falcon's Wings_, chronicling the star-crossed romance between Norman and Saxon lovers before the Battle of Hastings. Lisa has also written four novels in a six-part series set in Moorish Spain, _Sultana_, _Sultana's Legacy_, _Sultana: Two Sisters_, and _Sultana: The Bride Price_ where rivalries and ambitions threaten the fragile bonds between members of the last Muslim dynasty to rule the country. Her short story, _The Legend Rises_, which chronicles the Welsh princess Gwenllian of Gwynedd's valiant fight against twelfth-century English invaders, is also available.

Born in Barbados, Lisa currently lives in New York City. She is also an avid blogger and moderates at Unusual Historicals. She is also a contributor at Historical Novel Reviews and History and Women. Her personal blog is The Brooklyn Scribbler.

Learn more about Lisa and her writing at the website www.lisajyarde.com. Follow her on Twitter or become a Facebook fan. For information on upcoming releases and freebies from Lisa, join her mailing list at http://eepurl.com/un8on.